Donald Thomas and The Murder Room

》》 This title is part of The Murder Room, our series dedicated to making available out-of-print or hard-to-find titles by classic crime writers.

Crime fiction has always held up a mirror to society. The Victorians were fascinated by sensational murder and the emerging science of detection; now we are obsessed with the forensic detail of violent death. And no other genre has so captivated and enthralled readers.

Vast troves of classic crime writing have for a long time been unavailable to all but the most dedicated frequenters of second-hand bookshops. The advent of digital publishing means that we are now able to bring you the backlists of a huge range of titles by classic and contemporary crime writers, some of which have been out of print for decades.

From the genteel amateur private eyes of the Golden Age and the femmes fatales of pulp fiction, to the morally ambiguous hard-boiled detectives of mid twentieth-century America and their descendants who walk our twenty-first century streets, The Murder Room has it all. **》》**

The Murder Room
Where Criminal Minds Meet

themurderroom.com

T0351828

Donald Thomas (1926–)

Donald Thomas was born in Somerset and educated at Queen's College, Taunton, and Balliol College, Oxford. He holds a personal chair in Cardiff University. His numerous crime novels include two collections of Sherlock Holmes stories and the hugely popular historical detective series featuring Sergeant Verity of Scotland Yard, written under the pen name Francis Selwyn, as well as gritty police procedurals written under the name of Richard Dacre. He is also the author of seven biographies and a number of other non-fiction works, and won the Gregory Prize for his poems, *Points of Contact*. He lives in Bath with his wife.

By Donald Thomas

Mad Hatter Summer: A Lewis Carroll Nightmare
The Ripper's Apprentice
Jekyll, Alias Hyde
The Arrest of Scotland Yard
Dancing in the Dark
Red Flowers for Lady Blue
The Blindfold Game
The Day the Sun Rose Twice

As Francis Selwyn
Sergeant Verity and the Cracksman
Sergeant Verity and the Hangman's Child
Sergeant Verity Presents His Compliments
Sergeant Verity and the Blood Royal
Sergeant Verity and the Imperial Diamond
Sergeant Verity and the Swell Mob

As Richard Dacre
The Blood Runs Hot
Scream Blue Murder
Money with Menaces

The Blindfold Game

Donald Thomas

An Orion book

Copyright © Donald Thomas 1981

The right of Donald Thomas to be identified as the author of this work has been asserted in accordance with the Copyright, Designs and Patents Act 1988.

This edition published by
The Orion Publishing Group Ltd
Orion House
5 Upper St Martin's Lane
London WC2H 9EA

An Hachette UK company
A CIP catalogue record for this book is available from the British Library

ISBN 978 1 4719 0442 4

www.orionbooks.co.uk

For Carol

Adown the stricken capes no flare –
No mark on spit or bar –
Girdled and desperate we dare
The blindfold game of war.

The Destroyers, Rudyard Kipling

1

PROLOGUE:
VICTIMS OF
CIRCUMSTANCE

1

Peirce Mahony, servant to King Edward VII and the Viceroy of Ireland, was the first to die. His friends saw to that. Or rather, since he was judged a traitor to the Irish cause, his friends united with his enemies against him.

Mahony knew, as a matter of fact, that a court of patriots had been convened to try him. Probably he knew them all, and even the well-built house in south Dublin where they met. He was not invited to attend the proceedings, and, by the same token, there was no opportunity to appeal against sentence. Courts of this type knew only one sentence, the judgement of death. To be carried out when and where the executioners found an opportunity.

Such rules were common knowledge to a young man like Mahony, who had served the Irish cause in his time. Still, he protested his innocence to anyone who would listen, hoping that his words would be passed back to the judges. There was never an answer from them. Then months went by and he began to think that his accusers were too deeply involved in the struggle against England to care for his imagined crime any longer. Perhaps even they saw his total and demonstrable innocence. The months became years. During long periods he felt the same security which he had known before the nightmare began. Never more so than behind the walls and beyond the broad lawns of his father's estate, Grange Con, in County Wicklow.

Tall and fair in his sportsman's tweeds with gaiters and cap, he came down the wide staircase in the late-July sunlight. The man in the hallway was Athanas Blagoff, a Bulgarian secretary who had returned to Ireland with his master after the O'Mahony's service to the Czar of Russia.

"Tell them I shall be gone across the water for tea," said Mahony casually, not pausing to receive the reply of his father's secretary. The journey was less than it sounded. In this case, the water was a small lake on which waterfowl bred and which divided Grange Con from its neighbours.

The O'Mahony's mansion belonged as much to the world of

race-week and duck-shooting as to the formal society of Wicklow, the county club, and the ceremonial of the Viceroy's court in Dublin. Beyond the cream-and-gilt library with its leather bindings and deep chairs there were little rooms of casual furnishings and sporting prints on the walls. Peirce Mahony went to the gun-room. He took an old ornamented shot-gun from the rack. It resembled a twenty-bore, quite good enough for his purposes. He slipped a box of cartridges into the pocket of his belted Norfolk jacket. Though the little lake was thronged with water-birds by late July, the season had not yet opened. Mahony carried his weapon as a matter of habit and prudence.

He crossed the green-marble flag-stones, opened the heavy door, and went out on to the terrace. The afternoon was hot and still, as if the oppressive strength of the sun had stunned the world of grass and trees into silence. With a military stride the young man turned from the lawns towards the edge of the lake. To deter poachers, a barbed-wire fence ran along the margin of the water, except where the little boat-house stood. Mahony came to the door of the building and realized that he had forgotten to pick up the key which unlocked it.

Glancing round quickly, he saw no one else to whom he could shout for his key. Still, he was tall and agile enough to try the fence rather than go back and make himself half an hour late. Gently negotiating the upper strand of wire, holding it clear of his grey tweed suiting, he swung his leg over and then let himself down on the far side. The water came up almost to the posts of the fence, and there was hardly more than a narrow path to the boat-house on the inner side. But Mahony went sure-footedly along to the wooden platform where the squat shell of the rowing-boat was moored.

He laid the shot-gun carefully on the planking and began to unwind a cord which held the boat by its stern. No movement of air stirred the lake. On all sides there was a deep silence of expectation. Mahony stood up with a sudden pulse of alarm and saw the stranger step out from the shadows of the boat-house.

Or perhaps not a stranger. Mahony turned and stared at the other man, who held a shot-gun in his hands. He had the illusion very briefly of looking into a mirror, the victim of an optical trick. The other man was tall and fair, as he was. The grey tweeds might have passed for Mahony's. Both men shared the same look and bearing of a subaltern in civilian clothes. Mahony looked bewildered, as if at his own reflection.

In itself the illusion was more frightening than the shot-gun in the other man's hands. There was only one reason why another man should take so much trouble to look like him. Not to be recognized at a distance, not to be suspected or challenged. And that left no doubt as to why the young stranger had come to Grange Con.

The gun was more powerful than Mahony's, a twelve-bore of recent design. Mahony thought of his own weapon, now lying so close to him that it was like an agony to realize he could never reach it in time.

"Peirce Mahony!"

The stranger's words had the tone of a statement, not a question. Questions were not needed, and denials would have been futile. The young man would have learnt to recognize his quarry beyond any risk of error. That apart, Mahony was not going to deny his name. If he must die, he would do so as himself, and proudly.

He was brave, very brave. The executioner reported this to his superiors afterwards, as if it made his killing of the condemned man more creditable. Yet Mahony had nerved himself to bravery for the simplest of all reasons. Courage was unlikely to save him, but cowardice would certainly seal his fate. That being so, he turned and faced the man with the gun squarely.

"I am not a thief!" He made the words quiet but intense. "Whoever sent you and whatever they may have told you, I stole nothing. Still less am I a fool who would rob his own family of its diamonds."

"No," said the stranger gently, "it was never supposed that you did that."

For the first time Mahony realized that the man's voice was not Irish at all. An Englishman must be either a hireling, which was bad, or a convert to other men's causes, which was even worse.

"I have proof," he said, but the quietness in his voice was an echo of despair.

"Then you shall offer it," said the stranger coolly, "and you shall be heard by your judges. If you have done nothing wrong, then you have nothing to fear."

For the first time Mahony felt a quick pulse of hope. If he was to be taken somewhere to face his accusers, there was a chance that he could convince them. If that was what the young man intended.

"They will believe me," he said firmly. "When they hear me, they will have to believe me."

As he spoke he listened for a sound, any sound which might serve his purpose. Better than anyone, Mahony knew that his judges were unlikely to see him alive. The young man with the shot-gun might be speaking the truth, but it was almost certain to be otherwise. Mahony's fears were being soothed merely in order that he would walk quietly through the trees, where the execution could more safely be carried out.

He was right to listen. From the willows on the far side of the boat-house there was a sudden crashing of undergrowth, enough to deflect the other man's attention for an instant. In that moment, Mahony took a step backwards on the wooden platform and his hand went for the shot-gun in the boat as he dropped down, crouching. He had the barrel in his grip, his fingers curling on the trigger, as the other man fired, scarcely bothering to take his aim. The dull roar of the gun and the hardly-felt pang in his left breast merged as the pellets riddled Mahony's heart. Even as his body was thrown, arching back into the water, the stranger fired the second barrel. But Mahony was dead already.

The two pigeons which had broken from the undergrowth by the willows rose high over the lake and wheeled effortlessly against the warm sky towards the Wicklow hills.

There was no sound of commotion, no indication that anyone had heard the shots, or that, if they had, they thought of anything more than shooting pigeons. The stranger watched Mahony's body turn in the water, floating face-down. He took Mahony's own shot-gun from where it had fallen on the planking, fired both barrels, then dropped it into the shallows by the stern of the little boat.

Stillness returned to the hot afternoon. A tall, fair-haired figure, which might have been that of Mahony himself, faded into the warm shade of the woods. In the shadow of the boat-house the corpse floated with arms thrown out, rocking gently in the disturbance which the impact of its own weight had created. Presently that, too, died away and the lake resumed its brackish calm.

Mahony was not expected to return early from his visit. On the following morning, when his servant saw that Mahony's bed had not been used, inquiries began, and then a search. It was Athanas Blagoff who found the body, still floating on the dark shallows by the boat-house.

4

To the Wicklow coroner, the cause of death was never in doubt. Mahony's boat-house key was still in his room. Despite the dead man's care, a thread of cloth from the grey tweeds had caught on the barbed wire of the fence round the lake. It matched a tiny blemish on the leg of the trousers. There was also a scratch on the trigger of his shot-gun.

Mahony had climbed the fence, leaving his gun propped on the landward side. Then he had reached over to draw it after him, the muzzle pointing upwards. A careless but not a foolhardy procedure. By mischance, a barb on the wire had caught the trigger, discharging both barrels upwards into Mahony's heart at a range of no more than twelve inches. There was no blackening by powder round the entry wound, but with smokeless amberite cartridges that need not be expected, even at close range. The jury obediently returned a verdict of accidental death.

Mahony's tragedy was briefly reported in the Dublin press, and the papers in the case were passed to the Home Office. There they were glanced at briefly and then filed. As a matter of protocol, copies of the papers were forwarded by the Home Secretary to the Military Intelligence Department in Queen Anne's Gate. They arrived, bound with cherry-pink ribbon, on the desk of Major William Purfoy, assistant to the Director of Intelligence.

Major Purfoy already had a file on Peirce Mahony, a file opened eight years earlier. The young Irishman's death came as no surprise to him, though he hesitated to think that the Intelligence Department had had anything to do with it. Not in any direct sense at least.

But as Purfoy read the papers in his sunny room overlooking St. James's Park, he felt a sense of incredulity that bordered on downright amusement. How could they have missed it? How could any of them?

Of course, it was Purfoy's business to know a good deal about guns, their history and development. Especially small-arms. Mahony's shot-gun had been dredged out of the mud and examined just sufficiently to find that its barrels were discharged and its trigger scratched. A note in the evidence identified it as an Imperiale sports gun made in Vienna some twenty years earlier. Anyone would assume that such a weapon must take "Prussian" smokeless cartridges.

Purfoy could hardly believe his luck. He unhooked the ear-piece from its stand and put his mouth to the speaking-tube.

"Lieutenant Collins," he said. There was a pause. Purfoy spoke again.

"Imperiale sports gun. Karl Ranke works, Vienna. About 1890. Twenty-bore. Any model or modification known to take amberite smokeless cartridges?"

He paused again while Collins checked the details. The answer came back.

"None?" Purfoy's normally humourless face broke into a mild grin of satisfaction. "At what distance might the gun be discharged to cause a wound without blackening of the skin?"

He listened to Collins and then wrote on his blotter: "Minimum six feet." It was utterly impossible that Mahony could have shot himself accidentally with his own gun. Not that the public would be disturbed by the information. A note added to the file before it was closed would be quite sufficient.

"Someone," he said down the speaking-tube, "has been very lucky. Very lucky indeed."

Collins asked a facetious question. It was in his nature to do that.

"No," said Purfoy humorously. "Not one of us. Not that I know of, anyhow."

For some time after Mahony's death a chill of apprehension fell upon another Irish estate, Kilmorna House, and its occupant, Sir Arthur Vicars. Better than Major Purfoy, better than any man but the victim himself, he knew the innocence of Mahony. As Ulster King-of-Arms until 1907, he had presided over the ceremonial of the English Viceroy's court at Dublin Castle and the Viceregal Lodge in Phoenix Park. Sharing none of Mahony's passion for Ireland's freedom, certainly not his allegiance to the patriots of Sinn Fein, Sir Arthur Vicars had none the less been a companion in his disgrace. Dismissed from office by King Edward after the robbery of a few baubles in his care, suspected as a thief by the Irish rebels, he had withdrawn to his house at Kilmorna in County Kerry. There he lived among the remote hills of south-west Ireland. Like Mahony, he was often able to believe that the world had forgotten him.

For all the disgrace which had been apportioned to him, he was by no means a broken man. Little older than Mahony himself, he possessed a rather fine, aesthetic face and brown curls which made him look more youthful still. In his withdrawal from society he had even married and developed his haphazard antiquarian interests.

For all that, he woke from time to time with the sudden shock of a condemned man for whom the noose and the trap have been postponed but not remitted. He stood in greater danger than Mahony, not for what he had done but for what he knew. Alone among the fallen angels of the Viceroy's court in 1907, Vicars had seen dispatches and jewel-cases which testified to the deceit of governments, to the great struggle for military supremacy in Europe. Distant but clear, he had heard the dance of death by spies and diplomats which signalled the approach of a great war.

In that fateful summer, when the press clamoured about robberies and breach of trust, Vicars alone among the victims had guessed the truth. It was not his privilege to see the contents of the dispatch-boxes awaiting King Edward's arrival in Dublin, but the ciphers stamped upon them were enough. Those and the hints as to the royal yacht's subsequent destination.

Even the sight of the boxes, before the scandal broke, had carried his mind back eight months to the previous October. He had been staying with friends in England. A party of them had stood with other sight-seers on the sloping downland above the Dorset cliffs of St. Alban's Head. There, with hearts beating in high expectation, they waited to see "England's Pride" in all her beauty and in all her menace. Union Jacks flew from the two marking-posts which rose above the turf at either end of the measured mile. The Admiralty observers on the ship watched for them keenly, binoculars raised and stop-watches in their hands.

Vicars had little interest in ships, but he had never forgotten the scene on that fine October morning with the sun glittering on a patch of waves beneath the cliffs. Farther out, a thin mist still veiled the Channel distances, giving the effect of gauze curtains edging a spotlit stage.

The throb of her engines came first, two or three minutes before she rode into view. A heavy beat of turbines woke the still morning like the drums of a war-god. Looking into the sparkle of mist which covered the Portland anchorage, he had seen her quite suddenly, bearing down like a bird of prey with the sun upon her. The bright, colourless sky gleamed on her flanks of new pale-grey steel, the massive armour which was the talk of Europe. *Dreadnought.*

Vicars had expected some lumbering iron-hung monster, an armadillo of the sea. She was, after all, the biggest warship the world had known. But she had the long, clean form of a destroyer, unlike that of any battleship he could have envisaged. The deck was swept free of all the conventional clutter of a capital ship. There was no organ-pipe row of unwieldy funnels, no overhanging levels, no untidy and miscellaneous armament. Amidships there were two modern rectangular funnels, a tripod mast between them giving a command-ing view to the covered control platform. That apart, the entire length of the great ship was a smooth, clear gun platform.

And what guns they were, Vicars had thought. Mounted in massive armoured turrets, they rotated through formidable arcs of fire. The mighty barrels were ten-inch and twelve-inch, enough to destroy any other ship in the world at six miles' range or to riddle the thickest armour at three miles. There was no lighter ordnance apart from the rows of monstrous gun-muzzles with, here and there, ranks of the most modern torpedo-tubes.

Even to Vicars, the plain statement of truth was clear enough. There was not another ship in the world, not even in the German High Seas Fleet, which could live for half an hour in the face of such weaponry. The British press was full of it, of course. Berlin was reported in a state of panic at the advent of such an antagonist as this. German naval planning was paralysed by the futility of building conventional navies to face this new adversary. Not a single capital ship had been laid down in German yards since *Dreadnought*'s launching. More to the point, five more monsters of her kind, the inspiration of Sir John Fisher, the First Sea Lord, were being built on the Clyde and the Tyne.

Vicars had read such boasts with scorn until he saw the great ship for himself. The stark efficiency of her decks was matched by the most daunting speed and manoeuvrability. As she came up to the start of the measured mile he stared in astonishment at the bow-wave, where shining steel sliced through the glittering waters off the Dorset coast. Eighteen thousand tons of armour was moving with the speed of a destroyer, turning with the tight agility of a torpedo boat. He no longer disbelieved the brag that *Preussen* and the most powerful battleships of her class would be helpless against Fisher's protégée.

It was not just that *Preussen* and her sisters would be blown out of the water before they could get near enough to fight. The British builders had somehow adapted the turbines of a destroyer to drive a battleship. The sleek new ship, audacious and elusive as a gnat, would cut circles round an entire squadron of enemies.

Several weeks before, at a household dinner in the Viceregal Lodge, Lord Aberdeen had reported to his staff the new boast of Sir John Fisher. With five such ships, he would sink the German fleet, seize Kiel and its canal, and occupy the whole of Schleswig-Holstein with Royal Marines. All that within two weeks of war being declared. Such bravado had irritated Vicars; it still did. Yet the sight of *Dreadnought* persuaded him of its truth. If there was dismay in Berlin, it was felt with every justification.

Even then, as he stood on the cliffs and watched the ominous beauty of Fisher's new battleship, Vicars would have thought it laughable that he could ever be personally concerned in the future of *Dreadnought*. Even when it happened, he alone, outside the Intelligence Department and the government, guessed that he had been involved. Not merely involved but sacrificed to the expedients of British security. And not merely sacrificed but reviled by men who must have known his innocence. They might have saved him, had they wished to do so. Certainly they could have saved Mahony by some means. But Mahony had never been a favourite at court, always suspected as an "Irish rebel."

So when he read of Mahony's death and the story of an "accident" with his shot-gun, the chill of unease tightened again upon Sir Arthur Vicars's heart.

He took care, as he had always done, never to put himself in deliberate danger. That was all a man could do. The house with its Victorian gables and castellated towers was remote enough for a stranger to be conspicuous in the area. He was probably safer at Kilmorna than in Dublin or, for that matter, in London.

In the end, of course, there was no safety. That was no surprise to him. It happened after his valet brought him his morning tea and Vicars, having drunk it, fell into a light sleep again. He dreamt of his wife, who was no more than twenty feet from him in the next room, how they had been at a reception in the Viceregal Lodge when the Viceroy, for a joke, threw his plate at the window and broke both glass and china. Vicars frowned in his dream and then woke to a confusion of voices.

He was still alone in his bedroom, but someone was shouting below the window. Then he knew that the crash had been the breaking of a pane in the green-house. Irritated by such careless-ness, he tied the cord of his dressing-gown and went across to the window. Whoever had been below was gone now. But crossing the lawn were three men dressed like gamekeepers with caps and leggings. It was almost as if they had been in uniform.

He screwed up his eyes, looking harder, aware of his wife bursting in from her own bedroom.

"There are men on the lawn," she said, breathless with the terror of it. "Six of them with guns in their hands."

He looked again and saw only three.

"Nothing to worry about," he said easily. "It's all right."

Then he understood why there were now only three. From the floor below he heard a shout and the muffled sounds of a struggle. They were in the house already. Wood breaking, that was the next thing. Vicars glanced across the angle of the building and saw the pale ghost of flames dancing behind his study windows. In the desk which the fire now began to engulf lay forty or fifty neatly-written folio pages, setting down all that he knew of the Dublin scandal and the truth behind it. At the time he had regarded the document as his insurance against such acts as this. Now he saw the flames catch hold, the curtains alight and a yellow tongue licking out through the aperture where the window had been opened a few inches.

"The pictures," he said suddenly. "I shall have to save the family pictures."

Lady Vicars tightened her hold on her husband's arm. Gently but decisively he took her hand and drew it away.

"We shall be all right," he said quietly. "Nobody will do anything against us. They have no reason to."

The commotion which had broken out on the ground floor now seemed closer. Blows of a fist echoed on the panelling of the bedroom door, and Vicars could hear his valet calling to him above the din.

"We will go down," he said to the frightened woman. "Go through the kitchens to the back. Stay with cook until I follow you. I must have the pictures."

He shepherded her out and down the stairs, calling out instructions to the valet over his shoulders. The main hall of the house was still untouched, though drifts of smoke hung just below the ceiling like the steam from a wash-boiler.

At first Vicars opened the study door, but the room inside was bright with flames from floor to ceiling. Tall blooms of fire rose from the carpet, and the desk was already ablaze. The heat was unbearable, even in the doorway, and there was a smell of petrol. Vicars turned to the valet again.

"The dining-room," he said, breathless from the heat. "I want the family portraits. My brother's and Lady Rossmore's. We shall have time to put them out through the window on to the terrace. If necessary we will go that way ourselves. But we must be quick."

Of all the downstairs rooms, it was only the dining-room which the fire had not yet reached. The two men ran into it, Vicars locking the door after him to prevent any pursuit. There was no fear, hardly any sign of agitation in his features, merely a taut determination.

"Now," he said sharply. "Before they throw a bomb in here as well!"

Taking opposite walls, the two of them unhooked the first four portraits from the rail. Vicars gave his orders with the precise authority of a platoon commander under fire.

"Stand outside on the terrace, where I can hand them to you through the window!"

He watched the valet throw up the tall sash-window and swing himself out. Smoke was gathering in the dining-room itself now, already as thick as a mist, and he knew from the heat that the full rage of the fire was just beyond the door. He handed out the four oil-portraits and went back for another, probably the last. It was Lady Rossmore's. Lifting it gently, he crossed to the window again. From the windows on either side the smoke of burnt upholstery was drifting in clouds across the terrace, so that he could see nothing beyond the edge of it. From the hallway he heard a hoarse rush of flame, saw the smoke eddies round the door grow to billows, and caught the first bright flickering of the fire's advance.

Beyond the window he heard the servant's voice.

"Sir Arthur! Sir Arthur! You must come now! Before the smoke—"

It was the sudden interruption of the voice which decided him. Leaning the portrait against the wall inside, he eased himself out on to the terrace, then drew the picture awkwardly after him. He turned with the framed canvas in his arms, about to say something to the valet. But it was not the valet who stood before him now. The man was tall and fair, dressed in the gaiters and cap which his companions wore. Vicars, facing him in dressing-gown, seemed like a figure in a Feydeau comedy.

"Who is this person?" said the tall stranger to someone behind him. Despite his predicament, Vicars felt a sudden small flaring of angered pride at the man's tone.

"I am Sir Arthur Vicars," he said bitterly. "And who the devil are you?"

The stranger ignored the question. With the revolver in his hand, he gestured at the painting.

"Put that thing down and come with us."

To Vicars's surprise he was not nearly as frightened as he had always believed he would be. Or rather his fear was submerged by a greater anger and contempt for the smooth-spoken young man. He held the picture fast until the two other men came and took it from him. They led him to the end of the terrace and turned him to face the man with the revolver.

"Arthur Vicars, you have been charged before a court martial of the Irish Citizen Army with treason to the Irish people. On the evidence of your activities as an informer and a spy, the presiding officers have found you guilty on all counts. The sentence passed upon you is that of death. Confirmed by myself as officer commanding the County Kerry Brigade."

Vicars was not a brave man, had never supposed himself to be. Yet fear had not mastered him completely. They would have to shoot him to silence him. He raised his voice so that the other men could hear.

"Irish?" Scorn and incredulity tightened his mouth in a grimace. "You? Your voice is English, your birth is English, your loyalties are English. Your commander is not in Dublin, not in County Kerry. He is in the Military Intelligence Department of the British Army in Queen Anne's Gate, London. If there is a traitor to your comrades anywhere, you are he. Mahony knew it and he was killed. I know it, so you would kill me. The proof of your treason was written down in my own hand, kept in the drawer of my study desk. Small wonder you had to burn the house first!"

But the tall stranger was not listening. He nodded to the other men.

"Put it on him."

Vicars tried to brush it away, but they fastened the cord round his neck and the crude cardboard sign hung on the lapels of his dressing-gown.

SPY. INFORMERS BEWARE. IRELAND NEVER FORGETS.

Now he was frightened, deeply and convulsively. The defiance in his voice shook even in his own ears.

"You and your masters betrayed Ireland to England, and England to Germany. You stole the most precious possessions of your country for your own greed. I will tell you the game and players—"

He took a step forward and was thrown down by a mighty and agonizing blow in the chest before he heard the sharp echo of the revolver shot. Still he lived, lying on the terrace, the smoke sailing like clouds in the sky above him, unable to speak for the drawing pain of the wound in his breast.

If he lay very still, perhaps they would leave him for dead. While his body was torn by the spasms of suffering, his mind broke loose, running haphazardly back along the web of his fate, the web of other men's weaving. The audience with Lord Aberdeen, his warning of what he knew, and his dismissal none the less. The flags and crowds in the Dublin streets, cheering King Edward on a warm July day. The sight of the King's anger when news of the great robbery was given him. The house in Merrion Square with a plausible young rogue called Shackleton and a beautiful girl named Tonia. A drawing-room at Buckingham Palace with the band of the Irish Guards playing, the frogged tunics of the diplomatic corps and the women in their summer dresses like beautiful ships under sail. Faster and faster the thoughts ran back, beyond Kilmorna and Dublin, beyond the Viceroy's little court and the grander London season. Back to the suspicion and treason, the dark winter days of Berlin where it had all begun.

The pain came in a spasm which brought a brief involuntary movement with it. There was a footstep. Dark, hideous muzzles. Armoured steel. *Dreadnought*. A flash and a roaring like the guns of a great ship in battle. And then it was all over.

CAPTAIN WUNDER'S
LUCK

3

Captain Richard Gaudeans took a wax crayon and darkened his thin ginger eyebrows. Surveying the effect in the copper-stained mirror at the rear of the canvas booth, he frowned, moistened the pencil with his tongue, and repeated the lines once more. His public appearances required that he seem darker, more saturnine than nature had made him.

Without such aids as the crayon, the face reflected in the mirror had a faded fairness, a foxy sharpness in its lines and movements. It bore an habitual expression of shallow, "sporting" honesty. The quick, toothy smile and the scant moustache were the properties of a military man gone to seed. They seemed like souvenirs of a doggy fellowship among third-rate subalterns, men who swapped jokes and card-tricks in the drab mess-rooms of colonial exile. To see Gaudeans walking, his baggy swaggering optimism, was to wonder whether such a man could ever have held a commission in any regiment known to the British Army. But he had done so. That, at least, was not a lie.

Satisfied that the crayon had done its best, he adjusted a mask, a thin black domino, over the sockets of his eyes. It gave a certain air of danger and mystery to the hungry, inquisitive features. Leaning forward to the glass, Gaudeans inspected the weak line of mouth and chin, pursing his fat little lips. Nothing to be done there.

Still, he thought, the men and women sitting on their rows of benches in the tent had not come to admire his physical beauty. That could be bought cheap enough in a dozen side-shows up and down the length of the lake-side fair-ground. Gaudeans, as "Captain Wunder," offered something far beyond beauty, a pair of miracles, the like of which were not to be seen in the Specialita Theater, the Lietzensee Park, or anywhere else in Berlin.

As always, he was ready in good time, eager to get the night's performance done with, dry himself off again, and go home. From the roar of encouragement in the tent he knew that Miss Juno May, "The World's Champion Lady Wrestler," had not yet finished her exhibition bout with the Berlin challenger. Gaudeans stepped into the open air and lit a cigarette, peering out between the booths like a small, expectant rodent from its cage.

To either side of him, the striped canvas and the brightly-painted façades of the other shows lined the worn grass of the Lietzensee fair-ground. About the carousels and the steam-organs, shabbily dressed families from the dim streets and bleak tenements of Charlottenburg gathered in the shadowless glare of the Saturday-evening gas-light. Girls in flounced dresses and tall straw hats screamed as the grey wooden horses of the carousels whirled them round and the arms of their escorts tightened about their waists. A party of schoolgirls with broad-brimmed hats and coloured sashes round their white dresses stood wondering in front of the painted plywood which advertised Annita, "The Original Tattooed Lady."

As he listened, Gaudeans heard Wilk issue yet another challenge on Juno May's behalf. The little man cursed mildly to himself. Ten or fifteen minutes to wait yet. He trod his cigarette into the wet December grass and headed for the improvised beer-hall with its walls of palings and canvas roof.

The fair-ground stood on the edge of the city, where the park gave way to heathland and rubbish-dumps, old women in dark, voluminous clothes piling their hand-carts with fire-wood from the trees at the edge of the Grunewald. A tram whined and rattled along the cobbled Sophie-Charlotten Strasse, whose tall buildings looked out from the city's verge upon the flat, desolate land.

Here and there, of course, were representatives of the rich and imperial metropolis two or three miles eastward. Young women in light-coloured silks, their groomed and moustached admirers in tall polished hats, might have stepped straight from one of the fashion advertisements for Berliner Chic. Their destination lay beyond the shooting-galleries and the photographers' stalls, where silk flags and the white peaks of marquees rose in the grounds of the Berliner Grand Hippodrom.

In his dark cloak and satanic eyebrows, Gaudeans thought, he was a match for any of them. Captain Wunder, the star of the Specialita Theater, death-defying and miracle-working. Far off there was the screech of a whistle, a faint glare and thunder in the sky as the Paris express pounded over the Charlottenburg tracks into the heart of the city. By all the rights of nature, that enclosed, expensive world was the one to which he must belong. The buttoned plush of first-class saloon coaches and the shadowy encounters with beautiful, enigmatic women. It was what Colonel Lindemann had promised him. Almost promised, at least.

The beer-hall was crowded by men in dark, cheap suits and the caps of porters or navvies. Above the tables hung a silk banner on which the Münchener Brauhaus wished its patrons a happy Christmas for 1906 and a prosperous new year. At that moment, the bandy little man in the magician's cloak could almost believe in the possibility of such things.

He beckoned the waiter, who knew him by sight, and was quickly served. Gulping down the pale yeasty beer, he slapped a coin on the wood and went out again. A prosperous new year. It might be that, indeed.

For the moment he would have been content to get his performance done with and rest. They must be waiting for him now. He buttoned his thin black cloak over the dark tights and vest, setting the tall hat at a raffish slant. That was how they liked to see Captain Wunder, a suggestion of the man-about-town, debonair and devil-may-care. To complete the image he lit the cigar of which, in the interests of economy, he smoked a little each night. It tasted acrid and foul. Still, he was good, very, very good indeed. Far and away the best turn that Wilk had ever hired for the Specialita Theater.

He was within twenty yards of the tent when he saw the young woman and the man standing outside it. They had come to watch him, no doubt of that. But the sight of them filled him with simultaneous excitement and apprehension. He stepped back into the shadows to be quite sure that he had identified them correctly.

There was no doubt about the girl, he decided. Tonia Schroeder. His eager little eyes gazed gratefully upon her fine, high-boned face, the beauty of the dark-gold hair. The elegant coiffure, the tight-waisted coat, and the flowered hat dressed her to perfection. Gaudeans had met her when she was in Colonel Lindemann's company, strolling in the long shopping arcade of the Panopticum, off the Friedrichstrasse. He had assumed at once that she was one of Lindemann's "clients." Not a spy, perhaps, but certainly a suborner of spies.

The man he was less certain of, especially in civilian clothes. In appearance he resembled a young lieutenant called Eisner, an aide who had been present during Lindemann's examination of Gaudeans at the General Staff building in the Königsplatz. If it was Eisner, then their presence could only mean they were checking carefully on

Captain Gaudeans. And they would do that only if Colonel Lindemann really and truly wanted him. At the possibility of it, Gaudeans's heart seemed to bound with exhilaration.

As in the fashionable arcade of the Panopticum, a sense of deprivation filled him at the sight of Tonia Schroeder. For two nights afterwards he had dreamt of her, the pale gloss of hip beneath tight silk, where his hand seemed to run like a skate on ice. His possession of her in imagination was more real than any of the furtive liaisons with other women in reality. A bride fit for Captain Wunder. A nuptial fantasy made him smile in the darkness, the little teeth overhanging his lower lip.

Once after their first meeting he had glimpsed her far off down an alley of the Tiergarten, walking with a young officer. The sight had taken his breath, like a pang of enforced separation.

Looking again, he saw that the girl and her escort had passed into the tent, to stand at the back behind the benches. She had come to see him, and so she should. Captain Wunder at his magnificent, satanic best. He heard the applause which called him to his fifteen minutes of glory in her presence.

He loped on to the stage in a dozen running strides and then performed a florid hand-rippling bow in the manner of an eighteenth-century courtier. They liked that. He could hear genuine excitement in the applause from the tented auditorium below the crude wooden stage. The three-piece band which the Specialita Theater employed was performing an introductory drum-roll now, and Wilk, red-faced in his bottle-green evening coat, was preparing to whisk aside the curtain at the rear of the stage. Every man and woman present knew what was behind it. There was no secret; indeed, they had paid their money because they knew what was going to happen. Gaudeans was about to walk through a wall of armoured steel, in defiance of every natural law.

With a clash of cymbals and a wide fling of the curtain, the wall was revealed. A large carpet covered the boards at the rear of the trestle-stage. On the carpet lay a short steel beam, no more than two metres in length, running from the front of the stage to the back. Rising from it, bolted and cemented to the beam itself, was the "wall," placed so that the audience could see either side of it. It was a thin, rigid sheet of steel, some two metres square.

Wilk invited a dozen members of the audience on to the stage to inspect the steel wall, to satisfy themselves that it was immovable and impenetrable. Gaudeans walked up and down before the footlights, the languid and elegant debauchee with his hat askew and the cigar held languidly in one hand. When the twelve volunteers were satisfied with the wall, even to the extent of crawling under the stage and testing the solidity of the wood, Wilk drew their attention to the carpet. It was without a single cut or tear. There was, then, no means by which a man could get down through it and under the wall by going beneath the stage itself. Finally, Wilk insisted that the men should stand in a circle on the edge of the carpet to ensure that it was not moved or rolled back. They and the audience would have a clear view of the top of the wall, both sides of it, and the beam on which it rested. There was no doubt, of course. Gaudeans must pass bodily through the steel.

Wilk's assistants brought on two folding screens and arranged each of them like a small cubicle on either side of the steel wall. They were careful to leave the top, bottom, and ends of the wall in view. How Gaudeans passed through was to remain his secret, but all means of trickery were to be scrutinized by the audience. The three-piece orchestra, which had been playing a subdued waltz tune, fell silent as Wilk held up his arms.

"Ladies and gentlemen! Before your eyes, before the eyes of twelve independent witnesses, Captain Wunder will now attempt a feat of magic unsurpassed in the history of the Specialita Theater! An act of wizardry so stupendous that no other theatre in Germany or the world can show its equal! In order to accomplish the miraculous passage through steel, Captain Wunder must first render himself invisible. May I ask you, therefore, to keep silent during this most difficult and dangerous procedure?"

Gaudeans stepped into the first little booth formed by a screen against the steel wall. The orchestra struck up another drum-roll. He flourished his cigar above the top of the screen to show them that he was still there. Then Wilk swung the screen back and there was a gasp. Gaudeans had vanished. The drum-roll increased in tempo. The cymbals clashed. Gaudeans, top-hatted and cigar in hand, stepped out from the other screen on the far side of the wall.

A storm of applause filled the tented space. Gaudeans bowed his acknowledgement, knowing that it was no more than his due. It was a good trick, after all, and the fact that it was exceedingly simple to perform ought not to diminish his reward. After all, it did not appear simple, and that was the main consideration.

Whatever his reputation in other respects, Gaudeans never be-grudged his admirers a full performance of his magic. As the clapping died away, he prepared to pass back through the steel wall again. It was so easy. Stepping back into the second screen, concealed from view, he put down the hat and the cigar, took off the cloak and folded it. A trickster! He remembered how General Thorneycroft had called him that, the tall, red-faced commander, his mouth so contorted with fury that he looked as if he might spit in Gaudeans's face. To Gaudeans there was a concealed pleasure in the word, even as they ripped off his insignia of rank, cut off his buttons, and left him mauled and dejected to face his punishment. Had he only been more courageous he would have reproached them for the scantiness of their praise. He was not a mere trickster. Richard Gaudeans was the best trickster of them all.

In the concealment of the screen, he dropped to his knees and touched the carpet. It was still slack where one of Wilk's men had removed the trestle and the section of stage-boarding underneath. That was the secret of the trick. The witnesses knew that the carpet was unbroken, that no man could get through it to pass under the steel beam of the wall by going below the stage itself. But once a narrow section of boarding under the centre of the beam was removed, the carpet would sag at that point. The woven material would give just sufficiently for a man of Gaudeans's compact build to wriggle under the centre of the beam and reach the far side of the wall.

He wriggled through on his stomach, the beam pressing on his shoulders as he surfaced behind the folded screen on the other side. Having done that, he waited for Wilk to open the first screen, to show that Gaudeans had become "invisible" but that his hat, cloak, and cigar were still there. Mingled amusement and dismay came from the auditorium. Then, as the screen was replaced, Gaudeans reached back for his possessions, attired himself, and waited for Wilk to open the screen which concealed him. The final frenzy of the drumming and the singing clash of the cymbals drowned any sound of the boarding and the trestle's being slid into place below the stage.

While the stage was being prepared for the second miracle, Gaudeans went down among the audience with a pack of cards. Their faces were shadowed by the oil-light which diffused a glimmer-ing yellow twilight among the benches on the grass. The sight of the masked figure so close to them affected some with curiosity and some with apprehension. He grinned to reassure them and fanned out the cards, inviting and coaxing. Each time, a card was taken, returned, shuffled, and then rose from the pack like an accusing ghost to confront Gaudeans's victim. He did the trick a dozen times, identifying the card correctly on each occasion. Wilk's voice recalled him to the stage, where a large zinc tank was being filled with water from two hoses. The unmistakable shape of a coffin lay on a trestle, level with the top of the open tank. To one side there was a heap of chains and manacles.

Wilk, the bottle-green coat bursting with pride, cracked his showman's whip for silence.

"To end this evening's entertainment, ladies and gentlemen, Captain Wunder will perform his world-famous escape from certain death. This feat of daring has been performed before no less than six crowned heads of Europe, at the Kaiserhof and Windsor Castle, the royal palaces of Madrid and Saint Petersburg. You shall see Captain Wunder manacled hand and foot, bound with three lengths of chain, each of them padlocked, and the locks then filled with tiny shot so that no key on earth will open them. He will be placed in the coffin, and that casket itself will be locked. Only then will the same coffin be lowered into two metres of water. Captain Wunder will thus be beyond all human aid. In two minutes the coffin will fill with water. In five minutes Captain Wunder will be dead unless he can free himself from the most cruel locks and handcuffs that science has yet devised. Ladies and gentlemen! Captain Wunder!"

As usual, Gaudeans began by asking for half-a-dozen volunteers to inspect the locks and chains, to see that they were placed on him properly. There was some perfunctory pulling at the steel links, casual manipulation of the locks and steel cuffs. One pair imprisoned his wrists, another his ankles; the three chains bound his arms and legs tightly. Last of all, the chains were locked and the padlocks themselves jammed by the insertion of tiny lead shot.

Wilk's two men lifted Gaudeans into his coffin. There was no drum-roll this time, only a complete and intense silence on the part of the audience. Gaudeans saw Wilk looking down at him; then the lid closed and he was alone in his shell of darkness, like a disobedient child locked in a cupboard. The strong lock on the coffin fastened with a click quite loud enough for the witnesses to hear.

Gaudeans went to work at once. To wait until the coffin was sunk into the tank merely increased the danger. As a matter of fact it was really quite easy and not at all perilous so long as the rules were observed. First the chains with the padlocks that could never be opened. One link in each chain had been carefully prepared in a vice. It was twisted to and fro until it became so weak that a man could work it to the point of fracture with his own hands. To the witnesses it did not look weak; that was the secret. With practice, it was simple to find the link in the dark. The scratches which the vice left were easily felt.

He worked quickly on the first chain across his waist and felt it give. Able to move his handcuffed wrists more freely, he found the second. At that moment, the coffin was tilted on its trestle as the volunteers prepared to launch it like a ship into the tank. Gaudeans felt his feet sliding downward until the wooden edge touched the bottom of the tank. Then, as the heavy box settled, his head was laid gently backwards. He was alone now, two metres below the surface of the water, the first cold moisture trickling in, soaking the back of the tights and vest which he wore for his escape.

Still, he had the second link broken now and was reaching for the third. He was on time this evening, no doubt of it. A single key, hidden in the lining, fitted the locks on his handcuffs and ankles, as well as the lock on the coffin itself. He felt a sudden impatience to get the thing over with, collect his money, and go home.

The third chain gave at last. He moved his body more easily, knowing that it was now only a matter of turning a key in three locks. For some reason, the wooden shell was flooding more quickly than usual. His head and face were clear, but the water had covered his shoulders and he could feel the coldness beginning to close across his chest. There was no question, Gaudeans decided, the time had come to get out. With a mental reservation that he would insist on Wilk's having another contraption built if this one was being warped by immersion, Gaudeans stretched out his manacled hands. The key to both sets of cuffs and the coffin lock was hidden in a fold of the lining level with his waist. His fingers felt for its hard, reassuring outline.

It was not there.

In the first seconds of his realization, Gaudeans was incredulous rather than horrified. Then the horror came and with it a cold terror in which he screamed above the rising water yet at the same time allowed his mind to work through the logic of possibilities, eliminat-

24

ing them one by one. But logic gave way as the cold flood touched his jaw and he pressed his face hard against the wooden lid. He was the witness of his own death.

It had fallen out, then. Into the coffin. Must have done. It had been in its place beforehand. He had seen it, felt it. But his fingers delved to one side and found nothing. Now the water was at his lips and he dared not even cry out in his dark graveyard shell. The sharp brain in the foxy little skull raced at the last possibilities, hurdling them and scampering on in a final desperate search.

Suppose it was not an accident about the key. But it would have to look like one. If no key were found in the coffin, it would be plain murder. What, then? It must be there. Put where he could not reach it with his handcuffs on. Where? Beneath him! Make it look as if it dropped out and lay there and he could never reach it. One hope, then. Breathe deep and turn over, face-down in the water. If it's not there, he thought, Gaudy's a goner.

Drawing the last air into his lungs, he squirmed over. Cold engulfed his mouth and nostrils in the darkness, the water singing in his ears. The neat little fingers scrabbled and clawed. He was nearly done for now. Down at his feet, of course. That was where it would slide when the box tilted off the trestle. Too far. Too far for his manacled hands to reach. The stunted body doubled, in part from the agony of holding in the air. Just below his knees the bony fingers touched the hard shape, and the bursting brain flashed a final message.

His ankles could be free in a second, the easiest cuffs for his hands to reach now. Then the coffin lock. Only when he was free of the wooden shell would there be leisure to attend to the cuffs on his wrists. With the wooden lid unlocked, he pushed upwards with hands and knees, opening it with the force of his back. He floated up from what seemed to him a great depth in the last dribbles of air from corners and crevices. Two of Wilk's men seized him and hauled him from the tank. This time there was no applause, the audience being too frightened or too intrigued to clap. With water spattering convulsively from his lungs, the handcuffs still dangling from one wrist, a drowned spectre of Captain Wunder was supported from the stage.

They laid him in the partitioned area at the back of the tent and waited until he had coughed the worst of the water on to the grass. Then, once they were assured that he was recovering, the two men left him. Gaudeans sat up, hugging his knees, sniffing and spitting alternately. Presently he began to look quickly about him, this way and that, as the agile little mind came into play again.

If he was right—and Gaudeans knew he must be—the disaster with the coffin had been contrived deliberately. But by whom? And why? He already knew how. Someone had removed the key from its place and hidden it farther down in the coffin, where it might have proved to be beyond his reach. Moreover, someone had prised open the edge of the box so that it would flood at twice or three times the normal rate.

Fright and indignation were under control now, held in check by the sharp wits of the fugitive animal. Who, then? And why? Lindemann? Tonia Schroeder? The man he thought was Lieutenant Eisner? A test of his true ability before he was entrusted by them with his first important assignment?

One of Wilk's men, perhaps? A grudge? There had been quarrels over money in the Specialita Theater, trivial thefts, even a bitter jealousy when a plump young dancer of Wilk's, the blond girl Janina, had preferred him for several weeks.

No, he thought, make light of it. The drama in the coffin would remain his secret. If Lindemann had indeed put him to a test, with death as the penalty for failure, then Lindemann had learnt his lesson. So, indirectly, had Tonia Schroeder. If it had been one of Wilk's men, or women, they would hardly try it again. Gaudeans would see to that, by a hint as to his suspicions, and the information carefully written down and filed. In many ways, he thought, it was a woman's trick. Janina? If so, she had handed him the advantage now.

Not a word to Wilk, of course. To make such allegations to the proprietor would be the end of his employment and his nightly payment of fifteen marks. A week or two, Lindemann had said; then there might be something at last. No use complaining to anyone, in that case.

Gaudeans pulled himself together and took a green chemist's bottle from his Gladstone bag. Drawing the cork, he tilted the neck to his mouth and felt a comforting fire burn from his stomach up through his chest. By the time Wilk appeared, Gaudeans had stripped off his wet costume, towelled himself, and begun to dress. Wilk propped his whip against the canvas wall, sat down, and looked at Captain Wunder.

"So what happened to you, my friend?" he asked softly.

Gaudeans shrugged indifferently.

"That box needs seeing to," he said sulkily. "Leaks like a hole in a bucket. Damn thing needs stopping with pitch to keep the water out altogether."

Wilk spread his hands out jovially.

"The bubbles! They like to see the bubbles coming up. It adds to the suspense. Where's the thrill if they know you can stay down there all night and not get wet?"

Gaudeans pulled on his coat and turned up the fur collar round his neck.

"It only wants a concealed pocket at one end to give them all the bubbles they need. If you'd care to advance me twenty marks or so, I can have the work done before Monday night."

Wilk's head was lowered. He was counting out coins as he spoke.

"I don't mind a concealed pocket, so long as it makes the effect. I don't mind a little pitch in the seams, so long as it doesn't show on the outside. But if you remember, our agreement stipulates that the properties and their upkeep are your responsibility." He looked up with a fat, strained smile. "All the same, you can have five marks now. A good joiner will do the work for that. Deductible from your fee on Monday."

"Twenty marks," said Gaudeans firmly. "Otherwise I may not be here on Monday. Find someone else to go down in that death-trap."

Wilk returned the coins to his pocket. He stood up, reached for his showman's whip, and shrugged.

"As you please, my young friend. But if you do come back, see to it that you don't finish next time with the cuffs still on your wrist and your guts full of water. The customers don't like it. Looks botched to them. Even scares them. They pay to be entertained, not frightened. Remember it, won't you?"

He turned to go, but Gaudeans stepped forward, indignant and imploring.

"Stop a bit!" he said. "There's fifteen marks for tonight."

Wilk turned back, a weary smile on the broad red face.

"If you recall, Captain, that was advanced to you three days ago. As it stands, I think you'll find we're all square now."

"I need to buy things," said Gaudeans with a vague helplessness.

"Then if I were you," said Wilk gently, "I should make a point of being here on Monday. Good night."

Gaudeans swore to himself and returned to collect his Gladstone bag. Yet it was not in his nature to remain downcast for long. Indeed, he was buoyed up by the thought that perhaps he would not be coming back on Monday after all. He moved cautiously and expectantly round to the entrance of the tent, to gaze again upon Tonia Schroeder and her escort. They had gone. He was disappointed, and yet it confirmed his hope that they had come to see him and that, even now, they were carrying back a favourable account of him to Colonel Lindemann. Very soon, Lindemann had promised. Only be patient. Perhaps, then, before Monday.

He walked out of the Lietzensee Park and crossed the broad cobbled avenue of the Sophie-Charlotten Strasse, the denuded torsos of tailors' dummies standing like a ghostly regiment at the centre of the deserted street-market.

Already the tautness in his face, caused by the fright in the underwater coffin, was easing away. As he walked, he thought of tricks and trickery, the easy, plausible swindles, and his features were animated by the doggy self-confidence of the professional cadger. Thieving, of course, was a more serious matter. He had done one or two little jobs for Lindemann, acquisitions whose importance he had never truly understood. They, too, were probably tests of his loyalty and ability. On the whole he was a good thief, though it had nearly done for him twice: first when his school kicked him out, the second time in the army. Still, that was far enough in the past.

Thinking of the possibilities, he slipped away through the streets of Charlottenburg with their tall tenement blocks on either side. A full moon shone down the length of the tree-lined Schloss Strasse, catching the tall green dome of the castle tower and flooding the fore-court with a thin, misty radiance. There were so many opportunities to combine justice with profit. He had not even forgotten the grudge over Janina. At the right moment she might be destitute enough to turn a penny or two for him in the introduction service which old Frau Becker ran from her house near the Kantstrasse. As his optimism soared, Gaudeans resumed his bandy-legged swagger, the cocksure foot-work of a clown approaching a banana-skin.

Beyond the tree-lined avenue down which he had passed, the streets became meaner and greyer. Gaudeans's billet, as he thought of it, was near the Charlottenburg Stadtbahn, where the overhead railway rattled to and fro between the centre of the city, the woodland of the Grunewald, and the lake-side resort at Wannsee. He possessed a single room, small in area but considerable in height, looking out on to a sunless court-yard.

Lighting the gas, he stared into the reddening porcelain of the fire. *Please find something for me quickly. An attempt was made to kill me at the Lietzensee this evening.* That was the message a fool would have sent to Lindemann now. Perhaps, indeed, that was the message which the colonel and his minions awaited, Gaudeans's failure of the ultimate test. But either Lindemann knew already, in which case he also knew that Gaudy had beaten him, or else he was innocent. What use in telling him if that were the case? No one would employ a thief whose life was threatened.

The fire burnt up more fiercely, and he felt the heat beginning to scorch him. Gaudeans walked away and closed the curtains across the window. It really mattered very little who had tampered with the coffin, he decided. His only safe course was to assume that they had all been involved, and treat them accordingly. This was no more than a tribute which he paid to the uniqueness of his position. With a sudden sense of pride, he thought that among all his acquaintances, past and present, there was scarcely anyone who might not prefer to see him dead. And that calculation, of course, most certainly included Colonel Lindemann.

4

F ar to the west, beyond the square arches of the Brandenburg
Gate and the dark trees of the Tiergarten, the fading December
day flashed a thin gleam of storm-light under the dark bank of
cloud. A single ray glimmered down the long prospect of the Unter
den Linden, the Athenian splendour of libraries and Opera House
rising on either side. It died at last in a brief flicker on the bayonets
of the guards saluting outside the Dorian portico of the Neue Wache.

The moment passed. With stamping precision, the sentries of the
Imperial Guard in their blue, gold-faced tunics and black, gilt-
filigreed helmets resumed their taut stance. By now the object of
their salute had passed by, a dove-grey carriage drawn by a pair of
bay geldings. It was rolling sedately beyond the pillars and pink-
washed, lamp-lit walls of the opera, the open squares of the Royal
Library and the university, moving steadily towards the last plum-
coloured flush of sun framed by a central arch of the Brandenburg
Gate.

To a soldier of the Imperial Guard, the pale-grey carriage was as
familiar as that of the German Emperor himself. It bore the tall,
portly figure of the new Chief of the General Staff, Colonel-General
Helmuth von Moltke. True, he had yet to win a reputation equal to
that of his uncle, the great Moltke who had crushed the Austrians in
1866 and the French four years later. For all that, he would have
time to prove himself in the great war that must one day come. And
prove himself he would. It was in his blood.

As on every Thursday afternoon during the Emperor's residence in
the capital, Moltke was driving back to the Königsplatz, the
headquarters of the General Staff, from his weekly conference at the
Berliner Schloss. There, in company with the Emperor and the
Emperor's Adjutant-General, the grand strategy was discussed.
What that strategy consisted of was known only to a handful of men
in the General Staff building and the palace itself. Yet the Thursday-
afternoon discussions exercised imaginations at the Neue Wache no
less than in Whitehall and the Quai d'Orsay, or the foreign ministries
of St. Petersburg and Vienna. The Imperial Guard trusted to it for

the downfall of the nation's enemies. It was enough to picture the scene in the sombre grandeur of the Berliner Schloss, the Kaiser and his generals under the gilded ceilings and the unlit chandeliers.

Most of his subordinates would have been surprised to learn with how little enthusiasm Helmuth von Moltke looked forward to his Thursday afternoons in the heavy baroque splendour of the Berliner Schloss. With the conference over for another week, he now sat upright on the buttoned leather of the carriage-seat, defensively ignoring his present companion.

In his tight grey uniform with the carmine of his trouser stripes and collar tabs, the insignia of a General Staff officer, he felt an oppressive discomfort. More than that, at fifty-eight years old he was admitting to himself that for the first time he had felt extremely unwell during the military conference. The pain around his breast-bone, though not acute, had been persistent. There had been moments, too, in the heavy atmosphere of the rich, over-furnished room, when breathing had become a conscious labour, as though the air about him were being drained of its oxygen.

Protected by the privacy of his carriage, he loosened the tall scarlet collar, from which hung the single decoration of the Knight's Cross. Unbuttoning the grey coat, he carefully lifted from his head the black Prussian helmet with its ornamental gold spike. He laid the helmet on the seat beside him and drew off his gloves.

They were at the western end of the Unter den Linden now, approaching the Brandenburg Gate. The linden-trees with their bare branches stood at equal distances down either pavement and in a double row down the central promenade with its iron seats and pillars pasted over with theatre-bills. At the Friedrichstrasse crossing, the ornamental stonework of the Hotel Victoria and the Café Bauer, the blinds drawn out over the tall windows, rivalled the opulence of any Parisian boulevard. After the austere classicism of the military and academic buildings to the east, it was an agreeable change to see brightly-lit shops, men in frock-coats and silk hats, women in furs and coquettish little boots. They thronged the pavements between the tall iron posts of the lamps, or stood in groups before the richly laid-out windows of jeweller and perfumer.

Even as he looked out upon the scene, Moltke's attention was drawn to the reflection of his own face in the glass of the carriage-window. It bore the appearance of a tired stranger. The lines of the cheeks and jaw sagged not with age but with exhaustion.

At moments like this he knew that he should have resisted more determinedly when he had been nominated as successor to Count von Schlieffen. His family name and the expectations of what he might do to justify it had doomed him to office.

"You will find that I lack the habit of rapid decision," he had said to Schlieffen, knowing that the words would be repeated to the Emperor. "I am too reflective, too prone to second thoughts. In a sense I am more conscientious than a Chief of Staff should be. I am not a gambler who can risk everything on a single brilliant throw."

The only consequence was that they turned even this self-criticism against him. It was merely the modesty to be expected in a hero of the second generation, the descendant of the great Moltke who had led the German armies to Paris and whose statue now stood among the trees of the Siegesallee, white marble lettered in gold.

He turned from the window and felt that the air which he now breathed deeply through his mouth was hot and dusty as in midsummer. Of course he was the ideal man for the appointment, even by his own standards. Neither the Emperor nor the field commanders had any need of an originator of strategy; that had been made plain enough to him. His single occupation must be to preserve and perfect the great design of his predecessor, Schlieffen.

When he had at length opened the leather-bound memorandum which was Schlieffen's legacy, Moltke had been first shocked and then enthralled. It was the paradigm of victory against Republican France, Imperial Russia, and Liberal England. Even so, he was unnerved for a time by its moral audacity, the simultaneous invasion of neutral Holland and Belgium with no declaration of war. Mobilization of troops to this end must begin two weeks earlier in the full knowledge that such an action against international law and feeling was to be committed.

Once he had learnt to accept this initial necessity, Moltke was gripped by the detailed ingenuity of what followed. In a matter of days the German advance would have swept through the ill-defended north-east of France, falling upon Amiens and severing the French Army from its British reinforcements. Within a week or two, the philosophy of preventive war would be vindicated. Violation of neutral territory would no longer be an insult to world opinion. Because it had succeeded it would be regarded instead as a strategic master-stroke. Prussian armour and infantry would be west of Paris even before the words of condemnation could be uttered. The heartland of France would be encircled. Her army, all that mattered of it, must be grouped to face an attack across the Rhine. But the Rhine would be crossed in Holland, the French divisions by-passed and then attacked simultaneously from east and west.

France would collapse while Imperial Russia was still mobilizing its scattered units. With victory secure in the west, eighty crack divisions of the German Army were to be released for a single annihilating offensive against the unwieldy regiments of the Czar.

Despite his first misgivings, Moltke had found in the grand strategy both an outlet for his energies and a haven of refuge. Schlieffen's design offered him an intellectual consolation which he had ceased to find in his youthful enthusiasm for the music of Bach and Mendelssohn, the reading of Nietzsche. The magnificence of it comforted him even in moments of sickness. It nerved him against the cold realization that his wife's new religious enthusiasms and his own increasing scepticism had made a marriage of two familiar bodies now possessed by the souls of strangers. His work, after all, had saved him. In it he found the safe stronghold which the Lutheran hymn of his childhood described. "Ein feste Burg . . ."

The grand design had been Schlieffen's, bold and sublime in its way as Beethoven, complex and inevitable as a Bach fugue. Moltke was not the composer, merely the interpreter. He was to embody Schlieffen's vision in railway time-tables and movement orders, routes and loading instructions, maps and elevations. This consuming drudgery had little in common with the popular conception of battles and glory. For all that, he knew that it would decide the fate of Germany and Europe in the coming war. And war must come so long as France brooded on her defeats of 1870.

Therefore, during busy days and sleepless nights, his mind seemed absent from his body, an astral form haunting the Belgian fortress towns of Liège and Namur, the French cathedral cities of Amiens and Reims. There were distant railway junctions in Flanders or Picardy, lonely crossings on remote tributaries, which he knew better than the streets of Berlin. He had never seen them in reality, any more than the hills and bridges beyond the frontier which stood clearer in his thoughts than the remembered scenes of his own childhood.

Schlieffen had bequeathed him not merely a plan but a salvation. With hindsight, Moltke knew that his masters had been right in their judgement of his appointment, though he lacked the self-knowledge to see it at the time. There was in him a monk-like capacity for surrendering his soul to the obduracy of his predecessor's demands.

The carriage passed through the central arch of the Brandenburg Gate. High above, the bronze chariot of Victory mounted in its triumph towards the east. Moltke refastened his collar. He took the black-and-gold helmet from the seat beside him and set it on his lap. For the first time since leaving the Berliner Schloss he looked directly at his companion.

"There was quite a little sensation at the conference this afternoon, Lindemann," he said triumphantly. "A matter to be handled by your department."

"Excellency?"

"Political Intelligence at the Wilhelmstrasse has managed to intercept a third British memorandum. This one addressed from Sir John Fisher at the Admiralty to Lord Lansdowne at the Foreign Office. It elaborates the proposal for a British naval attack on Kiel to cripple the Imperial Fleet without declaration of war."

Colonel Lindemann nodded, and the blush of satisfaction which came into his cheeks seemed all the deeper by contrast with his pale-blond hair. The light-blue eyes moved quickly, betraying the question almost before he asked it.

"How was the interception effected, Excellency? Is the source proven?"

Moltke laughed casually at Lindemann's innuendo.

"His Majesty alone knows how, and you may be sure he will not share the secret with me. It was done under his own supervision, and he vouches for the authenticity of the document. Had he not done so, I should assume the entire discovery to have been manufactured in the Wilhelmstrasse for purposes of personal advancement. No, it is clearly genuine."

"What is the nature of the memorandum, Excellency?"

Moltke allowed his lips to tighten in brief resentment.

"This madness of Fisher's! This *Dreadnought* foolishness!"

Lindemann sat back, understanding at once.

"Ah," he said softly, "*Dreadnought* again."

"Precisely!" The Chief of Staff was getting visibly heated by indignation at the thought of it. "Does Fisher imagine that he can attack us at Kiel, attempt to cripple the High Seas Fleet, and all that without committing Europe to the greatest war for a hundred years?"

Lindemann attempted to soothe his commander's feelings. "We

know that Fisher attempted to enlist King Edward's support for an undeclared war, Excellency, and that he failed. He will not get the support of Lord Lansdowne or Sir Edward Grey in opposition to the King."

"Tell them that at the Berliner Schloss," said Moltke scornfully. "See if they believe you. Tirpitz asks why the English want Fisher's new ships if they have no intention of such an attack. *Dreadnought* and five more! Why does Fisher repeat his foolish boast that with a fortnight's notice he could destroy our fleet, seize the Kiel Canal, and occupy the whole of northern Germany between the Weser and the Elbe?"

Lindemann had no answer to this. Moreover, it was not greatly to his taste that he should be drawn into the rivalry of army and navy which the antagonism of Moltke and Tirpitz represented. He sat in subdued silence. Beyond the carriage-window the ornamental lamps and chestnut-trees of the Tiergarten shone wet in the falling rain. Impressionistic images of street-lights and carriage-lamps lay like scattered jewels down the long black surface of the main axial road.

Moltke put a hand on the coach panelling to steady himself as the horses turned into the great square of the Königsplatz. A veil of falling rain blurred the massive outline of the Reichstag on the far side, the familiar dome and square corner towers. From the trees and shrubs of the central garden the Siegessäule, the victory pillar of 1870, rose from its red-marble base. Golden against the storm-clouds, the winged figure held aloft its famous laurel wreath.

"With respect, Excellency," said Lindemann cautiously, "it is only a question of time before the secrets of *Dreadnought* and her kind become common property. That is the lesson which history teaches us about all innovations in armament."

Moltke's composure gave way, his voice rising as he snapped back at his subordinate.

"This is not a matter of history lessons at the Staff College, Lindemann! The future, not the past, concerns us now! If Germany were to build ships of such size and design—when those secrets become common property, as you call it—we should straightway find two things. First, the new ships would be trapped in the Baltic because the Kiel Canal cannot take them. And when we had spent years and millions enlarging the canal, you would find that no port on the North Sea could take them, either. And when you had spent more years and more millions enlarging Bremen and Wilhelmshaven, you would merely have made those waters navigable for any attacking squadron of the British Navy." He dropped his voice and looked away. "Make no mistake, Lindemann, unless he is countered very quickly indeed, Fisher has won the first battle of the next war already."

"If he is to be believed, Excellency." Lindemann's tone mingled consolation with gentle reproof. Moltke looked up, his eyes milder now as if he recognized the injustice of relieving his irritation upon the young colonel.

"They believe him at the Berliner Schloss," he said quietly. "They believe him as if he were Holy Writ. The Kaiser is summoning the British Ambassador this evening to make a formal protest about Fisher's activities. It can do no good, of course. For the rest, we have more to fear from Tirpitz and the Navy League than from the British."

"Excellency?"

"They would starve the army to rebuild the navy," said Moltke simply. "It is precisely what Fisher wants. Germany to follow England step by step, always behind. To imitate one's enemy is the first error of strategy. Tirpitz and Bülow have almost been tricked into it. They argue that, if Fisher were to succeed, a German army advancing into northern France would find a British expeditionary force landing in its rear. By the time it had dealt with such a threat, Russia would have mobilized and we should face war on two fronts. The very thing we have learnt to avoid."

"And are they not right, Excellency?"

Moltke glanced out of the darkened window and began to button his coat again.

"They could scarcely be more wrong. Fisher and a fleet of *Dreadnoughts* can be beaten by simple means, once we know their secrets. A new design of torpedo may sink the greatest ships afloat. Japan showed that against Russia two years ago. It was torpedo boats which sank the battleships and cruisers at Port Arthur. Damn it, Lindemann, in our case we need only strengthen the shore-batteries. Even a block-ship sunk in the path of a *Dreadnought* will stop it as a last resort!"

"If a landing were attempted," Lindemann agreed.

Moltke swept on.

"And for this they would weaken the army! The strength that Germany must have to break France before Russia can be ready!"

The carriage had drawn up outside the General Staff building. Now that the hoof-beats had stopped, the rain drummed on the roof of the dove-grey coach.

"His Majesty will surely not support the Navy League against us openly?" For the first time Lindemann sought reassurance against the worst.

"No," said Moltke thoughtfully. "His Majesty remains neutral. Indeed, he inclines to our side a little. We and Naval Intelligence in the Königgrätzer Strasse are to be given one chance. If we fail, funds will be diverted to the building of German *Dreadnoughts* with disastrous consequences to the army. A failure would please Naval Intelligence, so we can hardly look for much support from them."

"Support in what, Excellency?"

Moltke looked up, surprised, as though not realizing that he had kept from his subordinate the most important secret of all.

"In acquiring the *Dreadnought* papers from wherever the British Admiralty keeps them. Plans of her hull design and turbines, together with reports on their performance. Details of her armour and armament. Most important of all, the reports and papers prepared for battle-practice. Not the fleet manoeuvres. Those are mere ceremonial for naval attachés and visiting kings. No, the documents for the real battle-practice held in secret, far out in the Atlantic."

"And how are these papers to be acquired, Excellency?"

For the first time Moltke smiled, a wan and chill grimace of irony.

"By your own section of Military Intelligence. With full authority to act as you think best and employ whomever you choose. By all means at your disposal—those were the Emperor's words. In other terms, Lindemann, by fair means or foul. In view of Sir John Fisher's conduct to date, I confess that I should almost prefer them to be foul."

5

Sir Frank Lascelles stood alone in the long, narrow splendour of the Parolesaal, the outer threshold of the private royal apartments. With the stiff gold frogging of his dark-blue tunic, the bicorne hat and sword, he looked more like an elderly admiral of the fleet than an ambassador. There was little comfort in the grandiose decoration of the room, the heavy mouldings of the ceiling, the plaster bas-reliefs of Michelangelo angels set in pink-marble facing, which had the colour and pattern of nougat. Between the two sets of double doors at the far end of the chamber, a diminished copy of the *Pietà* from the Duomo at Florence stood white on a black pedestal.

He pulled himself upright, ran a finger round the inside of his high collar, and waited for the doors in front of him to open. Neither the manner in which he had been summoned nor the length of time they had kept him waiting suggested that the news was good. There was not a single chair in the Parolesaal, only the gold-inlaid mahogany of the polished Empire tables with their marble busts of Frederick the Great and his successors. No sitting down, then, he thought; no informal conversation between the ruler of the great empire and the ambassador of a friendly power.

It was so unfair that he sighed audibly at the injustice. And it was so unnecessary. After years of impeccable negotiation in Bulgaria, Romania, even Persia, he had come to the Berlin Embassy in the flower of achievement, his last ten years before retirement. Anglo-German understanding—he had even founded a society to promote it. Everything had gone so well. When the old Queen was dying, the German Emperor and the future King of England had knelt together at her bedside, first to pray and then to weep. England and Germany united were to be the joint guarantors of European peace by their irresistible strength.

What had gone wrong? Nothing that he could have prevented. It was the greed and ambition of other men which had caught him, in the last two years, in the skirmishing of rivalry and recrimination. He had hoped that the election victory of the Liberal party in England, the arrival of Sir Edward Grey at the Foreign Office, would have made for an improvement. After a year it had merely made matters worse. He would be glad to go when the time came.

The double doors were opened on the far side by two flunkeys who remained out of sight, and Sir Frank Lascelles bowed before the approach of the familiar youthful figure. Not that the Emperor was any longer so very young, forty-seven by quick calculation. Yet, thought Lascelles as he stood upright again, he hardly looked it. The dark hair, cut short and flat, its line razor-straight, had the style of youth. The clean-shaven cheeks and jaw helped as well, despite the moustache with its preposterously upturned ends which had been the joke of Europe. Not any more, though. The dapper, straight-backed figure, the long nose, the fine brows, the fierce sideways glance of the dark eyes, were recognized the world over, as easily as was his portly uncle, King Edward. The truth was, Lascelles thought, that Edward was the old man and Wilhelm the new. Perhaps that was why one still thought of him as young.

The Emperor acknowledged Lascelles's bow with a brief nod. He began to speak rapidly and without bothering to refresh his memory from the document which he held in his hand. Never before had the ambassador noticed such ferocity in those dark eyes. There was no flicker of recognition to suggest the same two men had sat together a dozen times and talked at leisure over the problems of Europe and the mutual interests of their countries. Lascelles felt a chill through the stiff woollen tailoring of his court-dress and thought that the room must be cold as a mausoleum. The Emperor was clearly very angry indeed.

"I therefore request Your Excellency to convey this protest in the strongest possible terms from my government to that of your own country."

The words broke harshly upon Lascelles's private thoughts, and the eyes with their flash of insulted pride never left the ambassador's face.

"My government is in possession of a memorandum of a meeting held at Sandringham two weeks after the appointment of Sir John Fisher as First Sea Lord of the British Admiralty. The purpose of that meeting was to reveal to King Edward the existence of a plan, drawn up on Fisher's instructions, for an attack upon Germany by the Royal Navy without declaration of war. Do not deny it, sir! I have Fisher's own words in my hand!"

Lascelles blinked at the sharp, fierce eyes. He hardly knew

whether to be frightened or amused at the outlandishness of what he was hearing. Still, "Cousin Willy" was well into his stride.

"According to that plan, the Royal Navy would choose a time when the High Seas Fleet was concentrated in Kiel. Fisher's proposal was that the British squadrons would launch their attack under cover of Baltic manoeuvres and that they should—to use his own foolish term—'Copenhagen' the Imperial Navy."

The ambassador blinked and tried to interrupt.

"So outrageous a proposal, Your Majesty, would be dismissed not only by the King but by any British government of any party."

The Emperor rattled the paper and looked still more grim.

"It was not dismissed. Neither was Fisher. King Edward merely said"—the eyes flicked down to the paper at last—" 'By God, Fisher! You must be mad!' "

"A dismissal of the plan, surely, Your Majesty?"

"No!" Lascelles listened gloomily to the growing shrillness. "For the past year, Fisher has remained at the Admiralty as First Sea Lord. Every facility and encouragement is given him to prepare a cowardly and vindictive assault upon the German Empire and its people. Wait! There is more to come! In a memorandum to the Foreign Secretary, subject 'Naval Necessities,' Fisher boasts that his undeclared war would give England the German fleet, the Kiel Canal, and Schleswig-Holstein within a fortnight. You doubt me, sir? There is proof to come! In another secret British Admiralty memorandum, dated the fifth of July, he defends last spring's decision to order manoeuvres by the British Navy in the Baltic. I will quote you his exact words." The paper rattled again. " 'Our drill-ground should be our battle-ground.' What is this but the most blatant and inexcusable provocation?"

In the fraction of a second before he replied, Sir Frank Lascelles thought it was even more appalling than he had feared, worse than anything in his diplomatic career since his first day as consul-general in Bulgaria almost thirty years before. Either the German Emperor had gone mad and fabricated the whole thing—which the staring eyes almost suggested—or else the allegations were true. He hoped it was only madness.

"I assure Your Majesty, upon my most solemn word, that I have never heard of these discussions or memoranda. Indeed, I venture to hope that Your Majesty has been misinformed as to their occurrence. There are not wanting those individuals who would seek to make mischief between Germany and England, for the benefit of third parties. Your Majesty will see how such deliberate interference might benefit certain European powers."

"The German Secret Service was not created to make mischief for this country," said the young man bitterly. "The Political Intelligence Department, my direct responsibility, is my informant."

At last Lascelles saw the chance of a moral advantage. He seized it quickly.

"Where such things are done outside the channels of normal diplomatic exchange, Your Majesty, I fear there is every likelihood that you may be misinformed. While a nation relies upon espionage, which may in some cases be necessary, she must deal with men whose integrity is rendered suspect at once by the nature of their profession."

For the first time he noticed the hint of a smile under the dark moustache, but it suggested triumph rather than conciliation.

"Then, Sir Frank," said the Emperor more gently, "I will tell you for your information that your own country has relied upon its own Secret Service for many years. If you find that hard to believe, I will also tell you that its present director is Major-General John Ewart, and his deputy is Colonel William Macpherson. It has four Foreign Intelligence sections and an Imperial Defence section, housed near St. James's Park, in Queen Anne's Gate."

"Your Majesty is mistaken," said Lascelles blandly. "General Ewart is director of all military operations, a staff appointment. Colonel Macpherson was merely a British observer in the Russo-Japanese War. The department in Queen Anne's Gate is concerned only with mapping and topographical surveys of areas in which the army might be committed in the event of an imperial campaign."

"Then so much the worse for it," said the Emperor bitterly.

"I will convey Your Majesty's observations on the conduct of Sir John Fisher to Sir Edward Grey at the Foreign Office. Yet I must remind Your Majesty that the Foreign Office has no authority in the appointment or dismissal of the First Sea Lord."

The Emperor ignored both the promise and the reservation.

"One further point, Sir Frank, the most relevant of all. On the fifteenth of June next year, the Hague Peace Conference will open. Its principal topics are to be disarmament and mutual guarantees of non-aggression. I have nominated Dr. Philipp Zorn and Baron Marschall von Bieberstein as German representatives. If, however,

I am informed that either the British government or the British Admiralty has proceeded with plans for an attack upon Germany, I shall order the withdrawal of our representatives from that conference. And you may be sure that I shall inform the world of our reasons for doing so, as fully as I have informed you now. There is no more to be said. I trust you will acquaint Sir Edward with our conversation as a matter of urgency."

Before Lascelles could reply again, the dark, straight-backed figure had turned about and marched the length of the ornate room with an air of military pride. The ambassador walked slowly away as the chamberlain came in to escort him back to his carriage. As he was driven to the chancery, on the corner of the Leipziger Strasse and the Potsdamer Platz with its grand hotels, he pieced together his fragmentary memories of the conversation. There was no doubting the glacial intensity behind that burst of royal rage. If that rage were justified, then the words spoken at a private meeting between King Edward and his First Sea Lord had become the property of the German government. How? Equally, he was asked to believe that two highly secret memoranda, one in the Admiralty, the other only for the eyes of the Foreign Secretary, had been intercepted word for word by the Wilhelmstrasse.

The carriage turned and Lascelles stared thoughtfully down the remaining stretch of the Leipziger Strasse. At the far end the baroque grandeur of the Hotel Palast with its tall windows and mansard roof dominated the Potsdamer Platz. It was surely impossible that a secret service—German or not—could achieve that degree of penetration unaided?

Lascelles considered a further possibility, one which had lingered in his mind uneasily during his more trying interviews with the Emperor. He would mention it in his dispatch to Grey at the Foreign Office. The Hohenzollern dynasty had always been a rum lot. Not quite balanced, one might say. In the case of the Kaiser, his twin obsessions with personal messiahship and the military power of Germany made a disturbing and unstable combination.

The ambassador relaxed and felt greatly eased by the thought. Of course, such manias would triumph in the end, as they always did. It had been clear to him throughout the interview that "Cousin Willy" was deaf to any argument based on reality or common sense. Personally, Lascelles regretted the young man's tragedy while relishing the phrases he would use to describe it. Mania was the key word. He lay back against the carriage-cushions, toying with the rich diplomatic cadences which came smoothly to his trained mind. As he did so, his normal sense of easy contentment grew more secure. He thought with special anticipation of the pleasure he would have in summoning his First Secretary next morning and telling him that "Cousin Willy," Emperor of Germany, had gone foaming mad.

Major Purfoy came out into the December evening. A trench of thin white fog stretched away down Pall Mall towards St. James's Palace. It hung in a sluggish vapour over the horses and hansoms at the cab-rank in Cockspur Street. By the corner of the Athenaeum, the gas of a street lamp popped and spluttered, blurred to a fitful halo.

Purfoy, in full regimentals, stood on the steps opposite and glanced at his watch. It was just about time. He turned up the collar of his great-coat. Then he began to negotiate the crossing, where an ambassadorial landau moved stately as a swan among lesser water-fowl. High over the cabs and victorias, the horse-buses bore their damp, wrinkled placards for Nestlé's Milk, *The Doctor's Dilemma*, and *The Belle of Mayfair*. As he reached the far paving, a tune from the *Belle* rose unprompted in his mind.

> *Wear a blank expression*
> *And a monumental curl,*
> *And walk with a bend in your back,*
> *Then they call you the Gibson Girl. . . .*

By the time that he passed the pillared entrance of the United Service Club he was humming the melody to himself. Uncurtained windows showed the splendid Regency ceilings, the long full-dress portraits of England's generals, from Waterloo to Mafeking. Far behind him, beyond the coffee-stalls and theatre signs of the Haymarket, the clatter of a barrel-organ drowned his humming with its tune.

> *Take me on the Flip-Flap*
> *Oh, dear, do . . .*

From the din of traffic and organ, Purfoy crossed Waterloo Place to the darkness of the Duke of York's Steps. He dropped a silver coin in the hand of the flower-girl near the German Embassy. After the noise and the electric brightness where the world of the theatres began, the Mall stretched in welcome silence through the damp parkland of the winter evening, from Admiralty Arch to the palace gates. Purfoy crossed Horse Guards Parade at a quick stride, past the end of Downing Street. In that wide, deserted space he looked more like a rising barrister or a successful schoolmaster than a soldier. The dome of his skull was almost comically accentuated by its central baldness and the two black flaps of hair which seemed to hang like a clown's wig on either side. There was a look of contrived intellectuality in his appearance, an absence of anything which suggested the swirl of cannon-smoke or the thunder of battle.

The appearance was entirely justified. Purfoy's entire service had been passed as military secretary, staff officer, aide-de-camp, and finally as an assistant to the Director of Intelligence in Queen Anne's Gate. His first experience of such work had come earlier, of course, on Curzon's staff in India. But then there had been the implacable hatred of Curzon and his Commander-in-Chief, Kitchener, for one another. Purfoy, caught between the Viceroy and his C.-in-C., had found the position extremely distasteful. He had heard with dismay that Curzon had written to the King, threatening resignation if Kitchener were not removed. And with still greater dismay he had learnt that the resignation had been accepted, to the utter consternation of Curzon himself. Purfoy had come home with the Viceroy, had witnessed Curzon's tears of mortification. "Lord Alabaster," Kitchener had called him behind his back. Not bad, Purfoy thought. Smooth as monumental alabaster. His lordship was all of that: sleek, supercilious, utterly self-confident. Still in his early forties, he had been the best Viceroy that India had ever known.

Purfoy's meditation came to an end as he reached the steps of the Foreign Office. He was not greatly looking forward to what lay ahead. At this time of the evening, most of the building was in darkness, corridors ill-lit, lights burning only behind the nobler windows of the upper floors. Those who worked as clerks or assistants, drudging for their living, had long since gone home. The building was left to the amateurs, those men of power for whom there was no home but this.

Inside the great hallway, Purfoy stripped off his top-coat and handed it to a liveried messenger. In his dark-blue regimentals with their blue-and-gold piping, he was escorted up the main stairway to the grandeur of the first floor. A young man in frock-coat and formal

45

dress awaited him at the top. The face was more familiar than the name, with its fresh complexion, narrow-rimmed glasses, and fair curls. An overgrown choir-boy, Purfoy thought as he held out his hand.

"I'm Purfoy," he said. "You must be Delahaye. I saw your team whip the House of Commons at the Hurlingham pigeon-shoot last year." He thought gratefully of the sunlit lawns and Linda Reeves who wore a yellow rose, the crowded paddock, the band of the Coldstreams playing.

"Ah," said Delahaye, as if it surprised him. "You were at Hurlingham?"

"Just for the day," said Purfoy lightly. "Now, what's all this nonsense about German spies in the Foreign Office?"

Delahaye gave him a look of agonized reproach for mentioning the matter so publicly. He hurried his guest away down the corridor, muttering as he went to forestall another indiscretion on Purfoy's part. Purfoy noticed that a positive blush of embarrassment coloured the young man's smooth, patrician cheeks.

"Certain difficulties were reported by the Berlin Embassy," said Delahaye quickly. "When Lord Lansdowne resigned after the election, he recommended to Sir Edward Grey that your department keep a watching brief on matters in Berlin. Sir Edward spoke to your Director, to Colonel Macpherson, and to Lord Curzon for an opinion of you. They all confirmed that Berlin was your speciality."

"The whole of northern Europe is my speciality," said Purfoy helplessly. Delahaye ignored him.

"Lord Curzon, knowing your staff work in India, recommended you."

"You make me sound like a grocer," said Purfoy pleasantly. "What about your German spies? Have you got one on the premises for me to inspect?"

Delahaye glowered at this flippancy.

"Whatever else you need to know will be told you by the Foreign Secretary himself."

Purfoy blinked. He had no idea that he was to be interviewed by Sir Edward Grey. When the summons to the Foreign Office had arrived, he had assumed that his discussion would be with Delahaye or another of Grey's "new young men" appointed after the Liberal election victory of the previous year. For a moment he felt overawed.

Before he could recover himself sufficiently to question Delahaye further, a white double door with gold inlay was opened for him. Purfoy saw what might have been an elegant drawing-room or library. Upright chairs were scattered about the rich red and green of the Turkey carpet. Two tables, each large enough for a dinner-party, were cluttered with books, papers, and ink-stands. Sets of bound reports filled the shelves of ebony wall-cases behind glass doors. On the carved marble of the mantel-piece four candles in tall gilt sticks were reflected by the broad mirror above the fire-place. Only a large globe atlas on a mahogany stand indicated that this was, after all, a government office and not a Park Lane apartment.

Another man was sitting casually on the edge of a table, folding the newspaper which he had been reading. At Purfoy's entrance he stood up and came forward. Only then did the visitor realize that the youthful appearance and casualness belonged to the new Foreign Secretary himself. At close quarters, Sir Edward Grey combined the smoothness of a schoolboy and the strong, broad face of a country-man. His photographs aged him. In reality, he looked like a boy who might have overstayed his time at school by a year or so in order to captain the cricket team.

"Major Purfoy?" Grey came forward to greet his visitor and then withdrew to the table. Purfoy came to attention, uncertain of how else to respond. He was aware of Delahaye, still there behind him. Like the escort for a defaulter brought up on a charge, he thought. Not hard to see, he supposed, why they had chosen Grey for the job. The honesty, the calm blue eyes, and the smooth dark hair gave him the appearance of a young and energetic diplomat.

The Foreign Secretary settled himself on the edge of the table again.

"Major Purfoy, since you already have a general idea of why you have been seconded to these duties, I will not waste your time over that. You have, I understand, a reliable contact in Berlin?"

"I believe we have, sir. So far it has hardly been necessary to put the matter to the test."

"Reliable, in your own judgement?"

"In my judgement, yes, sir."

"Good." Grey patted the table with his hands and leant forward slightly, as though at any moment he might begin to swing his legs to and fro. "You are aware that the Germans have intercepted confidential memoranda relating to Admiralty and Foreign Office affairs?"

"I believe a paper has been intercepted, sir. I understand it has."

Grey looked surprised.

"Not *one*, Major. Three, that we know of. Others, perhaps, that we do not. The earliest did not directly concern this office. The first was a Sandringham memorandum, recording a private meeting between the King and the First Sea Lord. The second was an Admiralty paper, Sir John Fisher's, on naval strategy in the event of war with Germany. With those I am not immediately concerned."

"No, sir."

"If they concern anyone, it should be the Director of Naval Intelligence."

"Indeed, sir."

"However"—Grey edged himself off the table and stood up—"we now have a third breach of secrecy, more serious to me because it directly concerns this office. Before the election, Sir John Fisher, as First Sea Lord, drew up an appraisal of British action to be taken against Germany in the event of war. That paper was directed to my predecessor, Lord Lansdowne. It was brought under seal from the Admiralty by two King's Messengers. The seal was not tampered with. Both the bearers are naval officers of long and unblemished service. The document was read by Lord Lansdowne alone. It was then placed in the most secure vault in this building, in a safe to which only two men have access. One is the permanent under-secretary. The other is the Foreign Secretary himself."

Purfoy nodded. He had not known precisely what arrangements were made with regard to security, but he had supposed them to be something of the kind.

"Now, Major," said Grey carefully, "that paper has not been missed from the safe. It is still there. No attempt appears to have been made against the vault or the safe. Yet last week, in Berlin, the memorandum was quoted, word for word, by the Kaiser to the British Ambassador."

Several answers lay ready in Purfoy's mind. Some of them would be extremely unpalatable both to Grey and, for that matter, to Sir John Fisher. Chief among these involved the fact that a German-born aristocrat, Prince Louis of Battenberg, had been appointed Director of *British* Naval Intelligence. True, the appointment had been made in the Victorian zenith of German popularity. All the same, Purfoy doubted if it would have been made now, not in the present state of relations between the two countries. For the time being, he decided to offer other and safer explanations.

"How? I ask you, Major Purfoy. How is it possible?"

Purfoy clasped his hands lightly behind him.

"To speak the truth, sir," he said quietly, "I doubt that it is possible by the means you envisage. Of course, it is *possible* for the contents to have been communicated to Berlin by the First Sea Lord or by the King's Messengers, if they had access to the seal-ring."

"Which they could not," said Grey smoothly.

"Or," said Purfoy stubbornly, "there remains the possibility that it was communicated by the Foreign Secretary or the permanent under-secretary."

Grey looked across Purfoy's shoulder at Delahaye standing behind him. He spread out his hands hopelessly.

"You see?" he said.

Casually, he sat down on the edge of the table again, for all the world, Purfoy thought, like the captain of a school house addressing his team.

"I know, Major Purfoy, that your suggestions are well meant and reasonable. But you will forgive me if I do not bring charges of treason against Lord Lansdowne or the First Sea Lord, least of all in the case of Sir John Fisher."

He was about to continue, but Purfoy interrupted him.

"There is a further possibility, sir. A copy may have been made of the memorandum for Admiralty purposes, and it is that which has somehow come into the hands of the German intelligence departments."

"There was no copy," said Grey shortly. "The entire purpose of addressing the document to the Foreign Secretary was that it might be more securely kept here than at the Admiralty. That was decided after the matter of the Sandringham document and the first Admiralty paper itself."

Purfoy reversed the clasp of his hands.

"Then, sir, I suspect that the document from which the German Emperor quoted may have been a conjecture at the contents of the true one."

At last it was Delahaye at his back who interrupted him.

"The words were quoted in English, sir. As Sir Frank Lascelles reports them, they are identical. So, too, are the tactical proposals."

There was a pause. Then Grey spoke the word which he had evidently been keeping for this moment.

"Burglars," he said gently. "Are they not among your suspects, Major Purfoy?"

"A man who could penetrate the safes of the Royal Household, the Admiralty, and the Foreign Office would be a remarkable burglar, sir." Purfoy tried quickly to think of a reason for ruling out the possibility. He failed to do so. "If there is no traitor, however, there must presumably be a thief."

"Very well," said Grey emphatically. "We—or rather you and your representative in Berlin—will look for both. Traitor and thief. If three departments of state have been plundered, the answer must be sought in Berlin rather than London. Here, as soon as one hole in the bucket is stopped, another may appear. There, we may find the source of the problem."

"Sir," said Purfoy deferentially. "If I may make a suggestion, we may already anticipate the nature of the next attempt—"

Grey nodded impatiently.

"Dreadnought," he said sharply. "Yes, Major, we understand that. Your Director has been kind enough to indicate that the German intelligence services would sell their souls for the *Dreadnought* papers to play leap-frog over us with some new weapon."

"Then, sir—" Purfoy began.

"Then, Major, we will agree on this. We, for our part, will investigate with all diligence the possibility that there is a spy among us. I know we shall have Sir John Fisher's co-operation in the matter, too. You have *carte blanche* from your own Director and myself to alert your representative in Berlin as to the matter we have discussed. Kurier, I believe, is his name?"

"The name under which he operates, sir."

"Good," said Grey enthusiastically. "The deeper he can penetrate their organizations the better. And the sooner the better."

For the first time in the conversation Purfoy felt alarmed by Grey's expectations.

"With respect, sir, one man cannot do everything. There are, to our knowledge, three German intelligence services. Military Intelligence at the General Staff building, Naval Intelligence in the Königgrätzer Strasse, and Political Intelligence in the Foreign Ministry. One man can hardly do so much."

Grey sighed, as if despairing of his visitor.

"Rule out Political Intelligence, Major. That is concerned exclusively with Germany's internal security."

Purfoy stood his ground.

"It is also the one branch of the service directly responsible to the Kaiser, sir. His personal involvement in these matters suggests we ought not to overlook a change in its functions."

Grey sighed again.

"Very well, Major. We have sought your advice, we must abide by your judgement. In return, we beg your discretion. Germany and her leaders are in a dangerous and mischief-making mood just now. When all this is over we must hope for a return to normal and amicable diplomatic relations. First, they must be shown that such conduct as this cannot be tolerated and will not succeed. That apart, Major, I should be grateful if your activities do not make the present mood worse than it is already. Tread warily, I beseech you."

Ten minutes later, Purfoy had been dismissed by Grey and had taken his leave of Delahaye. As the messenger escorted him back down the grand staircase, he thought of the Foreign Secretary's suppositious burglar. It really was not as absurd as it sounded. A corrupt messenger and a professional cracksman between them might penetrate any government department in the length of Whitehall. He doubted, from his knowledge of them, whether even the Admiralty and the War Office would be proof against that.

Buttoning his coat again, he went down the steps into the broad street with its monumental façades and statues, the long carriageway deserted at this hour of the evening, stretching in a long gas-lit perspective to the Victoria Tower at the far end.

He walked slowly, worrying at the possibility which had never been raised in the discussion. The worst of all. It seemed that no one would have known of the three memoranda in German hands but for the Kaiser's outburst in the presence of the British Ambassador. That being so, how many more papers were now in the possession of the Berlin intelligence services without the knowledge of Whitehall? He winced at the thought.

Purfoy followed Birdcage Walk, turned past Wellington Barracks, and came to the elegant eighteenth-century houses of Queen Anne's Gate. Here, too, the iron railings and ornamental lamps presided over a deserted street. Of course, he thought, there had been a final possibility, the most outrageous of all. As he went up the steps where the two men of the night-watch waited behind the illuminated fan-light, Purfoy almost wished he had possessed the courage to confront Grey with it.

The story of the memorandum held under maximum security, seen only by three of the most important men in the country, then suddenly recited word for word by the Kaiser, savoured of tawdry stage-magic. As a matter of professional training, Purfoy was not a believer in magic. Deception, yes. Magic, no. Suppose, then, they had simply not told him the truth. Either there had been no such memoranda or else there was nothing secret about them. They— Grey, Fisher, Lansdowne, and the rest—had fabricated either the story or the circumstances. The excuse? England's interest. The reason? To employ him and Kurier against Germany for their own ends, without ever revealing to him what those ends were. Such things happened from time to time. Purfoy knew that better than anyone.

He nodded to the two men of the night-watch. They sat at either side of the main door in the spacious hallway, each accommodated in a strange covered porch which looked like a cross between a sentry-box and a sedan chair. He went up the stairs to his own room. Now that the opportunity was safely past, he relished the idea of confronting them with their own falsehood. Curzon would have done just that. On the spot. Purfoy grinned to himself, imagining the flawless arrogance of Lord Alabaster's languid contempt.

7

Kurier was his man, known always by the name which gave the code its key. For eighteen months Purfoy had cared for him, nursed him into position. Now, it seemed, Kurier's value was to be squandered merely because the Admiralty and the Foreign Office failed to keep order in their own houses. It was a waste; Purfoy knew that. Kurier's chance would be used up and that would be the end of it. On the other hand, Grey had put the matter plainly to the Director of Intelligence, leaving Purfoy with no alternative but to obey instructions.

He closed the long green curtains of his room and switched on the brass table-lamp, flooding the leather desk-top with a pool of tawny light. He sat down in the swivel-chair to encode Kurier's alert.

The coded alert was first telephoned to the Admiralty, to be tapped out from the Whitehall transmitter and relayed again by a destroyer of the Home Fleet flotilla somewhere off Harwich. For all that Purfoy knew, the wireless signal was picked up and relayed a second time by another warship of the Baltic squadron to ensure that it came in strongly across the Danish islands and the north German plain. Kurier would be listening at half-past midnight to catch the shrill, twittering bursts of Morse.

Once contact had been made, specific instructions would be dispatched on the following night at eleven o'clock. Only in an emergency would they follow immediately on the first broadcast. Purfoy could, of course, compose the message and forward it to the Admiralty's Signals Department at any time. Only the hour of its final relay by the Royal Navy, in the North Sea or the Baltic, had to remain consistent.

The code name and the key to the cipher were the same word: *Kurier*. The message would begin with that word, as a call-sign, tapped out twice over in the code. After that, the circumspect wording of the alert was composed by use of a code chart. This was an alphabet, written out six times in as many lines, beginning each time with a successive letter of the code word. Above it was the alphabet in normal sequence.

A	B	C	D	E	F	G	H	I	J	K	L	M	N	O	P	Q	R	S	T	U	V	W	X	Y	Z

K	L	M	N	O	P	Q	R	S	T	U	V	W	X	Y	Z	A	B	C	D	E	F	G	H	I	J
U	V	W	X	Y	Z	A	B	C	D	E	F	G	H	I	J	K	L	M	N	O	P	Q	R	S	T
R	S	T	U	V	W	X	Y	Z	A	B	C	D	E	F	G	H	I	J	K	L	M	N	O	P	Q
I	J	K	L	M	N	O	P	Q	R	S	T	U	V	W	X	Y	Z	A	B	C	D	E	F	G	H
E	F	G	H	I	J	K	L	M	N	O	P	Q	R	S	T	U	V	W	X	Y	Z	A	B	C	D
R	S	T	U	V	W	X	Y	Z	A	B	C	D	E	F	G	H	I	J	K	L	M	N	O	P	Q

Purfoy took the oblong chart from his desk and laid it on the blotter, next to the bright-blue paper containing the message he was to transmit. During the Indian Mutiny, the Intelligence Department's predecessors had been content to transliterate uncoded messages into the script of Classical Greek, baffling to Asians but clear at once to an educated Englishman. The present state of European political rivalries required something more refined.

For all that, the code was essentially simple to operate. In the first of the six lines, K stood for A, L for B, and so on. Purfoy wrote down the alert for Kurier, vertically at one side of the chart. It was couched in the absurd, stilted language by which the department guarded against imposture. *Kurier, Kurier. Make yourself visible.* The two sentences were encoded separately and Purfoy wrote them out beside the chart.

	A	B	C	D	E	F	G	H	I	J	K	L	M	N	O	P	Q	R	S	T	U	V	W	X	Y	Z

K K M u v e	K	L	M	N	O	P	Q	R	S	T	U	V	W	X	Y	Z	A	B	C	D	E	F	G	H	I	J
u u a r i	U	V	W	X	Y	Z	A	B	C	D	E	F	G	H	I	J	K	L	M	N	O	P	Q	R	S	T
r r k s s	R	S	T	U	V	W	X	Y	Z	A	B	C	D	E	F	G	H	I	J	K	L	M	N	O	P	Q
i i e e i	I	J	K	L	M	N	O	P	Q	R	S	T	U	V	W	X	Y	Z	A	B	C	D	E	F	G	H
e e y l b	E	F	G	H	I	J	K	L	M	N	O	P	Q	R	S	T	U	V	W	X	Y	Z	A	B	C	D
r r o f l	R	S	T	U	V	W	X	Y	Z	A	B	C	D	E	F	G	H	I	J	K	L	M	N	O	P	Q

The first stage of the encoding was straightforward. K in the first line was represented by U, U in the second line by O, R in the third by I. Working patiently down the columns, Purfoy encoded. UOIQII . . . Then the result was refined again by moving each letter back through the alphabet according to a prearranged number. In Kurier's case, 1066 successively repeated. So U went back one letter to T, O remained in place. I and Q went back six letters. Then the sequence resumed. Simple and unbreakable, Purfoy had been told. He hoped it was. For Kurier's sake.

In an hour or two more, on the far side of the North Sea, the listeners in the German intelligence posts would be confronted by a riddle whose possible answers ran almost to infinity. Indeed, as the Director of Intelligence had once demonstrated to him, it was even better than that. Among the millions of possibilities there might always be more than one. Some other key would produce a comprehensible message from the babble of Morse. So even if the enemy, by a fluke that was hardly to be envisaged, should break the message down, it might still be the wrong one. The Wilhelmstrasse and its rivals had been given to understand as much. That being the case, the general opinion was that they had now ceased any concerted effort to decipher the messages of British Intelligence. This news brought no comfort to Purfoy. Quite simply, he did not believe it. All the same, the simplicity of old-fashioned Victorian mathematics compelled his admiration.

He adjusted the brass table-lamp and assembled the words in cipher. First there was Kurier's name, twice. Then, going back to the start of the process, there came the message. For his own benefit he wrote this out in separate words. By the time that it reached the German interceptors in Bremen or Hamburg, it would be an unbroken flow of letters, repeated monotonously for ten minutes. *Kurier, Kurier. Make yourself visible.* He looked at the oblong chart and checked the letters back. TOCKHI OIHQCC VUVG BFYFIMJQ ECDKECI.

When he was satisfied with its form, Purfoy put the alphabetical chart back in its drawer and turned the key in the lock. He drew the sheet of blue paper from the blotter, tore off the edge with his scribble on it, and set a match to it. Last of all, he picked up the telephone-receiver from its stand and asked for Admiralty Signals. He was struck by the irony that the Intelligence Department was obliged to send out its coded signals through the very organization which appeared to have been penetrated on three occasions by the German Secret Service. Not that it mattered. Soon after midnight this alphabetical lunacy would be broadcast for anyone who cared to listen.

He waited until the sequence of letters had been read back to him and confirmed. At any moment it would be tapped out from the

Whitehall mast, joining the nightly babel of cackling and crackling messages which filled the air of seven oceans, linking the Royal Navy from Dover to Darwin, Hong Kong to Heligoland. He looked at the message again. TOCKHIOIHQCCVUVGBFYFIMJQECDKECI. Crossing to the window, he drew back the curtains and his gaze rose above the damp parkland to the roofs of Whitehall, mistily outlined against a pale flush of gas-light. In his mind he thought of the cipher as some strange, invisible bird of night. It would chirrup its way high above the fog of the Essex marshland, out across the dark rollers of the North Sea where the Harwich flotilla performed its nightly destroyer sweep. In a fraction of a second more it would pierce the cloudy night over Jutland and the islands, across the obscure sluggish waters of the Baltic, coming in above the long, luminous crescents of breakers on firm sand, the flat, bleak coast-line of north-eastern Germany.

Walking back to his desk again, he picked up the torn slip of paper and set a match to that as well.

8

"**H**ow ghastly for you! How absolutely ghastly!" The ex-Viceroy put down his glass and stood behind the arm-chair, resting his hands on its back as he looked across the fire-place at Sir Edward Grey. "When you asked me about Purfoy's reliability in such matters, I had no idea that the Foreign Office, too, had suffered one of these depredations."

His lordship's supercilious moon-face observed Grey with no trace of sympathy. The tall broad forehead and the handsome features of the great proconsul were matched by eyes which held the acute vision of a policeman or an interrogator.

"As matters stand," said Grey stolidly, "C.-B. felt that you had better know the complete story. The Premier did not think it necessary to obtain the sanction of the Cabinet."

His lordship nodded. Behind him the curtains were still open, and moonlight cast its ghost-paths across a garden quadrangle. A quarter of a mile away, towards the river, a college clock began the preliminary chimes of midnight. His fingers tightened on the back of the padded chair, his body unnaturally stiff and upright as the result of the corset he wore following a spinal injury in his youth.

He was, Grey thought, more impressive than ever in his "Tiger Tim" uniform with the floral gold of its high collar and tunic front. It was something to be ex-Viceroy of India at forty-six, an age when most men still strove after high office and, as a rule, strove in vain. Unlike some of his colleagues, Grey was unconvinced that, after the regal power he had tasted, Lord Alabaster would be content with the Chancellorship of the University of Oxford.

"You want my advice, of course?" Grey almost winced under the bland arrogance of the words. "If the Germans are inside Sandringham and Windsor, the Admiralty and the Foreign Office, you would hardly have come here again unless you wanted it."

"I should like to know how it was done," said Grey quietly. "That's all."

His lordship allowed his lip to curl slightly, as if he might snarl at his guest. But the snarl was no more than the lightest sneer at the suggestion that he should demean himself by taking on the work of lesser men.

"Purfoy will do that for you," he said contemptuously. "He is *trained* for it."

This time, Grey failed to check the wince. Despite the passage of time, he felt as uncomfortable now as when he had been a freshman and his lordship already a rising star of the college and the university. More than ever, Alabaster justified the rhyme composed about him as an undergraduate:

> *My name is George Nathaniel C———n,*
> *I am a most superior person.*
> *My cheek is pink, my hair is sleek,*
> *I dine at Blenheim once a week.*

It was with an effort that Grey reminded himself how their positions were reversed. Now it was he who held the power, while the man standing before him hungered for a beggar's portion of it. Yet pride and supercilious humour concealed that hunger behind a mask of flawless arrogance.

His lordship stepped back from the chair and picked up his glass.

"After all, my dear Grey," he said lightly, "what does it amount to? Fisher and this tiresome boat of his! Do you really intend that the great diplomatic game in Europe should be at the mercy of such a man and his contrivances? Fisher belongs elsewhere. His natural plumage is a pair of workman's overalls and his natural habitat is the stokehold. Cannot you and Campbell-Bannerman persuade the King that Fisher must go?"

Grey tightened his lips, as if biting back his anger at Alabaster's unsolicited opinions. His mission had been intended only to check Purfoy's credentials. That was all. Now, it seemed, Lord Alabaster was about to demand a seat in the Cabinet.

"First it was Fisher's plans," said Grey doggedly. "Now it will be the *Dreadnought* papers that the Germans want. All our own intelligence chiefs are agreed that it must be so. Berlin wants those more than anything else."

"Then it must have them," said his lordship coolly.

"I beg your pardon?"

Lord Alabaster made an expansive gesture.

"Since C.-B. and the Cabinet have asked for my advice in the matter, this is it."

"It was not advice—" Grey began, but his lordship talked him down effortlessly.

"There will be no peace until they have what they want. Your departments will be infested with German agents. They mean to have the papers of Fisher's wretched boat, and they will continue their efforts until they get them. Nothing can prevent that."

"Out of the question!" said Grey heatedly.

"Therefore"—the proconsular voice drawled on unremittingly—"I consider that your best course of action is to hand the papers to the Kaiser and have done with it."

Grey scanned the pale, supercilious features for some trace of irony. There was none.

"Preposterous!"

"You think so now," said his lordship smoothly. "In a little while, however, you will see that I am entirely in the right."

"A war between ourselves and Germany has never seemed more likely!"

"Precisely." Alabaster favoured his guest with a bleak smile. "In which case it is quite the best thing to provide your enemy beforehand with those facts you wish him to know. While you are still at peace, there is a chance that he may believe what you choose to tell him. Once the war begins, his suspicions will be thrice-armed."

Grey looked moodily at his host. Seeing this, Alabaster attempted to comfort him, without modulating his own habitual tone of suave arrogance.

"Sleep on it, my dear Grey. See if you don't concur in my view by breakfast. What I would suggest will not prevent war. But if there should be a war, it may go some small distance to ensuring that we win it."

9

Captain Gaudeans braced his narrow shoulders and trod the light Berlin snow with sporty panache. Two weeks after the drama of the coffin there was a renewed jauntiness, an irrepressible bandy optimism in his walk. This time they had a proper job for him. He knew it. No more spying on the nightly indiscretions of military attachés with Frau Becker's fat nymphs. No more hawking of passions on scented note-paper to Lindemann and his rivals. Now he was going to be all right. They had summoned him.

He cantered down the iron steps from the platform of the elevated railway at the Hallesches Tor station. It was a good time of day, always lucky for him. The shops were lit, the city's pleasures spread like a jewelled Babylon before him. And it *could* have been an accident over the key, rather than a victim's revenge. No sense in raising a rumpus, anyway. A chap who let himself get croaked like that would hardly do for his new friends.

Gaudeans repressed an urge to whistle like an errand-boy in his enthusiasm. He crossed the intersecting streets where the mounted policeman sat solid as a church-tower in his saddle. Green-and-brown trams screeched and rumbled in a lumbering procession, following the iron geometry of rails across the broad canal bridge, through the grand architectural circle of Belle-Alliance Platz, and down the lamp-lit avenue of the Wilhelmstrasse with its Grecian government offices.

Glancing about him, he skipped across the road, dodging the cabs and bicycles, coming safely to the arcaded entrance of Belle-Alliance Platz. He turned aside from it, moving in the rainy dusk with the suggestion of a caper, the genial excitement of a performing animal in anticipation of its reward. He rattled his stick on the pavement with the dexterity of a café entertainer as he passed a shabbier row of buildings. Gaps in their terraces showed where sites had been left empty, like missing teeth.

Quick, audacious as an insect and as easily crushed, Gaudeans swung round the corner into a darker street of railway stations and cheap entertainments, the green iron trellis of bridges crossing high above the traffic of cars and electric delivery vans. This was the Königgrätzer Strasse, dominated by Berlin's main-line stations, Anhalter and Potsdamer, a pair of stone and terra-cotta palaces standing in Venetian splendour behind their shrubs and trees.

Just beyond the play-bills and the electrically-lit foyer of the new Hebbel Theater stood a plain building, unmarked except by its number: Königgrätzer Strasse 70. It was a drab block of dark and sooty sandstone, the type of premises to which less important government departments were being moved from the pillared elegance of the Wilhelmstrasse.

Gaudeans took the steps two at a time and presented himself at the window of a little room just inside the main doorway. It reminded him of the porter's lodge in the only London club of which he had been a member. It had been a rather brief membership, many years before.

"Captain Gaudeans," he said, the affability of his tone tempered by an edge of command. "Captain Gaudeans to see Captain Tappken, by special appointment."

He waited while the porter, every inch a petty officer in civilian clothes, uncorked an old-fashioned speaking-tube and passed the information to his superior. Once again, in his rising sense of excitement, Gaudeans had to make a deliberate effort not to twirl his stick and whistle.

His escort, by Gaudeans's guess, was no more than a naval rating. They went up to the next floor in a lift, a gloomy little cavern lit by a single light-bulb. Gaudeans had never been in the Königgrätzer Strasse building before. As they passed through outer offices and ante-rooms he was interested to see the way in which German protocol had divided the duties of Naval Intelligence between serving officers and civilians.

Both the porter and his escort were obviously service personnel in plain clothes. Yet in the offices themselves there was a decidedly civilian air about the men who worked there. Gaudeans detected it at once. He was never wrong about such things.

It seemed, then, that only the most exalted and the most subordinate members of this branch were serving members of the Imperial Navy. Gaudeans found it singular but not astonishing. The actual work of espionage was regarded as unsuitable for men of honour. His optimism took another leap, seeing how well his own reputation might serve him in that case. As a door was opened for him, he looked forward with true pleasure to the encounter which lay ahead.

Then the door closed behind him, and his optimism faltered. This was not what he had expected, not at all. For the past two days, ever since the offer had been made through Lindemann, he had pictured the scene quite vividly. A genial meeting alone with Tappken. A friendly discussion over matters of mutual interest. Arm-chairs before the fire, perhaps. And then the offer of employment, well-remunerated and offering ample scope for Captain Gaudeans's special talents.

He saw instead a round table of polished walnut, four men in leather chairs sitting at it. One of them wore captain's undress uniform of the Imperial Navy, a dark man with thin features and an odd little beard which looked as if it had been glued on for the part of Mephistopheles in an amateur production. This was Tappken? Gaudeans looked once more. This was Lindemann's friend?

"Captain Gaudeans!" Tappken was standing up now, motioning him forward with the impatience of a band-master. "Take your chair, if you please!"

There was no humour, no geniality. Gaudeans sat down and felt a deep unease. This was alien to him. In soil of this kind, his natural charm and ability never throve. Still, he would do his best. He glanced at the table. The ashtrays were full, and the air was laden with smoke. They had been questioning and interviewing men all day. Now they had come to him at last, a name perhaps added to their list merely out of courtesy to Lindemann. Tappken gave him a brief, formal nod and made the only introduction that was necessary.

"These are my three colleagues," he said quickly. "Each one is an instructor in his own branch of intelligence work. They will question you upon those aspects presently. First, though, there are certain matters which are puzzling." He glanced at a paper before him. "You are *Captain* Gaudeans? It seems a remarkable rank. For a man in your situation."

Gaudeans smiled, a desperate little grin of honesty, and wondered if he could get away with a lie. Surely they would not have set a trap so early, and in such a little thing. Still, one never knew with these jokers. He gave them all the helpless look of a decent fellow who has caused misunderstanding through no fault of his own. Taking the blame for it, all the same.

"Temporary," he said quickly. "Temporary rank, to tell you the truth."

Tappken drew a line on the paper.

"Ah," he said thoughtfully. The syllable had an uncomfortable sound to Gaudeans. A trap, of course. There *had* been a trap, then.

"Lieutenant Steffens." The man at the far end of the table introduced himself. "But you claim to have served with Military Intelligence in your 'temporary' capacity. Do you?"

"No," said Gaudeans, surprised. "Never did." Let them work out whether he never had served or never had claimed it. See which way the ball bounced before committing himself.

"'M.I.'"—Steffens looked at his own paper again—"the British Army's abbreviation for Military Intelligence. 'Captain Gaudeans, M.I.'"

"No," said Gaudeans again. "Sorry. Also stands for Mounted Infantry, d'you see. Mounted Infantry. Eh?"

"Cavalry?" asked Steffens sceptically.

"No!" Gaudeans went for the word like a hungry pigeon in his anxiety to seem frank and open with them. "Mounted Infantry are chaps who ride into battle, then dismount and fight as infantry."

"A horseman fights in the saddle!" Steffens held his gaze coldly. "He does not fear falling out of it when the enemy confronts him!"

"Now that's the thing, don't you see?" Gaudeans wagged a lightly reproving finger. "Carry rifles, not swords."

Tappken interrupted, still worrying at his own question.

"Then you never held a Regular Army commission, Herr Gaudeans?"

"No," said Gaudeans with quiet regret. "Never did."

"Mounted Infantry!" snapped Steffens. "Where in the British Army List does one find the Mounted Infantry?"

"One doesn't!" Gaudeans judged it time to give a little display of tightening his jaw with pride. "Irregulars. Raised in the veldt to fight in General Thorneycroft's brigade." That was better. It sounded convincing, even to him.

Tappken sat back in his chair.

"And this was the formation from which you parted company in so dramatic a manner?"

"Yes," said Gaudeans, beaming at them with the relief of having clarified the point. "That's it. Rather than peach on a friend."

"To become a circus performer?" Steffens finished Tappken's question for him. "A conjurer? A juggler?"

"An illusionist," said Gaudeans reproachfully. "That's what you want, isn't it? What's it to you whether I can ride a horse or not? As I see it, I'm more use to you this way. Passing through walls. Springing open locks and boxes. Dash it all, I said to myself, I might be made for work like this. And here I am. Eh?"

That was more like it, he decided. More the tone of jovial authority he had imagined himself using.

"Tricks!" Steffens answered him in a word.

Gaudeans bore the disparagement with a shrug. These people needed tricks as much as he did. Then Tappken spoke again.

"More precisely, Herr Gaudeans, what qualifications do you hold in, let us say, trigonometry?"

No doubt of it, he was no longer Captain Gaudeans to them. Trigonometry? The word was so unexpected, so jarring in the context of his thoughts, that he had to stop and think for a moment as to what it meant. Then his eyes turned devotedly to Tappken, imploring belief.

"To be quite honest with you, to be quite honest I wouldn't say I had qualifications in the subject. Not if you mean *paper* qualifications." He kept the disparagement light but well aimed.

"Naval architecture and drawing?" asked one of the other men. "Topography?"

Gaudeans snatched at the opportunity.

"Topography." He laughed at the word. "Now that's what we call in English a horse of a different colour!" They looked blank at the explanation, and he felt that, for the moment, he held the upper hand. "A man can't survive in the veldt without topography. And survive I did! Indeed I did! Map and compass. Nothing a man can't do with map and compass."

They looked at one another hopelessly, and he guessed that it was some other kind of topography. Tappken's narrow blue eyes rested on him, and the little forked beard seemed more devilish than ever.

"In other words, Herr Gaudeans, you have no acquaintance with the basic tools of naval intelligence?"

Gaudeans tried to look amused and reasonable in the face of such pedantry.

"Intelligence is intelligence!" He spread out his hands with the forbearing of an expert. "If a man can get you what you want, does the name matter?"

"It does here," said Tappken more gently. "German intelligence is carefully co-ordinated. There is no secret about that. They will tell you in London if you ask them. The Königgrätzer Strasse is not concerned with political or military intelligence. Nor is it interested in feats of deception which involve walking through walls and escaping from handcuffs. Naval intelligence. Just that."

"But surely . . ." Yet his defiance of their pedantry lacked all conviction now. They had done with him, he could see that. Even Steffens, at the far end of the table, spoke more sympathetically.

"It would take months for your preliminary instruction, here and at the Zeughaus. Then you would need more specialized training in recognition until you could distinguish at a glance the silhouettes of battleships, cruisers, destroyers, their class and nationality. Believe me, I'm telling you no secrets. Every intelligence officer on a modern warship undergoes instruction of that kind. You would also be taught to recognize uniforms and ranks, signal flags and codes."

"That's all right," said Gaudeans easily. "I'd pick it up in no time. You'd see. Try me."

"There are tests and examinations," said Tappken quietly. Gaudeans smiled to himself, thinking of the dozen ways a chap could crib his way through things of that kind. But Tappken had yet to reveal the worst. "When you had passed these, you would serve a short apprenticeship at the naval yards in Kiel and Wilhelmshaven. That would continue until you could talk fluently about every unassembled part of a gun, mine, or torpedo-tube. Then you would be tested again. You would be expected to tell by the pitch of its whistle, for example, whether a torpedo which was discharged was a Whitehead or a Brennan. If your performance in all these tests was exceptionally good, you would be considered for employment by Naval Intelligence. Your first year or two would be spent sitting behind a desk in one of the offices out there."

"But look here," said Gaudeans greedily, "I'm English! I could be much more use to you than that!"

Tappken nodded.

"Your nationality carries a problem with it. What happens to you, a non-German, if you are instructed in so many confidential matters and then fail to satisfy us as to your skill? You could hardly expect to be provided with a ticket to London—to offer your information, perhaps, to the British Admiralty."

For the first time that afternoon, Gaudeans saw death, glimmering like a distant light on a dark horizon. Of course they would never let him go just because his performance was unsatisfactory. He thought of the stories men told in South Africa: the figure bound to the post, the eyes blindfolded, the cloth target pinned on the left breast, and then after the volley the writhing, wounded creature put out of its misery by the provost-marshal's pistol to its head, as if it were an injured horse. He drew a deep breath, but now he had no answer for them.

Tappken reached out, as if he might touch him gently on the arm.

"You see why, Herr Gaudeans, any intelligence service in the world is reluctant to employ those who are not its own citizens. In your case, you have forfeited your reputation in England. We accept that. But for us, the problem remains."

Gaudeans was of two minds, angered by their treatment of him, unnerved by the chill in Tappken's gentle apology. All the same, there was only one way out. Take it on the chin. Like a sportsman. Leave them with an impression that Gaudy wasn't such a bad type after all. It might be useful one day.

"Yes," he said, with his easy decency, "I see that absolutely. You're quite right, of course you are. I'm only sorry that my talents can't be of some use."

Tappken nodded consolingly. Gaudeans made no attempt to leave his chair.

"Was there anything else you wished to ask us?" Tappken inquired.

The spaniel eyes looked at him again, shining with the faintest reproach.

"Silly of me, really," said Gaudeans coyly. "Sure you'd have had something for me to do. Used my last five marks, the Stadtbahn ticket and all the rest. Thought there might be a retainer. Of course, I appreciate there can't be. Still, if there was some entitlement for expenses of the journey . . . An advance? A very small one, of course."

Their unease in his presence had turned to unconcealed disgust. They wished only to see the repellent shrewdness of the insect crushed and disposed of. Tappken drew some coins from his pocket and handed over five marks.

"I say!" said Gaudeans, the eyes wrinkling with gratitude. "That's most awfully decent of you. It really is."

He rose from his chair and made an obsequious little bow to each of them, as if he had just finished a private performance at the Specialita Theater. Tappken saw him to the door, the dark features tightened with embarrassment at the little wretch's final self-abasement.

Gaudeans returned the way he had come, towards the canal and the Hallesches Tor. He went more slowly down the Königgrätzer Strasse, under the iron railway bridges, looking like what he was. A dyspeptic, shambling old subaltern, an old horseman broken in wind and warped in limb. The features of his face drooped like a tragic mime's. Only the eyes continued to question those who passed him with a moist, cadging intimacy.

In the room he had just left, Tappken's three subordinates collected their papers and departed. Tappken watched them go and then crossed to a door which communicated with his private study. Inside that inner room a green leather arm-chair was drawn close to the door. Colonel Lindemann stood up from it, fair and imperturbable as Tappken was dark and intense.

"You heard him?" The annoyance in Tappken's voice was hardly concealed.

Lindemann nodded and let out a long breath.

"Hopeless," he said. "Quite hopeless. My apologies for taking up your time. I thought he might have been of some use to you."

They went down the stairs together, and Tappken's evident irritation seemed mollified by the time they parted company below. A plain cab was drawn up outside. Lindemann, subdued but philosophical, went down the steps. A young officer who had been sitting in the cab sprang out to open the door for him. When they were both inside, Lindemann's mood changed, his eyes brightening with enthusiasm.

"Well?" he inquired. "What news, Eisner?"

"The man's rooms were searched carefully and thoroughly while he was on his way here this afternoon, sir," said the young officer proudly. "Nothing at all. One or two tools of the burglar's trade. Otherwise, nothing at all. You were right all the time, sir, if I may say so."

Lindemann nodded.

"That's good," he said emphatically. "Tappken and his naval colleagues were not pleased with Gaudeans. Indeed, they appeared to regard the interview as a total waste of their time. I even sensed that the honest Tappken himself bore a resentment, as though considering he had been used for someone else's purposes."

"Was he not, sir?" There was a hesitant reproach in Eisner's voice.

The force of Colonel Lindemann's laughter filled the tiny space of the cab.

"My dear Eisner! How better to ensure that Captain Gaudeans was not at home when your men called upon him? And how better to ensure that after this humiliation he will now be grateful for any consolation offered him? Keep a watch upon the little reprobate for two more days. Bring him to me the day after tomorrow. In the evening. With courtesy, if possible. But bring him, anyway. The time has come for us to have a conference with our brave captain!"

The cab jerked forward, Lindemann holding the braided velvet cord to steady himself as he watched the passers-by on the Königgrätzer Strasse. Then, to Eisner's astonishment, the colonel began to sing gently to himself, as if with the exuberance of sudden romance.

10

Beyond the arched window-recess of Lindemann's study, the rain blew in windy drifts across the lamp-lit Königsplatz, veiling the Siegessäule column, the Bismarck statue, and the distant front of the Reichstag. The storm fell with such force that the water bounced back like a hail of marbles from the lights reflected on the road's surface.

Lindemann's room was similar in design to that of the Chief of Staff immediately below. Yet it had none of Moltke's monastic simplicity. At this time of the evening a fire sputtered in the grate. Leather chairs were drawn up on either side of a table which was burdened with decanter, glasses, and a chess-board of onyx pieces. The white globes of the central gasolier were unlit. Only the pink-shaded gas-mantels above the fire-place cast their warm, hissing radiance on the intimate scene. It was a pool of warmth and comfort in the rain-swept night, as the storm-clouds tore and swirled above the north European plain.

In the subdued fiery glow of the gas, where the shadows seemed thicker, the fire-light gave an almost aquiline handsomeness to the sharp, inquisitive cut of Gaudeans's features. Lindemann reached out to the chess-board.

"Pawn takes pawn," he said lightly. "No intelligence service in the world would ever employ you, except as what you are already. You should have known that. Tappken was quite right to dismiss you. Such a man as you would be employed only as a thief. Forgive me for speaking so bluntly, but the term is a precise one."

Gaudeans cocked his head to one side, like a small bird.

"Sticks and stones may break my bones but names shall never hurt me." He spoke in a monotone, as if reciting an incantation. "We used to say that at school."

"Quite." Lindemann pointed to the chess-board: "By the way, you must take my knight with your bishop now. You have no choice. If you simply wanted to be a thief, now that would be a different matter altogether."

Gaudeans appeared not to hear this last sentence.

"Chess!" He shook his head wearily. "Not my game. Knew lots of chaps at school who played it. Clever chaps. Brains galore. Never my forte, I'm afraid. I'd call myself an illusionist rather than a thief, to be accurate." He looked up at Lindemann, tapped the side of his nose, and winked. "Thieving is just what you steal. Illusion is how you do it. See?" He looked at the chess-board wistfully, but Lindemann was right. Gaudeans removed the knight and put his bishop on the empty square. Lindemann took it at once with his queen.

"Now you must take my pawn with yours."

"Oh, dear," said Gaudeans, lightly distressed, but he obeyed the instruction. "What d'you want stolen?"

"Anything, more or less." Lindemann surveyed the state of the game. "It depends to what extent you can persuade me of your abilities."

Gaudeans chuckled.

"First time I ever met a chap who didn't care what was stolen for him."

Lindemann frowned. He picked up a pawn and then put it back. His gaze came up to meet Gaudeans's.

"Anything," he said softly. "And everything!"

An uneasy pause followed this, but Gaudeans perked up again almost at once.

"How about this for a game?" he said enthusiastically.

From his pocket he took a pack of cards, still unopened, whose wrapper advertised Leistbräu of Munich. He tore the paper off, shuffled the cards, and fanned them out towards Lindemann, face-down.

"Take a card!" he pleaded. "Any card!"

Lindemann stared at the little man, curiosity in him stronger than distaste. Gaudeans's eyelid moved, halfway between a twitch and a wink.

"Go on! Be a sport!"

Lindemann drew a card from the centre of the fan. He glanced at its face secretly and then held it against his chest. Gaudeans tapped the pack together and arranged it neatly on the table, still face-down.

"Slide it in," he said encouragingly. "Anywhere you like."

Lindemann pushed it in about halfway down the pack, so that its face was still concealed from Gaudeans. Then Gaudeans picked up the deck, shuffled and jiggled it, tossed it on the table and scooped it up again, until the card which Lindemann had chosen was irretrievably lost in the confusion. At last he held the pack very tightly in one hand, the faces towards Lindemann. From the closely compressed slips of card, the ten of clubs rose by the magic of a concealed thumb-nail.

"Your card?" he asked hopefully.

Lindemann nodded, and Gaudeans chuckled with sheer happiness.

"Show you how?" he suggested, not waiting for Lindemann's reply before he continued. "Chap takes a card. Right? While he's looking at it, you turn the bottom card of the pack the wrong way up. Now, whichever way the pack is, it looks as if it's face down. Only it ain't. Chap puts his card back. Only his card and the one you turned are the wrong way round. Spot it easy. Then, of course, you cut and shuffle, toss 'em about anyhow you like. 'Cause you know already which one it is. See? Still, looks clever, don't it? After a minute or two of the fancy stuff, just for show, you push the right one up from the pack with a bit of thumb-nail. Easy to keep track of it in the shuffle, once you know which card it is. Not bad, eh? I used to do tricks for the fellows in the mess, that's how I got started."

"Excuse me," said Lindemann bleakly, "you got started on the day you were dismissed from your school for theft."

Gaudeans twisted his mouth dismissively.

"That!" he said indifferently. "Lots of chaps get the sack like that. One reason or another."

Lindemann nodded and his tone became more conciliatory. It seemed to Gaudeans, for the first time, that he was no longer treated by the young colonel as an engaging little animal to be indulged or abused for no evident reason.

"No one expects you to betray your country's essential interests," said Lindemann casually. "Even if you were willing to do so, it would be impossible to ask it. No man can be relied upon in such matters."

"I see that, of course," said Gaudeans quickly, though as a matter of fact he did not. What, after all, he wondered, was the debt which would prevent such betrayal in his case?

Lindemann lifted a carved pawn from the chess-board and weighed it in his hand.

"I should be prepared to employ you only as what you are," he said presently. "A thief. If you can convince me that your accomplishments in that profession are sufficiently impressive, you shall be both employed and well rewarded."

Gaudeans displayed his neat little teeth in a quick, lop-sided smile.

"What for?"

Lindemann looked at him for a moment.

"You would have no objection, I take it, to stealing from the King of England? Something well known to the public but of no essential importance?"

The smile faded from Gaudeans's face.

"By Jove," he said pensively. "There's a trick now. What?"

"As to that, we shall see. No one expects you to ransack Buckingham Palace or the Tower of London. What matters is that the items should be well known to the public and their loss a matter of embarrassment to British security."

Gaudeans smiled again, very quickly, like a flicker of light.

"You'd have to tell me why. And I'd need a free hand. Even so, it might be odds against the idea. But I'd have to know why you wanted me to do it. All right?"

Lindemann shrugged.

"Call it devilment, if you wish. During the past few months there has been a good deal of unpleasantness in matters of security between ourselves and the British. There has been much foolishness. Left unchecked, such incidents make trust between two great powers impossible. That, in turn, brings closer the point of more general conflict. You see?"

"Oh, yes," said Gaudeans. "Plain as day. What do you want me to do?"

"Convince the British that in a duel of this kind they will be the losers."

"And how would I do that?"

"By penetrating one of their strongholds, removing its most famous treasure, and then allowing it to be returned by our own intelligence service."

Gaudeans's foxy face expanded in a crooked grin again. He was frank but amiable.

"I don't believe you," he sniggered. "Not the giving-back part. I never knew a fellow who could bear to part with spondulicks like that once he got his hands on them."

Lindemann flushed slightly but kept his pride under control.

"In that case," he said lightly, "our conversation is at an end."

Gaudeans looked thoroughly alarmed.

"All I meant," he said quickly, "is that I'd never known it. A chap who pays me the price is entitled to the goods, of course. What he does with them is his own business. Come to think of it, you couldn't do much else with royal treasure except hand it back, could you? No fence would touch it. No market. Too easily recognized. What exactly is it you want stolen?"

Lindemann put the pawn back on the board.

"We shall come to that later," he said. "Before we do, I shall need to be further convinced in the matter of your own peculiar expertise."

"I'd need priming, too." Gaudeans's amber spaniel-eyes apologized for raising the matter. "The salvage money. I'd need to know, d'you see, how much was on the table." Another quick little smile showed that he meant no harm.

Lindemann shrugged, as though money were unimportant in the agreement.

"Shall we say the current market value of whatever precious metals and stones you obtain from the place decided on?"

Gaudeans let out a long, soft whistle.

"Now there's a thing!" he said admiringly. It was a trick, of course; it had to be. No one paid a thief the market value of anything. It crossed his mind that Lindemann might have launched his own private scheme for international burglary, under cover of his appointment in General Staff Intelligence. A chap who directed the thieving of codes and secret treaties from palace vaults might do a very nice line in jewellery and bullion as well. And if that were true, a clever little animal like Captain Gaudeans would be the best partner in the world. So Gaudeans thought. He began to see himself and Lindemann as colleagues, the big man and the little chap.

"You have been, after all, a safebreaker," said Lindemann reasonably. "To my own knowledge."

Gaudeans licked his lips.

"Oh, yes," he said sincerely. "Rather." He was going to be anything that Lindemann wanted him to be from now on. By instinct he knew that this was the chance of his life. Nothing would make him surrender it. Nothing. It was the only promise he ever kept, a promise to himself.

"But," said Lindemann, "can you open a modern vault-safe?"

Gaudeans's tongue was still running on his lips with anticipation. "What sort precisely would that be?"

Lindemann's face was expressionless now.

"Double-locked, six tumblers, million-number combination, bomb-proof doors, armoured steel?"

Gaudeans gave a snigger of relief.

"*That* sort of safe!" He beamed at his interrogator. "Yes, of course. Anyone can do that. Anyone, at least, who claims to be an illusionist."

"And the proof of your abilities?"

The little man tapped the side of his nose confidentially.

"Now there's the trick, d'you see? It's like asking you if you could win a battle. You can't prove till you try. Can you?"

"Safes are more easily procurable than battles."

"Yes," said Gaudeans nervously. "To be sure they are." There was nothing for it now but to take up the challenge and hope for the best. "I imagine you must have some pretty good ones in a place like this. Real corkers."

Lindemann nodded. So there was no going back now.

"Tell you what," said Gaudeans sportingly. "You take me to the best of all. A hundred per cent snorter. See what I can do with it. I can't say fairer than that, can I?"

Lindemann went to the phone at the far end of the room and spoke too quietly for Gaudeans to overhear. He walked slowly back.

"It seems your wish is to be granted," he said laconically. "I trust for your sake that your skill as an illusionist goes somewhat beyond the cheapjack displays of the Lietzensee."

"Oh, it does," said the little man reassuringly. "In lots of ways. For instance, since we've been sitting here playing and talking, you haven't had your eyes off me longer than it takes to blink. Eh?"

"So? You tell me now you have my watch and chain in your pocket?"

"Goodness, no!" Gaudeans smiled. "But if you was just to take another look at the chess-board, I think you'd find yourself as checkmate as you've ever been in your life. See?"

Lindemann gave him a short glance of contempt for this mean and unimpressive manipulation of the pieces. Gaudeans held his gaze with a hard and bright sincerity.

"Speaking of the Lietzensee," he said softly, "that's where your young lady goes of an evening, ain't it?"

Lindemann's frown might have been displeasure or mere incomprehension.

"Miss Tonia Schroeder," said Gaudeans helpfully. "Golden tresses, skin like peach, dimples. Eyes that look sometimes blue and sometimes green. Fine figure of a woman. With you in the Panopticum that day. Remember?" He sighed wistfully.

Lindemann grunted, as if it were of no consequence.

"At the Lietzensee," Gaudeans continued. "Funny thing, saw her there one night when something went wrong with my little box. Key not in the right place. Someone could have drowned me if I wasn't up to snuff. See?"

"No," said Lindemann derisively. "No. I don't see. I have no idea whatever—"

"I think you have," sniggered the ugly little man confidentially. "Still, all water under the bridge and down the river now. Eh? Thing is, I rather fancied Missy Tonia was up to no good."

"Oh?" Lindemann waited with an expression of supreme indifference.

Gaudeans giggled again.

"Then I saw otherwise. Not her style. And you know what?" He waited for a response, but there was none. "She wasn't there because of you. Oh, no. Other times, she may do what you tell her. Frightened not to, perhaps. But the Lietzensee was different. She came to please herself. Give her eyes a feast. All the way out to Charlottenburg just to see a sharp little fellow like me!"

Still there was no answer from Lindemann, and Gaudeans, meeting his gaze again, saw in the eyes of the young colonel the resolute, impassive look of the hunter for the vermin in his trap.

11

Gaudeans felt quite sick with the apprehension and excitement. This was going to be the big one, he thought, but if he could do it, there was no limit to the possibilities. He had asked for the best, the hardest, because he knew that would be a Kromer and he had a general idea of what to expect. If he could open this, young Lindemann would be eating out of his hand.

Lindemann led him out of the high panelled room which served as a study, towards the main staircase of the General Staff headquarters building. Gaudeans glanced quickly at the rows of narrower corridors running off the main passage-way. No wonder, he thought, that the place was known to the army staff as "The Rabbit Warren."

"Mind you," he said reproachfully, "I'm not saying I *can* open it, not just like that. But if you were just to lead me up to the beast and show me the action of the door, there's no knowing what we might not do. Is there?"

Lindemann looked contemptuously at the foxy whiskers and the neat, predatory teeth as Gaudeans tried to make him an unwilling conspirator in the matter.

"There is no knowing what may happen if you prove to be a braggart and a scoundrel," he said quietly.

Gaudeans winced. The cold promise reminded him of something that Tappken had said two days before, a vaguely defined threat whose words now escaped him. He plucked up courage, however, and chattered on, a nattily-dressed little cheat in his sharp, old-fashioned Gladstone collar with its high pointed corners.

"Now I don't *promise!*" he admonished Lindemann coyly, like an adult with a tiresome child. "If it was a question of keys, I wouldn't even try. Not without my equipment. I wouldn't even look at double locks and armoured steel. But million-number combinations ain't the same at all. Eh? So much of that is just in the head. Brain-work. Wouldn't you say?"

Lindemann strode smartly beside him, and Gaudeans almost had to skip along to keep pace.

"And what does your equipment consist of, Herr Gaudeans?"

Gaudeans chuckled bravely.

"That'd be telling, eh? Bits and pieces. Odds and ends. Still, I don't mind letting a chum in on it. Never hold out on a chum. Never peach on a chum. That's the golden rule of life."

"What instruments precisely?"

"Plumber's ring-saw," said Gaudeans earnestly. "Lovely job, that. Cut a round hole through metal, big enough to put your fist through."

"Through armoured steel!"

"Ah!" Gaudeans conceded the point. "That's a trick, though. Eh?"

They went down the main staircase to the basement area of the General Staff building. At this level there was a large open space which duplicated the dimensions of the entrance-lobby above. Two uniformed N.C.O.s, the warders of this territory, sat at a desk in its centre. They stood to attention as Lindemann appeared.

To Gaudeans the rigmarole seemed extraordinarily complicated. First of all, Lindemann handed a key to the warders. With this they opened a small steel safe built into the wall and handed another key to him in exchange.

Lindemann then opened an iron wicket which led into a low-ceilinged corridor, and switched on an electric light. It reminded Gaudeans of the cellars at Ladysmith, the improvised military prison with which he had been briefly and uncomfortably acquainted.

They passed several doors whose grilles showed small white-washed rooms inside which might easily have been jail cells. Then the apartments which opened off the long low-ceilinged corridor appeared more spacious. One, dimly-lit, was hung with two cards bearing concentric circles, like targets at a rifle range. None of these glimpses did anything to reassure Gaudeans of his safety.

Almost at the end of the passage-way, Lindemann stopped. He used his key to open the last door in the row, a solid piece of armoured steel with no grille or Judas-hole to weaken it. Despite himself, Gaudeans was impressed. At least his request had been granted; Lindemann was about to bring him face to face with the tightest crib that the General Staff possessed. A new sense of dignity warmed him at the thought of it.

Lindemann unlocked the door, switched on the electric light, and ushered Gaudeans inside. Easy to see, Gaudeans thought, why they used electricity down here. Gas too dangerous. The vaults were air-tight, no ventilation. No gas, then. When he looked about him at the room they had entered, it seemed to him to be carved out of solid rock. It wasn't, of course. He was sure of that. The truth was that it nestled in the foundations of the massive building, giving it a five- or six-metre thickness of concrete round its walls. The ceiling, too, was solid. Never dig through to this from the level above or below. Very good. Gaudeans paid his professional tribute to such workmanship.

The room itself, windowless and tall, was almost cosy, for all that. The nearer area was lined by book-shelves bearing handsome leather-bound volumes identified only by numbers on their spines. Yet the shape of the vault was long and comparatively narrow, the dimensions of a passage-way. The far end was closed off by an iron-barred partition with a sliding gate at its centre. Through the bars, Gaudeans saw the tall, steel-grey shape standing in dramatic isolation under the harsh electric glare of the farther light, which was turned on, like the nearer bulb, by the switch at the door. Gaudeans looked quickly and noticed that the two lights could both be operated either from the door or from a second switch inside the vault where the safe stood. He murmured his approval. They were good, he conceded; they really were very good.

Lindemann walked ahead of him, Gaudeans close at his heels. Nothing to tell him what the book-shelves contained. Volumes big and small, bound uniformly in blue leather and distinguished only by their numbers. Codes, perhaps? Not his concern, anyhow.

He watched Lindemann unlock the iron grille and slide the gate aside. Gaudeans admired the way it moved so silently. Like oil on ice, he thought. Like a hand on a silk dress. He also noticed that Lindemann used the same key for the grille which he had used to open the previous door. That told a chap something, a chap like himself, Gaudeans thought. Whoever could open the steel door could get all the way to the safe. Not many fellows privileged to do that. He was about to ask how many, and then he paused. Too pushing. What did it matter how many? Two, at a guess. Chief of Staff and senior aide-de-camp, Lindemann. Not bad. Only two men on earth knew the secret of the million-number combination, and they were inviting old Gaudy to join them. His heart jumped at the thought. Excitement spiced by just a little terror.

The grey Kromer safe seemed almost dark against the immaculate whitewash of the bare walls. As was customary in such places, it stood sideways to the gate, its door and combination dial better concealed from casual view in this position. Smooth and sleek, were the words that rose in Gaudeans's mind. For all that, the armoured steel of its outer shell, bound with concrete in the manner of Krupp's armour-plating, would blunt the keenest bit almost before it chipped the paint-work. Its door, two metres high and almost as wide, would withstand an explosion that might bring down the entire building.

"What a beast!" said Gaudeans proudly, for Lindemann's benefit. "What a beauty, too!" He stood before the door, the smooth steel broken only by the spindle of the combination dial at its centre and the bolt-handle to one side, which could be operated as soon as the correct numbers were dialled.

"Beautiful!" Gaudeans's rhapsody rose a tone higher. "No frills, you see. No projections, no crevices. Couldn't get a gnat's whisker between the door and the edge. No leverage, no toe-hold. Nothing. May I just touch her?"

Without waiting for Lindemann's consent, he ran his fingers up and down the steel edges with a loving, anatomical professionalism.

"Beautiful," he said again, in the same wistful, moist-eyed way. "She's the girl for me, all right."

"Are you ready?" said Lindemann sharply.

"Just the action of the door," Gaudeans murmured. "If you wouldn't mind. I only ask because, frankly, I've never had the pleasure of a Kromer before."

He stood with arms folded while Lindemann spun the spindle to and fro, quick and expert, picking out the sequence of numbers to right, to left, and to right again. He turned the projecting knob a final time to the left, stepped across to the bolt-lever, pressed it down, and opened the door. Gaudeans shook his head in wondering admiration. Not a click from the spindle, not a sound from the lever.

Lindemann made no effort to open the door wide. He drew it back just a little. Gaudeans caught a glimpse of the interior, like a small room lined with shelves and bound volumes whose blue calf was uniform with those on the ledges close to the strong-room door.

He watched Lindemann close the safe.

"Look," he said, in his best imitation of a decent sporting fellow. "I think I ought to turn my back now, or anything else you like. Then I'd like you to set the combination to a new number, if you don't mind. Make it a stinker, if you can. Hardest of them all. Then let's see what I can do. Mind you, though, I don't absolutely promise. Not with a machine like this."

He turned his back and let Lindemann see how he buried his face in his hands, beyond any possibility of watching the new combination that was being chosen. Only when Lindemann finished did he turn around, his eyes still languid with their pathetic admiration of the safe, the damascene beauty of its steel hide, the silent power of its hinges, the sensuous elegance of its heavy, silent movement.

Lindemann watched him. With an instinctive gesture of reverence Gaudeans touched his finger-tips together as he stood before the massive steel door. Taking the spindle gently, he turned it one notch in either direction, feeling the slight movement of the cogs through his sensitive fingers and the ligaments of his hand. He repeated the exercise, this time with his ear close to the mechanism, tongue pressed out between his teeth in the agony of concentration. He listened, shook his head doubtfully, then began to hum a little tune as he tried the bolt-lever. It held fast.

Undefeated, he wiped his fingers on the lapels of his oatmeal tweed, as if the ordeal might be bringing him out in a sweat. Then he began to turn the dial again, even more slowly than before.

Lindemann stood beside him, watching in complete silence. With his ear to the mechanism all the time, Gaudeans turned the spindle this way and that, picking out one series of numbers after another. He chose a dozen combinations, his face looking more like a forlorn little animal with each failure. Lindemann made no attempt to conceal his scorn. At last Gaudeans looked up at him, still crouching with his hand on the spindle. The eyes were hopeless and apprehensive in their dog-like misery.

"Sorry," he said, trying to make light of the whole thing. "Can't seem to make the jolly old 'fluence do its stuff. Funny, that. Never had bother like this before."

Lindemann motioned him aside. Gaudeans once again turned his back and hid his face in his hands so that he should not see the combination reset. He looked almost as if he might be weeping with the humiliation of it all. Yet when he turned round at last, his sporting optimism still flickered with life.

"Look," he said, in a fresh access of frankness and decency, "I really am most awfully sorry. To have put you to all this trouble." His voice rose in a wail of misery. "What must you think of me?"

Lindemann made no reply. He tested the bolt-lever a second time to make absolutely sure that the safe was securely locked.

"Listen!" Gaudeans's voice quavered on a double tone, imploring and self-abasing. "Let me make it up to you!"

Lindemann looked at him with a grimace of repulsion.

"Make it up?"

Gaudeans nodded and swallowed greedily. There was no limit to his willingness to make amends.

"Let me do something for you. Show you something. Lock me in this end of the vault, behind the sliding iron gate. No tools, no keys. I'll have it open again in two minutes or so. See if I don't!"

"What with?"

Gaudeans held his fingers up and wriggled them in the air.

"Absurd!" Lindemann waited for Gaudeans to precede him out of the area containing the safe so that he could slide the metal grille across and lock it again. Gaudeans stood still.

"Please!" he said, his tone reasonable but insistent. It seemed that Lindemann would either have to accede to the request or carry him out bodily.

"Why?"

"To show you what I can do!" Gaudeans, from the sound of his voice, was on the verge of tears. "I *can*! One difference of opinion with a Kromer safe don't signify! There's no end to the things I can do!"

"Including the opening of a double-action military strong-room lock with your *fingers*?" Lindemann's scorn was fraught with amusement despite his annoyance.

"Among other things," said Gaudeans with quiet modesty.

Lindemann sighed.

"Get it done, then!"

With a nervous tweak of his lower lip between his teeth, Gaudeans bounced back to full self-confidence.

"Right!" he said, rubbing his hands enthusiastically. "Right you are, then!"

He watched Lindemann step out of the strong-room area and slide the grille across. The key turned twice. Double lock. That was good, thought Gaudeans, very good indeed.

"Now," he said gently, "I want you to hold that key in your hand. Make sure you've got it where I can't reach it. In fact, I want you to walk away slowly as far as the door of the vault at the far end. Take a couple of minutes. Make sure you're so far away you couldn't help me even if you wanted to."

"I should prefer to stand here and watch you," said Lindemann coldly. But Gaudeans shook his head.

"Fair is fair," he said reprovingly. "I don't want to know your secrets. You've no right to know mine."

Lindemann shrugged and walked with slow, measured steps up the length of the vault towards the door which opened on to the main subterranean passage. After all, there was nothing lost by granting Gaudeans this final indulgence. Perhaps there was a true magic in the fingers of the little trickster. If so, the best he would do would be to open the iron grille. He would hardly dare to attack Lindemann from behind. If he did, if he could get the key and open the door to the passage-way, there were still two armed guards to meet him at the other end.

These were the thoughts which passed through Lindemann's mind as he walked, step by step, farther away from the grille which sealed off the strong-room. All the same, he was beginning to feel tired. The air was never very good down here, stagnant and enclosed as it was. Gaudeans wearied him, too. The bogus joviality, the mindless chatter.

He had almost reached the door when he heard Gaudeans's voice, richly falsetto in its new enthusiasm.

"I say! I do believe I've done it!"

Lindemann swung round. The iron grille was still closed, as he had expected it to be. Indeed, Gaudeans was nowhere near it. He was propped by one elbow on the door of the massive Kromer safe. The door of the safe was, of course, wide open.

For a second or two Lindemann stared at him, not angry but dumbfounded as he tried to envisage a sequence of events which would account for what he saw. His imagination failed him. Then he pulled himself together as Gaudeans disappeared from view behind the open steel door and there was a clatter of files and document-cases. Lindemann raced down the length of the vault, key in hand, unlocked the iron grille, and slid it aside with a crash.

"I did tell you," said the voice of the invisible magician reproach-fully. "I did tell you that I could have that grille open in a couple of minutes."

Lindemann ignored the taunt. To slam the door of the safe and lay hands on Gaudeans were now the conflicting priorities in his mind. He pushed ahead of him with his palms, throwing his weight at the smooth grey steel and feeling the heavy door swing smoothly into place. He looked for Gaudeans, but Gaudeans had gone. That made no sense at first. Then Lindemann knew that the nimble little trickster had somehow got behind him. He had begun to turn defensively when, to his astonishment, all the lights went out.

Only then did he realize the tawdry fair-ground deceptions to which he had fallen victim. None of them was remarkable in itself; it was the rapidity with which they followed one another that had bewildered him. Hardly ten seconds before, he had been walking calmly towards the outer door of the vault, musing on his own weariness. Through the rush of his own breath and the confusion of his movements, Lindemann was aware that he had just missed hearing distinctly the solid impact of a metal bolt closing. He had a fleeting image of himself, in his moment of panic, turning the key to open the grille and leaving it in the lock as he raced for the open door of the safe.

"Hello!" said Gaudeans amiably, not ten feet away as Lindemann judged. "I'm out here now!"

Lindemann stood still and silent in the darkness. Anger was useless. His best chance was to leave the initiative with Gaudeans until the little man, in his turn, made an error of judgement. There was no need to go to the grille and try it. Lindemann knew that it was securely locked, that he was a prisoner behind it, and that Gaudeans was safely on the outside with the key.

"Nothing to worry about," said Gaudeans through the darkness. "I just thought you'd like to see what I can do when I've got to."

Lindemann frowned and waited. Presently he heard Gaudeans turn away and walk slowly up the length of the vault to the other door, which opened on to the passage-way. Again there came the heavy, resonant sound of a bolt's being turned by a key. The outer door opened, showing a silhouette of Gaudeans against the glow of the passage-way. He stepped out, closed the door, and then locked it from the far side.

Alone in the darkness, Lindemann swore to himself. Not only had he fallen for the easiest tricks of a fair-ground charlatan, he was no longer even certain of the charlatan's motives. However, the bars of the grille were wide enough for him to stretch his arm through and reach the light switch on the wall just beyond. Moving cautiously in the darkness, he did this, blinking in the renewed brightness of the white-shaded bulb.

He had no idea of what Gaudeans might be doing in the passage-way, or indeed of what Gaudeans *could* do in the passage-way. His principal fear was that the guards at the far end would suspect what had happened and might find the senior aide to the Chief of Staff locked up in his own strong-room. Quickly he checked the contents of the safe. Nothing was missing; nothing was out of place. Indeed, it seemed that Gaudeans had only made the sounds of rummaging to draw Lindemann to the place more quickly and surely. Lindemann closed the steel door and set the dials to a new combination.

In the electric-lit passage-way outside, Gaudeans decided to take a stroll down to the far end and back. Have a word with the guards there through the locked gate and then turn back again. He owed himself that much. It also occurred to him that Lindemann might, after all, be angry with him. A friendly word with the guards and a pretence that all was well would be good insurance. After all, Lindemann had made a bit of an ass of himself. Only too glad to say no more about it, he supposed. As he walked, still unnoticed by the two guards outside, Gaudeans took a thief's professional interest in the security of the underground cells. Unobserved, he tried Lindemann's key to see if it fitted any of the other doors. Interesting to know what might lie within them. Unfortunately the only doors well out of sight of the guards in the vestibule were the two little cells immediately inside the passage-way, hidden by the jut of the main stone lintel. The key certainly fitted both. So, the keys in the vestibule wall-safe had common and varying teeth. There were officers who might have access to a prisoner but who would never be allowed in the vault where Lindemann now awaited him.

He came into view of the guards and raised a reassuring hand.

"Colonel Lindemann's compliments," he said smoothly. "Asked me to wait in the corridor while he consulted certain documents. All in order, I hope?"

The guard who had stood up now sat down again. There would be no quarrel with Lindemann's orders.

Gaudeans walked slowly back. At one point he took out his pipe and began to fill it from a tin of Ogden's Flake. Then, remembering the lack of ventilation, he seemed to think better of it, putting pipe and tin away again. With his back to the main gate, he unlocked the outer door of the vault, opened it, stepped through, and closed it again behind him.

"Hello," he said casually. "Here I am again."

Lindemann said nothing. He stood tall and fair in his field-grey uniform behind the grille of the strong-room, his arms folded.

"Aren't you going to ask me to let you out?" inquired Gaudeans pleasantly.

Lindemann shook his head.

"You are quite as much a prisoner as I, Herr Gaudeans. You would not get beyond the gate at the end of the passage-way."

Gaudeans, leaning back against the closed door, took out his pipe and lit it. He waved away a cloud of fragrant smoke.

"D'you think not?" he asked anxiously. "I don't see it that way. In fact, the reason I went and walked down the corridor just now was to see what the guards would do. And what did they do? Nothing. Surprised to see me, of course. Not pleased, perhaps, but certainly not hostile. Suppose I'd said, 'Colonel Lindemann's compliments, and I'm to fetch the ink-stand from his room'? Or just asked for an escort to the cloak-room? I could have been out and away with the key to the vault. And it would have taken heavy artillery to blast you out of here. Eh?"

"You would never get past them," said Lindemann quietly.

Gaudeans shrugged, as if at the futility of arguing with one so obstinate. He turned to the shelves of bound leather files, each identified only by a number, and drew his finger along them. Then he waved his pipe-stem at the array.

"Nice little library," he said pleasantly. "Very handsome."

Lindemann unfolded his arms and slipped hands into his trouser-pockets.

"If you remove one of those volumes from its place, I will have you shot."

"All right," said Gaudeans indifferently, "if you feel that strongly about it."

He sauntered down towards the locked grille which divided them and stood, confronting Lindemann at last.

"Only goes to prove what I can do when I have to," he said. "Not so bad, was it? At the most, I could be out and clear with the key to the General Staff strong-room. Copies to French and British military attachés, and one to your old guv'nor Moltke, for good luck."

"Never," said Lindemann coolly. "And if you could, then every lock would be changed within twelve hours."

"At the least," Gaudeans persisted, "I've got into the strong-room, opened the safe, and locked up the aide-de-camp instead. No doubt about that, is there?"

"Not the least," said Lindemann equably. "Is that all?"

Gaudeans looked at him with reproach.

"Of course it isn't," he said. "I haven't even mentioned the most important thing of all. Imagine all this done *for* you, against whoever you have in mind. Tell me what it is you want, and let me get it for you. Don't you see? I can do it! That's my trade. But you wouldn't have believed me without a bit of a show like this, would you?"

Without waiting for Lindemann's reply, he unlocked the grille and handed over the key again. Lindemann stepped out and closed the gate once more.

"Would you?" Gaudeans was hurrying along beside him now, like an insistent child pestering its parent. "I had to show you!"

Lindemann nodded, as if the explanation were no longer important.

"Just because it was easy to do!" There was a faint whine of accusation in Gaudeans's voice now. "It's only practice and timing that makes it easy! I knew you'd go for that safe door. So fast that you'd never bother jiggling with the key in the lock. And I was round that safe and behind you before ever you got the door shut. Knocked off the light in passing and had that grille closed and locked quicker than you could turn your head."

"Evidently." Lindemann was preoccupied, scarcely attending to the explanation.

"Of course," said Gaudeans generously, "I could never have done it if you were expecting what happened. But you weren't, you see. Nor will they, whoever they are. They won't know which side I'm coming from, nor how, nor when. They won't even know what I look like. There's a trick now! Eh?"

They had reached the outer door of the vault.

"Wait outside!" said Lindemann irritably. Gaudeans stood obediently in the passage-way, the door almost closed between them. He could hear Lindemann moving some of the bound volumes on the shelves just inside the vault. Gaudeans was displeased by this. It showed a lack of trust on Lindemann's part. After all, he had done no more than look at the handsome bindings, run his finger along them, and wave his pipe-stem at the collection. Still, he knew that he had discovered a thing or two in the past twenty minutes. Enough to embarrass even Colonel Lindemann if the need should occur. This thought sweetened his mood. He smiled both in recollection and in anticipation. For all his cringing and humility, he decided, it was the little man who would be master now. His mind raced with ideas and inspirations so exciting that he longed to tell someone about them. That was impossible, of course. With all the strength at his command, Gaudeans controlled his exuberance. For the time being, all the momentous discoveries and ambitions would remain securely locked from the world, in the narrow fox-skull under its ragged ginger curls.

12

T he pain of the first blow had been so intense that Gaudeans
cried out even before Lindemann hit him the second time. That
second blow, when it landed on the side of his face, knocked the
pipe from his mouth and snapped the bowl from the stem as it fell on
the hearth. They were in Lindemann's study again.

Lindemann himself stood with feet firmly planted before Gaudeans's chair, watching impassively as his victim blinked away
involuntary tears and wiped moisture from his nose on the back of
his hand.

"This will continue," he said quietly, "until you answer the
question. From side to side. And when that has failed to make an
appeal to reason, we shall go back downstairs to somewhere very
private. Things will happen there which, frankly, would make it
impossible for you to be set free even after you had answered the
question."

Gaudeans made a sound of distress in his throat, his head still
singing from the blows as he tried to comprehend the horror of what
Lindemann was promising him. His hesitation was an error of
judgement. Lindemann took it for deliberate obstinacy. He hit
Gaudeans again with a full swing of his shoulders, knocking him off
the chair. In his fall, Gaudeans crashed against the table, scattering
onyx chess-men across the carpet and rolling the tin of Ogden's
Flake into the fire-place. The little man landed on his spine,
performed an involuntary backward roll, and caught his temple
sharply on the crest of the iron fender. He put his hand up to the tiny
welling of blood, and then looked at his fingers with the wide-eyed
shock of a tormented animal.

"Come," said Lindemann reasonably. "This will not do. There are
some secrets which no man has a right to keep to himself."

"I tell you!" shouted Gaudeans, almost in anger rather than in fear.
"It was a fluke! A guess! I wish I'd never done it!"

The toe of Lindemann's military boot came forward, short and
sharp. Gaudeans let out a muted howl of anguish as his adversary
stood over him, poised to do the sort of damage which could never be

repaired. It was absurd to see the face and whiskers of a middle-aged man looking up from the body of a frightened child. Still, Captain Gaudeans had better reason than anyone to know what a well-aimed kick might do to him.

"Yes!" he shouted suddenly, above the throbbing nausea of his spine and the ringing in his head. "Yes!" The surrender was complete now, and the dishonour to himself was easier with every syllable which followed. Lindemann stood over him, quick to deal cruelly with any deceit. Gaudeans, wiping blood on his hand, snuffled and almost wept.

"Don't you understand?" he wailed. "Can't you see? As soon as I twigged there was only two of you had the combination, I knew I could open that safe! You're supposed to be an intelligence officer, ain't you? Surely you can see how!"

"Don't tell me what I'm supposed to be," said Lindemann coolly. "I should not wish to be angry with you now. Continue."

Gaudeans gulped for breath and sniffed pathetically.

"You let me watch you open the safe, first time," he gasped. "So I could get a look at the mechanism. See? All right? Then I turned my back and you set it to another number. One in millions. Right? 'Course I couldn't find it! Who could? All that stuff about listening to the clicks of the spindle, no one ever opened a safe that way!"

"But you did open it in the end." Lindemann spoke as if Gaudeans needed to be reminded of the fact. "Now you are going to tell me how. Your back was turned and your eyes covered when that combination was set."

Gaudeans pulled himself on to his knees, as if he might embrace Lindemann's shins and weep for forgiveness. Lindemann took a step backwards.

"Don't you see? If only two of you had the number, it was odds-on you'd set it to the first one again. The one I'd watched you open it with. Suppose you set it to a different one and something went wrong with you. Badly wrong, I mean. Accident in the street. Sudden seizure. Anything like that. Someone else has to know the number, too. But then, I thought, if you went and left the safe with a new combination, how could they? I don't suppose you'd get a chance to tell General Moltke before tomorrow. See?"

"Go on," said Lindemann quietly. Gaudeans sat back on his heels. He was recovering from the ill-treatment rapidly as his pride began to swell and he described his own cleverness.

"When I turned my back and covered my eyes, I guessed you were setting the combination to the same one. The one you used when I watched you open the safe at first. Otherwise, you only need a little clot of blood in the brain while you sleep, a bit of a stumble on the street-rails when one of those tram-wheels comes slicing along—and where's your old Moltke then? Eh? He'd need a ton of dynamite to budge that door if you snuffed it and took the new combination with you. Simple, really."

"No, no." Lindemann helped Gaudeans back into his chair. "Not simple. Ingenious."

It was a little painful for Gaudeans to smile, but he did so.

"Mind you, I wasn't sure, not certain!" The wet lips were babbling confidentially again. "That's why I made up that little story for you about being able to get the grille unlocked and open. Wouldn't do to say I could open the safe straight off, would it? You'd have caught on fast to that. And, be fair now, I did get that grille open—with your assistance—didn't I?"

He looked up at the man who, a few moments before, had knocked him to the ground, and his mouth opened in a ghastly little smile of self-congratulation.

"Turn out your pockets," said Lindemann gently.

"I say!" The broken smile withered. "I thought we were friends again."

"Turn out your pockets!" There was no mistaking the promise of retribution in the quiet, clipped voice.

Gaudeans obeyed. On the table beside him he deposited a small leather pocket-book, a comb, a pencil, several coins, a latch-key, and a handkerchief seamed with dust along its folds. Lindemann thumbed through the contents of the pocket-book; then he nodded at the clutter of articles.

"Put them back," he said gently. "Now we can talk sensibly again." He filled a glass from the decanter and handed it to the little man. Gaudeans took a gulp from it before going down on hands and knees to find his broken pipe and tobacco tin. He opened the tin and held its fragrant brown contents towards Lindemann.

"Take a fill?" he pleaded, indicating himself. Lindemann nodded. Gaudeans tried to join the two fragments of his pipe, shrugged, and gave up. He took another pull from the glass, his eyes brimming at the raw spirit.

"Rewards and penalties," said Lindemann. "How you are treated for the future depends on which you earn. Do you understand?"

Gaudeans nodded and mumbled gratefully.

"Good." Lindemann laid a hand firmly on his shoulder. "Then I shall find something for you. Not Buckingham Palace or the Koh-i-noor diamond. But something better than the Lietzensee."

Gaudeans snuffled humorously, as if to confirm his restored trust in Lindemann.

"Anything's better than the Lietzensee."

"First of all," Lindemann continued, "something well within your capabilities rather than something which may be just beyond them."

"Nothing's beyond Dicky Gaudeans," said Gaudeans proudly, "not once he sets his mind to it."

"You shall prove that. In time."

Gaudeans seemed satisfied with this, apart from one suggestion of his own.

"I'd like a chum." He made the appeal deferentially, as if still wary of Lindemann's recent anger. He knew that Lindemann would kill him if it ever became necessary. He promised himself never to doubt that. "It's easier with a chum. There's no end to what four eyes and four hands can do. A girl chum, if possible." He was daring Lindemann to make Tonia his partner.

Lindemann took the empty glass and set it down on the table.

"Yes," he said thoughtfully. "Why not? But a companion of my choosing, not yours. One who will remind you of your duty, should you ever be inclined to forget it. You shall have the best."

"A clipper, eh?" Gaudeans held the twisted little grin a moment longer for Lindemann's benefit. The reply was not quite all he had wanted, but there was nothing to be gained by argument. Then Lindemann took him by the elbow and led him to the door, where two messengers would be waiting to see Gaudeans off the premises. Before the door opened, the little man turned to his companion with a look of self-conscious admiration.

"Listen," he said gently. "I haven't been quite straight with you. Not altogether. There's something else about that safe, how I knew the number at the end had to be the same one that you began with. I'd like to tell you about it."

Lindemann looked down at him expressionlessly, waiting.

"You see," said Gaudeans, with an endearing narrowing of the eyes, "if you'd changed it, that'd mean telling your guv'nor so. General Moltke. And then you'd have to tell him that you'd been down there. What's more, you'd have to tell him that you'd let me open the safe and rummage in it. Not to mention our little joke with the grille. I was sure you wouldn't want him to know. See? That's how a sharp fellow always looks at these things."

The moist animal eyes looked up gratefully. Lindemann nodded.

"I wanted you to know," Gaudeans persisted, "now that we're going to be together in this. We'll get on like a house on fire, you and I. You see if we don't."

Lindemann closed the door on him and stood quite still, possessed by an involuntary shudder. He went across to his desk in the window-recess, unhooked the telephone, and asked for a number.

"Lindemann, Excellency. Gaudeans has gone. He performed so well that it was necessary to change the combination code after he had finished. Not well enough for a first-rate target, perhaps. But probably a second-rate, and any third-rate without question."

In response to his commander's summons, Lindemann entered the bare monastic study, vaulted like a baroque tomb, ten minutes later. The two men sat at either side of a table, Lindemann prompting himself from a file of papers in his hand.

"The first opportunity, Excellency, occurs in early January. King Edward's visit to Chatsworth as the guest of the Duke of Devonshire. For the shooting."

"Too soon."

"Until the end of February, it is unlikely that there will be anything of value to us in the dispatches. After that, of course, there is *Invincible*, launching and trials."

"Within Gaudeans's reach?"

Lindemann frowned.

"On the fourth of March, King Edward travels overland to Biarritz. For a month, his entourage will occupy the south wing of the Hôtel du Palais. Unfortunately, Excellency, communication with London has always been via three Royal Navy destroyers. After our earlier success, it is unlikely that confidential dispatches will be sent by courier."

"And then?"

"The whole of April is occupied by a Mediterranean visit in the royal yacht, *Victoria and Albert*. A meeting with King Alfonso at Cartagena. A crude attempt to involve Spain, Italy, and Greece in the encirclement of the German peoples. May and June are divided between London and Windsor. My own preference is for July."

Moltke looked across at his subordinate uneasily.

"That is seven months away!"

"True, Excellency. It also precedes immediately the manoeuvres of the Home Fleet in the Western Approaches. Including speed, gunnery, and target exercises. King Edward will be present at the Atlantic battle-practice after the royal visit to Dublin."

"Where and when do you propose to employ Captain Gaudeans?"

"Dublin," said Lindemann simply. "At the beginning of July, King Edward will make an official visit to Ireland. The occasion is the Irish International Exhibition at Ballsbridge, a few miles from the centre of the city. Our information is that the King's bodyguards fear for his safety. They believe that Irish nationalists may attempt his assassination. Therefore he must live on board the royal yacht, putting to sea each night and steaming off shore."

Moltke shook his head.

"Gaudeans could never reach the royal yacht. Let alone carry out a robbery on board. This is all a schoolboy's dream!"

"A moment, Excellency." Lindemann pushed a sheet of paper across the table. "In all their security arrangements for the next few months, there is one weakness. During the Irish visit, official communications will pass through Dublin Castle. It is the headquarters of the British garrison and the Dublin Metropolitan Police. That is the one place where a man like Gaudeans might succeed."

"Against the British garrison and the entire police force?" There was a new weariness in the Chief of Staff's voice, as if he might dismiss Lindemann and the entire scheme at any moment. "The man has done nothing so far which could not have been accomplished by luck and cheap trickery."

"There is a way, Excellency, in Dublin during July. He may fail, indeed. But we shall hardly acknowledge him in that event! He will be a common thief. He may plead that he was acting on behalf of German Intelligence. In which case the court will condemn him both as a poor thief and a poor liar."

"Whom we shall have to trust meantime!" Moltke's face tightened.

"By betraying us, he would betray himself, Excellency. I have offered him the market price for whatever treasures he brings. There is no one else who will pay him half as well."

"For what?"

"The Mahony diamonds, Excellency. Even the Irish state jewels. Mahony has been cultivating our embassy in London, seeking sympathy for his Sinn Feiners. He seems quite proud of having made the British Army stand guard over his family heirloom in Dublin Castle."

"There is no possibility of employing Mahony himself in this matter?"

Lindemann shook his head.

"Neither Mahony nor his cause is yet ripe, Excellency."

Moltke nodded and then looked sourly at the blond young colonel.

"It goes against conscience, Lindemann! Common robbery upon whatever pretext!"

"Once we have what we want, Excellency, it would always be possible to return the jewels. We might do so discreetly and without even identifying ourselves."

The Chief of Staff nodded again, unenthusiastically.

"And the girl? Someone must keep a cur like Gaudeans on a leash."

Lindemann laughed, attempting to lighten the mood of the discussion.

"That was the most extraordinary part of it, Excellency! The little scoundrel asked for a chum—that was his word. A girl chum. He almost went so far as to name her."

"Then you did well to put her in his way at the Lietzensee," said Moltke grudgingly.

"If your Excellency will permit"—Lindemann beamed at his commander—"I believe we might favour our own cause by obliging him in this. Your Excellency will recall how well Fräulein Antonia Schroeder has served us in small matters of this kind. She might do more. I judge her as being loyal, capable, and dedicated. Let her be given the leash to which the cur is attached. And let him think he has lured us into the choice by his own cunning. We shall know how to keep him at heel."

Colonel-General Helmuth von Moltke looked up. For the first time since Lindemann had entered the room, the Chief of Staff's face was softened by a sense of relief.

"Very well," he said finally. "It shall be as you suggest."

13

A swelling had begun to appear on his hip where Lindemann had kicked him, the promise of a deeply-coloured bruise. He limped up the stairs to his tall, narrow room, which vibrated distantly to the trains on the elevated railway passing through Charlottenburg station. The pain itself was nothing new. Worse things than that had happened every week of his life at school. Gaudy, the white and bony dwarf with absurd ginger curls, his air of bitter and brooding privacy. Even the other weaklings had turned against him in the knowledge that he was easy game. By pointing him out as a target, they saved themselves into the bargain. Such was his childhood.

The little man winced and drew breath sharply as he lowered himself into the shabby chair. Someone was going to pay for this. Lindemann. Tall, supercilious brute. Arrogant young swine. The phrases came easily to Gaudeans's mind, for he had applied similar descriptions to so many acquaintances in the past. Lindemann. Swaggering peacock in grey regimentals with the coveted carmine stripe of a General Staff officer. Easing his leg where the boot had caught him worst, Gaudeans promised himself that the young colonel would occupy a very special place in his thoughts from now on.

Leaning back carefully, he continued to think of this, his excitement drawing attention from the pain of the blow. He knew there would be many approaches to the problem, many tactical withdrawals and delays. Endless patience. Yet there was no doubt what the objective must be. The destruction of Colonel Lindemann. Not yet, of course. Not until Lindemann had yielded all that was so far promised. But then, certainly. No question of it.

To be fair to himself, Gaudeans thought, it was not often that he was possessed by this wish to accomplish a man's destruction. Quite rarely, in fact. He had not felt it with such intensity, perhaps, since the cases of Granger and Pratt. They were two splendid young blades with flash families and easy athletic prowess who had made his schooldays a living hell. Gaudeans could remember his own voice at twelve years old, blubbering and imploring, the commands of Granger and Pratt obeyed by their hangers-on. The water scalding and the brushes like wire. Dark places where he was doubled up from the spasm of a blow, so far as the grip on his arms permitted. "What are you, Gaudeans? Say it again, please. Much louder this time!"

They had harried and tormented him with the exhilaration of riders after a fox. But he had got the better of them in the end. When the matter of thieving came to light, he was brought before them all to be disgraced and dismissed. During these proceedings he had looked from time to time at the faces of Granger and Pratt. There was contempt, of course. But deeper than that lay incomprehension and unease. It was almost as if they had begun to fear him. He chuckled bitterly at the memory. Such were the creatures who now strutted upon the adult stage, proclaiming it the duty of lesser men to shed their blood for the England of Granger and Pratt against the Germany of Colonel Lindemann.

Lindemann. There was one more thing to be done tonight, safeguarding Gaudeans's plan. Even from the grave the power of Captain Wunder must have its effect. Heaving himself out of the chair, Gaudeans found a sheet of paper and sat down at the bare wooden table under the gas-mantel. Just a precaution, he thought, that was all. The cheap pen began to scratch.

Your Excellency,
As one who is now to work in your interests, I wish to offer a record of certain events which have passed. Colonel Lindemann has tonight betrayed to me the present combination of the Kromer safe No. 465381 in the strong-room of General Staff headquarters. He has also divulged to me the system upon which new combinations are selected and which I describe in the appended note. I have been provided by him with a copy of the key to all doors intervening between the vestibule and the strong-room grille. An examination of the original will show traces of the wax left by the process of taking impressions.

Colonel Lindemann proposes, by my aid, to sell the key and information to British Military Intelligence. My services are to be rewarded by the proceeds of certain robberies carried out under his protection. You will receive this letter only if, when my purpose is accomplished, Colonel Lindemann becomes my murderer. Your

Excellency may therefore more easily believe this last testament of your humble servant, Richard Gaudeans, late Captain, Mounted Infantry, Natal.

It was not quite a lie. He knew the system for choosing the safe-combination. It was not the one which he had "confessed" to placate Lindemann. In a sense, he did have copies of the keys. He added a note on this and folded the two papers into an envelope addressed to Colonel-General Helmuth von Moltke. He put this in a second envelope, marked *To be forwarded in the event of my death.* The entire package was then directed to Scott, Fowler, and Scott, solicitors of Lincoln's Inn Fields. Its arrival would cause little surprise. Several other envelopes in the Gaudeans family deed-box already awaited similar disposal.

In the event of my death. That was the phrase which now possessed him, even in sleep. Since childhood he had been prey to recurring dreams. In the past seven years they had become The Dream: the memory of the first time that he truly believed he was going to die; it haunted him still. He lay down, exhausted, curtains drawn against the flare of street-lights and the rumble of the Stadtbahn over the Charlottenburg bridges. Presently he was lost once more in the silent landscape of sleep, the dumb menace of phantoms.

Now it had the terror of reality. At the time there had been an unreal, dream-like quality even in the bleak subaqueous light within the bell-tent. Rain had fallen steadily throughout the night, to be followed by a sudden sunlit morning. The canvas was dark grey with moisture, though its threads were penetrated by the saffron flush of early light. Captain Gaudeans, hatless and defeated, sat on an upturned box and stared wistfully at the young lieutenant and the sergeant-major who had been ordered to guard him. He was senior to both of them, and much difference did it seem to make. Lieutenant Clarke refused to answer his inquiries at all; Sergeant-Major Stone responded with a beefy relish, making the word "sir" a protracted sneer.

When it was fully light, an orderly brought a mug of hot sweet tea, pressed beef and biscuit in a mess-tin. Even in his dream it seemed to Gaudeans that he could taste dry flakes of food again. When the flap of the tent opened he glimpsed the troops outside in their khaki uniforms, puttees caked in a cast of clay. Some of the relieving force still wore the bristles of a week's beard, their cheeks hollow with exhaustion, eyelids seeming fat and heavy. Far off he saw the outline of the hills among which the little town of Ladysmith lay. Signal flags blinked from the rises, confirming the continued retreat of Kruger's Boer farmers. Pickets with fixed bayonets dotted the ridges of Caesar's Camp, Telegraph Hill, and Lombard's Kop. Beyond the mounted patrols riding in pairs over the high ground, the wave-like South African veldt was green with budding mimosa thorn.

In his panic, Gaudeans could scarcely swallow the strong tea, let alone the hard pellets of beef.

"Listen," he said in the tented nightmare of his dream, "I had no idea that Laszlo was a thief, less still that he was going to trade with the enemy. It was nothing but ordinary barter. See? Box of ammo for his own use in exchange for a few tins of grub. Damn it, man, he'd already got a gun. He needed a box of cartridges to defend himself. That's all!"

"If you say so, sir!"

"Well, then," Gaudeans concluded feebly, "I do say so. If you don't believe me, ask Laszlo."

"Mr. Laszlo executed last night by firing party, sir. Pursuant to sentence of field court martial, approved by General Thorneycroft."

That was when the horror of the dream always began, as it had done in reality seven years before. Yet, to his own surprise, Gaudeans reacted to it with a shout of anger.

"Then you murdered him! You can't shoot a man without having the sentence confirmed by the Commander-in-Chief at the Cape!"

He was shouting to save his own life, of course. Lieutenant Clarke looked at him with silent contempt for his cowardice. It was Sergeant-Major Stone who answered again, eyes gleaming and red moustache bristling.

"Martial law, sir! Looting punishable by summary execution on conviction. Confirmed by General Thorneycroft, general officer commanding mounted brigade of Ladysmith relief force, sir!"

Under the ginger bush of the moustache there was the curve of a smile just discernible in the line of the sergeant-major's mouth. They were enjoying his predicament now, laughing at him in the moments before his death.

"I don't believe you," he said quietly. "I don't believe he was shot."

"One volley, sir. Found to be still respiring when examined. Officer's field-pistol to back of head, sir."

Gaudeans was about to argue when there was a movement outside the tent, a shadow falling across the wet canvas, and then the flap was opened once more. General Thorneycroft stooped through the entrance. He straightened himself inside, a massive and monstrous figure, well over six feet tall, barrel-chested and red-faced.

"Get him ready," he said angrily.

Sergeant-Major Stone stepped across, and Gaudeans got instinctively to his feet.

"Please," said the sharp-featured little man in his dream, "please don't murder me."

They led him out of the tent into the sunlight of the windy morning. He found himself, blinking stupidly, at the centre of a square of men, the troopers of his brigade drawn up and facing inwards to witness his initial humiliation.

"Prisoner to be stripped of rank and insignia, Sar'-Major!" yapped Thorneycroft in front of him.

Gaudeans made a slight movement, about to voice his protest.

"Stand to attention in the presence of your commanding officer, sir!" yelped Sergeant-Major Stone at his back.

Gaudeans gave up that particular struggle. Stone walked round in front of him, carrying a pocket-knife with a sturdy blade. He held Gaudeans's tunic by the top button and then cut the button away with a flourish. The lines of troopers looked on in total fascination at the degradation of one of their officers. Stone took the second button and treated it in the same way. He worked his way down the tunic, then cut away the two pocket-buttons. Last of all, he wrenched the epaulets from Gaudeans's shoulders with a force that nearly pulled the little man off his feet.

Gaudeans stood with his tunic flapping open, the ragged crests of his shoulders confirming an appearance of clownish disarray. Half-a-dozen riflemen had formed up on either side of the little group, which now consisted of General Thorneycroft, Lieutenant Clarke, Sergeant-Major Stone, and Gaudeans himself.

"Prisoner and escort! Right turn! By the left . . . quick march!"

Gaudeans moved instinctively with the others. Keeping step, he thought, all the way to death. He had no idea where they were taking him as the formation marched between the lines of bell-tents, the encampment of the relieving force which had reached Ladysmith three days earlier and ended the long siege. At least he could try to call their bluff.

"You can't shoot a man without a court martial," he blurted out, "not without a trial. Unless you want to be hanged for it."

Thorneycroft, marching massive and brutal beside him, ignored Gaudeans and addressed himself to Stone.

"Law of looting, Sar'-Major?"

"Shoot on sight, sir, where circumstances afford sufficient cause."

"Very good, Sar'-Major. Carry on, please."

"You have no proof—"

But this time they ignored him completely, only the regimental sergeant-major singing out the steps to the detachment which formed his escort.

"Left, left, left, right, left!"

They were out of the tented encampment now, marching the short distance down the muddy road towards the little town of Ladysmith itself. The sun was hotter in the sky and the first perspiration had begun to show in dark patches on the khaki uniforms of the men. Even in his terror, Gaudeans noticed that General Thorneycroft reeked of sweat, as though he were proud of it.

The procession passed the tents of the commissariat stores, reddened by the dust which blew with every dry wind from the changeless yellow-brown of the South African landscape. Just ahead lay the single main street of Ladysmith, behind it the tin roofs and sunny gardens of English exiles. It was a settlement of ramshackle bungalows and stores, a typical frontier town on any continent of the globe. Only the town hall and the Royal Hotel reflected the pretensions of European architecture.

"Wait!" pleaded Gaudeans in the silent drama of his sleep. "I need to see a priest. If I must die, let me have a priest!"

It was a trick, of course, a vain hope of delay and reprieve. They would hardly dare shoot him if he could find a neutral witness who might testify against them later. He was sure that what they were going to do to him was illegal, but certain that it would happen just the same. A priest, though. That was a good idea, and even in his fear he gave himself marks for it.

Thorneycroft turned to Stone again.

"How many R.C.s in the Mounted Infantry, Sar'-Major?"

"Three Baptists, sir, eight Methodists, all the rest Church of England, sir!"

"Very good," Thorneycroft sang out. "Carry on, Sar'-Major."

Their cool indifference knocked the breath from Gaudeans for a moment. They cared nothing for his excuses, true or false. And now, from the rear of the procession, came a derisive fluting sound. Thorneycroft's musicians were piping the "Rogue's March," the shrilling triumph which had first played the mutineers to their deaths in India more than forty years earlier. It was more frightening than Gaudeans could ever have imagined, to hear all these men rejoicing in his suffering and the end which awaited him.

"Stop!" He went on his knees, in tears, the sharp, foxy brain knowing that contrition was the only hope now. If he could disgust them enough, promise them enough, they would be so eager to be rid of him that they would not even want to go ahead with the execution. The procession halted and the music stopped. "Don't kill me!" He grovelled in front of Thorneycroft. "If you kill me, you'll never know the truth." Here, in his dream, he contrived to draw breath in a howl. "It wasn't just a box of cartridges."

"Get up!" said Thorneycroft contemptuously. "Get up and act like a soldier or I'll blow your brains out here and now."

"There were guns!" The dishonest little eyes brimmed with tears as they looked up, begging their judge to be a deliverer from death. "And there were boxes of ammunition supposed to have been fired off at Spion Kop. Gone to Colonel Schiel and the German Volunteer Corps on the Boer side. Please let me live, just till tomorrow, and I'll tell you everything!"

It was good—he appreciated that in his dream more than he had done at the time—but it was nothing like good enough. They pulled him to his feet and thrust him onward. For some inexplicable reason, a new solemnity came over them all, the musicians at the rear striking up a shrill rendering of the "Dead March" from *Saul*.

By that time they were in the main street of the little town, where pyramids of beef boxes and flour-sacks filled with earth rose in front of the doors. These were the rudimentary blast-walls built during the siege as a protection against the Boer artillery which had been ranged on the hills above the town. Gaudeans allowed his distress to subside to a steady grizzling sound. Then, where the town hall with its belfry and pillars stood beyond the porches of the general stores, the detail came to a halt.

They led him into a yard behind the town hall building. There was a single post in the ground at the far end, sawdust scattered about it and two officers with short leather straps standing by it. The men of the Mounted Infantry lined the walls on every side. Six more troopers stood at ease in a row, facing the post with rifles held at a slight angle. Gaudeans's heart beat faster and more powerfully. This, then, was what had happened to Laszlo after all. No doubt of it.

As the walls of the yard closed him in, the nightmare reached its climax. Only once in his dreams had it betrayed reality and moved on to the final chill ritual of the firing-post. As a rule it proceeded, as now, to the appearance of a tall, erect figure in the uniform of a staff officer, the face blue-eyed and beak-nosed, the head high and domed with a promise of baldness under the head-gear. Thorneycroft strode across at once, stamped to attention, and saluted, more like a junior N.C.O. on a drill-ground than a man who had been promoted in the field a week or two before.

The two men exchanged several sentences. Gaudeans felt a surge of hope as he caught the words "court martial" from the new arrival. Sir George White, he thought. It must be he, the commander of the Ladysmith garrison during its siege. Thorneycroft's face grew redder; with a note of whining frustration he made a final appeal to Sir George, in which the words "shoot the brute" were clearly audible. Sir George gave his final instructions and turned away.

Gaudeans was almost ready to chuckle secretly to himself. They had shot Laszlo the night before, that was clear enough. Yet in doing so, they had destroyed the major witness against him in any court martial. It was a chance in a thousand, but with his bandy, shop-worn optimism he saw it coming up. There was nothing they could prove against him and they knew it. The only other witnesses were Colonel Schiel and the German officers of the Volunteer Corps. The war would be over before they were found and invited to tell their story.

Still, when Thorneycroft walked back towards him, Gaudeans held his pathetic, tearful, hang-dog expression, as if he quite expected to be shot after all. Thorneycroft towered over him with his large red face contorted in an agony of inexpressible rage. That was the ultimate assurance of safety, or so it seemed. Gaudeans, from nervousness, relief, and a dawning enjoyment of the situation, emitted a half-smothered giggle. Thorneycroft turned to Sergeant-Major Stone.

"I want this man kicked out of the regiment," he said gently. In the evaporation of Thorneycroft's fury, Gaudeans sensed danger again. The order given to Sergeant-Major Stone was no mere figure of speech. The junior N.C.O.s were yapping out commands, the men of the Mounted Infantry coming forward from the walls of the yard to form two lines, facing inwards, stretching from where Gaudeans stood to a side gateway which opened on to a rutted road beyond.

When they were all in place, there was a brief silence, soon broken by a rising clatter of bayonet-scabbards beating on mess-tins. As the noise grew louder, it became more regular, a rapid clashing of metal in which each man kept time. Gaudeans, the light breeze catching his thin ginger curls, his clothes hanging raggedly about him, drew back with instinctive alarm. Someone, either Stone or perhaps Thorneycroft himself, drove him forward again.

In panic, he tried to run, to pass the gauntlet before its members were fully prepared to do their worst. He had hardly floundered beyond the first two pairs when a foot thrust neatly between his own sent him sprawling. A cry, beginning as a howl and ending with a cheer, broke above the sound of the drumming. Still no one touched him. They waited until he stumbled to his feet. Then, from both sides, the boots lashed out at him, grotesque and swollen from the clay which adhered to them at every march through the muddy trails of the perimeter defences.

When he ran, the blows landed on his upper legs and hips; if he fell, they kicked him in the ribs, which was far worse. He was driven from side to side, buffeted by the force of their revenge. Some kicked him half-heartedly, inflicting little more than passing discomfort. Others drove the full force of their feet against him. Once when he fell, there was a crushing impact upon the right side of his chest, not far below the armpit, and a sick, brittle sound as if one of his ribs had been broken. Ahead of him the last men waited, expressionless and almost anxious, as if they feared they might misjudge the aim. Even in this tumult the sharp little brain struggled to reason out what must be done. Let them think he was finished, then make a dash for the open gate with all his remaining strength.

He sprang up with the pain of his bruises flaring like renewed fire over his body. Next he lumbered past them, closing his mind to everything until he tripped again in the gateway and fell prone in the mud of the cart-track beyond. The gate slammed behind him with a derisive cheer from the assembled troopers. Then something came flying across the wall and landed beside him. It was an old knapsack with the remains of his personal possessions inside.

When they had finished with him, it was as much as he could do to crawl forward and stretch his forearm to touch the webbing of the knapsack. Yet his mind was possessed by the thought that he was, after all, going to live. He was frightened still, and injured, but even that was relatively unimportant. The moment when he knew he had won was when he ceased to be the imploring Gaudeans who would have been Thorneycroft's slave for life as the price of continuing to live. Already, even as he spat the thick, powdery mess of mud from his teeth, his thoughts turned to the things he might do to General Thorneycroft in the years ahead.

As his spirits began to rise, the closed black carriage which had been waiting at the junction of the track and the main street moved forward. It was as inconspicuous as a hansom cab, one of the few conveyences whose horse had survived the siege while others were slaughtered for food. It drew level with the damaged little man who lay in the mud clutching his bundle of possessions, and there it stopped. The door opened and a hand reached down to him. It was a delicate gloved hand, beyond which he glimpsed the sleeve of a black silk dress, a feather boa, and a pair of eyes that were green rather than blue. He raised himself and was helped into the carriage.

Stirring in his Berlin sleep as the dream ended, Gaudeans, half-waking, thought of General Thorneycroft. Life was now dedicated to certain unpleasant things which could be done to General Thorneycroft, Colonel Lindemann, and their kind. The strong men who triumphed over the frail and the meek, the petty thieves and the underlings, and who then demanded respect and honour for their arrogance. But was it not the meek who must inherit the earth? By force, if necessary? Gaudeans smiled at the thought with the simple malice of a child. Then he went back to sleep.

III

THE SUMMER OF
CAPTAIN GAUDEANS

14

The Irish International Exhibition of 1907 opened on 4 May. In the cool spring morning, the Viceroy's carriage passed through the arch of Dublin Castle gate to the salute of the sentries on either side. As the four guardsmen grounded their weapons again with slapping precision, the glossy geldings turned down the short incline of Cork Hill into the length of Dame Street. Ahead of the Earl of Aberdeen and his lady rang the hollow hoof-beats of two squadrons of hussars, their dark fur shakos with upright plumes, red tunics laced with gold, sabres bumping against the dark-blue thighs of their overalls. Behind the Viceroy and the Countess of Aberdeen came two more carriages bearing the officials of the viceregal household; Sir Arthur Vicars, the youthful Ulster King-of-Arms; and the Viceroy's aide-de-camp.

It was not the fresh, gusty wind blowing from the heather-covered hills above Kingstown which dictated the choice of closed carriages. One day, as a matter of inevitability, Ireland would emulate India in assassinating an English Viceroy. The murders of the Chief Secretary for Ireland, Lord Frederick Cavendish, and his assistant in Phoenix Park were a prelude to it. The revolver intended to dispatch Judge Lawson at the doors of his club in Kildare Street was a further ultimatum. Now within a frail elegance of eighteenth-century coachwork, the viceregal cab was protected by a thin sheeting of steel. The double thickness of the window-glass was indicated by a taint of bottle-green.

Along Dame Street, past the coloured glass of the Empire Music Hall and the arcaded elegance of the banks, the crowds on the pavement clapped and cheered the procession. The Viceroy doffed the cocked hat of his court-dress in formal acknowledgement, his grave, bearded face looking out through the glass with distrust and regret. Lady Aberdeen, plump and motherly, smiled out at the well-wishers with visible relief. The minds of actors and spectators alike were possessed by the thought that the King's representative could no longer drive from the castle to Herbert Park without

107

policemen lining the route and two squadrons of cavalry with a detachment of riflemen to clear the way.

They were turning again now, taking the curve of College Green into Grafton Street, passing the prison-grey classical front of Trinity College on their left. The smile faded from the face of the Vicereine. Where the trams were drawn up to allow the procession past, there was a glimpse of lawns and chestnut-trees in Trinity court. Behind the outer railings rose a jeering outburst. Above the surge of the struggle, clenched fists were lifted at the dark carriages with their gilt scrolls. Two uniformed policemen moved in that direction, and an obscure scuffle began among the onlookers.

In Grafton Street itself, Lady Aberdeen's smile returned, though with reluctance. Here was wealth and elegance, as surely as in London's Bond Street. Gracefully-bowed windows offered the best and most expensive that saddler, costumier, or perfumer could devise. On the crowded pavements the women waved and the men stood bareheaded as if with the respect due to a funeral cortege.

As the procession came out into the vast square of St. Stephen's Green, past the lake and band-stand of its central gardens, the officer commanding the mounted troops gave a prearranged signal. The horses broke into a trot, the three carriages picking up speed at the same time. While the foot-guard of riflemen fell back, a detachment of riders from the Dublin Metropolitan Police, drawn up in readiness outside the yellow brickwork of the Gaiety Theatre in South King Street, trotted out to form a new rear-guard.

It had always been the contention of the Intelligence Department and the Dublin Special Branch that the danger to the Viceroy and his entourage was less in the crowded streets of the city's centre. In the outlying areas, a marksman would find cover among the trees of St. Stephen's Green or the long Georgian terraces and quiet gardens of Morehampton Road. There the Viceroy was a moving target, and there was security only in speed, riding so rapidly that an assassin would have neither the time nor the aim to be sure of hitting his mark.

Without slackening speed once, the carriages and their escort passed down the long avenues where the pavements were almost deserted. In the broad suburban thoroughfares, where the trees of Herbert Park began, the pace slackened at a second signal as the squadrons of hussars reached the high walls and the grand archway of the exhibition grounds. The ornamental park was filled with reconstructions of African villages and Canadian settlements, an Indian theatre, Helter-Skelter, and children's amusements. The International Exhibition itself was housed in ornate temporary buildings. Four large galleries in the style of Renaissance basilicas radiated from a vast central concert hall whose massive dome might more properly have crowned an Italian cathedral of the fifteenth century.

The procession curved round the grand fountain of the fore-court and drew up outside the splendid Romanesque doors of the main entrance. With a blaring of trumpets for the arrival of the King's representative, the Viceroy stepped down from his carriage and stood with his Countess while the Marquis of Ormonde clutched an official address of welcome. In the cold May wind, the flags of a dozen nations whipped and snapped on their poles above the outer wall. Each gust of wind blew clouds of sand in a blinding storm from the newly-laid paths.

From inside the great domed hall, as the procession formed up, came the massive, soaring chords of the *Tannhäuser* overture for organ and full orchestra. The Viceroy, waiting to bring up the rear of the procession, was suddenly aware of Colonel Ross of the Dublin Metropolitan Police speaking softly.

"Mahony is missing, Your Excellency. The other heralds are in their places. We presume he is ill."

"What does Vicars say?"

"He knows nothing, sir," said Ross impassively.

The Viceroy nodded.

"Very well. Carry on, as arranged. If his Fenians planned some outrage now, Mahony would scarcely draw attention to himself by his absence."

Ross gave a quick little bow.

"The entire hall has been searched twice, sir. Nothing was found. Each of the guests has been required to show an invitation card, and the Special Branch has made a note of every name. There is no ground for suspicion."

"So be it!" The Viceroy sighed. He stepped forward slowly as the long procession in front of him began to move. Beyond the members of his household and the Knights of St. Patrick in their richly jewelled collars, his gaze picked out the men on whom his resentment fell. Chief of them was the slim, youthful figure of Sir Arthur Vicars, Ulster King-of-Arms, his herald's coat blazoned with the royal coat of arms in gold. Vicars, as chief of viceregal ceremonial, was His Excellency's aversion, a legacy from a previous viceroy, Lord Houghton. Worse still, Vicars had made two appointments of his own. Peirce Mahony, one of his protégés, was a young man who was rich as Croesus and dangerous as a keg of gunpowder. Even in the confines of Dublin Castle or viceregal receptions at the lodge in Phoenix Park, young Mahony made no secret of his fierce attachment to the cause of Irish republicanism.

Why the devil had Vicars appointed him? Distant family connections were too frail a reason. The Viceroy heaved another sigh and thought of blackmail. Not difficult, he would imagine, with a young man of Sir Arthur Vicars's type. What made the whole thing even odder was that Vicars had given permission for the great family heirloom, the splendid Russian diamonds belonging to the O'Mahony of Kerry, to be kept in the official safe, within the strong-room of Dublin Castle itself. Very odd. Colonel Ross and the Special Branch had been watching young Mahony with considerable interest. Must ask them to see if the rich, self-opinionated youth could have some hold over Vicars.

Nor was the Viceroy much consoled by Vicars's other appointment, the still more youthful figure of Frank Shackleton, who now walked as Dublin Herald behind the Knights of St. Patrick. He was the younger brother of the famous explorer Sir Ernest Shackleton, and Colonel Ross's report on the Dublin Herald showed him to be chiefly remarkable for his escapades with money and women, in that order. On the proceeds of financial speculation, young Shackleton had bought a fine house in Dublin and a mansion in Park Lane between those of Lady Grosvenor and Sir Rufus Isaacs. It was no secret that this second home had been on the market for forty-four thousand pounds. Where the devil was the young scoundrel getting his money from? Ross was of the opinion that Shackleton lived off women, but that seemed absurd. No woman or combination of women could provide him with an income of that size.

The Viceroy realized that he was frowning and quickly resumed his official appearance of grave, bearded dignity. He would wait until the season was over, and the summer of the Irish International Exhibition. Best leave it that long. Then he would cleanse the Augean stables of viceregal ceremonial. First Shackleton and Mahony. Give it a month or two and then get shot of Vicars, too. No need to sack him outright. Simply advise H.M. to make a replace-ment as Ulster King-of-Arms. Old Lord Pembroke had been rather keen to see his son-in-law have the job. Captain Rodwell Wilkin-son, Coldstream Guards. Not too bright, unfortunately. Bit of a duffer, in fact. Honest, however; decent and straightforward. None of this business about living off women or buying bombs for the damn Fenians. Other thing, of course, old Pembroke was the biggest landowner in Ireland. Friend at court. No harm in that nowadays.

By the time the procession emerged into the great hall, Lord and Lady Aberdeen were both smiling a faint acknowledgement of the applause on either side. *Tannhäuser* had ended. They stood motion-less now, facing the massed choir, the men black-suited, the women in white silk dresses and brimmed hats, the great batteries of organ-pipes beyond. On every side the spectators rose from their seats like the mighty congregation of a vast cathedral. The sudden bellow from organ, orchestra, and choir was almost terrifying in its volume.

> *God save our gracious King,*
> *Long live our noble King . . .*

The Viceroy winced, thinking that a pistol-shot from one of Mahony's friends would have gone unnoticed in the uproar of voices. He noticed Shackleton's dark head turn and allowed his own eyes to follow the young man's gaze. Once a fellow permitted himself to be led that way, there was no keeping him. To his satisfaction the Viceroy recognized the girl with whom Shackleton was exchanging distant glances of admiration. Tonia someone or other. Foreign, of course. Still, strikingly pretty in that lilac silk gown and the matching hat which looked like a triumph of confectionary. An *elfin* prettiness, the Viceroy thought, that was the word for it. Pert and lively, fine well-marked cheek-bones and straight nose. A little girl's mischievousness in those dark-green eyes and the deep-gold curls which framed her face and brushed her shoulders. What on earth could such a treasure see in a sallow young gigolo like Shackleton and his hangers-on? Oh, there were hangers-on, his lordship told himself, plenty of them. Tonia herself was escorted by one of them, who stood next to her now. Absurd little fellow, middle-aged and balding, ginger curls like an overgrown choir-boy's. Watery eyes, shifty little mouth, comic moustache. Broken-down old horse-trader. Another leech fattening itself on Shackleton, who in turn fattened himself on the body politic.

The Viceroy shifted his feet slightly, easing a spasm of cramp, and looked about him. Colonel Ross had really done rather well with the security arrangements. The way the kilted Highlanders from three regiments lined the processional route, it would have been extremely difficult for a single shot with a pistol to find any certain mark. Hardly more than the heads of the dignitaries visible in some cases, military men with plumes, Admiral Custance, Commander-in-Chief of the Channel Fleet, with his cocked hat, velvet court-dresses and swords everywhere, the Provost of Trinity, Dean of the Chapel Royal, French and Italian consuls. No Germans, of course. Not to be expected, as things were. Not like the last great exhibition in Dublin, opened by Prince Albert in 1849.

The anthem was over and, in a forgetful moment, the Viceroy prepared himself to sit down. It was not to be, of course. Organ, orchestra, and choir gave out a jigging blast of sound, the first "Hallelujah!" of Handel's famous chorus. The tension at the back of the Viceroy's left knee became so invasive that soon he could think of nothing else. Then the chorus of shrill soprano and roaring bass was over. Ormonde was rumbling on with his address of welcome. Bouquets of flowers were presented, roses oddly mixed with lilies-of-the-valley.

To the sound of applause on all sides, the Viceroy took his place on the platform, flanked by Ulster King-of-Arms and the Dublin Herald, whose coming dismissal cheered Lord Aberdeen's mind at every moment. He took a slip of paper, directed to himself, and read aloud its contents.

" 'I trust that the exhibition you are to open today may prove a success and demonstrate international progress made by Ireland. Edward R.' "

There was a veritable pandemonium of cheering. Sardonically, the Viceroy wondered if such enthusiasm would have been tempered by the knowledge that the message was dated from Paris, where His Majesty had announced his intention of remaining until all danger of having to open the exhibition himself was over. Looking about him, waiting for the applause to die away, His Excellency doubted that anything could stem the enthusiasm now. Of all those in his view, assembled under the central dome, only the girl at whom Shackleton had looked sat quiet and indifferent to everything which passed. Odd, the Viceroy thought. Decidedly rum. He returned to the text of his speech.

From his place beside Tonia Schroeder, Gaudeans looked down over the ranks of feminine hats, their brims gay with light net and waxed colours of artificial flowers. The splendour of the music—the anthem, the great chorus of hallelujahs, the fine hymn-like swelling of Wagner's overture—all this had fallen like nourishment on his shrivelled little soul. When he looked down at the magnificent procession, scarlet and gold of plumed military peacocks, robes of the peerages, court-dress, and the ornate tunics of the heralds, he almost despised himself for the manner in which his heart was stirred.

But it was stirred, no doubt of it. Always a weakness in him, he thought, to feel the blood surge and the spine tingle at the brash, jigging optimism of "Rule, Britannia" or "The British Grenadiers." The land of Britannia and the Grenadiers, its judges and its commanders, existed by virtue of grinding most of its citizens into poverty and subservience. Any fool could see that. Worse still, in the person of General Thorneycroft and his kind, it had beaten and reviled Gaudeans himself. Still, it was the most splendid occasion he had ever seen. Two infantry battalions in ceremonial dress; two hundred uniformed police officers, to say nothing of the plain-clothes men of the Special Branch. All this to guard the Viceroy and the officers of state from assassination.

He beamed down on the panoply of the occasion as the trumpets rang out again. Even at this distance he caught the gaze of Frank Shackleton for a moment with a weak, affectionate smile. There was something about Shackleton, the proud young features and the fierceness in the eyes, which reminded him of Laszlo. Poor old Laszlo. Gaudeans smiled and exchanged a gentle look with Tonia, beside him. It was not the intimate glance of lovers, Gaudy took great care about that. If Shackleton was looking he would see only the expressions of two people, each of whom was deeply but separately attached to him. Decent of old Frank to get us tickets for the show, they seemed to convey to one another.

It was over now and the procession was about to turn away. With a final tremendous blast of sound, the great organ, choir, and orchestra sent the viceregal parade on its way.

Land of hope and glory!
Mother of the free . . .

The din was magnificent, the great "Pomp and Circumstance" march making goose-flesh up and down Gaudeans's back while his heart surged with the thought that they and all their hope and glory would be damned in hell if he had anything to do with it. For now, as they turned, he caught sight of the one thing which meant more to him than all the martial music and patriotism in the world. Glittering and flashing like fire in the summer light, the crown jewels of the Irish kingdom shone like coloured fire on the robes and tunics.

The Viceroy's robe bore the finest of all, the Star of St. Patrick. From this distance it looked the size of a soup-plate, a great shamrock of rubies and emeralds set in solid gold. Its border consisted of white-hot Brazilian diamonds, each the size of a walnut, and the eight points of the star were encrusted with Indian diamonds of slightly smaller size. Gaudeans licked his lips and transferred his gaze to Frank Shackleton. The Dublin Herald was walking before the Viceroy now, bearing on a black velvet cushion the great Badge of Viceroyalty. The badge was similar in size and grandeur to the star, though it bore the motto *Quis separabit?* round its circumference, picked out in rose-tinted diamonds which the British commanders had looted from the tombs of Golconda.

The poetic justice of what was about to happen filled Gaudeans with a quiet glee. Shackleton was preceded by the Knights of St. Patrick walking in pairs, first the Earl of Mayo with the Viscount Iveagh, then the Earl of Kilmorey and the Marquis of Ormonde. Round each noble neck hung a "collar" of the order of knighthood. Each consisted of finely-worked gold links, and every one was set with precious stones. Lindemann might prove to be rather mean in the matter, might try to beat down Gaudeans as to the value. Still, he was prepared for that, even resigned to it. There was no point in being greedy. Greed had nearly done for him in South Africa. One thing no one could argue, not even Lindemann. A man with eyes in his head must see that the state jewels of Ireland were worth quite enough to set up a modest fellow like Gaudy for the rest of his mean little life.

And there was Tonia as well, of course. Gaudeans cadged another sidelong glance at the beautiful young face, the fine high-boned structure of it which testified to good breeding, the coquettish golden curls which clustered about her cheeks and forehead, softening the severity. Yes, indeed. So far she had held out nothing but the vaguest of promises. Still, that was little to go by. Her duty, plainly put, was the seduction of a swaggering and jumped-up jackass called Frank Shackleton. When it was all over and when she saw precisely how well Gaudeans came out of it all, there would be no argument.

He smiled out across the scene of that solemnity. Even on the allowance which Lindemann had made him, he was already a dapper little man, hardly recognizable as the moist-eyed, capering buffoon of the Königgrätzer Strasse. There was a certain sleekness in the ginger curls, a more spirited line to the moustache. He was every inch the Captain Wunder of the Lietzensee, capable, alert, well able to take care of himself. Young men of Tonia's own age were dull and stupid as tailor's dummies by comparison. Let her once see a man who knew his way around, a man who could open locks and vault-doors with such coolness and expertise! Let her see all that and the promise of more to come! By Jove, thought Gaudeans, there would be no holding her. Even as it was, though Lindemann had put her on to him as a spy, he was master of the situation.

The musicians were purple-faced with exertion now, the strident notes echoing among the iron girders and the dome, the sounds rolling away down the pavilions of the exhibition building, through the halls of machinery and the galleries draped with velvet where the finest paintings of the royal collection hung on loan. By now the great procession was passing into shadow, away from the sunlight of the dome towards the improvised robing-rooms. The emeralds and rubies, clustered diamonds set in thick gold, seemed to glow and sparkle all the more dramatically in the gathering gloom. Gaudeans watched their final display with a sense of personal pride.

> *Truth and right and freedom,*
> *Each a holy gem,*
> *Stars of solemn brightness*
> *Weave thy diadem . . .*

His throat filled with an emotion beyond anything that the anthem or the great chorus from the *Messiah* had been able to stir in him. Now they were singing of tangible possessions, of gems and diadems which burnt and flashed in the dying light. More to the point, he

115

thought, they were singing of gems and diadems which were his. At last the little man had come into his own. Truth and right and freedom were neither here nor there. Give him locks and vaults and ciphers any day. He was only to steal the holy gems and diadems from people who had robbed the true owners in the first place. He looked for a last time that morning on the treasures of the Kingdom of Ireland, the loot which George IV had bequeathed by way of one of his mistresses. Gaudeans grinned. Every stone that had been on display in the opening of the Irish International Exhibition was his already, as surely as if he had them in his pocket.

15

Even in the vestibule which served as a temporary robing-room there was no escape from the sounds of "Pomp and Circumstance," pumped out with unflagging energy by the musicians in the main hall. The Viceroy glanced up and met the gaze of Colonel Ross, who was standing directly in his path.

"Mahony, sir," said Ross quietly. "No sign of him at his lodgings or anywhere else. If he was merely indisposed we would have expected to find some news of him there. There are two officers watching the house, but Mahony seems to have disappeared completely."

The Viceroy sighed.

"What do you advise?"

"A change of plan and an alteration of the route for the return to the castle, sir." With his clipped moustache and slick grey hair, Ross looked like what he was, a lifelong professional in such matters. The Viceroy failed to conceal his growing irritation.

"Is that really necessary? With an escort of this strength?"

"It would be *prudent*, sir." For all his deference it was clear that Ross was not going to be budged. "With the ceremony over, there will be less interest and less caution taken on the return journey. If Mahony should be in league with the republicans, that is precisely when they would be most likely to strike."

"We have no evidence of that kind against him as yet," sighed his lordship.

"With respect, sir. If you wait until there is evidence, the damage may well be done." Ross lowered his voice slightly. "If not for your own sake, I should be grateful if you would consider my advice on behalf of those who accompany you. And for the safety of the state jewels. There is a story put about that the Fenians intend to show their strength by a spectacular robbery of some kind. The jewels are a very likely target."

"In the middle of Dublin garrison and the police headquarters?" inquired his lordship sceptically.

"Perhaps, sir, on a deserted suburban street in the confusion of a well-armed attack." Ross had made his point and he knew it.

117

"Then do as you please," said the Viceroy sulkily. Of course Ross was right, but it irked him to think that the mere threats of Fenianism could dictate what pageantry was permitted and what was not, whether the Viceroy returned in procession to the castle or skulked back in concealment. His decision, in the end, had been made in the knowledge that King Edward's state visit to Ireland was only eight weeks away and would certainly be cancelled if something went badly wrong now. Fenianism's greatest triumph would be in showing the world that the King dared not set foot in this part of his own dominions.

Twenty minutes later the first of the carriages carrying lesser dignitaries began to leave the exhibition grounds. The viceregal coach, empty now, followed them. The red leather jewel-cases, locked by separate keys, were loaded into a plain black police van drawn by two horses. Ross and two senior officers accompanied them. The Viceroy and Lady Aberdeen were escorted to an anonymous closed carriage, which followed the van with a dozen police outriders. Ross had rejected the Viceroy's suggestion of using a motor van. An engine which broke down left the vehicle as a sitting target, miles from safety and with no means of signalling its distress. A good pair of horses was far more reliable.

The Earl looked at his Countess and gave her a faint smile of reassurance. He had lately been under pressure to resign his office and resume the presidency of the Western Insurance Company. Today he felt more than ever inclined to accept the offer.

All traffic had been stopped by the police on the far side of the exhibition grounds. Already moving at a trot, the horses of the black van and the plain carriage clattered out past the long pillared front of the Royal Dublin Society's show grounds. Swinging north, the two vehicles and their mounted escort raced down the length of Northumberland Road, past the wide lawns and shrubberies of handsome red-brick villas. Ross had sent mounted police ahead to clear the route, and now the few bystanders on the pavement looked with mild astonishment at the two vehicles which plunged past them as if the horses were bolting out of control. If the guns of Fenianism were anywhere around, it would be half a mile away, waiting in vain along the leafy elegance of Morehampton Road.

They crossed the Grand Canal Bridge and presently came out of the commercial shabbiness of Mount Street into the vast Georgian splendour of Merrion Square. The Viceroy felt a new sense of relief, and an agreeable superiority in knowing that Ross had taken all these precautions unnecessarily. Mahony was clearly the associate of some very undesirable people. But to credit him with the ability to stage an attack on the Viceroy in the middle of Dublin was quite outlandish.

The vehicles had slowed down again, rolling more gently along Nassau Street with its shops on one side. Chestnut-trees were in full leaf opposite, beyond the high wall and the iron railing of Trinity. There were crowds along the pavements in College Green and Dame Street, but now they hardly spared a glance for the van and the carriage which ran inconspicuously towards Cork Hill and then in at the castle gateway. The mounted police detachment, riding behind them, no longer seemed to be part of the little procession.

In the long quadrangle of the upper castle yard, the Viceroy stepped down from his carriage and walked slowly across to where Ross stood by the police van. The van was parked immediately outside the Bedford Tower with its safe and strong-room. Two armed sentries stood guard at its doorway. Next door to it was the guard-room of the Dublin garrison, and close by the headquarters building of the Dublin Metropolitan Police.

"Now tell me, Colonel Ross," said the Viceroy pleasantly. "Am I to thank you for saving us all from assassination?"

Ross was subdued but unrepentant.

"I hope there was no need, sir. But your route and time-table were extremely well advertised in the press. With respect to Mahony, however . . ."

"Ah, yes," said His Excellency. "Mahony and his Irish *banditti*. Well, Colonel, I will tell you what, with respect to them. Every day I am to travel—what? two miles?—between the castle and the Viceregal Lodge. Two miles to Phoenix Park, would you say? At any point on that road I might be a target for a gunman, if they choose. They have half a mile of trees and perfect concealment in the park itself."

"We have a plain-clothes patrol in the park day and night, sir."

The Viceroy nodded.

"And even so, there is probably nothing you or they can do to prevent Irish rebels from firing a gun or pitching a bomb into my carriage if they choose to do so. For the future, then, I will not be made to hide myself away in plain carriages on side-roads, to go as if in fear of men like Mahony or the men behind him. No, sir! I am damned if I will."

Colonel Ross inclined his head in a slight gesture of submission. For all that, he was visibly displeased.

"Now," said the Viceroy briskly, "I should like to see the state jewels checked and put securely where they belong."

It was unusual, but not unprecedented, for the King's representative to be present when the vault in the Bedford Tower was opened. The time had come, Lord Aberdeen decided, to satisfy himself that the treasures of the kingdom were being held where no harm would come to them, neither the harm promised by a knave like Mahony nor that invited by a young jackass like Shackleton. As for a fool like Vicars, in whose care the Bedford Tower was supposed to be, the Viceroy thought, the less said about him the better.

The Bedford Tower was a Georgian building just inside the castle gate. It consisted of two main floors, an attic level above those, and a tall, pillared cupola with windows and a green bronze dome. Its front was pillared and arcaded, the strong-room being on the ground floor to one side of the main entrance. The building also contained the library of the Office of Arms, over which Vicars presided with a fussy, pedantic querulousness.

The Viceroy himself had insisted on the location of the strong-room when it had been constructed a few years earlier. It could be approached only through the main front door of the tower, which was in any case the only entrance to the building. Outside this door, two armed sentries of the Irish Guards patrolled day and night, having a clear view at the same time of the outer wall of the strong-room with its heavily-barred window. A few yards to one side were the guards on the main gate of the castle. On the other side, the strong-room actually adjoined the guard-room of the Dublin garrison. For good measure, the entire building with its massive walls and barred window was in full view of the police headquarters and the viceregal apartments on the far side of the upper yard.

But that was only the beginning of the formidable security which surrounded the vault and its contents.

Unlike the other rooms of the Bedford Tower with their white-painted panelled doors, the strong-room was sealed off by a hermetically tight door of Harveyed Krupp armour plate. It was almost identical to the armoured belt of a warship's hull, and at four and a half inches, it was half the thickness of a heavy battleship's armour. It had twin locks of the latest Bramah pattern, one key held by the commander of the military guard, the other by the duty superintendent of police. Neither man could open the door of the vault alone.

Its resistance to force had never been put to the test. However, the Viceroy was consoled by the Chief Secretary for Ireland, who described how an identical vault-door had withstood a direct hit from a one-hundred-pound nickel shell, fired from a six-inch gun at the devastatingly close range of fifty yards. If the republicans ever acquired six-inch guns and nickel shells, the Viceroy thought, the fate of the vault-door in Dublin Castle would be the least of anyone's worries.

Immediately inside the vault-door there was an iron grille, a gate which also carried two locks and required a second pair of keys held by the guard commander and the duty police superintendent to open it. It was, of course, quite possible that a thief might somehow evade the sentries and enter the Bedford Tower secretly. He might be equipped with the finest probes and the subtlest skills of any locksmith. It would matter very little. The locks of the vault-door had been adjusted with gyroscopic precision after it had been built into place. Within the mechanism itself the levers had a mirror-like polish and a hair-trigger balance. Even if it were possible to take impressions of the keys, which would require the complicity of the guard commander and the duty police superintendent, it was unlikely that duplicate keys could be made to a fine enough likeness. The least irregularity in a key, or any other interference with the locks, produced two results. First, the bolts locked tight; and second, an alarm was triggered, sounding in the guard-room next door. When electric lighting had been installed in the castle, an alarm system had been wired to it.

Even a cracksman who could open the vault-door would then have to perform the same miracle again on the iron grille within. If he could succeed, against every law of science and security, he would find himself in the strong-room, with its single barred window at the sentries' backs and the guard-room on the other side of the partition wall.

The room itself was furnished like a small library or study, with a number of handsome display-cabinets and breakfront bookcases round the walls. In the far corner, no more than six feet from the sentries on the far side of the window, stood a tall Milner safe, turned with its door to one side so that the opening and closing of it was concealed both from the window and from the strong-room door. The Milner safe was something of which the Viceroy felt particularly proud. It was built of two-inch armoured steel, proof against any force short of a direct hit by a six-inch shell.

The key to the safe was kept by Sir Arthur Vicars, Ulster King-of-Arms, who was reputed to wear it in a locket round his neck, day and night. But without the guard commander and the duty superintendent of police, Vicars was unable to enter the strong-room. And those two men, though they could between them open the vault-door and the iron grille, had no key to the safe.

Could Vicars make mischief if he chose? The Viceroy looked sidelong at him. He, not the Fenians, might be the true danger. There were no weapons in the hands of the Irish rebels which could overcome such defences. Several bundles of dynamite would bring the entire Bedford Tower down on their heads before they could shift the steel door. Far and away the easiest method of breaking in would be to blast a hole in the outer wall where the sentries patrolled.

However, if the wall had to be blasted open, it was more likely to be done by the British Army. The obsession with security had gone so far that an entire set of duplicate keys—for the steel door, the iron grille, and the Milner safe—were locked in the safe itself. Ross had insisted on this. Two sets of keys at large doubled the risk to the strong-room. A Fenian or any gang of criminals would not need to use a copy of the keys. They would merely substitute a copy for the set of genuine keys not normally employed and make their way in by using these originals.

To the Viceroy the argument had seemed absurd, though he had allowed Ross to have his way. Even with the original keys, no thief would dare to try the steel door. Except when the strong-room was visited, as now, the electric alarm was switched on. As soon as the vault-door opened, there would be an explosion of alarm-bells heard distinctly throughout the castle and probably all the way to College Green. Fifteen seconds was the time allowed for the guard to reach the scene and surround the Bedford Tower. In rehearsals for such an emergency, it had rarely taken them more than ten.

In the upper yard of the castle the group of men walked towards the door of the Bedford Tower, which housed the offices of Vicars, Shackleton, and Mahony, as well as the strong-room and the old heraldic library. The guard commander, in dress uniform of the newly-formed Irish Guards, walked beside the plain-clothes superintendent of the Dublin Metropolitan Police. Behind them came Vicars, still dressed in the pageant-costume of Ulster King-of-Arms, with Colonel Ross at his side. The Viceroy watched the jewel-cases carried up the steps and placed on a table just outside the vault-door. He spoke quietly to the guard commander.

"Major Tolland."

"Sir!"

The Viceroy winced slightly at the stamping precision with which Tolland came to attention before him, the suggestion of ill-concealed aggression.

"Would you please make quite sure that the electric alarm has been turned off at the guard-room switch."

"Sir?"

"Today of all days," said the Viceroy patiently, "we do not want a commotion in the centre of Dublin. Moreover, the existence of an electric alarm is supposed to be one of our secrets. If it goes off for the wrong reason, it will be secret no longer."

"Sir!"

Tolland stamped about smartly and strode, arms swinging high, in the direction of the guard-room.

"It went off," said the Viceroy lamely to Ross, "last time. Fortunately the door was being closed. Only a brief clatter. Commander in the guard-room thought someone had left the switch off by mistake."

Ross nodded indulgently, and the Viceroy cursed privately for having explained himself to his inferiors. Never apologize, never explain. Tolland returned, and the ritual of the crown jewels began.

Ross and the superintendent turned their keys in the twin locks, one at the top and one at the bottom. Only then could the two levers be moved which allowed the massive steel arm on the inside of the door to run back on its rails and open the vault to their view. It was only a view until the next obstacle, the iron grille, had been unlocked as well. Then the sunlit room with its mahogany bookcases and white paint-work was accessible. Vicars, closely accompanied by Colonel Ross, opened the safe and stood the door ajar so that the interior was concealed from those on the threshold of the room.

Each jewel-case was opened and its contents checked. Then, when the necessary signatures had been added in the minute-book, the cases were taken singly by Ross and Vicars and replaced on the shelves of the safe. The Viceroy gazed with bleak indifference at the pale fire of Brazilian diamonds, the gold of their settings. One by one, the pieces were accounted for and packed away: the great Star of St. Patrick, the Badge of Viceroyalty, the collars of the order, each

123

with the name of its individual knight engraved among the precious stones and the golden links.

When the last of these had been stored away, the Viceroy himself stepped into the strong-room and walked across to the open door of the safe. He had always felt misgivings over the appointment of young Vicars. Only now did he realize how much he distrusted Ulster King-of-Arms. It was the disappearance of Mahony that had done it.

The shelves of the safe were now full, each bearing its jewel-cases, and at the top, two red leather boxes stamped with the royal monogram. They were empty, the Viceroy knew that. Give it another eight weeks, when the royal visit began, and there would be so many dispatch-cases of this kind that the Milner would hardly hold them. The safest place in Dublin, according to Chief Inspector Kane and King Edward's bodyguards—therefore the place in which official papers would be held.

What to do with the state treasures then? The Viceroy looked about him. There was an old safe in the library of the Bedford Tower; perhaps that would do. Those responsible for the King's safety would value dispatches and intelligence above precious stones.

"Close the safe, please," he said quietly to Vicars and watched his command obeyed. As was customary on these occasions, Vicars and Colonel Ross, as the carriers of the jewels, submitted to having their pockets patted by the guard commander and the duty superinten-dent. As the Viceroy followed, he saw that Major Tolland was hesitating.

"Well?" said His Excellency sharply. "I'm a thief for all you know. Get on with it, man!"

Major Tolland sheepishly and ineffectually patted the blue velvet of the court-dress. The Viceroy sighed with irritation. In company with Colonel Ross he watched the iron grille and the steel vault-door closed. Sir Arthur Vicars withdrew to his office, the guard command-er and the duty superintendent returned to the guard-room. In company with Colonel Ross, the Viceroy went out past the Bedford Tower sentries. The two men crossed the upper yard towards the pillared and arcaded front of the viceregal apartments.

"Mahony!" said the Viceroy with abrupt bitterness. "I want something done about Mahony. I require to know where he was today and precisely what he has been up to for the past month. I shall need to know quickly. Long before the King's visit."

Ross drew down the corners of his mouth doubtfully.

"It may not be easy, sir. The past month is a long time."

He paused as Lord Aberdeen gave him a bleak, unsympathetic glance.

"It will be a sight less easy for us, my dear Ross, if a bomb goes off under King Edward with Mahony's connivance."

"Of course, sir." Ross responded with a quick confidence which he was far from feeling.

"And Vicars!" The Viceroy stopped in mid-stride and faced his companion. Having begun, he felt inclined to give his misgivings full rein.

"Sir?"

"Vicars. There's something in the pricking of my thumbs about him."

"If Your Excellency has any information connecting him with Mahony," said Ross coolly, "I should be most grateful for it."

"Evidence?" said his lordship scornfully. "How should there be evidence with a man like that? By the time we have evidence, the worst will have happened. No, I sense there a defect of character. That's all."

At the Italianate portico of the apartments he turned to Ross again.

"Have the goodness to go back and send Vicars to me. It's high time we tightened up the regulations here. For everyone's sake. Including his own."

16

The hansom cab pulled up on the north side of Merrion Square. Tonia Schroeder stepped down with the natural elegance of a dancer. Late-afternoon sunlight glistened on the turquoise silk of her tea-gown with its narrow waist. Her fine high-boned face and golden curls were shaded now by a rakish broad-brimmed hat with a crown of feathers. She looked very expensive and, at the same time, not quite proper. Every eye seemed intent on catching the impudent coquetry of her glance, each admiring wistfully the stretch of turquoise silk on thigh and hip as she swayed, wasp-waisted, up the steps of a Georgian red-brick villa with its walls softened by Virginia creeper.

While she waited for an answer to the bell, she half-turned, looking out across the wide lawns, shrubberies, and rockery of the central gardens, children's voices rising from among the tall trees beyond the railings. A manservant opened the door and Tonia vanished from view. The society of Merrion Square, which had held its breath at the sight of her, now breathed again and went about its normal business.

"Mr. Shackleton is not yet home, ma'am."

There was no need to invite her to wait. The servants knew her too well by this time to think such an invitation necessary. In the town-house which young Mr. Shackleton shared with his friend Sir Arthur Vicars, Fräulein Schroeder was almost one of the family. To be accurate, they should have called her "miss" rather than "ma'am," a tribute to her maiden status. But, as they said, the way it was with her and young Mr. Shackleton, "ma'am" seemed better all round.

Tonia inclined her head in acknowledgement and walked through to the drawing-room, which overlooked the square.

"You will take tea, ma'am?" They no longer said "will you?" because that would have sounded like a concession to a stranger. Mr. Shackleton had given his instructions as to that.

Tonia finished unpinning her hat.

"Yes," she said. "Thank you, I will." It was a lightly-accented

126

voice, high-pitched and carrying a self-conscious refinement in its tone.

The manservant gave a slight bow and withdrew. Tonia sat down and looked about her. The main reception room of the bachelor home was as unlike a drawing-room as she could imagine. The furniture was all black horsehair and club chairs in dark leather, more like a smoking-room or even a billiard-room. The prints on the walls reflected Frank Shackleton's tastes rather than Sir Arthur Vicars's. There was a large colour print of Ingres's harem painting *The Odalisque and the Servant*, facing a more gaudily tinted piece of the Prince of Wales leading in Persimmon after his victory in the Derby of 1896.

With a half-hearted interest, the girl sifted through a pile of papers and magazines: the *Tatler*, *Irish Society*, the *Illustrated London News*, the *Freeman's Journal*. . . . She had hardly made a choice before the tea was brought and set down on a smoking-table.

After that, as was usual, the servants took care not to disturb her again. On an ordinary day, she thought, Frank Shackleton would have come back to her long before this. But it was no ordinary day. Even after the opening of the exhibition, it was part of his duty to return to Dublin Castle. It was precisely for this reason that she had chosen to arrive early. No one but the servants would be in the house for the next hour or more. Sir Arthur Vicars was, if anything, likely to be still later than his friend.

When she finished her tea the shadows were lengthening eastward across the square. It was no longer the time of day when a young lady wore a tea-gown. Tonia stood up, her face rather more flushed with excitement than the highlights of rouge on her cheeks would have accounted for. The green eyes, too, darkened by a touch of mascara on their lashes, now shone with a childish devilment. She opened the drawing-room door and went slowly up the stairs, one hand on the polished walnut rail of the wrought-iron balustrade. The servants would not question her decision. For any number of reasons, this was the time at which they would expect her to be going in such a direction.

On the landing above, two white-painted panelled doors opened into adjacent bedrooms overlooking the square. One was allocated to Vicars, the other was Shackleton's own. Tonia stood quite still for a moment, listening to ensure that she was alone on the first floor of the house. There was not a sound. In any case, a servant who heard her from downstairs would naturally assume that she was opening the door of Shackleton's room. They were accustomed to that by now.

Turning aside, she curved her hand over the knob of Vicars's door. It was unlocked, there was no reason why it should be otherwise. No one expected him to leave the keys of the kingdom lying about there in his absence. Treading cautiously on the uncarpeted threshold of the room, Tonia crossed to the window, beside which there was a marble washstand with a bowl and ewer of veined porcelain. Just to the side of this the bottle of drinking-water with its inverted glass had been set.

Now it was safe to do what she had to. Long before this the bottle would have been refilled for the coming night; that was certain. Vicars had the habit, known to Shackleton and so relayed to Tonia, of drinking at least half of his bottle of water before going to bed. Sometimes, indeed, he would ignore the glass and tip the water into his mouth directly from the bottle. Listening all the time for the slightest sound which might betray the approach of a servant, the girl opened a small silk reticule embroidered to match her tea-gown. She took a neat paper packet, shook its white powder into the water-bottle, and then replaced the glass over it. Looking again, she satisfied herself that the powder had dissolved. It was a gentle enough sedative, an opiate compounded with sodium. In Vicars's case it would be more than enough. If his weak-headedness with drink was any means of judgement, a quarter of the contents of that bottle might now cause him to sleep the clock round.

There was, of course, always the risk that for some unpredictable reason he would not take his drink of water, tonight of all nights. Even the dapper cunning of Captain Gaudeans was not proof against such contingencies. That was why she had to provide herself with a means of escape.

It was simple enough. Standing in the doorway, she looked back and made a mental note of the level of water in the bottle. If, when the time came, candle or moonlight showed the level unaltered, she could withdraw at once. It was just possible that the opening of the door might wake him if he had not drunk from the bottle. In that case, Tonia would explain with concern in her eyes that she had thought she heard him cry out in his sleep and had come to reassure herself. The bedroom door would not, of course, be locked. As it happened, the key had been missing when Shackleton first took the house. But in any case, the door was always left free for the servant to bring Vicars his early-morning tea.

So, the only unforeseen contingency would have been if Ulster King-of-Arms had a companion to share his bed. It was not a danger she was likely to encounter. She smiled faintly at the memory of a conversation with Captain Gaudeans on the subject.

Tonia looked round the room for a last time, holding in her mind the position of its furniture. The path from the door to the wash-stand, which ran past the bed, was clear. There was a carpet beside the bed, its edges curled a little and therefore to be avoided. That apart, there was nothing to impede her when the time came.

She opened the door to the landing and closed it quietly behind her, stepping sideways to the room which she shared with Frank Shackleton on her visits to the house. Not a board creaked. That was good. Unless she were extremely unfortunate, the whole thing could be done without a sound. One of the great advantages of opium, in addition, was its delusive power. Even if Vicars were not deeply asleep, even if he recalled some movement or touch in the darkness, he would never be quite certain afterwards whether it was a waking or a dreaming impression. Probably he would think himself the victim of wishful fantasy and would even feel a furtive guilt at his subconscious desire for her. She smiled again at the thought and let herself into Frank Shackleton's room.

"Franz" she called him when they were alone, bestowing the German form on him as an intimacy. It amused him, and pleased him as well. Everything about him seemed to her open and unconcealed. It was not, of course. She knew that. Yet he appeared to be what he was, like the room itself. With its pot-pourri jars and pink lamp-shades, its basket-work stools and chairs, a dressing-table like a high altar of beauty, it was designed for such nights as they passed together.

Standing before the mirror, Tonia scrutinized her face carefully, the high, lightly-rouged cheek-bones, the darkened lashes over the green eyes, the deep gold of the curls which clustered to her shoulder. Nothing too obvious, that was the secret of success in her profession and she had learnt it young. It was the apparent inno-cence of embarrassed beauty, the impromptu glimpse, and the sudden excitement which ensured the slavery in which her admirers were held.

The silk gown rustled as she unhooked and pushed, shedding the tight cloth as a caterpillar might shed its skin. The petticoats whispered in a flurry of cotton, and then she sat in a basket-chair, unhooking first one long stocking and then the other. It was all carefully calculated. Reduced to the black silk armour of an elegant corset with wasp-waist and embroidered fleur-de-lis, she crossed to the window and watched the square outside from the cover of the net curtains.

To remove the corset without the assistance of a maid was almost impossible. But there was a cameo to be staged and a precise moment for it. As soon as she saw Shackleton step down from a cab, Tonia rang the bell for the maid. The Dublin Herald opened the door of the room on a scene which caused him to gasp. The little maid was labouring to release her mistress, as if a handmaid of Venus attending the naked goddess. Shackleton could hardly wait to see the girl bustle away down the stairs. His enthusiasm was the more highly charged by the suggestiveness of the corset's elastic impress on the pale body-contours.

"Franz," she said later in her light, soft voice. "The necklace, my necklace, it is not safe in the hotel, is it?"

"Safer there than here," he said casually. Propped on his elbow, he repeated circular designs on her, here and there.

"It should be somewhere better." She was pouting sulkily, but she knew better than to press him too hard as yet. "A place where the Schroeder jewels cannot be stolen!"

"We'll see, old girl." The words were accompanied by the light resonance of a reassuring pat. "We'll see." Again the acoustics of the room caught the light, plump sound.

The reference to the Schroeder necklace, the family's heirloom, was really not important, just a reminder to the scapegrace young man of its existence. Tonia did not think he would steal from her. One never knew, of course. And in any case, it would really not matter whether he did or not.

Two hours later, dressing for dinner, she opened her dainty silk reticule and moved a second paper with its sleeping-draught. Perhaps it was mean to treat a lover in quite this way, but he had, after all, been well rewarded. In truth, she was quite fond of "Franz" after their weeks of acquaintance, though never forgetting the purpose to be served. It helped her to regard their affair as something apart from that. Of course, it would last no more than a few months, but then, she wondered, how many affairs outlived such a span, anyway?

A child could have tipped the powder into Shackleton's drink, it was so easy. Nor, as she had feared, did it have the effect of making him pass out too quickly. The Dublin Herald yawned a good deal and spoke of the tedium of the day's ceremony. When Vicars had gone upstairs, he followed with Tonia. Only when he was asleep did the fine-cut, sallow features seem still as in death. Tonia touched him, spoke gently, caressed him. There was no response. His breathing was hardly perceptible. She guessed that the sodium must delay and intensify the action of the drug. That was good.

Somewhere beyond St. Stephen's Green a clock chimed one. She lay very still, listening and thinking, until it chimed the next hour. By now she was certain that she was the only person awake in the house. Vicars, with his old-maidish preoccupation over his health, would certainly have gone to bed at once. Very slowly, she moved the bed-clothes and swung her feet out on to the floor. Her dressing-gown, which had been left in the room for the past two weeks, hung close by. While putting it on, she watched Shackleton's face in the window light. It was still as that of a crusader on a tomb. Without a sound, she opened the door to the landing, closed it behind her, and stood for a moment in the darkness. There was no strip of light showing under Vicars's door, no sound that she could hear. Holding her breath, Tonia turned the china handle and opened it steadily.

The room was faintly illuminated, like its neighbour, by the light from outside. It was as she had left it, except for the figure on the bed. Looking from the doorway, she was at first startled by the sight of him. The mouth was open, rigid and silent, like that of a corpse. In the twilight of imagination it seemed the eyes were open, too, but that was a trick of light and shadow playing on the contours of the sockets.

Because the light from the square seemed sufficient, she had not bothered with a candle. To carry one unnecessarily was to risk leaving tell-tale wax-droppings or drawing immediate attention to herself if Ulster King-of-Arms should wake from his sleep after all. Because of this she had to walk silently across to the washstand and examine the water-bottle more closely. Half of its contents had gone. That was more than enough, if Gaudy was to be believed. Indeed, she felt relieved that Vicars had not emptied it completely.

Keeping to the carpet, treading silently back to the bed, she stood over him like a spectre, looking down. At that moment, even with Gaudy's repeated assurances in her mind, it seemed impossible that she could do what she had to and not wake the man from his sleep.

She took another deep breath and held it, her hands gently turning back the sheet from his chest. Just then it occurred to her that the task would have been quite impossible if Vicars were in the habit of sleeping on his stomach, and, in a fit of childish nervousness, she wanted to giggle at the thought. But he had turned only slightly on to his side. She looked more closely and saw that the neck of his night-shirt was open at the front four or five inches below the collar. There was also the tiny metalwork thread of a locket-chain. In that case the locket itself must be very nearly in view.

Letting her breath out in a rush, drawing it and holding it again, she took the chain gently between two finger-tips and drew upon it lightly. There was no response from the body of the sleeper. She doubted that he would have stirred if she had begun to cut his appendix out. The little chain went taut, the locket snagged somewhere within the night-shirt itself. Again she felt a rising splutter of amusement and checked it at once with the memory of penalties for failure.

Lifting the edge of the linen, she at last pulled the pendant clear and held it above the man's chest. It was not a locket at all. In the faint light it looked more like a cartridge-case, about three to four inches long and the thickness of a finger. There was no indication as to how it should be opened. She felt the ridge round its top, pressing evenly on the circumference until, presently, the narrow lid snapped open with a faint pop. Tonia slid her little finger inside to withdraw the key, ready to press it into the square tin of wax in her dressing-gown pocket. Twice, Gaudy had said. Once for each side. Her finger probed further.

The key was not there.

It was so absurd that she thought at first her eyes or her sense of touch had played a trick on her. Was there another locket on the chain? Or had she not probed it sufficiently? A second glance convinced her that she had done all that she could. Wherever else the key to the Milner safe might be, it was not on the locket-chain of Ulster King-of-Arms. Yet Frank Shackleton had not been wrong when he boasted to her of the precautions taken at Dublin Castle. There was a chain and there was a locket. But no key.

The possibilities were daunting. Perhaps Vicars alone knew where that key was hidden. Shackleton, it seemed, did not. It might be somewhere else in the bedroom, or anywhere else in the house. For that matter, Vicars could as easily have concealed it in his office in the Bedford Tower or deposited it in a vault at the Bank of Ireland. Tonia looked round the room again, her pretty young face dimpling with a grimace that mingled despair and resentment. Still, there was nothing to be gained by remaining where she was. Lowering the locket and turning the sheet back, she went soundlessly from the room.

Shackleton stirred lightly in his sleep as she slid into bed beside him. Then he settled back into a profound slumber. Tonia lay staring at the faintly-lit ceiling and allowed the confusion in her mind to resolve itself. Half an hour before, she had been the intruder, the deceiver who held the household at her mercy. Now the case was entirely altered. She was the dupe, the deceived, the intruder who had taken an easy risk and had been, improbably, caught out.

It was much worse than that, the more one thought about it. To take an impression of Vicars's key had not even been part of the main business, merely a casual preliminary. As things were, there now seemed likely to be no main business. She thought of Gaudeans, then of Lindemann. The clock beyond St. Stephen's Green chimed three, and the sky began to lighten above the Irish Channel.

17

"**N**ot there?" Gaudeans looked at her with a grimace which was midway between laughter and outrage. "But it can't not be there!"

They had met outside the grand entrance to the Shelbourne Hotel in St. Stephen's Green. Before the red brick and pale stone facing of the luxurious building the slope of a white awning on cast-iron pillars provided shelter from the first hot day of the season. Tonia's smooth young forehead wrinkled in honest perplexity. She turned to the iron scroll-work, the bronze statues of Nubian princesses and their slave-girls with which the hotel front was lined.

"It is not in the locket round his neck," she said simply. "Not at night, anyway. Perhaps during the day he carries it, but I doubt that. Even if he trusts a woman in his room at night, she won't find the key there."

"Cunning young devil," said Gaudeans grudgingly. "Still, it must be somewhere, old girl. Stands to reason, don't it?"

"Somewhere?" She looked at him incredulously. "Anywhere! I think you should tell Lindemann and ask him to change the plan. Without the keys, the idea of Dublin Castle is preposterous."

They walked slowly along the north pavement of St. Stephen's Green, westward towards Grafton Street and the fashionable shops.

"Look," said Gaudeans suddenly; then he swung his silver-topped stick and paused before continuing, as if he had given the matter great thought. "No one ever makes a lock with only one key. There must be a duplicate, apart from the one Vicars carries—or doesn't carry."

Tonia turned towards him, pouting with a scorn which he found particularly attractive.

"The duplicates are locked in the safe itself, according to Frank Shackleton. In other words, Gaudy, if you could get at them, you wouldn't need them. They have no part in the plan."

"Oh, I don't know," said Gaudeans, faintly reproving. "I wouldn't say that. I wouldn't say that at all." He hummed a little to himself and swung the stick once more as they crossed Kildare and Dawson streets, turning at length into the sedate traffic of Grafton Street itself with its flags and elegant shop-fronts.

"You know," he said presently, "I rather think that's their mistake, locking the duplicate keys in the safe. I believe that's just where we might have them on the hip."

"Mistake?" Tonia looked at him with a coy and intimate scepticism.

"Yes," said Gaudeans cheerfully, "the biggest mistake they could have made."

At that point they turned into Brown, Thomas and Company, past the Victorian windows, bowed and plate-glass, the elegant front with its gold lettering on black gloss. The grand interior, the panelled ceiling above the counters, the rows of Grecian columns supporting it, would have graced Paris or London as easily as Dublin. A royal coat of arms proclaimed that the firm had been suppliers of millinery and haberdashery to Her late Majesty the Queen and the Prince of Wales.

Gaudeans watched Tonia move gracefully up the broad staircase, her gloved hand gliding easily on the mahogany rail with its white-painted ironwork. She lifted the folds of her dress, and his gaze was caught by the perfection of what was fashionably called a well-turned ankle. In her absence, he wandered jauntily among the counters, silk hat under one arm, stick swinging from the other hand. He winked casually at one of the girls on the millinery counter. She blushed slightly and was then caught by a convulsive giggle, as she might have been by indigestion. No good, he thought breezily, blushes and giggles were not in his line.

A long time later, it seemed, Tonia reappeared, giving her final instructions to a shop-walker who bustled along fussily at her side. Turning from the man as if dismissing him from existence, she accepted Gaudeans's arm. Outside in the sunlit street, he hailed a cab.

"Exhibition grounds at Herbert Park," he said loftily.

Tonia frowned, tightening the pressure on his arm.

"Tell Lindemann," she said petulantly. "Tell him it can't be done, then see what he wants instead."

"My dear young person," said Gaudeans with an attempt at facetiousness, "what he'll want instead is my head on a platter. And

135

your beautiful self, roasted and basted, carved into nice thin slices for his delectation. Colonel Lindemann doesn't allow for things that can't be done. It ain't in his book."

"That's ridiculous!" She detached her arm from his and stared out of the window at the houses of Leeson Street.

"You haven't known him as well as I." Gaudeans leered at her frankly. "And in any case, it can easily be done. You'll see."

But now she turned back, and the pretty face with its roguish delicacy betrayed her anger at his facetious confidence.

"You haven't a single thing!" she burst out. "There are two keys to the vault-door, and you haven't either. There are two keys to the iron grille, and you haven't either. There's a key to the safe which you haven't got and won't get. For that matter, even if there were no sentries outside the Bedford Tower, you haven't got a key to open that door to begin with."

"That's the easy part, keys," he said thoughtfully. "I'll have a key presently, you'll see. What's difficult in this life is dealing with types like Colonel Lindemann. If I wanted to, I could be standing in that strong-room this minute in front of the open safe, but Lindemann doesn't want that yet."

She tossed her golden curls impatiently.

"How absurd!"

Gaudeans sighed and murmured to himself, "Oh, ye of little faith!"

That was all he would say. Tonia stared out of the window again, suddenly aware that she was biting the thumb-nail of her right hand. She made a conscious effort to pull herself together, but the truth was that the events of the previous twelve hours had shaken her confidence. The absence of Vicars's key was merely confirmation of a distant haunting suspicion which she now acknowledged having felt from the start. The entire plan was preposterous. Worse than that, everyone but her intended that it should be preposterous. Worst of all, it might be a trap in which she was to be the necessary victim. Vicars knew that someone was about to copy or steal his key. So he had not worn it. Perhaps Lindemann was party to the cheat; at the very least, Captain Gaudeans must be.

She began biting at the thumb-nail again and this time made no effort to stop herself. If there was a traitor, she reasoned, it was more likely to be Gaudeans than Lindemann. Nationality, habits of dishonesty, absence of honour and moral scruple—all pointed to him. It was possible that he would reward himself by betraying the entire plan to the British Intelligence Department. Even more likely, he would use the cover and the funds which Lindemann had made available in order to perpetrate some crime of his own.

Glancing quickly at him, Tonia thought she might be wrong. But for her own sake there seemed only one thing to do. Write to Lindemann within the next twenty-four hours and confess her suspicions. It was she, after all, who had been sent to control and check Gaudeans. For the past week and more, the situation had been well beyond any control which she might have exercised.

The cab drew up outside the main entrance of the exhibition hall. In the bright morning the fountains played and the stone of the sham-basilicas threw back the heat as if the scene were a piazza in some north Italian city. Gaudeans took her on his arm again and led her to a seat.

"Stop here," he said gently. "I won't be half an hour. Then you see if I'm not right after all."

For his part, too, he was uneasy, torn between telling the girl more than was necessary and irritating her by explaining too little. Still, there was no point in boasting further until he had something to boast about.

Passing alone through the turnstiles, Gaudeans entered the pavilion devoted to engineering and manufacture. Large areas had been roped off and canopied for the main exhibits, including a massive railway locomotive in liver-coloured paint with black trimmings. A party of boys from Belvedere College swarmed round the engine, like Lilliputians about a quiescent and captive monster.

Gaudeans swaggered past, walking the long arcade of engineering marvels under the glass vaulting of the roof. He knew from the catalogue where the object of his quest lay. It was not one of the more impressive stands, not at least to the casual spectator. He found it in a corner site, almost at the end of the long, sunlit pavilion. Who, after all, was interested in a parade of metal boxes?

Like most companies of its kind, Milner's built everything from bank vaults to cash-boxes. Indeed, a man with money in his pocket could come to the exhibition and buy at once a small box for his petty cash or a massive cylindrical vault-door which the Bank of Ireland might have envied. The only difference, as Gaudy knew, was that a man could take the box away with him. The vault-door would have to be delivered from the works.

Dominating the display was a fire-proof, shock-proof, burglar-proof safe. It stood massive and brooding, a square tomb-like artifact, its front adorned by shielded keyhole, bolt-lever, and a metal roundel bearing the maker's name in gold. The only treasure a safebreaker would get from it, Gaudy decided, was the amount of gilt he could scrape off the name-plate. This was presumably the same model as that installed in the Dublin Castle strong-room. Merely to see it was no help in opening one. Interesting to have a glimpse of it, though.

For a moment, Gaudeans avoided the frock-coated representative of the firm who presided over the display. A look round first, he decided, that was the ticket. He walked slowly and admiringly round the safe itself, with the air of one who had never seen such a device before, let alone considered purchasing it. He was, as he had expected, ignored. For all that, he thought, Dublin Castle had the jump on old Lindemann and his jiggery-pokery with million-number combinations. Showed you the difference between Dublin and Berlin. The Germans trusted the man; the British trusted only the key.

Casually, avoiding the gaze of the man in the frock-coat, he crossed to the display of smaller strong-boxes and the even more diminutive steel tins for petty cash. Each was made from the same black-painted metal with the firm's distinctive design. Not only was there a similarity in design from the massive safe to the smallest cash-box; as Gaudeans had expected, the keys to the locks were also made in the firm's unique pattern, bronze-coloured with a heart-shaped finger-piece. Whereas the steel artifacts varied in size from the vault-safe to a box the size of a biscuit-tin, there was correspondingly little difference in the size of the keys. Each was cut to fit only the lock to which it belonged. That apart, it was hard to tell by sight which one belonged to the Milner safe and which to the cash-box.

He walked up to the frock-coated representative.

"I beg your pardon." Gaudeans assumed the air of quiet authority which he kept in reserve for such occasions as this. "I should like a cash-box. Nothing elaborate. Just large enough to hold a few bags of sovereigns."

The other man's self-importance vanished in his enthusiasm at a likely sale. He bowed slightly and led the way to the display of boxes behind the mesh of their shelf. Even the key with which he opened this grille was of identical pattern to the rest.

"That one," said Gaudeans abruptly, pointing at the smallest and cheapest. "That's quite good enough for what I had in mind." He felt the sudden uprush of a chuckle at the hidden truth of his words, and he checked it hastily.

"You will find, sir," said the representative with an air of faint reproof, "that even the smallest of our strong-boxes is made to the same exacting standard as the Milner safe." He held out the steel container for Gaudeans's approval. "The lock is proof against any pick or probe known to the criminal world. The lip which runs round the top of the box is so curved as to be impervious to any implement which might otherwise force open a container of this kind. The hinges, you observe, are concealed. As to the material itself, no drill or bit will penetrate it. This, sir, is made of the identical armoured steel used in our vault-safes."

Gaudeans played the ingenuous customer.

"Supposing," he said confidentially, "just supposing I were to lose the key. What would happen then?"

The man in the frock-coat pursed his lips slightly with the humorous pleasure of revealing some final measure of security.

"Were that to happen, sir, the box and its contents would have to be taken back to our works. There, and there alone, we have means of opening it. The firm's policy is absolute. We do not construct locks which may be opened in an emergency by an ordinary locksmith. A locksmith may be honest, or he may not. And what a smith can do today, the criminal will learn to do tomorrow. That, sir, is the experience of other firms. The box, by the way, is also resistant to fire."

"Very good," said Gaudeans thoughtfully. "That really is very good. D'you know, I think it's just what I need."

He took a small leather purse from his pocket and began to count out sovereigns into his hand while the man sent for another box and arranged to have it wrapped.

"Perhaps, sir, you would care to sign our visitors' book for the exhibition."

"Oh," said Gaudeans slightly startled. "Oh, yes, rather."

He had, of course, intended to do so, whether invited or not. The man opened the leather-bound volume with its neatly-ruled columns. Gaudeans pretended to find some difficulty with his pen, and in the moment that the man's back was turned, he flipped over the previous pages which had been filled since the opening of the exhibition. Then with an expression of innocent concentration he signed General Thorneycroft's name.

Five minutes later, with the box in his hand and its two keys in his pocket, he left the long pavilion of industrial exhibits, crossing the vestibule and coming out again into the bright May sunlight of the gravelled fore-court.

Tonia was still sitting where he had left her, a pink parasol now opened in a coquettish pretence of shielding her fair skin and golden curls from the noon glare. Gaudeans perched himself beside her and drew a small packet from his waistcoat.

"Milner key," he said casually.

Tonia looked at him, the green eyes narrow with suspicion.

"For the safe?"

Gaudeans laughed at the extravagance of the idea.

"These little jiggers? They ain't cut to open anything but a penny-box. Still, they *look* as if they'd open safes. That's it."

He would have to trust her now. The time had come to convince Tonia that, with what he had, he could empty the strong-room of Dublin Castle as easily as he could walk through walls or escape from underwater coffins.

Slipping one arm round her waist, he drew her close and gently described what must be done. He was careful to outline her own part, which was far simpler than his own. There were still a few details to be completed, but there was no doubt any longer. Captain Wunder could be past the sentries, the vault-door, and into the safe itself whenever it suited him.

At first Tonia's face remained strained in an expression of scepticism. Then she relaxed and grinned like a child. Presently she giggled. Gaudeans, with a clownish lasciviousness which matched the occasion, drew a narrow fold of flesh on her hip and pinched it lightly. To his delight she moved vigorously against him.

"Lindemann was wrong," she giggled. "He said you were a trickster, nothing more! But you are a safebreaker, a burglar after all!"

Gaudeans looked at the immaculate polish of his flashy little shoes.

"Ain't I the boy, then?" he said pleasantly.

But there was more to come.

"Mind you," he said, "there's a bit of bad in with the good."

The doubt returned to her eyes as she scanned his face.

"Visitors' book at Milner's stand," he whispered. "Fifty names or so, including a friend of ours."

"Who?"

"Peirce Mahony, Esquire. And why should that little squeak be interested in Milner safes? If he is, why can't he look at the one in the castle?"

"The diamonds," she said quickly. "The Mahony diamonds. He wants his own safe to keep them in?"

Gaudeans shook his head.

"No, old girl, he don't. The one thing about those diamonds is that if the castle safe is emptied, the sparklers taken, who'd look at Mahony? A fellow steal his own family fortune? If he wanted money he could sell 'em legal. You think the C.I.D. would fancy him for that?"

"Well, then?" she asked fretfully.

Gaudeans sighed.

"You tell me, missy. Tell me what a man's prepared to lose his fortune for. What he's ready to give everything for."

"How should I tell?" There was irritation in her tone. Yet in the shadow of the parasol her face showed a new timidity, as if for the first time in their partnership she was uncertain of the way ahead.

"The cause!" said Gaudeans sharply. "For the cause! Ireland! Don't you see it? He's a true patriot! No matter to him whether he's to pinch the state jewels or secret papers the C.I.D. keep on the rebels. Worth every last sparkler to him."

"Are you sure?"

"For the last twenty minutes," said Gaudeans solemnly, "I was never so sure of anything in my born puff. They're on the same path as us. They may be a bunch of bog peasants, for all I know, but they've got Mahony. A man on the inside. And they can pick their time. Any day from now till Christmas Tuesday. All the same to them. Lindemann had best look slippy. Unless he wants to come up with a handful of shine-rag and damn-all else."

"And you?" The pretty doll-face was imploring him now. "There is nothing you can do?"

Gaudeans liked this, the little girl gazing up at her hero. He liked it very, very much indeed. He gave a sharp sniff.

"Yes," he said, "there's one or two things I can do. First of all, I'm going to write a letter to a man called Colonel Ross. Chief of security."

"Yes?" Her timidity was profoundly exciting.

"Yes." He swaggered with his walking-stick a little. "I shall write and tell him that the safe in the castle strong-room is about to be robbed."

Because it was so obvious to her that he must be joking, Tonia registered no response at first. Then she saw it was not a joke.

"That's impossible!" she cried. "Lindemann will not allow you!"

"Lindemann ain't here to stop me, miss!" said the little man confidently. "Any case, I shan't be mad enough to tell him who's going to do it. Mahony and his potatoes."

"No!"

"Yes! A letter from an unsigned well-wisher, revealing that Mahony has been skulking in Dublin when he was supposed to be in England. They know half that already, according to Frank Shackleton. Story of Mahony drunk in a bawdy-house on the North Wall, boasting of how he'd rob the castle safe. Make him starkers. He's got a birth-mark and a stomach scar. They'd believe that."

"No!"

"Use your brain!" snapped Gaudeans. "They can't make the security any tighter than it is. And all their attention goes to Mahony. He won't so much as pick his teeth without a report going to Colonel Ross. See?"

"No." But there was defeat in her voice and he knew it. As they walked back down the leafy Georgian avenues of south Dublin, he saw how everything might be turned to his own advantage. From time to time he glanced at the pretty high-boned face shaded by the pink parasol and felt the gratifying pressure of her gloved hand on his arm. But in his mind he was composing the opening sentences of the letter which Colonel Ross would receive next morning. Unsigned, of course.

Dear Sir,

As a loyal subject of His Majesty and a soldier of the late and gracious Queen, it is my duty to acquaint you with certain threats uttered in my presence by a man claiming to be Peirce Mahony of the Royal Household. . . .

A bit of polish here and rephrasing there. Not too elegant. The work of a senior N.C.O., perhaps. As they strolled on towards St. Stephen's Green he thought with gratitude of Mahony and the inspiration which the young man had provided. This was going to be good, Gaudeans decided, with another appreciative glance at Tonia. This was going to be a bit of all right.

18

Gaudeans lurched confidentially against Shackleton as the two men turned into the leafy gas-lit boulevard of Sackville Street. With its broad carriage-way and tall trees, pillared elegance among fine hotels and splendid shops, it might have been Paris or Berlin rather than Dublin.

"Old man," he said clumsily, "I don't want to intrude in the matter, but you ain't thinking of marrying little Tonia? Are you, old man?"

Shackleton turned to his companion with a sharp, dark glimmer of humour in his eyes.

"Wouldn't I just!" he said softly. "Wouldn't I, though! Not cutting across your bows, is it?"

He did not sound as if he cared much whose bows he cut across, Gaudeans thought. And that was good. Gaudy gave a snuffling little laugh.

"An old fellow like me?" he asked modestly. "A man mayn't marry his own cousin, anyway. Not any more. Mind you, though, she's a clipper. Ain't she?"

They crossed over the Talbot Street turning, where the urbane procession of Sackville Street society gave way to a bright glimpse of riot and tawdriness in the little roads and alleys which ran towards the stations and the docks. An open carriage bore four girls in petticoats with two bullies, the girls shrieking their invitations at the bystanders. A soldier with his tunic torn open stumbled from a shadowed doorway and went sprawling on the pavement. As the open carriage with its girls vanished round a corner, two men began to fight drunkenly and ineffectually in its wake.

"I'm not poor," said Shackleton suddenly, "and I'll be a sight richer when the Mexican loan's funded."

"And she's not Tonia Schroeder for nothing," said Gaudeans proudly.

Shackleton's dark, aquiline features turned quickly again, eyes narrowed as if to penetrate Gaudeans's meaning. Gaudy smiled; he and Tonia had agreed that it would be more plausible if the story was left to him.

144

"Tonia *Schroeder*!" he said delightedly. "My old ma's a Schroeder. That's what makes us cousins. See?"

"What if she is?"

"Schroeder!" whined Gaudeans impatiently. "Dear old Shacky! Ain't you the boy for a spec and a run with the bulls and bears? And don't you know the Schroeder works in Dresden? Chemicals! Stinks! Whiz-bangs!"

Shackleton stood still in the middle of the broad pavement, as if transfixed by lancing agony.

"*That* Schroeder?" For the first time in their shallow companionship Gaudeans saw the young man's composure broken. Greed, cupidity, and lust struggled behind the sharp, sallow features.

"Dear old Shacky!" The words were as patient and affectionate as Gaudy could make them. "You never knew? She never said? Don't you see? The only reason I'm escorting her this season is because I'm her cousin and can't marry her. And my old guv'nor mayn't be rich as Schroeder but he can spend pound for pound with him a deuced long way! So the old man knows I shan't want her fortune!"

It was going even better than he had hoped. Shackleton was a trickster, of course, but not in Gaudy's league. He had nosed at every possible flaw with the professional suspicion of a cheat and found nothing but the promise of gain. No one asked him to lay out a sovereign of his own money. Instead, money was offered him without conditions, on all sides.

"She ain't just the old man's only daughter," Gaudeans added casually. "There's no sons, either."

For the past fortnight he had woven a double thread in his conversations with Frank Shackleton, his new chum. One strand was the pathetic and comic envy of an older man for a lucky young scoundrel in his possession of such a treasure as Tonia. The other consisted of hints about the fortune in the hands of a Schroeder uncle and an equally mythical Gaudeans father, the payer of his son's debts.

Shackleton recovered himself sufficiently to say the thing which decency required.

"A gentleman don't take a girl for her money, Gaudy. Not in my book he don't. Any case, when the Mexican loan business is funded and paying, I'll have more of it than your old guv'nor and hers put together."

Gaudeans's sharp little features tightened with suspicion.

"Not without me, you won't," he said quietly, as if reminding Shackleton of his power. "Ain't it you and I that's going to be rich together from the certified Mexican loan? Me first, Shacky. When you've taken my little investment, I'll squeeze all the juice you need from my old guv'nor and Missy Tonia too, if you want."

Shackleton tried to conceal his satisfaction at the urgency with which his companion was forcing money upon him. He nodded at the grizzling little figure.

"Play fair, old man!" pleaded Gaudeans. "You take a great bundle of oof from her and my old guv'nor first—and what happens? Sours the milk! Price goes up and the game's spoilt! You promised you'd let my little bit get a start on them!"

"All right!" said Shackleton reassuringly. "All right! A man makes a bargain! Stands by it! You as well as me! Remember?"

Gaudeans gave a sniggering little grimace of mock-bashfulness.

"Oh, that!" he simpered. "That!"

"Just for tonight! She won't come to the house when Vicars has company there. I can't go to her at this hour of night. Not unless I'm going to the Shelbourne to see you."

Gaudeans nodded contentedly and gave him a knowing smile. He had been working for an opportunity like this, knowing it must come in his dealings with a cheat like Shackleton. Even a foolish son so easily prepared to part with his money had to be tested and proved. He accepted that. It was what he would have done in Shackleton's place.

"Dear old Shacky!" he said, shaking his head as if in affectionate despair at the antics of the young scamp.

They crossed Carlisle Bridge with its dark river flowing from the slums of Kilmainham down to the docks and the open sea. Past the front of Trinity they turned into Nassau Street and came to the ornate red-brick splendour of the Kildare Street Club with its elegant windows and porticos, the retreat of judges and politicians. In St. Stephen's Green, Gaudeans escorted his companion into the grand vestibule of the Shelbourne Hotel and up the wide sweep of the staircase. Shackleton was right, of course. No establishment of repute would have allowed him in at that time of night to visit a young lady.

The suite which the two "cousins" occupied consisted of a pair of bedrooms with a day-room intervening. There was no internal communication among the three. Gaudeans led Shackleton into his own bedroom and put up the gas. He now appeared to be increasingly uneasy.

"Old man," he said quietly. "You won't mind, old man, if I leave you here and make sure that the coast is clear? It won't do for you to be seen going to her. Not for her, not for you, and not for me! Not if old Schroeder and my guv'nor get told the tale!"

He slipped off his jacket and hung it carefully on a chair. Shackleton smiled obligingly and contented himself with admiring the polished mahogany and ormolu inlay of the apartment. Everything about it, from the silk curtains to the ornate gilding of the lamps, spoke of quiet affluence and easy contentment.

Gaudeans put a finger to his lips and went out into the corridor. The sound of his footsteps moved gently in the direction of Tonia's door. He was away for about five minutes, returning with a look of indulgent envy on his face. He stood in the doorway and whispered.

"All right, old man! No time to lose, though."

Shackleton walked quickly away and let himself in through Tonia's doorway. Gaudeans's heart beat quickly with expectation. He was certain of what he was going to find now. But, then, he had been certain once or twice before and had been disappointed just the same.

He knelt down in front of the chair on which his jacket hung, looked carefully at the inner lining, and smiled. Of course, he had been right. When arranging the jacket there, he had taken great care with the note-case in the inside pocket. A slip of cloth stitched to the bottom seam of the pocket had been pressed between the halves of the case. Any attempt to take the leather case out would draw the slip of cloth free without the person's knowing it. Gaudeans made a quick inspection with his fingers and felt the cotton tag now flattened on the pocket seam.

That was excellent! Frank Shackleton had done exactly as Gaudeans had hoped, inspecting the papers of his victim to ensure that the mark was worth hitting. With affectionate care, Gaudeans examined the compartments of the note-case, the letter from a loving but anxious Gaudeans senior, receipts for items of jewellery bought at West's in Dublin. And, of course, the tickets and passes of a gambling man.

He turned to the desk, which had been left unlocked. The top drawer was the one which mattered. He hardly dared hope that Shackleton had searched it and found the cheque-book for Coutts

Bank in London. The stubs showed that Gaudeans had apparently paid several thousand pounds for his summer pleasures as if the amount meant nothing to him. A spendthrift fool with a wealthy father. The account at Coutts had been opened with Lindemann's money, of course. In reality, not a single cheque had been drawn upon it.

Gaudeans drew open the desk drawer. He had left the cheque-book positioned with great care so that its corners just touched certain letters of a printed dividend voucher lying underneath. He need not have bothered. In his hurry, Shackleton had tossed the cheques back so carelessly that it was obvious at a glance.

So that was that. Gaudeans sat down in an easy chair, shut his eyes, and tried to doze. There was no justice for poor old Shacky, he thought. A young trickster was never a match for an older one. Youth was a time for athletic prowess and lyric poetry, he supposed. But there were some things which required time to bring to perfection. Like trickery and making love. Young Shackleton could boast nothing better than his guaranteed Mexican loan, a fraud which reeked like old cheese. On the other hand, it was possible to feel a gentle indulgence towards him. Perhaps because in the young man Gaudeans saw himself, ten or a dozen years earlier. He smiled at the thought and slept.

Though he woke several times, hearing movements outside the door, he was still dozing when Tonia came in the next morning. She was radiant in pink embroidered with pale blue, and he felt a pang of true envy for Shackleton at the sight of the pretty high-boned face with its china delicacy.

"Well?" she asked coyly.

Gaudeans stood up, flashed a debonair smile, and walked across to her. He took a fold of skin on her cheek and pinched it roguishly.

"Hooked!" he said jubilantly. "Neater than apple pie!"

She was not as pleased as he had hoped. It concerned him that she might allow herself to become too fond of the young man. Not likely, though. Lindemann had picked her carefully. Must have done. For her it was no different from enjoying the taste of caviar, though eaten in the presence of someone to whom she was indifferent. Such a degree of self-possession was beyond his own comprehension.

"He wants me to go to London with him," she said casually, "for a few days later in the month. London and Ascot."

"So you shall," said Gaudeans indulgently. "So you must. Ascot, eh?"

"The Royal Enclosure."

"Can we do it?"

"Lindemann can. Of course. Franz seems to think he might meet your father at Ascot. Is that so?"

"Ah!" said Gaudeans thoughtfully. "Now there's a trick, d'you see?"

She began to button his shirt, which he had undone the night before, pouting up at him.

"You haven't got a father."

Gaudeans reached round, pinched her again, and winked.

"Wait till Ascot!" he said knowingly. "Then you'll see!"

He watched her turn away indifferently, swinging her hips and dancing her hand along the backs of the chairs.

"By the way," she said, as if it were a matter of no consequence, "I asked Franz about my necklace again."

"Oh, yes?"

"He was evasive. But he did tell me where Vicars's key is kept."

"Yes?"

"Yes!" she echoed mockingly. "In a wall-safe in the Viceroy's private study. He has to report there and sign for it when he wants it. They took it from him on the day that the exhibition began. You see, they don't trust him, either."

She liked him, Gaudeans thought. All this display was for him. He risked another pinch.

"That's good news," he said lightly, close to her ear. "The more they don't trust people, the easier it'll be. Mind you, if I was Viceroy, I don't suppose I'd trust anyone, either. Especially not you."

19

Nobody looked at a coachman on occasions like this, not at his face. Certainly not if all that could be seen was a dark bushy moustache and a hat pulled well down at the brim. It was the first time that Gaudeans had ever been a coachman, but the problem was minimal to one who had driven drags and four-in-hands. The line of closed carriages stretched in the dusty gold of a twilit evening from the castle gate, down Cork Hill past the pillared elegance of the Royal Exchange, and halfway down Dame Street. It was the evening of the Viceroy's reception.

Tonia was going as Shackleton's guest. No one had invited Gaudeans, though his partnership in Shackleton's financial fraud was flourishing. It had been so easy to milk Gaudeans, or at least to know that milk would shortly be yielded in gratifying quantities, that an invitation to a viceregal reception was quite superfluous. That suited Gaudeans. He preferred to be Tonia's coachman.

Since this was likely to be his only glimpse of the castle inside its gates until the moment of the robbery, he made the most of it. They were certainly checking the arrivals with great care, he gave them marks for that. There was a double sentry detail in the bearskins of the Irish Guards, with an officer who scanned the gold-printed invitations as each lumbering black coach drew level. Half-a-dozen uniformed policemen lined the immediate approach to the castle gate, a solitary Georgian arch with a figure of Justice whose back was turned upon the city of Dublin. Behind the policemen small groups of spectators watched the waiting carriages with mild curiosity. They were mainly women admiring the dresses of the Viceroy's female guests.

The arch was joined to the buildings on either side by a short wall with a small gate. To one side, almost touching the Royal Exchange, there was a high, shabby Georgian block with barred windows. On the other, the wall joined the rear of the Bedford Tower at right angles. From the outside there was no means of entering the tower, the sole door being in the castle yard.

He need not have feared identification; it was already growing

150

dark by the time that the last of the carriages approached the arch above Cork Hill and were admitted to the yard. Even then, it was only Frank Shackleton who was likely to spare him a second glance. Gaudeans guessed that the Dublin Herald would be far too preoccupied with his other duties, as well as with the impression he hoped to make on Tonia.

The uniformed officer of the Irish Guards waved them through, and Gaudeans flicked at the two horses. Their carriage rumbled under the arch, into the long space of the upper yard. On the far side, opposite the Bedford Tower, the viceregal apartments were brightly lit, with a glimpse of glass chandeliers through the upper windows. The rest of the yard was built round by tall flights of Georgian brick, a quadrangle which suggested the administrative quarters of government in Ireland rather than a castle in the usual sense.

One of the flunkeys opened the carriage-door and handed Tonia down, the delicate beauty of her face and figure matched by the silver-blue of her evening gown. Then Gaudeans was directed through a wide arch which led down to the lower yard.

Here the carriages of the guests were drawn up in line to await the end of the reception, at midnight or later. The lower yard was the bigger of the two, though like the other it was enclosed by a jumble of buildings. Down one side ran the narrow, pointed windows of the Chapel Royal, in Victorian Gothic, with a massive round fortress tower at one end which was almost all that remained of the mediaeval castle.

Gaudeans, in the wide-brimmed hat and long, heavy coat of his coachman's uniform, took his place. Despite the precautions at the castle gate, no one seemed greatly interested in the drivers once they were inside. In the lower yard they were out of harm's way until the reception ended. In the upper yard, every door and window was under surveillance by the two sets of sentries, as well as by the footmen at the entrance to the viceregal apartments.

Soon afterwards Gaudeans heard the faint strains of a military band from the long throne-room, where the reception was being held. Not that there would be dancing, of course. The minuets and the quadrilles, the salon music of high society, were mere background to the rising murmur of gossip as the guests formed a patient queue and waited to be presented to the Viceroy and Lady Aberdeen. All the same, he judged it was now safe to leave the line of deserted carriages and take his place in the concealment of the archway which led from the lower yard to the upper.

The position was well chosen. From where he stood in the shadows, he could see both sides of the upper castle yard, the brilliant illumination of the viceregal apartments and the Bedford Tower in darkness. To anyone who noticed him, he was a loyal servant proudly but distantly sharing the social triumph of his young mistress.

They would be a long time yet. The last of the men in their dark, sharply-cut suits, the women in a glitter of jewellery and the warm colours of their gowns, had scarcely passed through the Italianate portico of the apartments. The line stretched up the grand staircase with its French tapestries and its chandeliers of Waterford glass. Through the tall windows of the throne-room, Gaudeans glimpsed a section of ceiling-paintings and gilt Corinthian pillars. In a gallery at one end, the military flautists and violinists in their scarlet tunics now discoursed tunes from light opera for the benefit of the assembled guests below them.

The officer of the Irish Guards who had scrutinized the invitations at the gate marched busily to and fro between the apartments and the guard-room on the opposite side of the yard. It was difficult to see much of the guard-room. A single light burned above its closed door on the outside. The windows, though barred on the outside, also seemed to be shuttered within. Somewhere in that room was the wall-safe in which, presumably, the guard commander's vault-key was kept.

Gaudeans began his watch at nine o'clock. The Bedford Tower would have closed by four o'clock at the latest. In that case it was unlikely for the guard commander and his police colleague to have made their rounds already. As a matter of habit, such things were done at about ten o'clock, the hour at which barracks and guard-rooms were accustomed to settle down for the night. They might vary the routine in this case, but Gaudeans doubted it. For the time being, there were three sentry watches within his view. First there were the men on the main gate, then the two guards on the door of the Bedford Tower, and finally two more in sentry-boxes at either side of the door to the viceregal apartments. This last pair did duty only when the Viceroy was at home, according to Tonia's information from Shackleton.

Someone had opened a window of the throne-room. The rumble of conversation and the inconsequential melodies of the band grew more distinct. Shackleton would by now be showing off Tonia like the young braggart that he was. Gaudeans hoped that the Dublin Herald would say nothing of the link between Tonia and the Schroeder chemical works at Dresden, which he had fabricated for his dupe's benefit. In all probability he was safe. Shackleton's natural instinct for deceit in matters of money would surely prevent him from confessing to Tonia that he knew of her supposed wealth. Better to be the decent fellow who loved her for herself alone, and then be agreeably surprised at the discovery of her parentage. Yes, Gaudeans thought, that was rather more like young Shackleton's style.

Despite the warmth of the summer day, he was distinctly cold by half-past nine and began to grow impatient for the ritual which he had come to observe. When it began, just after ten o'clock, it was so unobtrusive that he almost missed it. A tall man in a plain dark suit came very quietly from behind him, walking from the lower yard through the archway to the upper. Gaudeans, hearing just in time, drew to one side, so that the man's back was to him as he passed. The plain-suited figure walked slowly across the upper yard to the guard-room door, knocked upon it, and was admitted. So, then, even the guard-room was locked at this time of night. The security was more formidable than Gaudeans had supposed, and that pleased him.

Less than five minutes passed before the officer of the Irish Guards, who was evidently guard commander for that night, came out of the entrance to the viceregal apartments and followed the first man. For ten minutes more, the guard-room door remained shut and there was no sign of activity. Gaudeans prepared to move. An oblong of light slanted across the yard as the guard-room door opened again and the two men came out. One of them looked across the brightly-lit windows of the apartments and said something which made his companion laugh.

On the far side of the upper castle yard was a single line of coaches. Gaudeans emerged from the shadows, walking across to them in a businesslike manner. It must have looked natural enough to the sentries, he supposed. In any case the men at the door of the Bedford Tower were occupied in saluting the guard commander. A single syllable was spoken. A password? Gaudeans admired them for that and felt more pleased than ever. The door to the Bedford Tower was opened for them and closed again as the two men went in.

153

Now it was easy; he had only to watch the windows of the tower from the corner of his eye. As he walked he saw that the light in the vestibule went on and stayed on throughout their visit. No curtains were closed in the building, and this made it all the easier to calculate the two men's route. Another yellow patch of brilliance fell on the wall by the guard-room. So that was the method, then. The inspection began with the vault-door and the strong-room. Its barred, lighted window showed Gaudeans the upper part of the room, majestic breakfront bookcases standing against the side-walls. He knew the type well.

Casually he approached the line of coaches beyond the tower.

"All right?" he shouted to one of the drivers. "Doing all right?" The man looked back without speaking, but Gaudeans made a great show of waving his arm cheerfully for the benefit of the sentries. Then he turned and started back across the yard.

The strong-room light had gone off. Now it was the windows of the offices above which were lit, one by one. No one trusted Mahony, not Shackleton either, not even Vicars. None of them was permitted to spend a night alone with the treasures of the tower. The windows of the Georgian clock-tower remained unlit except by a glow from the floor below. That made sense, too. Easy enough to glance up there without climbing all the way.

He timed his return across the upper castle yard as carefully as he could, waiting for the light to go on in the library of the Office of Arms before he passed its windows. None of the sentries would think it odd that he should glance at the windows as he walked by. The library was the daily centre of activity in the tower, with nothing particularly secret about it.

Gaudeans walked in a careful, leisurely arc, taking a long view of the windows, keeping his gaze well up at the level of the top shelves which lined the inner walls. He knew from something which Shackleton had said to Tonia that he must find what he wanted there. He saw it almost at once. An oblong mahogany box which might have contained Corona-Coronas.

So that was where the fuses were. Easy to get at in an emergency. The alarm system was bound to be wired to it, but only a fool would believe that it was as simple as that. As a double precaution the alarm would be attached to another circuit, probably the guard-room's, in case one or the other should fail.

There was really very little more that he needed to know.

154

Gaudeans walked with the slow, even step of a bored but patient servant until the shadows of his archway once again concealed him. Just one little calculation had to be done. He watched carefully until all the lights had gone off in the Bedford Tower except for that in the vestibule. When that, too, was turned off, he began to count with the same deliberate measured pace as his walk. "One, two, three, four . . ." The two men came out, and the main door to the Bedford Tower was closed. They walked back, and Gaudeans counted past fifty as they went.

Afterwards he went back to the coach, intending to pull his coat about him and fall into a doze. To his surprise, he found that he was far too excited to sleep.

It was soon after midnight when the Viceroy's guests began to leave the reception. Gaudeans took his place once more in the line of vehicles and waited for Tonia to be escorted to her carriage. Shackleton accompanied her out, too engrossed in the girl's company to glance at the figure muffled in hat and coat on the box of the coach. Moreover, as Gaudeans had known, it was dark enough in the castle yard, despite the lamps which had been lit outside the main doorways of its buildings.

Shackleton went back to take his leave of the Viceroy. Whistling quietly to himself, Gaudeans turned the horses' heads towards the castle gate, following the sedate progress of the other carriages down Cork Hill. Propriety required Tonia to be seen driving back alone to her rooms at the Shelbourne Hotel. And that put young Shacky quite out of court for the moment.

Afterwards Gaudeans drove back alone, returning the carriage to the livery-stables behind Parliament Street. He bundled up the coachman's hat and coat, walked down to the quays, and lobbed them into the Liffey. As the coat spread on the water, drifting in the current down to Carlisle Bridge and the sea, he leant his elbows on the low wall above the river and tested Frank Shackleton's remarks to Tonia against the view of the strong-room which he had seen for himself.

All that he knew fitted exactly with what had been said. In his mind he constructed a plan of that room. First there was the door of armoured steel, with two separate keys for its two separate locks. Immediately inside it was the iron grille, also with two keys for two distinct locks. The purpose of the grille was presumably so that it was possible to open the vault-door and see into the room without opening its secondary protection, which the iron bars represented.

Inside, the plan of the room seemed essentially simple. The two walls to either side of the doorway were solid, with the majestic breakfront cases on broad pediments standing against them. The wall opposite the door was pierced by the single window, closely barred and guarded outside by the sentry patrol. At the centre of the room, according to a remark of Shackleton's, there might be a table and one or two chairs. Finally, there was the safe. If the table was, presumably, under the main electric light which he had seen, Gaudeans knew where the steel carcass of the Milner safe must be. It would be well away from the vault-door and the grille immediately within. As a matter of routine it would be turned so that its door faced the side-wall against which a breakfront case stood, not the entrance to the strong-room. In that way, only the man who opened it would see the operation of the door and the interior of the safe.

It would not, of course, be directly under the window. In other words, it must be sideways to the outer window wall, its door facing a side-wall and breakfront case, probably at a distance of a few feet. It must be so. And in that case, Gaudy thought, he had been right. From the very beginning. He turned from the wall of the quay and performed a quick little dance of exhilaration, like a sea-side minstrel.

In his mood of well-controlled excitement, he sauntered back down the gas-lit length of Dame Street, College Green, and Nassau Street like the dapper little "cousin" who was escort to the young heiress Tonia Schroeder. In his buoyant humour he was ready to burst into song. That was impossible, of course. The Shelbourne was not the sort of place to which a fellow could return singing at two o'clock in the morning.

Tonia was waiting for him in their day-room, the lights full on and her shimmering gown still undisturbed.

"Well?" Her lips were parted with expectation, just enough to show a glimpse of her teeth, even and delicate ivory.

Gaudeans chuckled.

"It's done!" he sang out. "Sure as if I'd gone in tonight. We could do it alone. Only I think it's best that Shacky should be in it, too. Up to his neck!"

"And the keys?"

He flung out his arms with complete self-confidence.

"Keys? No one needs them! Think of them at each other's throats!

Mahony and the Viceroy! All the guards and sentry-go! Vault-doors and armoured safes and alarm-bells! D'you know what a chap really needs to do the trick? One thing."

"One thing?" The doubt in her eyes conveyed a forlorn and puzzled prettiness.

"That's right," he said encouragingly. "Easiest thing in the world to get. Not keys or dynamite or any of that nonsense. To tell you the truth, I was never very good with keys."

"What?" she said impatiently.

"Oh," said Gaudeans, as if he had simply forgotten to tell her. "A very ordinary box of matches. Any sort would do."

"Matches?"

"That's right," he said cheerily. "Lucifers. So, tell Lindemann we know the way in, when the time comes. And tell him something else. I promised to take your young friend Shackleton to Ascot races. Next week. Tell Lindemann that. He'll know what it means."

She looked at him again, colouring slightly as if at his flippancy.

"Is that really necessary? Ascot?"

"Oh, yes," said Gaudeans, suddenly earnest. "We mustn't miss that. What I thought was this. Shacky, being as keen on money as he is, he'd be no end taken with the notion of going racing with my old guv'nor."

"But you have not got an old governor."

He burst into laughter at the charming solemnity with which she imitated his slangy speech. And in his good-natured fit he told her everything that he was going to do.

20

ajor Purfoy frowned. He looked at the message to be encoded and frowned again.

Kurier. Kurier. Subject now believed to be British. Imperative report all names British nationals known contacts of Political Intelligence/General Staff HQ/Naval Intelligence.

How the devil had they done it? he wondered. Or, rather, how had Kurier done it, since it was presumably on his information that the deduction was based. A British subject. That was no surprise at all. If the British Admiralty could have a German prince as its Director of Intelligence, why not an Englishman as a German intelligence officer? Or Irish? Or South African? The world was full of political grudges.

Purfoy's role had become extremely unrewarding. In the past weeks he had pumped out messages, night after night, never seeing the answers. Whatever information Kurier was sending back from Berlin—and there was evidently a lot of it—went straight to the Director or to Sir Edward Grey. It was clear that neither the Foreign Office nor the Admiralty had decided to trust him. Not that Purfoy was disturbed by that. Personally, he would not have trusted either of those establishments to spread butter on muffins.

One thing was obvious, though. It was no secret that, after six months, *Dreadnought* and *Invincible* were at sea. Five more like them on the slip-ways of the Clyde and the Tyne. Yet Germany had still failed to follow suit. And that meant one thing. There was to be a short cut, a theft of the *Dreadnought* secrets and the development of a new weapon to render Fisher's battleships obsolete. Cheaper and quicker. That, at least, was Purfoy's reasoning. Whether it was shared by his masters he had no idea.

He turned the shade of his brass lamp, directing the light squarely on to the grid before him. With his pencil he began to write the words. The first ones were so familiar that he no longer needed the grid for them. TOCKHI OIHQCC BOMLHTX BEE . . . The truth was that

158

he had long since grown bored with the entire operation. To judge by appearances, the Director was bored, too. Even Sir Edward Grey, amid the buttoned leather and polished mahogany of the Foreign Office, must have grown weary of it by now. Purfoy yawned, checked himself, and worked back through what he had written. At least the tedium of the others was relieved by answers to the cryptic messages. Well, he supposed it was. Presumably Kurier answered them. Or was he dead? Had he never existed? What, in any case, did it matter now? The whole thing was over.

With bland imperturbability, Purfoy lifted his phone and spoke to the Signals Department of the Admiralty. In another hour or two, his lunatic babble of Morse would join the chatter above the North Sea. Far below, the destroyers of two navies cut the dark waters with their bows. Their business was to watch and disengage with all the courtesy and menace of professional duellists.

21

From Piccadilly to Pall Mall the heat of the London afternoon shimmered on the black lacquer of the court carriages.

"Old man," said Gaudeans cautiously. "Old man, do you know a fellow called Mahony? Same line of business as yours?"

"Yes," said Shackleton abruptly, as if the mention of the name woke disagreeable recollections. "I see him from time to time. Why?"

They were standing in the window of the smoking-room of the St. James's club to which Shackleton had introduced his new friend. It was a gesture of appreciation for the way in which Gaudeans had interested his "old guv'nor" in Shackleton's "Mexican" loan. A carriage passed down the broad street outside towards the darkened Tudor brickwork of St. James's Palace with its famous clock. It was a bright yellow carriage picked out with glossy black, and its trimmings were polished brass. The dappled bays which pulled it were sleek as butter, every white hair so clean that it might have been laundered.

"Why?" said Shackleton again.

Gaudeans gazed thoughtfully at the fringe of trees which bordered the park beyond the palace towers.

"My old guv'nor's got one almost the spit of that." He nodded after the carriage. "Tall and fair, is he? Mahony?"

"Yes," said Shackleton. "Why?"

"In London just now?"

"Quite likely. Why?"

"Got anything against you? Rival for the fair lady, perhaps?"

"Look here," said Shackleton irritably, "what is all this?"

"Well"—Gaudeans paused and thought about it a little longer—"since we've been here, I think we've been followed. Not all the time, but quite a bit. Tallish cove with fairish hair. Similar to one pointed out to me in Dublin as being of your profession. A herald of sorts."

"Mahony's a herald. Look, this is absurd."

"Not out to catch you and Missy Tonia in a spot of amorous indiscretion? Bit of a bounder is he?"

"Not that sort of bounder."

Gaudeans grew interested.

"Oh? What sort of a bounder, then?"

"As far as I know," said Shackleton finally, "he's not a bounder at all. He's probably in with the Fenians. That's all."

Gaudeans laughed in mock-outrage.

"I don't call having a bomb put down a fellow's trousers such a little thing!"

"The point is," Shackleton persisted, "Mahony—if it's him—has no interest in Tonia."

"No," said Gaudeans with a sudden access of decency. "Absolutely. Not to be mentioned again. Say no more. Mistaken, that's all."

It was the following evening just before dinner when Tonia looked out of the window of Shackleton's bedroom in the Park Lane house. In the last hour before dusk the sun-blinds were still pulled out at an angle above the graceful bow. Warm trees in full leaf, doves in the park elms, imparted a stillness to the late summer day.

"There's a man walking away through the gate of the park," she said with mild curiosity. "He was standing on the other pavement half an hour ago. I think he must have been there all the time. Almost as if he were watching the house."

"What sort of man?" Shackleton paused in fastening a collar-stud.

"A few inches taller than you. Light-brown hair, I think."

Shackleton dropped the stud and crossed quickly to the window. There was a tall man with fair hair walking away through the trees. It might even have been Mahony, though distance now made it hard to tell. The light summer coat was certainly of Mahony's kind.

"How long did you say?"

"About half an hour." She looked up at him innocently. "But why should he watch the house? He doesn't look like a burglar. I'm sure he was just waiting for someone who never arrived."

For the first time, Frank Shackleton felt himself stirred by profound unease. There was no obvious reason why Mahony or anyone else should be following yet. When the trouble over the Mexican loan began, there would be plenty of men wanting to follow him, but they would have to find him first. Still, it was all rather unnerving.

His nights were spent with Tonia, but on the following day Shackleton and Gaudeans were taking an afternoon rest in the deep leather chairs of the smoking-room.

"The fellow with the fair hair," said Shackleton suddenly. "The one you saw following us."

Gaudeans tapped the side of his nose confidentially.

"Not a word, old man. Say no more about it. Gaudy made ass of self. All right?"

"No," said Shackleton, "it's not all right. I think it needs to be checked."

Gaudeans shook his head vigorously.

"Waste of time, old boy. Look, you and I and Tonia, what were we doing? Walking about, seeing the sights, showing the young lady the town. Think about it. Other chap out to do the same thing. Of course, he'd very likely be going the same way, the same places. Not following at all."

"Possibly." Shackleton received the explanation without enthusiasm.

"No." Gaudeans shook his head. "Not possibly. Certainly. Certain sure. Come to think of it, fellow had little box camera. Just like chaps do when they're touring about."

The mention of the camera did little to reassure Shackleton. Gaudeans persisted.

"Old man! If it was this fellow Mahony and his Irish rebels, why the devil should he bother following you round Nelson's Column to take pictures of you with Tonia and me? It don't add up, Shacky! Not two figures of it don't add up!"

"If you see him again . . ."

Gaudeans nodded reassuringly to his new friend. He allowed Shackleton a moment's contemplation and then pulled from his pocket a pack of cards. He leant forward and tapped Shackleton lightly on the knee.

"Old man," he said quietly. "See this one?"

Shackleton looked at him blankly, not understanding. Gaudeans smiled and unwrapped the cards.

"*Écarté*," he said pleasantly. "Play for a shilling a cut?"

He shuffled the cards briskly, allowed Shackleton to do the same, and then held them out for his friend to cut. Shackleton cut the deck and held up the eight of hearts. Gaudeans cut a king. First Gaudeans held the cards, then Shackleton. Each man cut for himself; each man cut for the other. No matter how, it was almost always the case that Gaudeans cut a court card and Shackleton one of lower value.

"Rum things, cards," said Gaudeans genially. "That makes about two sovs you owe me. See the trick?"

Shackleton shook his head dumbly. Gaudeans held up a card for his inspection.

"Never heard of cards they call *arrondies*?"

Shackleton laughed.

"Bridge is my game. Baccarat went out with the cheating at Tranby Croft in 1891."

Gaudeans gave him an honest little smile.

"Look at the craftsmanship, though. See? They cut these cards so that the high ones are rounded at the ends and the low ones rounded at the sides. A fellow that knows the dodge can cut high for himself and low for the other chap every time. Even when he holds out the pack for the other man to cut, he knows that man is more likely to lift from the sides of the pack rather than the ends. It's natural."

"It might work once," said Shackleton sceptically.

Gaudeans grinned like a schoolboy.

"Once is enough," he said. "Chap gets introduced to a club. Other fellows get to playing cards. He joins in. Slips his own pack into the game. Wins handsomely. Promises them their revenge next night. Never seen again. Gone somewhere else to try the same dodge. Fellows make a thousand pounds a week that way."

Shackleton's scepticism gave way to a sudden alarm.

"You haven't played with those cards here!"

Gaudeans laughed reassuringly.

"Not here. Not anywhere. When you meet my old guv'nor at the races on Tuesday, you'll understand. Old Gaudeans was all for me being a varsity man when I was a boy. Taught me all the tricks that the fast men play on a fellow there. He gave me these cards as a lesson. Took them off a man who tried to cheat him once out at the Cape. Left him something to remember, too. My old guv'nor can spot a cheat easy as a fly on whitewash. Swat!" Gaudeans thumped a fist into the other palm. "A man that tries to fleece him never does it again. Not ever." And he smiled as if in affectionate reminiscence of his mythical parent.

During the remainder of the afternoon, Frank Shackleton seemed uncharacteristically apprehensive. From time to time he questioned Gaudeans obliquely on the manner and personality of his "old guv'nor," the interests and habits of Gaudeans senior. At every inquiry, Gaudeans replied with a jovial pride, seeming only too glad of an opportunity to flaunt the old man's oddities.

They turned into Park Lane as the fine summer afternoon began to thicken with dusty light among the trees.

"Mind you," said Gaudeans cheerily, "you'll get off lighter than most. I mayn't be all that the good old man is himself, but he generally reckons that if a fellow's square enough for me, he's all right. You won't be roasted nearly as fine as a chap he'd never heard of. If you'll take my ten thousand pounds, Shacky, I can promise now that he'll plunge much deeper. A hundred thousand or more. And then, when he knows whose brother you are, the great Ernest Shackleton, why then you might ask him for what you like. So cheer up, old fellow, you're good as home."

As if sharing in his friend's good fortune, Gaudy twirled his stick and began to whistle. The sky was blue and cloudless, the park elms billowed with the fresh green of June, the chestnut-fans flirted and their flower-candles swayed in a light breeze. In the warm golden air the girls in their narrow-waisted dresses of pink or pale blue, lilac or saffron, seemed part of nature's display. It was perfect weather for Ascot, Gaudeans thought, and in the same instant he realized that he had not been as happy as this for years.

22

"**I**t's the life, though, ain't it?" said Gaudeans cheerily. It was, after all. The excursion trains with their Cockney trippers and racing men, their card-sharps in the third class and club-men in the saloon coaches, were pulling into Ascot station from Waterloo every ten minutes. On the platforms of little country stations on the Windsor branch line, valets and ladies' maids stood among the piled luggage of the house-parties, waiting for the baggage-brakes which would fetch them and their impediments away to the estates of the titled and the famous.

From Windsor to the race-course there was not a public carriage to be had. Gaudeans in morning dress, Shackleton in the plumage and pride of his regimental uniform, got down from the excursion train at Ascot station. A cool wind scattered the clouds, promising a clear blue sky for the first day's racing. Over the trees of Windsor Great Park rose the familiar round tower of the castle. From its flag-staff flew the red and gold of the sovereign's standard.

Gaudeans turned gallantly to assist Tonia. Around her, the women wore their muslin, laces, nets, and soft silks. White and ivory dresses, subtle mauve, black millinery, fine net embroidered in bold raised patterns, long coats and hats trimmed with osprey feathers, flowers, or silk bows were the fashions of the day. As always, Tonia was distinctive. Gaudeans gazed with admiration still undimmed at the willow pattern of blue and white silk, the wide sash of Chinese blue girdling her waist and hips, tied in a bow at the back.

On the heath the usual Gypsy fair had set up camp. Men on stilts and girls in Oriental costume touted for custom at the canvas booths. Jugglers in plumed hats, organ-grinders, even a fire-eater, were already on view. The card-sharps were everywhere, their competitors varying the three-card trick with three thimbles and a pea.

"My old guv'nor's no end sorry," said Gaudeans wistfully, "missing all this. First time the Royal Enclosure ain't seen him for a good dozen years."

"Really?" said Shackleton politely. His distaste for the increasingly loud, slangy manner of his acquaintance was still concealed.

165

"Awfully browned off not to meet you, of course. Some other time, I expect."

"I hope so," said Shackleton lightly. "I should like that."

Gaudeans chuckled.

"Not that you'll lose by it! The old fellow's struck on your Mexican loan. Especially when he knew who your brother was. The deal's as good as done, Shacky. So long as you don't mean him to go in for more than a hundred thousand. He might jib at that. And there's a condition."

"What's that?" Shackleton covered his unease by a blankness of expression as he turned to Gaudeans walking beside him.

"You know, old man!" There was a quiet, humorous reproach in Gaudeans's tone. "If you want his money, you must take my widow's mite, too."

Shackleton laughed away the supposition that he would ever have done otherwise. They were close to the course now. On one side of the turf were the grandstands, the lawn of the Royal Enclosure immediately below the stand from which the King and his party would watch the racing. Admittance was by ticket only. Lord Churchill, on behalf of the King, was reputed to sort all applications for tickets into three baskets: "Certainly," "Perhaps," and "Certainly not." Shackleton, as Dublin Herald, went into the first basket by right of rank. Despite the current hostility towards Germany, the intervention of the embassy had assured a ticket for Tonia Schroeder of Dresden and her escort. In the end, it had all been much easier than Gaudeans had feared.

Already the Royal Enclosure itself was crowded, its perimeter guarded by uniformed officers of the Metropolitan Police and patrolled by a handful of detectives in plain clothes. Opposite, beyond the white rails on the far side of the course, a number of marquees had been erected in the equally exclusive area reserved for club tents. These were erected for the sumptuous lunches consumed by their members in the intervals of the racing. From the canvas peaks streamed the standards of the Guards Club, White's, the Cavalry Club, the Tiffin, the Badminton, and the Grosvenor.

Gaudeans smiled upon the scene with a satisfaction beyond anything which he had expected to feel. It was all working so well. The sunlight and the sense of affluence, the immaculate turf and the beauty of the clothes, buoyed him up. He could almost have liked a sly, shallow brute like Shackleton.

Beyond the tents the bright summer sky gleamed upon the fine old coaches of the Four-in-Hand Club, the Coaching Club, and the antique snobbery of the racing set. Farther still the humbler cabs and carriages, even omnibuses and traps, were drawn up with hardly a space between them where the mass of racegoers crowded towards the rails or watched from the height of their vehicles.

"My old guv'nor"—Gaudeans edged confidentially towards Shackleton—"my old guv'nor says, if he lives till next June, he's something-well coming to the first day of Ascot whatever his man in Harley Street may say. And if the old misery of a sawbones don't like, he may be jolly well damned. That's what my old guv'nor says."

Shackleton kept himself between Tonia and Gaudeans as he spoke.

"Suppose," he said softly, "suppose all shouldn't go well with the old party. I mean it shall, of course, but suppose it don't. Must you step in and run all that business?"

Gaudeans's heart beat faster. Fortune had been kinder to him than he ever deserved. He laughed at the absurdity of Shackleton's supposition.

"Me? Not likely, old man! Takes more brains than I've got to keep ahead of the market the way Josh Gaudeans did these last fifty years. Not me! Put a man in to run the business, what else can a chap do?"

He could almost hear Shackleton's gasp of anticipation at the prospect.

There was a sudden silence over the great crowd which stretched to either side. As if by some unspoken command the course was cleared. The spectators pressed to the rails, all eyes on a moving bit of colour which had come into sight across Windsor Great Park from the gates at the end of the New Mile. King Edward in procession was driving from the castle to open the first day of Royal Ascot.

Despite himself, Gaudeans could feel a patriotic tightening of the throat as the royal cavalcade swept up the course. At its head rode the royal huntsman and whippers-in, Lord Churchill as the King's representative, splendidly mounted with silver leashes as his mark of office. Next came the scarlet-coated outriders and finally five landaus with cane-faced sides, drawn by four horses with postillions. The sight of the King, with Queen Alexandra and his guests, was announced by a long roll of cheering which continued until the procession had turned in past the enclosure and the party disappeared into the Royal Stand.

"Hurrah!" said Gaudeans, acting a comic but lovable enthusiasm. "Hurrah and God bless 'em!"

One or two of the well-dressed men and women nearby looked round at the noisy little man. But it was so evident that his expression was genuine, naïve but sincere, that they forgave him. A mistake to allow such an ill-controlled stranger into their enclosure, but they would tolerate him for this year. Lord Churchill had an eye for such eccentricities. The little man would not appear in their company again.

Gaudeans nudged Shackleton.

"What I fancy, old man, is Slieve Gallion for the St. James's Palace Stakes."

Shackleton had been talking to Tonia, and he was clearly put out by Gaudeans's interruption.

"If you fancy horse-flesh," he said coolly, "there's the Prince of Wales Stakes first. Try your hand at that and see how you do before you plunge deep."

Gaudeans chuckled amiably, showing his indulgence of the young man and the girl in their self-absorbed romantic passion.

"See you presently," he said and sauntered away. Neither of them took any notice of him.

It was really far more like a garden-party than a race-meeting, he thought. Elegance and casual conversation surrounded him. A vast bed of rhododendrons glowed with deep colour in the centre of the enclosure lawn. There were rows of wooden seats, but they were so widely separated that there was ample room for groups of men and women to stand between them gossiping. He turned to observe the Royal Stand itself, the stairway with its wrought-iron balustrade curving upwards, guarded at top and bottom by two stalwart men in plain suits. The balcony of the stand would have done credit to a flower-show. Pink and mauve carnations were massed together among lilies and geraniums, golden privet and bay-trees in tubs. The sun came out more strongly and warmed the back of his frock-coat. All the people were so beautiful and gentle. The sight of their opulence filled him again with a sense of well-being, and he felt a genuine gratitude to them for allowing him to be there. It really was a shame what he had to do to them all.

Now that the sun was at its height, he was more than comfortably warm. It had become rather close in the packed assembly of men and women. A disagreeable band of perspiration had begun to collect along the top of his forehead, just where his silk hat rested. It was a very special silk hat, Gaudy had seen to that. Indeed, for all its routine appearance it was probably the most remarkable topper that any man had sported in the whole two centuries of Ascot. Still, for the moment he could do without it. He took it off and held it under his arm. No other gentleman in the Royal Enclosure was bareheaded. No one but Gaudeans was bare-headed. Even the plainclothes policemen wore their bowler hats. One or two of the others looked at him, disapproving, even contemptuous. Perhaps they were not so nice after all. That made his task all the easier.

He walked up to the curve of the iron balustrade, where the stairs went up from the lawn to the Royal Grandstand itself. To one side of the two policemen who stood at the foot of the graceful steps was a table covered with green baize. The reason for its closeness to the plain-clothes officers was evident at once. Three miniature but exquisite examples of the goldsmith's art stood there on display for the admiration of the approved guests in the Royal Enclosure. On the left-hand side of the table was a fine double-handled cup with a flat cover. It might have been the work of a seventeenth-century Florentine goldsmith with its gleaming flanks and intricate festoons of laurel. Yet, as the card proclaimed, it was the product of Messrs. Garrard of the Haymarket. Engraved at its base in plain letters was a simple inscription: THE GOLD VASE, THE GIFT OF HIS MAJESTY, ASCOT 1907.

Gaudeans smiled with pleasure and pride. He was in such good spirits that he wanted to speak to those who stood near him, to draw their attention to the solid elegance of the piece. But that would have been excessive.

The right hand of the table was occupied by a taller yet more graceful cup, heavily ornamented with reliefs of Orpheus charming the animals with his music. Its cover was surmounted by the royal coat of arms ingeniously supported. Messrs. Garrard claimed the credit for this, too, the Royal Hunt Cup.

But Gaudeans's full admiration could go only to the simpler and most majestic design of all. Behind and above the other trophies on the table was an almost plain Grecian vase of gold with double handles. He recognized it, of course, its precise size and shape having occupied him in his researches during the past few months.

This time, the engraving said only ASCOT 1907. There was no need for more. The entire racing world would recognize at a glance the most coveted prize of all, the Ascot Gold Cup, trophy of the season and the turf.

He shook his head in final admiration. What other country in the world would have displayed these treasures so openly? Where on the face of the earth was there such another society as that of the Royal Enclosure? Everywhere about him there was nobility, breeding, and honour. To Gaudeans such things were far more remarkable than any mere gold filigree.

From his pocket he took a small paper-covered coil. A Captain Wunder special, he thought. It was harmless enough. Unnoticed by anyone he lit a cigarette and waited for the drum-beat of hooves which announced that the runners in the Prince of Wales Stakes were approaching the winning-post. All eyes were on the course, but that was not good enough. The two plain-clothes men seemed shifty in their allegiance. Self-interest drew their attention to the horses on which their money rode, but duty compelled sudden sidelong glances.

Not good enough. Gaudeans took the paper-covered coil, touched it with his cigarette, and dropped it unobtrusively at his feet. He walked back and approached the two policemen.

"What price the favourite?" he said genially. They stared back at him, silent and suspicious, from their dark eyes and well-filled faces. Just then, there was a report like a pistol-shot from somewhere to the front of them, then another. Women screamed and scattered, the heads of the two plain-clothes men went forward like game-cocks', though their feet remained planted firmly in the place of duty.

"My hat!" said Gaudeans mildly. No one bothered to glance at him. He drew back timidly, standing behind the table now, his eyes following those of every other person near him, as a third explosion rang like a whip-crack. He lowered the silk topper, clasping it against him as if in fear. Then, straightening up with courage renewed, he walked away.

It was a full minute before either of the plain-clothes officers realized that the exhibition table now contained only the King's Vase and the Royal Hunt Cup.

"Old man," said Gaudeans at Shackleton's side, "how's this for first place?"

He held out a handful of sovereigns.

"Not bad," said Shackleton politely, "not bad at all."

"One other thing, old man," said Gaudeans confidentially. "Would your friend Mahony be here? Ticket for the enclosure and so forth?"

Shackleton's dark face looked gratifyingly apprehensive.

"If he wanted to be. Why?"

"Chap by the Royal Stand. Tallish cove with fair hair. Might be mistaken but don't think so. Bet bottom dollar, in fact. Same fellow that was walking near us in town."

There was a rising commotion in the direction which Gaudeans had indicated.

"What's that?" said Tonia suddenly.

Gaudeans laughed.

"Some ass let off a fire-cracker for a joke. That's what it sounded like."

This last remark seemed thoroughly to unsettle Shackleton.

"Look," he said reasonably, "I know it's early but I really do think I fancy a bite of lunch. If it's all the same to you two, I don't want to see Mahony and I don't want him to see me."

"Come on, old fellow!" said Gaudeans reproachfully. "What can he do?"

Shackleton showed signs of growing irritation.

"I don't know what he can do. Whatever it is, I'd prefer to be somewhere else when he does it. And I'm damned if I'll be followed everywhere by him. What's his game?"

The sunlight caught the clustering curls under the broad brim of Tonia's hat.

"Whatever it is," she said gently, "let him play it." The hand which rested on Shackleton's arm gave the arm a gentle squeeze.

"All right, then," said Gaudeans obligingly, "lunch it is!"

They walked together to the restaurant at the back of the stands. Gaudeans excused himself for twenty minutes and came back wearing his top-hat at a jaunty angle. He noticed that Shackleton ordered with indifference and ate without enthusiasm. It would be a pity to let the thing go too far, but Mahony's presence seemed to be satisfactorily established now.

"Look," said Gaudeans with the open decency of one who longs to be helpful. "If you've had enough of the enclosure, what say we cut it for an hour or two and go round the fair?"

171

Shackleton nodded with the same dumb indifference and left Gaudeans alone with Tonia. She drew off a glove and opened the small embroidered reticule.

"If you do that," said Gaudeans amiably, "everyone'll know you're not a lady. Then we're for it."

She looked up at him, the green eyes sparkling with incomprehension and annoyance.

"Do what?"

"Pull off a glove without unbuttoning it. A lady never does that in England. Always unbutton it first."

"How very foolish," she said, her hostility softening at once into coquetry. "By the way, there is a story going round the crowds here that the Gold Cup is missing. Already."

Gaudeans laughed at her.

"Missing? Don't you believe it, old girl! It ain't missing at all. I've got it safe as anyone could ask for."

"Truly?"

"Only thing is, missy," he said very quietly, "I never believed a chap could do it so easy. Beats me why they don't pinch it every year."

By the time they reached Waterloo again, Shackleton seemed still more depressed.

"What you need," Gaudeans remarked several times on the journey, "is taking out of yourself. What you need, in fact, is an evening with the old Roman."

It was this suggestion which brought the three of them, just after nine o'clock, to Romano's in the Strand. From the windows of the hansom cab, Gaudeans noticed the first placards of the evening papers to carry the news: ASCOT GOLD CUP STOLEN. By comparison, he thought, the Prince of Wales Stakes or the win of Slieve Gallion in the St. James's Palace Stakes would be nowhere in it. On the whole he was relieved that Shackleton, in his mood of depression, seemed not to notice the bills. There was, of course, always the ubiquitous Mahony to carry the blame. But, then, a fellow ought not to work Mahony too hard. Not just yet, anyway.

The Café Vaudeville, as Romano had christened the establishment, was packed every evening by racing men, theatrical folk, coaching men, young brokers from the Stock Exchange, and every type of man-about-town. On either side of the long central window was a door, one leading to the ground-floor bar, the other to the restaurant above. As they approached, the bar seemed to be in the possession of Guardsmen back from their day's racing. Gaudeans had inspected the place in Tonia's company several nights before. He recognized several of the red-faced, overfed, roaring young officers and the names which they gave one another. "Billie," "Fitzditto," "The Windsor Warrior," and "Bonetwister" were well to the fore. The sight of them swept away any misgivings which Gaudeans would have felt about his allegiance to Lindemann.

He ushered Tonia and Shackleton through the other door, where a long fish-tank was displayed to the street. The surface of the water was covered by scraps of burnt almond, lemon-rind, and cigar-ash, on which the coaching men and the bloods tried to feed the fish. As they climbed the stairs, one clean-shirted bohemian was trying to force another into the tank itself.

On all sides the Vaudeville seemed to heave and throb with noise, quite sufficient for Gaudeans to talk to Shackleton in the pretence that Tonia would not overhear.

"What you are, old man," he said brightly, "is the luckiest dog that ever barked."

"Oh?" said Shackleton, still subdued.

"What I mean, Shacky, is the call of true love. Dash it, old fellow, it's you that Cousin Tonia's taken a shine to. If Mahony don't like it, tell him to go to the devil!"

Shackleton's face brightened at once.

"Gaudy!" he said, brotherhood breaking out as never before. "You never mean that's why the bounder might be watching his chance?"

"Don't I?" said Gaudeans happily. "Don't I just! Nothing plainer!"

"You really do think that?"

They were standing at one end of the long, narrow restaurant, waiting to be shown to a table.

"Word to the wise, old man," said Gaudeans, his lips close to Shackleton's ear. "Young Mahony's game to chuck his hat for Tonia. She won't have him. Good as said so to his face, I hear. And what I do know is this. If it's a choice between a man of sense and business like you, and a young rascal like Mahony, it'll be you every time. And I ain't just saying that because I want it to happen. It's the truth, old fellow. It's Uncle Schroeder's way."

From that moment it seemed that Shackleton's depression had

lifted. As they ate and drank, chuckled or roared with laughter according to their mood, hints became promises, and possibilities grew certain. All to the benefit of Shackleton. There was the certainty of Gaudeans's investment in the Mexican loan. The near-certainty of a much bigger investment by Gaudeans senior. And when the ailing "old guv'nor" had run his course, there was a man to be "put in" by his son. Added to all this, there was Tonia and the Schroeder fortune in chemicals.

Among the hock-and-seltzer, the French and Italian wines, the oysters and saddle of lamb, Shackleton grew confident and talked loud. He was well out of his gloom now and felt every right to think of himself as a devil of a fellow. Tonia was his, a couple of fortunes were his. He stared comfortably around him at the sporting aristocracy with its Gaiety girls, and knew that he was, in their own language, one of the "flyest flats in the village."

They left Romano's, Shackleton noticing that Gaudy seemed as flushed and rowdy as any of those who had been there on their arrival. In no time at all they were in Leicester Square, the gas-lights flaring bright as day before the front of the Empire.

"Tell you, Shacky," blurted Gaudeans. "If there's one hall in London where a fellow can get the best whisky, real old brandy, and a Rothschild cigar, this is it!"

Tonia, completely self-possessed, neither approving nor otherwise, went in with them. Shackleton liked that, the coolness of her behaviour. Inside the auditorium the din and the smoke from the cigars was stupefying. In the saloon at the back of the stalls and on the promenade of the music-hall there were clerks in top-hats like stage-door swells and red-coated soldiers with their girls hanging about their necks.

Two pretty sisters with their hair in comic curls held the stage, challenging all the men in the audience to a duel of words by the impudence of their song.

> *You men are deceivers and awfully sly!*
> *Oh, you are!*

And it seemed that Shackleton led the entire assembly in their roar of defiance.

> *Oh, no, we're not!*

The pretty sisters shrieked back at them:

Oh, yes, you are!
You come home with the milk,
Should your poor wife ask why,
"Pressing business, my pet," you serenely reply,
When you've really been out on the tiddle-y-hi!
Yes, you have!

The reply was enough to lift the roof and scatter its fragments across the square.

Oh, no, we've not!

The girls paused.

Oh, yes, you have!

Gaudeans watched Shackleton from the corner of his eye. The young man was rather slumped in his seat. Indeed, he seemed almost to be dozing. Ten minutes later he roused himself for just long enough to take a glimpse at Cissie Cinders and her lament.

Oh, my missus wouldn't let me wear no feathers in my hat,
So my sojer's gone and given me the chuck!

"Old man," said Gaudeans gently to his friend, "I rather think we'd better see you home. Put you in a cab. Eh?"

Shackleton mumbled something. He appeared to be in agreement, all the same. With an effort he pushed himself up on his feet, then sat down heavily again.

"That's all right, old fellow," said Gaudeans sympathetically, "happens to the best of us at times."

With Gaudeans on one side and the lighter, less certain support of Tonia on the other, Shackleton was helped out through the stalls into the cool darkness of Leicester Square.

"Look," said Gaudeans gently into his companion's ear. "Only one thing for it, Shacky. I must see Tonia safe home. Put you in a hansom, give the cabbie the address and the fare, let him see you to Park Lane. All right?"

Shackleton tried to form a protest at the way in which they were abandoning him, but now the words presented tortuous difficulties to his mind and tongue alike.

He need not have worried. The cab bore him away as in a waking dream. Considerate hands carried him and undressed him, no doubt the work of his manservants. He heard strange voices at one moment, and, at another, he thought they were taking him back to Ascot. Really he did not care. Before slipping finally into the soft refuge of unconsciousness, his mind was disturbed only by one thought. Without meaning to, he had made an exhibition of himself in front of Tonia. That might prove to have been the most costly error of all.

He need not have worried. Tonia, at that moment, was preoccupied by other matters. More precisely, she was crossing Waterloo Place with a package which might almost have fitted into a top-hat. It was addressed to the care of Colonel Lindemann, and her immediate destination was the German Embassy, near the Duke of York's Steps.

23

Gaudeans was solemn for the first time. Solemn and confidential. "Old man," he said softly, "this is about as bad as it could be." He and Shackleton sat on opposite sides of the Dublin Herald's desk in the Bedford Tower. It was the first time that Gaudy had been inside the building, though Shackleton had once taken Tonia there to show her the splendours of the Office of Arms library. Beyond the white-painted glazing-bars of the Georgian window the rehearsal in the upper yard of the castle was proceeding vigorously.

"Company! Royal salute! Pre-sent *arms!*"

There was a double *thwack* of palms slapping smartly upon rifle-butts.

"Should-er *arms!* As you were!"

In his misery Shackleton seemed to hear none of it. He looked at the three photographs which Gaudeans had laid on the desk, like a fan of cards.

The first showed Shackleton, Gaudeans, and Tonia crossing St. James's Street in London.

The second was a view, taken by an unnoticed intruder, of Tonia and Shackleton in the Park Lane bedroom.

The third was the worst of all. Shackleton sprawled stark naked in the corner of a room he could not identify. In his arms he clasped an elegantly simple golden vase. The light in that room had been good enough for the inscription upon the vase to appear quite distinctly: ASCOT 1907.

"Posted to me from London the day before yesterday," said Gaudeans simply.

Shackleton opened his desk. From the drawer he took out three identical prints and laid them out on the blotter.

"Posted to me from Dublin," he said wearily, "yesterday evening."

The two men looked at each other. Outside in the yard the voice of the N.C.O. continued to yap with belligerent hysteria.

"Pre-sent arms! Sl-ope arms! Pre-sent arms! Will you wake yourselves up!"

"Who?" asked Gaudeans, his shrewd face now downcast with dismay.

"Gaudy," said Shackleton softly, "I was wrong to doubt you, ever. That brute Mahony was in London all the time. Vicars says so. He was there the night before last, and here last night to be in time for the King's arrival. He posted them, I'm sure of it. What's more, he probably took them."

Gaudeans almost laughed at the preposterousness of it all.

"Mahony? Steal the Ascot Gold Cup? What the devil for?" And then he appeared to see the point. "By Jove, Shacky! It's not the cup he wants! It's you and me!"

Shackleton shook his head.

"No, just me. There was a slip of paper with these: 'Await instructions.'"

Outside, the military hysteria grew more shrill. It was barely another four summer days before the royal salute would be given in earnest. Shackleton went across and closed the window. He sat down again.

"Look," said Gaudeans thoughtfully. "I see the point of the photographs. This one ensures that old man Schroeder never lets you near Tonia again, if he ever sees it. I'm game to go in with you, of course, but I can't say as much for my old guv'nor if he should be sent copies of these. The worst of it is, Shacky, this picture of you with the Gold Cup. That's prison, and no two ways about it. Even though Mahony must have been the bounder who took it."

Shackleton nodded and sighed.

"That's about the extent of the damage."

Gaudeans appeared to think about this.

"See," he said reasonably, "see what these instructions are. If it's nothing much, do what they ask. Give us time to plan."

Shackleton leant forward across the table and looked at him intently.

"You still don't understand, Gaudy, do you."

The voice outside the window yapped its twentieth repetition.

"Roy-al sal-ute! Pre-sent . . ."

"My God," said Gaudeans softly, "the King! Is that what you think?"

"I've thought of nothing else since the damned things arrived!"

"Instructions?" Gaudeans thought again. "By Jove, old man, you're right! Chap takes your place as Dublin Herald, papers and all the rest. Goes to Kingstown, asks to be taken out to the *Victoria and Albert*. Urgent message from the Viceroy, danger to the King's life. Gets close enough to King Edward to put a bullet in him or leave a bomb under him! Blow the royal yacht to pieces! You can't, Shacky!"

"Do you think I haven't realized that?" In his misery, Shackleton began to snap at his friend.

"For the King's sake!" pleaded Gaudeans.

"Damn the King!" shouted Shackleton. "It's for my sake! Once the thing was done they wouldn't let me go free! A tenner to a tanner I should be found in the Liffey with my throat cut wide enough to sing through!"

Gaudeans sat silently for a moment, out of respect for his companion's predicament.

"Then you tell them to go to the devil," he said simply. "You lose your chance of a fortune, you lose Tonia, and you go to prison sure as Monday follows Sunday."

"No."

Gaudeans became urgent.

"Go to Mahony, then. Reason with him. He can't be as bad as that."

Shackleton shook his head.

"Tried it," he said thickly. "Denies everything. Smooth as pig-grease! Even if he wanted to, the others wouldn't let him do it. That's how a Fenian works. It's my head or his, and he knows it."

"You'll have to split on Mahony to the police, or else do as he says, old man," said Gaudeans coaxingly. "Stands to reason. See?"

Shackleton clenched his teeth and then appeared to relax.

"No, I won't, Gaudy. There's another way, and be damned to them. I shan't go to prison, old fellow. And I shan't have my throat cut by the hands of a Fenian. If it comes to the point, I've hands of my own. And that's all about that."

Gaudeans was now thoroughly and genuinely alarmed. For the first time since he had entered the sunlit room there appeared to be a real chance that his entire scheme would fail. He was more gentle with the Dublin Herald than ever.

"Tell me this, Shacky. Am I your friend or ain't I?"

Shackleton sighed again.

"You are, Gaudy. Best friend a fellow could ask for, even in a few weeks. Better than some fellows deserve."

"Right"—Gaudeans began to warm to his proposal—"then listen to this. What's the odds in us sitting here and blubbering as if Mahony was all the world? He ain't, old man. Now, you said there was another way. And so there is. But not your way."

Shackleton gave a tired little laugh.

"I mean it," Gaudeans insisted. "What you've never thought of is that we might get those photographs—the glass-plate negatives—and give Mahony the thrashing of a lifetime for his trouble."

"We might," said Shackleton wearily, "but I'll be damned if I see how."

Gaudeans coaxed a little more, like a nurse-maid with a child.

"I don't say we *can*, but I think we might. Mahony posted one lot of pictures in London just before he left, the second lot here just after he got back. And somewhere he's keeping the negatives. Only two likely places in Dublin. At his house or here."

"Here?" Shackleton sat more upright in his chair, as if this possibility had really not occurred to him.

"Of course," said Gaudeans, surprised at his friend. "You think of it, old man. Where's the safest place in Dublin? Not his house, which you might burgle to get the negatives. But here, locked in his desk, in his office. With a regiment all about to see that no one interferes. Choice, ain't it?"

"Absurd, more like."

"Exactly." Gaudeans brought a clenched fist down lightly on the blotter. "That's what we're supposed to think. Trouble is, Shacky, you and I have been sitting on our brains this last half-hour instead of using them. Now, when Mahony came back from London last night, he must have gone to his house in Dublin. True?"

"Yes," said Shackleton doubtfully.

"And he came here this morning? And then went away just now, probably to the house again?"

"I suppose so."

"Right," said Gaudeans enthusiastically. "Now, he'd keep those negatives with him. Too precious to leave in London. They might be at his house or they might be here. It's an odds-on chance, old fellow."

Shackleton had just begun to take an interest in the theory, like an invalid with his first solid food.

"What do you suggest?"

"Any chance of a look-see in his office?"

"You can't open the desk, it's locked."

Gaudeans raised a protesting hand.

"Just a look."

Shackleton led the way across the upper landing, tapped on the opposite door, and opened it. The little office with its book-shelves and desk, its swivel-chair and Turkey carpet, was unoccupied.

"Just try the drawers," said Gaudeans pleasantly. "You never know."

Shackleton pulled at the handles, one by one. The drawers rattled lightly and refused to budge.

"Book-shelves locked?" Gaudeans inquired.

Shackleton walked across to the glass-fronted shelves and tried them. They held fast. He turned back again.

"Waste-paper basket?" said Gaudeans. "Anything there?"

It was then that Shackleton's eyes opened wider. He picked up a small cardboard box from the basket, the yellow label of a photographic company upon it.

"Old man!" said Gaudeans proudly. "I do believe I'm right. If Mahony brought that box with him today, it must have been because it had negatives in it. And if he threw it away, that must have been because he had no further use for it. In other words, he left them in his desk. Didn't I tell you so?"

He at once began examining the structure of the desk, the way the back and the sides had been fitted, the likely extent of the drawers.

"With enough time," he said quietly, "a chap could have the back off this. He could reach the screws at the back of the drawer-locks and undo 'em, too. There'd be a bit of damage that Mahony would find when he came to open it again. But he'd be the last to squeal about it."

Shackleton was looking in exasperation at the desk.

"Ten minutes," he said. "Ten minutes from now the messenger Stivey comes round to see that all the rooms are empty and all the staff outside before he locks up and leaves."

Gaudeans sat down in apparent despair. For one moment he thought Shackleton had turned quickly enough to see him drop the box into the waste-paper basket, and the shock had taken his breath.

"No good," he gasped. "Not in ten minutes. And by tomorrow it's too late."

They looked at one another hopelessly. All Shackleton's temporary optimism seemed drained from him.

"And that's all about that," he said miserably.

Gaudeans appeared to think about the problem with great care. Presently he looked up.

"Would you call me a friend, Shacky? A friend that a fellow might trust?"

"Better than that," said Shackleton quietly. "A friend that any man might trust."

Gaudeans stood up.

"Then it ain't all over. Not even half over, if you'll let me do something for you."

"Meaning?"

"Meaning," said Gaudeans, "let me be the one to have the back off this bounder's desk and fish out the glass-plates. The prints, too, if they're there, as they're likely to be."

Shackleton sighed.

"Not in ten minutes—five minutes more like. It can't be done."

"Suppose a fellow had all night?"

Gaudeans was relieved to see that when Shackleton looked at him there was no trace of suspicion at all, merely the concern of one friend for another.

"You can't. I wouldn't ask it of you. In any case you'd be found here."

"Who's going to find me?"

"Stivey in five or ten minutes' time."

"Look," said Gaudeans. He stood behind Mahony's desk, crouched down, and squeezed himself into the knee-hole cavity. Pulling himself out, he straightened up again. "That's not the best, but it'll do if I can't find something smarter."

Shackleton remained unconvinced.

"The guard commander and the duty superintendent come round later on."

"When?"

"About half-past ten or eleven o'clock. They check every door, every room."

Gaudeans nodded.

"If they open the door of this one and look inside, that's the most they're likely to do."

He could see that Shackleton was almost convinced of the possibility. And once Shacky knew it *could* be done, he would have no scruples as to the propriety of it. There was too much at stake for him. But then came the true difficulty.

"Tomorrow morning," he said. "Six or seven o'clock. There's a cleaning-woman, Farrell, who comes in. There's nowhere in this room that she wouldn't look."

That seemed to settle the matter as far as Shackleton was concerned. Gaudeans had prepared his answer long before, but he waited a few moments to give the impression of further intense thought.

"Old man," he said, a gentle smile brightening the neatly-moustached little face. "I've got it in one. The cupola up there, the clock-tower. Any rooms up there?"

Shackleton shook his head.

"Well, then," said Gaudeans cheerily, "that's it. Whoever comes in, I go up there and wait. The cleaning-woman don't go up there to clean. The guard ain't likely to go up, and there's an end of it."

"Suppose they do?"

"Then, if I hear them coming, I open the window, step out on to the flat roof, and close it after me. Lie behind the parapet and wait till they've done. Step back in again."

"And if they close the window on you?"

"Then you must open it for me, Shacky. Come bright and early in the morning to work."

Shackleton thought about this, but he was very nearly convinced. Gaudeans gave him no leisure for doubt.

"What I want you to do, Shacky, is this. Leave me the key to your room. If the photos are in Mahony's desk, I'll take them to your room and lock them in. After the cleaning-woman's gone in the morning, I'll go there and lock myself in until you get here. That's unless there's an easy way out before. There might be, but I shan't take risks. Then tomorrow morning you and I can walk out of here with the pictures, like two old chums, and Mahony can go and whistle for his blackmail."

"He'll find his desk broken into."

Gaudeans laughed.

"Well, old fellow, he can't very well complain that his blackmail pictures have been stolen, can he? What's more, if he raises a rumpus and his pals in the Fenians should hear, they won't half be in a wax with him. I'd say he's the one who's likely to be found in the Liffey with his throat slit. No, Shacky, you and I shan't hear another word out of the little squeak."

"There's no call for you to take a risk like this, Gaudy."

Gaudeans's face broadened in an expression of facetious amazement.

"Ain't there just? Look at those penny snapshots, old man, and you'll find my phiz on one of 'em. I dare say I mayn't be doing worse than walk the London streets in it. But if there's a real old set-to about it, my old guv'nor's going to be told that I'm in with the fellows that stole the Ascot Gold Cup. You know what Ascot means to him. I'd be lucky if I was even cut off with the proverbial shilling!"

At last Shackleton saw the sense of it and the self-interest behind Gaudeans's offer. If Gaudy's own neck was in question, it was the best guarantee of his good faith.

"And if they find you?"

"Easy story about being locked in accidentally. Don't worry, I shan't be found. Any schoolboy could run rings round them in here."

Shackleton gave him the key, cut for his own door and Mahony's.

"Watch out for Stivey," he said softly. "He'll go the rounds at any minute."

Gaudeans nodded and began to speak rapidly.

"Old man, this is what you must do. If Mahony should sing the whole song ditto ripetto, you must show that you couldn't have been anywhere near his precious desk at the time. Right? Now, let them see you leave here. Go to the Kildare Street Club and make yourself conspicuous from now until midnight. Ask 'em for a room there and sleep, so that the night-porter can swear you never left the building. Anything to prove the point. But remember this. Whatever happens, however far things go wrong, you can't very well be much worse off than you are now. Savvy?"

Shackleton nodded. He seemed genuinely moved by the danger which Gaudeans proposed to incur on his behalf.

"I don't know that I can say—"

"You haven't time to say anything," said Gaudeans humorously. "You leave me the key that unlocks the rooms here, yours and Mahony's. I'll lock myself in. Then go and meet Stivey or whatever his name is and tell him it's all locked up. See if you can't stop him opening up this room again. It ain't likely he'll notice me even if he comes in, but if you can head him off, there's one less risk for us."

Shackleton looked at him, thunderstruck.

184

"Tools," he said, "equipment! You've got nothing to use on the desk."

Gaudeans smiled. He took a clasp-knife from his pocket.

"I'll get far enough with this. Now go and stop Stivey. If I can slip out in the morning, I will. If not, I'll be waiting in your room. Either way, so long as those pictures are in here now—which they must be—they'll be on your desk tomorrow. And so much for Mahony."

He was impatient now to be rid of Shackleton and do what must be done. The Dublin Herald gave him a final glance and went out into the corridor, pulling to the door behind him. Gaudeans turned the key in the lock with a feeling of the most stupendous relief. He truly could not have endured much more of Frank Shackleton's company. Now he was on his own, as he always preferred to be. Several times in the past hour he had feared that the blackmail story would fail him and that he would have to find some other way into the Bedford Tower. He had made provision for alternative plans, several of them. But this was far and away the neatest. It would have offended his sense of professional pride if he had started with anything but the best.

He stood quietly by the desk in Mahony's room, prepared to duck down and conceal himself if that should be necessary. The late-afternoon sunlight fell warm and drowsy in the pattern of the Georgian glazing-bars. Stivey was late. Either that or possibly Shackleton had gone to meet him on the stairs. Then he heard their voices, Shackleton's fluting and self-assured, Stivey's gruffer but obsequious.

Gaudeans listened. It seemed that Stivey was not to be put off even by the Dublin Herald's assurances. If there were any mistakes, it was Stivey in person who would be held to account. The footsteps approached. Gaudeans ducked down and prepared to crawl into the knee-hole cavity of the desk, which faced the window and was concealed from the doorway. A key rattled in the lock of the door, and he held his breath. Why did the messenger have to come in? The windows, of course! But they were locked already. Stivey came forward a few paces, close enough to see that the fastenings were across. Then, to Gaudeans's relief, the feet turned and headed back towards the door. He heard the catch close and the key turned in the lock again.

The first danger was past. He was where he was supposed to be at the time he was supposed to be there. Tonia's instructions were clear. Now there was nothing to be done until he was sure that the building was empty and that he could move about in comparative safety.

Shackleton's voice drifted up from the sunlit castle yard outside, the Dublin Herald wishing good afternoon to someone near the gate. The sentries, perhaps, or the guard commander. That left Stivey.

He heard footsteps going down the curve of the polished staircase to the vestibule of the Bedford Tower. A door, presumably the main one, opened and closed with a good deal of rattling and locking. With great caution Gaudeans stepped across to the edge of the window and peered down. A humbly-dressed little man with several packages in his hands was crossing the castle yard. He knew at once that it was Stivey, ex–petty officer of the Royal Navy. That was all right.

Give it another half-hour, he thought. After all, it was not yet five o'clock and he was not short of time. Moreover, though the Bedford Tower was ostensibly the Office of Arms, a museum indeed, which closed at four o'clock, one could not be quite sure that Stivey or one of the others might not come back for some reason in the hour following its closure. That, at least, was how Gaudy saw it.

He went back to Mahony's desk and sat down. For Shackleton's benefit he took out his clasp-knife and made some ugly little scratches along the joins at the back of the desk. Not too many. After all, there was no advantage in drawing undue attention to it. Then he took from his pocket a small packet wrapped in a handkerchief, an oblong the size of a pocket-book. He folded back the handkerchief and looked at the three glass negatives which had given poor old Shacky such concern. The indoor cameo of the Dublin Herald embracing the Ascot Gold Cup with an expression of stupefied infatuation was particularly good, he thought. So it ought to be for the price it cost. The conveying of the drugged and drunken Shackleton from the Empire Music Hall to a room not far from the German Embassy had been easy enough. It was the technique of photographing in such light which had been so expensive and so triumphantly achieved.

Captain Gaudeans sat back, relaxed, and gazed wistfully at the sunlight reflected on the whitewashed ceiling. Even Colonel Lindemann, he thought, would have reason to be proud of him now.

24

Now it seemed good as done. Gaudeans sat in Mahony's chair and watched the late sun move off the carpet and begin to warm a diagonal slant of the polished walnut which fronted the bookcase. Unless the rules of logic and simple arithmetic could be bent, it was done already.

He got up and went to the window again, taking another sidelong view of the scene outside. The upper yard of the castle was deserted, though he knew the sentries must be standing in their places. Evening light mellowed on the portico and columns of the viceregal apartments, which faced the Bedford Tower across the open space. No ceremonial occasions would be held there tonight; Frank Shackleton had told him that. The interior of the great hall was being prepared for the royal drawing-room which King Edward would hold there in a few days' time. That was good, too, so many unfamiliar people coming and going. But not to the Bedford Tower. Not yet, anyhow.

Gaudeans judged it was safe now to begin the first of his tasks, a very simple one to delay the raising of any alarm for as long as possible. Gently he unlocked the door of Mahony's room and stepped out on to the small landing of the first floor. Shackleton's office was on the far side of the tower, the twin to Mahony's in the eighteenth-century symmetry of the building. It was good that a single key had been cut for both. Easier, of course, in the administration of Vicars's department. Gaudy could have picked both locks with his fingernail, as it happened, but he was reluctant for Shackleton to be told of his expertise. Better this way, he thought.

There was not a creak or sigh of boarding anywhere in the tower as he opened Shackleton's door. Taking from his pocket the little package of photographic plates, he lodged them on the desk. They were well wrapped. No one would disturb them. They were now in an envelope addressed to Shackleton, and, as a last precaution, Gaudeans took a book from the case and laid it on top of them.

"Old man," he said softly to the absent Dublin Herald, "ain't Gaudy a fellow for keeping his word to a pal?"

But now matters became more serious. Once the entire contents of the viceregal safe were missed, there would be the father and mother of a search. Every technique known to the police would be used. For two years, to Gaudy's certain knowledge, that had included finding prints of a man's palms and fingers. A careless burglar named Stratton had clubbed an old man to death in Deptford High Street at that time. Even more careless, he had left a smudged print of his palm in the blood. Three months later they had hanged him at Wandsworth.

Gaudy sighed and pulled on a pair of thin suede gloves. His prints in Shackleton's office and Mahony's room were unavoidable. He could hardly have worn gloves all the time that he was in Shackleton's company. What mattered was that when they came to examine the inside of the strong-room, the only prints would be those of the guard commander, the duty police superintendent, and Ulster King-of-Arms.

He frowned, as if in his anxiety to omit nothing from his preparations. Going back across the landing, he locked Mahony's door, having no further need of that room. Then he came back, and left the key to both rooms under the book on Shackleton's desk where he had concealed the photographic plates. He locked the door from the outside, using a simple steel probe the size of a pencil. They were old-fashioned locks, no more than an iron catch, and it was easily done. As the probe went in he felt a single strip of metal. It took him less than ten seconds to find the catch which held this "tumbler," release it, and hear the bolt of the lock snap shut.

In the twilight of the landing he stood and tried to imagine how this would look to Shackleton the next day. The key inside, the door locked. Obviously, Gaudy had left the key with the photographs and had hidden in the cupola above. The cleaning-woman had come in the early morning and had locked Shackleton's room on leaving, with the key inside. Captain Gaudeans, with his usual resource, had found his own way out of the building. Yes, that was certainly how it would seem to a man like Shackleton.

From the landing on which he stood, a smaller and less handsome set of stairs turned upwards towards the attic rooms and the windowed cupola of the clock-tower above them. What no one would understand, of course, was how an intruder could get out of a building whose only door and two of its walls were constantly guarded. To pass through that sentry patrol was an impossibility.

Gaudy knew it could be done, however, as other impossibilities were. What he had to see now was exactly how it must be done.

Softly, as though there might, after all, still be someone else in the Bedford Tower, he slipped up the narrower stairs towards the octagonal cupola with an arched window in each of its eight faces.

In the grey-blue evening the view was magnificent; that was the first thing which struck him. Away from the castle the little streets sloped down towards the dark silver of the river, the bridge and the grandeur of Sackville Street marked by the gas-lamps, the North Wall and the smoke-blackened stonework of the quays. He seemed high above everything in the castle itself, even looking down on the ugly Victorian chimney-pots which had been added to the main roof of the Bedford Tower itself.

It was, after all, this less-appealing view which concerned him. A man who forced his way out by the cupola windows would have a drop of no more than eight feet to the main roof. True, he would be trapped upon it, having only the walls of the square tower to escape by and sentries posted at the bottom of them. But to Gaudy there had been another clear possibility. It was the one link which would save him if it held and destroy him if it broke.

The main gate to Dublin Castle was surmounted by a monumental broken arch with a statue of Justice on a pedestal enclosed by the two halves of the arch. With a loop of rope a man could spin himself across to the nearer slope of the archway and then make his way to the far side.

After that came the second part of the route, which was the first half in reverse. Down from the arch on to a brick wall, about twelve feet high. Along that, and then up on to another, easier roof. That far roof belonged to a decayed building of Georgian red brick which housed some of the minor viceregal offices. The gap between the Bedford Tower and the building was the challenge. The gulf in which the arched gateway stood. Once across that, he would be safe enough. The castle might be walled and guarded everywhere. But Gaudy had seen its one weakness. There was a point at which the roof of the decayed building almost touched that of the Royal Exchange, which stood in all its pillared splendour on Cork Hill.

A fellow who could reach the Royal Exchange, and find himself the drain-pipe which Gaudy had in mind, would come to earth out of sight of the sentries, two streets away from Dublin Castle.

Other men would have worried most of all about the rusted

189

brackets which clamped pipes to the walls, the soft Georgian facing-stone of windows and ledges, loosened and cracked by two centuries of acid, sooty rain. Gaudeans was rather more preoccupied by noise. He could envisage the route and its dangers, but he could not imagine how much noise it would make, or what other noises there would be to disguise his progress across the castle rooftops. There was only one other sound of which he could be absolutely sure, and, for that reason, he had to time his departure with the greatest of care.

He drew back from his survey of the triumphal arch and roofs below him, satisfied that for the time being he had done all that was necessary. Now, while it was still light, he must make his reconnaissance of the ground floor of the Bedford Tower.

He went down, past the landing, and followed the graceful spiral of the main staircase. It would not have surprised him in the least for the main door to open and for someone to come in from the castle yard. It would not have surprised him, and yet, at the same time, he knew it was not going to happen. No one but the guard commander and his police companion would be allowed into the tower that night. It was odd that they should permit a cleaning-woman to come in alone during the early morning. Perhaps she was not alone after all. He should have questioned Shackleton more closely while he had the chance.

There were three internal doors on the ground floor. Two of these, a dozen feet apart, led to the same room, the library which ran along one half of the building. The other door looked the same, panelled and white-painted in the style of the mid-eighteenth century. The difference was in what lay behind it.

Gaudeans took his probe and a second piece of steel, no stouter than a knitting-needle but flatter. He struck a match from the box in his pocket and held the probe in its flame. When the match guttered and failed, he struck another. Presently two inches or so of the probe had been covered by a thick, rather greasy deposit of carbon. Sliding it into the keyhole, he turned it gently and withdrew it. Two distinct scratches on the carbon told him all he needed to know. A double tumbler this time. That was no great problem, though.

Using the flat piece of steel, he edged it into the lock of the door and found the first lever easily. It was not a complex mechanism, merely the first of two hook-shaped iron tongues which held the lock bolted until they were lifted off the spindle. He eased the first one upwards, held it on his flat needle, and slid forward to the second. A minute was quite long enough to open this outer door.

Inside was a small room which had all the appearance of the messenger's office. Set in the wall to one side of it, where another door might have been, Gaudeans saw for the first time the vault-door which sealed off the strong-room.

It was far more impressive than he had dared to hope, tight and sleek like the flank of a battleship. The two little keyholes and the neat bolt-lever were the only ornaments upon its thick hide of armoured steel. But what Gaudeans had been quite unprepared for was the degree of polish. The steel glimmered in the fading light of the summer evening, as if the messenger spent all his time labouring at it with a duster.

Gaudeans longed to step forward and stroke the satin finish of the metal, as if it were living skin. But of course that was out of the question. Just in front of it, the linoleum which covered the floor of Stivey's room showed a very faint rectangular ridge. And that meant, Gaudy thought, that a man would not need to probe the lock of the vault-door before setting off the alarm. There was a pressure-mat at the very point where he would have to stand.

Reluctantly he drew back and released the lock-bolt on the office door. Since the doors on the floor above all took the same key, he assumed it might be true of those at this level. It was. The two doors of the panelled library yielded to the same treatment as that of Stivey's office.

Occupying the eastern side of the Bedford Tower, the library was now more deeply in twilight than the other rooms. For Gaudeans this had the advantage that his movements were unlikely to be noticed— let alone expected—by anyone outside the window. At the same time, there was only just enough illumination for what he had to do.

The window looked out on to the side of the triumphal arch which formed the main castle gateway. This meant that the sentries themselves were within the arch and not likely to see him. There was no one else in view. Deftly he picked up a small chair, among all the bookcases and display-tables, and carried it over to one corner. By standing on it he was able to reach the wooden box which was screwed to the wall in one corner and which carried four fuses.

At the worst, he would have to take out the most likely one and see if the lights on the ground floor still worked. Stivey's office was the room where a light was least likely to be noticed. But the worst was not to happen—not yet, anyway. He looked at the four porcelain fuses and the thin silver wires which crossed each one. On the back of the white glaze was lettering: GROUND, FIRST, SECOND, and ALARM. He understood at once. This was the last place where the garrison authorities would want confusion if the lights and the alarm-bells failed.

Later on, when the darkness was complete, it would be too dangerous to strike a match. He took out the porcelain fuse marked GROUND and stepped down from the chair. Using the shelter of a table and his coat, as if trying to light a cigarette in a wind, he struck another match and held it to the thin wires of the fuse until the slender web of metal seemed to bubble and curl apart.

Back on the chair, he exchanged FIRST for GROUND. All he need do now to plunge the ground floor into darkness was to change them back again.

From his observation of the guard commander's previous inspection he knew what the routine would be. Even if it varied he had made provision to cope with that. But it seemed that the two men went first to Stivey's office and the strong-room, opening the vault-door and the grille in order to check the well-being of the safe. In that case, Gaudeans thought, the best place for him to remain was in the library. For his own convenience, however, he would unlock the library door farthest from Stivey's office, the door through which a man would be less likely to come if he were hurrying back from the strong-room to inspect the fuses. It took him a minute or so to do this. By now it was almost completely dark outside, and that was not making it any easier to deal with locks.

Before committing himself to his long captivity, Gaudeans went quietly back up the stairs to the little closet on the first floor with its running water and flowered porcelain. After all, he conceded, it was going to be a long time and the idea of an emergency bottle was not greatly appealing.

After that, there was nothing to do but wait. By his own timing there would be fifty-eight seconds between the departure of two men from the guard-room and their arrival in the Bedford Tower. Say, somewhere between fifty seconds and a full minute. Not that it mattered to him just now, but it was going to matter a great deal tomorrow night.

He had waited only about twenty minutes when there were voices in the castle yard outside. They faded, and he thought he heard the door of the guard-room open and close. The silence was punctuated by the clock in the cupola above him striking ten, loud as a gunners' salute in the still evening. From time to time the sentries, as if at an invisible signal, turned and marched in a slow swinging stride to their opposite corner, stamped about, and then swung leisurely back again.

Abruptly there were footsteps, quicker and less disciplined, the sound of voices again. Gaudeans's heart beat faster, and he felt a galvanic shock of excitement as a key turned in the main door of the Bedford Tower. For better or worse, this was it. He felt no fear as yet, only a surge of anticipation at the prospect before him.

It began well. He knew in a moment that the two men were going straight to the strong-room, as before. Indeed, they were talking about it, and he guessed that it was the guard commander who was speaking.

"Why they should think papers safer here than on the royal yacht, I'll be damned if I know. Still, if this is good enough for 'em, they can't be that important. Eh?"

The other man laughed politely, and Gaudeans heard a key being inserted in the door of Stivey's office. Under the door which separated the library from the vestibule he could see a pale gleam of electric light. That was all right so far. Still more intently, he listened. From the acoustics he could tell when they were merely standing in Stivey's office and when they were in the barer and taller space of the strong-room itself. He let them get in there before be stood on the chair and, with the deftness of Captain Wunder himself, exchanged the two fuses so that the one marked GROUND was now in its correct place.

The illuminated strip under the door went black. From a long way off he heard the guard commander's voice say, "Damnation!" in a tone of exasperation which suggested that this was not the first time the fuse had failed.

Gaudeans moved with all the speed of Captain Wunder. The two men had not carried a lamp when he had watched them before. There was, after all, no reason to do so. Now they would be moving slowly and warily in the darkness for a precious moment or two before their eyes grew accustomed to the gloom. This was his chance.

He closed the box and swung the little chair back into its normal place. Without a sound he reached the unlocked door of the library, opened it, and slipped the catch of the lock with his probe as he stood in the vestibule.

While he stood back, concealed by the central staircase, he saw the faint outline of one of the men—the police superintendent, presumably—moving like a sleep-walker from Stivey's office to the first of the library doors. Gaudeans let the man enter and listened for the sound of another chair's being moved. He guessed that the guard commander must still be in the strong-room. It was no part of a gentleman's duties to understand the workings of the fuse system, least of all one who held a commission in His Majesty's Irish Guards.

Swift as a shadow, Gaudeans moved towards the open doorway of Stivey's office. He had hardly passed through it when he heard the guard commander moving in the strong-room and realized that the officer was coming out, in his direction. It was so dark that Gaudeans himself could hardly make out the shape of the open vault-door. He crouched down behind Stivey's table, on the side farthest from the strong-room door.

The guard commander came forward, his feet shuffling along the floor as though he feared that he might trip himself up in the darkness. Gaudeans could just see him pausing in the doorway of the strong-room. His heart sank. If that was as far as the man went, then the whole game was lost. Or, rather, Gaudy would have to take the worst risk of all.

But the guardsman grew impatient with his colleague's fumbling in the library. He took a step forward into Stivey's office and called out.

"Well?"

Gaudeans gathered himself like a cat watching a sparrow.

"Ground-floor fuse," said the policeman's voice distantly, "melted. Wires must have been going for some time, I suppose."

The guard commander let out a breath of frustration and swore to himself.

"Phone the guard-room," he said loudly. "Two lamps to be brought and a double detail on guard outside. And the garrison engineer. This will be a job for him."

"The phone's in here," said the superintendent indifferently, "unless you can find one where you are. Let me check the alarm fuse and I'll come back to you."

The guard commander seemed to mutter something uncomplimentary about the superintendent. He took another step towards the door to Stivey's office. Gaudeans calculated the distances.

"I want the guard-room phoned now! We shall need lamps and a double sentry!"

The superintendent got down from the chair, and the guard commander took another step or so to meet him in the vestibule. Against the faint flush of light in the vestibule, Gaudeans could see that the guard commander's back blocked the doorway. He moved forward, head down, and crept silently but steadily towards the vault-door. It was still wide open. Inside, the floor seemed to be solid and soundless.

Outside in the vestibule the two men were still arguing with official politeness over whether the garrison engineer could be fetched at once or whether the repair of the fuse must wait until the morning.

It was hard to make out much of the strong-room, though the metal hulk of the safe was unmistakable. Not that Gaudeans was interested in it for the moment. All his attention was on one of the breakfront bookcases which he had seen when the room was illuminated on his previous evening in the castle yard. Shackleton had described it to Tonia long before, in a boastful mood about the castle's security. Its massive pediment was a match for one in the Dublin Herald's own room. Gaudeans had known at once that the main body of the case would not fit flush against the wall. There would be a cavity eight or nine inches deep between the wall and the back of the case. His glimpse of the lighted window from the castle yard on the evening of the reception had confirmed all this.

There were alternatives, of course, as in all Gaudy's plans. And there was his supreme gift of improvisation, the natural talent of the successful trickster. He had concealed himself from Lindemann by using the bulk of the Kromer safe. But this was better. Much, much better. This was the way to a robbery which would leave the police stunned and the press gasping.

His tongue pressed between his teeth with the effort of concentration. He moved gently towards the tall, looming shape of the breakfront case. In the vestibule the two men had ended their conversation, and the superintendent was coming back. Gaudeans pressed himself between the back of the case and the wall. He was careful not to stir the creaking wood as he slid farther away from observation towards the centre of concealment.

It sounded as if the policeman was just within the doorway of the strong-room now, casually impatient. His foot tapped the hard floor rhythmically, a breathless little tune whistled between his teeth. Gaudeans relaxed. It was all over now. Either they would lock up and leave, or else they would bring in half-a-dozen guardsmen and search every inch of the building. In the latter case they would find him.

But, of course, they would not do that. Not without permission from the Viceroy to invade the strong-room. And Gaudeans very much doubted that the guard commander would phone the Viceregal Lodge in Phoenix Park at this hour with such a demand. Not for so trivial a matter as a melted fuse-wire.

Gaudeans smiled to himself in the darkness. That was where true artistry always paid off. When the policeman inspected the wire it would not be cut or snapped but melted, precisely the correct appearance of a fuse blown by overuse. He felt a great pride in these little things, in the care which he had taken to please his audience. As he used to tell himself at the Lietzensee, he really was good. Very, very good indeed.

The guard commander was making his phone call to the guard-room in the distance of the library. His words were not audible, but there was no mistaking his tone. Weary, Gaudeans would have called it; resigned, vaguely irritated. Had the fuse for the alarm system been melted, that would have been a different matter. But they had seen for themselves that it was intact. No danger there. And that, Gaudy decided, was just another little bit of artistry in its way.

Now, it seemed, the conversation on the telephone was over. Footsteps sounded outside the wall of the strong-room, somewhere in the castle yard. The main door of the tower opened, and pale oil-light flooded one of the outer rooms.

Still it was only the guard commander and the duty superintendent who were in the Bedford Tower itself. The man who had brought the lanterns was left outside. They were both in the strong-room now, and Gaudeans, hardly breathing as he listened, mapped their steps. One of them, the guard commander as he guessed, was looking at the front of the safe. He even heard the bolt-lever tried.

"Tight enough," said the superintendent, and the two men laughed.

Light caught the ceiling above him, and Gaudeans assumed that one of their lamps had made a final sweep of the strong-room. They walked in step, and his heart leapt with triumph as he heard the iron grille closed across the doorway. One after another their two keys were turned in its lock. Then came the softer, heavier thud of the armoured vault-door being closed into place. The quality of the sound suggested a seal that was hermetically tight. This time the thickness of the door was such that the turning of the two keys was inaudible. Only a metallic thump, muffled by the skins of steel, assured him that the bolt now sealed him securely from the world.

In his mind he began to count the seconds, still and motionless in his place of concealment. He had reached thirty-nine when he heard their footsteps in the yard. No doubt of it, then; they had gone straight back. Continuing to count, he reached fifty-four as he heard the guard-room door open. Still he listened, straining for the tiny sound which would tell him the most important thing of all. It came when he had counted to sixty-three: a faint electric click, perhaps more of a fizz than a click, he thought. They had switched on the alarm again. Even to approach the safe or the grille and the vault-door might set it off now. Any attempt to probe the secrets of their locks would certainly do so. A man might have the very keys which the guard commander and the superintendent had just used. And those would set off the alarm as surely as an attack on the lock with a hammer and chisel.

Gaudeans sighed with admiration and contentment. By just such precautions as these had his enemies delivered themselves into his hands.

25

For ten or fifteen minutes, Gaudeans waited and listened. Beyond the outer wall of the room with the narrow steel bars of its window, he could hear the sentries. They marched slowly to and fro, every few minutes. This exchange of standpoints relieved the stiffness of their limbs and allowed them a brief comment to one another from the corners of their mouths. Once, when they must have passed just by the window, Gaudeans caught the muttered words.

" 'Nother bleedin' hour yet. Watch out for old man Tolland!"

That was good, he thought. So they changed the guard at midnight. A moment or two later he heard the clock in the cupola of the Bedford Tower begin to strike eleven. If the guard commander and the superintendent were to come back at all that night—which was unlikely—it would probably be when the guard was changed. That gave him at least an hour in which to inspect his surroundings. Not that he would lack opportunity. The strong-room was likely to be his prison for the next twenty-four hours.

Edging his way out from behind the tall breakfront case, he looked at the room. There was moonlight in the castle yard and the yellow glimmer of lamps. Not a full moon by any means, but enough to show him a ghostly section of Georgian brickwork outside and several tall sash-windows in darkness.

His eyes were accustomed to the nocturnal gloom in the strong-room itself, and he looked about him carefully. Tonia had not pressed Shackleton too obviously on the matter of security. She had not, for instance, been able to discover without rousing his suspicions the precise extent of the electric alarm. Gaudeans could guess the least that would have been done. The alarm would be wired to two circuits, for instance, so that if the fuse or the installation in the Bedford Tower went, it would still operate. The vault-door and the iron grille immediately inside it would be wired. Set to explode with sound the moment anyone touched their locks. Except, of course, when the master-switch in the guard-room was turned off.

And when would that be? Every evening when the guard commander and the superintendent made their visit. And probably once, at least, during the day. With the approach of the royal yacht, *Victoria and Albert,* to Kingstown harbour, there would be no end of coming and going. Papers for His Majesty's perusal would arrive by King's Messenger while the yacht cruised leisurely off the Welsh coast or in the Irish Sea. There would, no doubt, be a good deal of fussy checking over the state jewels before King Edward's arrival.

So, the vault-door and the iron grille were dangerous. Outside the strong-room, he had looked constantly for any tell-tale wires from doors and windows. There was not one that he could see, not even on the main door from the castle yard. That made sense. It was almost impossible to get past the sentries. A man who succeeded would find himself confronted by the impregnable vault-door. No reason, then, to wire the outside doors and windows.

When, for a day or two, it had seemed that the blackmail dodge with Shackleton might not work, Gaudy had contemplated his other plan. It meant scaling the roofs of the Royal Exchange and the castle, attacking the Bedford Tower through the windows high in the cupola. At that time he had been seriously concerned that they might have been wired to the alarm. He need not have worried. If he had made one mistake in all his planning, it had been to suppose that his adversaries were cleverer than they had proved to be. In fact, not one of the British intelligence officers would have lasted for a single evening on the stage of Wilk's Specialita Theater in the Lietzensee.

He smiled in the ghost-light of the darkened room. Now that he knew the extremes of danger and security, he had only to map the unknown territory between. Had they wired the safe? Were there pressure-pads in the room itself which would set off the alarm if he put his foot on them? Was that why the guard commander and the superintendent had shuffled so cautiously when the lights went out?

Absurd, he thought. The alarm was switched off at the time. No pressure-pads, then? His eyes mapped the room. The walls were lined with high breakfront cases, similar in pattern to the one which had concealed him. Only the outer wall with its window was bare of them. In the centre of the room was a single flat table with two wooden upright chairs. It seemed, then, that the room was used for working in, for consulting documents. That was interesting. The documents might, of course, be the rare books and manuscripts kept in the wall-cases. But since the duty superintendent was a nightly visitor, Gaudeans wondered if the most secret of Special Branch files might not also be locked away in the vault. Files on Mahony and his kind, perhaps?

Apart from the table, there were four museum display-cases, arranged in pairs, at the room's centre. Gaudeans doubted if they were used for purposes of display in a room like this. Probably, he thought, they had been moved in there as a convenient place of storage. No doubt it was this clutter of furniture which the guard commander and the superintendent had been trying to avoid as they shuffled gingerly forward in the sudden darkness.

That left the safe. It was well concealed from the door of the room, standing close to the outer wall, not far from the window. As in the case of Lindemann's safe in Berlin, the Milner had been turned so that its front faced the side of the room. When it was opened, no one at the door of the strong-room could see into it. Indeed, even the man who was removing or replacing the contents would be concealed from inquisitive eyes by the open door of the safe itself.

Gaudeans had chosen his place of refuge carefully. The breakfront case ran along the wall which the front of the Milner faced. As he stepped out at one end of the tall case, he was hidden from the vault-door by the jut of the deep shelves. The front of the safe was about four or five feet ahead of him.

In the deep shadows of the room, the steel shape was outlined by a faint flush of light from the window. The safe looked the twin of the one he had seen on the stand at the exhibition. When he stood upright, it was quite as tall as he. The solid rectangle of its door was broken only by keyhole and bolt-lever, the Milner name-plate apparently having been removed. Or perhaps never placed there. Any embellishment of the plain steel door, the tiniest hole drilled for a screw, minutely diminished its total security. That, in terms of viceregal and royal standards, was unacceptable. By God, thought Gaudeans, they really must believe that they had taken care of everything.

With professional caution he resisted the instinct to reach out and touch the sleek metal skin of the monster. It was what any third-rate burglar would have done. But to do so he would have had to take a step forward. Even if that could be done, the moment he laid a hand on the Milner it might burst into sound as the alarm went off. That was what he had to know first. Could they have wired it so finely that the least pressure of a hand—let alone the ravishing of its lock—would detonate the alarm system?

There was more to it than that. When he had slipped into the strong-room the alarm had been turned off. Now that it was on again, he dared not take a single step from his hiding-place until he knew that the floor had not been laid like a mine field with pressure-pads or other devices.

He would have struck a match but for the faint glow that was bound to reflect on the ceiling of the room. The sentries outside would perhaps not see it, having their backs to the building most of the time. He could choose a moment when they had completed their little exchange-march and would be stationary for several minutes at least. But what of the other windows which looked on to the Bedford Tower? Might not someone notice from there? The risk was too great, and for the moment he decided to do without it.

Squatting down with his back against the wall, be brushed his hand in a circular movement over the floor in front of him. It was linoleum. That was good. To his sensitive fingers the ridge of such a pad as an alarm system required would be clear at once through the thin, waxy surface. Even without constant wear, linoleum adapted itself to the contours of whatever lay beneath it.

After several gentle sweeps with his hands, he knew that there was nothing under the smooth covering. But there was one further exploration to be made. The linoleum had been pushed into place along the skirting but not nailed down. His gloved hands took the rough edge of the material and pulled it back from the outer wall as far as the weight of the breakfront case would allow. Then he ran his hands under it, almost to the level of the safe. There was nothing to be found, no metal-rimmed pad, not even a trace of wiring.

With a long sigh of contentment, Gaudeans stood up and walked slowly, noiselessly across the stretch of linoleum which he had examined. The steel carcass of the safe was inches away now, but still he must not touch it. From his examination of the floor, he was reasonably sure that no wires ran either from the front or from the left-hand side. That was to be expected. Moreover, they had not bothered to place an alarm-pad under the linoleum in front of its door. That, after all, was the most likely place, the way to catch a burglar as he stood before it.

Alarm-pads were unlikely, then. But still they might have connected the door of the safe to the alarm system. In the darkness he could see no scar of wire on the safe-door. It was just possible that they had wired it inside, that the wires ran down through a hole at the rear of the safe, or even through the bottom of it.

Edging round with his back against the window wall, where there were no breakfront cases, Gaudeans eased back the linoleum square again from the room's corner. This time he rolled it back level with the side of the safe. His hands slid under, tracing the bare floorboards at the rear of the safe where the wires would have run directly to the wall which adjoined the guard-room. There was nothing.

That made it very unlikely that the safe had been wired to the alarm system at all. After all, it was hardly necessary that it should be. The strong-room itself was impenetrable; the vault-door and the grille were certainly wired. To wire the safe as well might even cause inconvenience. Suppose they ever wanted to move it to another part of the room? Suppose Vicars was ever left to work in there with the vault-door closed? He was entitled to open the safe. If it were wired, that would mean turning off the entire alarm system for hours at a time.

Gaudeans was almost sure that he was right. Almost, but not completely. In the faint flush of the star-light from the window, he could just make out the hands of his watch. Five minutes to midnight. He rolled the linoleum as far back as it would go and took from his pocket a small metal lever, short and stout, with a forked grip at one end. The two floor-boards closest to the window were nailed to the joists near his feet, just where the boards divided.

He almost heard the preparatory whirring of the mechanism, or thought that he did. Then the clock of the Bedford Tower began to chime and boom. Working with the deftness of a joiner, he jacked out the nails at the ends of the two floor-boards. The third and fourth strokes of the hour overlaid the faint squealing of wood as the boards themselves came up. Lying on his side, he slid his arm under the other boards, feeling along the joists to where the safe must be standing. There was steel reinforcing there to hold the weight of it. He could feel that. And short of a long tunnel from the street outside, there was no way anyone could come up into the strong-room from underneath. But there was no wiring from the bottom of the safe.

That was it, then. They had not bothered to connect its door to the alarm system. Gently he eased the boards back and slipped the nails into their holes. There was no need to do more than press them lightly into place and let the linoleum flop down over them. It would be months before anyone noticed what had happened—if they ever did.

Now there was little that he could do until the next day. Instead of going back to his hiding-place, he sat there on the floor with his back against the wall, just below the barred window. His feet, stretched out on the floor in front of him, almost touched the side of the safe. For several hours he had nothing to do but to think his own thoughts and listen, half-interested, to the movements of the sentries outside. He was not arrogantly confident now, not cocksure in his triumph, but there was a great tranquillity in the sharp little brain behind the foxy features. The outcome of it all hardly depended on him any longer. Whatever he did, it was all decided one way or another.

It was daylight soon after three o'clock, though the room itself was not fully lit until an hour later. Gaudeans sat there, staring at the grey steel flank of the safe. Later still, there were footsteps outside and someone opened the door to the Bedford Tower. Perhaps it was the cleaning-woman whom Shackleton had mentioned. For the first time it occurred to Gaudeans that she might be blamed for the crime when it was discovered. He hoped not. He had no quarrel with her, only with King Edward, the Viceroy, General Thorneycroft, and their kind. Still, it was odd that with all their sensitivity over the security of the Bedford Tower they should allow her to have the run of the place at this hour of the day.

Presently he took an apple from his pocket and ate it quietly. Eating and drinking was something he had to be cautious about during his stay in the room. He wrapped the core very carefully in a sheet of paper and returned it to his pocket. Apple cores were likely to give off a smell, and, when the moment came, a smell would betray him as easily as a sound or a glimpse of him.

It was after nine o'clock when the other movements began. The thickness of the vault-door made it difficult to distinguish voices, but he was reasonably sure that Frank Shackleton's must be one of them. Already the Dublin Herald would have found the packet of photographs and glass-plate negatives on his desk. By this time he was presumably swollen in heart and moist in eye with gratitude to his new friend Gaudeans, who had saved both his reputation and, very probably, his life.

Gaudeans did not even smile at the thought. He was gazing across the room at the interior of the vault-door, feeling a gratitude of his own to Shackleton for all that he had told Tonia, unwittingly, about the arrangement of the strong-room. In many cases a vault-door would have been made to open only from the outside, the keyholes being on that side alone. But the strong-room of the Bedford Tower was also an office or small library. As Shackleton had mentioned, it was sometimes necessary for two or three men to be in there—presumably Vicars and the two duty officers—while the state jewels or confidential papers were checked. They might work there for an hour or two. To have left the vault-door open for such a length of time would have made the strong-room vulnerable to any attacker who could find a pretext for entering the Bedford Tower. The door was therefore closed and locked, to be opened by the occupants of the strong-room when their work was complete. For that reason, if for no other, it had been equipped with a door which could be opened on either side.

As usual, Gaudeans had prepared an alternative plan, in case the door could not have been unlocked from within. But this would have involved tampering with the wiring in the room so that it would once again be in darkness for the nightly inspection. They would have assumed that the fault was somehow related to the blown fuse, and he could have got into another room under cover of temporary darkness. His ability to do that was never in question in his own mind. All the same, the risk would have been greater, and he was glad not to have had to resort to such means.

The morning passed in a succession of familiar noises. There were the movements of the sentries in the castle yard, footsteps and voices, the changing of the guard on the main gate and the Bedford Tower, a subdued murmur of everyday business in the heralds' offices. The afternoon, Tonia had said, was his most likely chance.

High above, the cupola clock struck noon. He had rationed himself strictly, but now he was entitled to a second apple. He ate slowly, once again wrapping the core in paper before he put it in his pocket.

The warning sounds which he waited for in the early afternoon were footsteps and voices again. But when it came, the signal was a light click, audible to him only because he was sitting there in complete stillness. It came from the direction of the vault-door and was an exact repetition of the little sound he had heard the night before when the returning guard commander had switched on the alarm again in the guard-room. Now they had switched it off.

Gaudeans moved without sound to the breakfront bookcase and gently squeezed himself into the narrow space between its back and the wall. It was possible, of course, that Shackleton had deliberately fed Tonia false information about the procedures which were followed now, but he doubted that. The tone of the Dublin Herald's boasting suggested that he was only too willing to impress the girl by his own part in the great pageant of state security.

He held his breath and waited.

They were a long time in reaching the vault-door, he thought, more leisurely than when he had timed them. But presently there was a smooth sound, the hiss of sleek metal hinges as the heavy steel swung upon them. Gaudeans edged as close as he dared to the end of the breakfront case, so that he could step out and confront the safe.

His blood beat harder in his temples, and there was a discomfort in his throat as though it tightened whenever he drew breath. The air passed his gullet like something hard and tangible.

The men—he counted four different voices—were in the open doorway of the strong-room. Only one of them came in. Gaudeans could not see him, but he knew it must be the young, foppish figure of Sir Arthur Vicars, Ulster King-of-Arms. There was a metallic slither of a key in a lock, the muffled thump of the bolt's being drawn back, and then the same gentle whisper of armoured steel moving slowly on its hinges.

Gaudeans knew that but for the breakfront case between them, he could now have reached out and touched Vicars on the shoulder. Yet he could not see or guess precisely what the other man was doing. Something which sounded like hard hollow leather bumped gently. Gaudeans ran his tongue over his lips and opened his mouth to ease the discomfort of breathing by drawing air through it. He had not expected this degree of tension, but the penalties for failure now were quite as severe in their way as the terrors of Captain Wunder's underwater coffin.

Vicars took whatever it was from the safe and crossed the strong-room again towards the door. In his hand Gaudeans already held the hard, warm shape of the cash-box key which he had bought at Milner's exhibition stand. He slid one foot out and trod quickly but deftly on the floor of the room. The door of the safe was wide open, its interior a series of shelves with leather boxes on them.

The open door reached to within two feet of him, providing a complete screen for that part of the distance. Ducking down, he was shielded from the gaze of the men outside by the tables in the centre of the room.

Gaudeans scanned the shelves inside the safe as if he had been reading a page of print. Dispatch-boxes and jewel-cases meant nothing to him. He was looking for something smaller and simpler than those.

"If you will sign the receipt, Colonel Molyneux, I will then release the papers into your custody. That is the normal procedure, is it not?"

It was Vicars who had spoken. The papers to be released were presumably connected with the arrangements for the King's security in Dublin. That, at least, was what Gaudeans hoped. The hungry little eyes saw at last what they were looking for. Four keys on a ring lay at the side of the top shelf. They were silver-coloured and quite large. Beside them was another key on its own, bronze-tinted with a heart-shaped finger-piece. It was identical to the key which now projected from the lock of the safe. It was so close in design to the one which Gaudeans held in his hand that only a careful comparison would show the difference.

"Thank you," said Vicars from the doorway. "Now, I must sign as receiving those dispatches which you wish to deposit here. There must, of course, be a serial number."

Even with his own nerves strained taut to accomplish what he had to do, Gaudeans disliked the voice. It had all the tones of fussy, pedantic precision. An old maid's querulousness in the body of a foppish young man.

They would be watching the exchange of signatures now. It was the best time. Ten seconds more and it would be too late. With head well down, he ducked into the concealment of the open door of the safe. In a few moments more, Vicars would finish and come back to restore the dispatch-case and turn the key in the Milner lock. For all that, Gaudeans dared not hurry. To rattle the spare key, or his own replacement, against the metal skin of the safe would be to have them all coming after him at once.

Gently he lifted the spare key to the safe from where it lay beside the duplicates for the vault-door and iron grille. He held it in his left hand and with his right set the cash-box key down in its place. That was all. He had done it and he was secure. Not once in a thousand visits would Vicars do more than glance at the spare set of keys which the Milner housed.

Vicars was thanking Colonel Molyneux crisply for the dispatch-list as Gaudeans turned and crouched towards the wall where the breakfront bookcase ended. He took a quick, silent step, missed his footing as he stooped, and instinctively put out his left hand towards the wall to save himself. The key to the Milner safe rang on the linoleum as it fell.

For what seemed like a full minute but was hardly a few seconds, he crouched there, motionless. They must have heard the key fall; there was no doubt of that. If they entered the room, if they even took a few steps forward so that they could see over the clutter of tables at its centre, he was done for. Gaudeans waited for the end.

Nothing happened. It was as if they had heard the sound but simply disregarded it. He snatched the key and pulled himself in behind the breakfront case again. How had it sounded to them? Was Vicars already entering the strong-room again, and did they think he had made the noise? Or did they simply believe that it must have come from somewhere beyond the room, perhaps in the castle yard outside?

He waited, squeezed behind the case, his mouth open as he drew air deeply and silently to ease the shock of the incident. In his mind he could think of only one thing. They were so sure of their security, so convinced that the measures they had taken were impregnable, that he could have beaten a drum in the strong-room and they would still not have believed that anyone could have been there to do it. Since the previous night the duties of the guard commander and duty superintendent would have passed to other men. Even if they had heard of the fuse which had failed, they would have had no more reason to feel suspicious than the others.

The steel door of the safe moved slowly into place, and Vicars turned the key in the lock. Gaudeans listened to the sound of the iron grille's being closed and the vault-door's swinging shut. His heart rose with an excitement more powerful than anything he had felt in his moment of fear.

Now he was sure that he would not be caught. He might be killed in completing the rest of the plan; the risk of that was extremely high, one way and another. But at least there would be no arrest or imprisonment. He would die, as it were, in action against the enemy.

For the first time that day he smiled at the thoughts which passed through his mind.

26

When Vicars left with the King's Messenger and the escort, Gaudeans listened very hard. He wanted to hear the tiny click once more which signalled to him that the alarm had been switched on again in the guard-room. It came quite distinctly. More than that, he was alert and expectant enough this time to know that it came from the vault-door, as he had guessed, not from the Milner safe. They had not wired the safe, he was more sure of that now than ever. There was simply no way they could have done it without betraying the fact to him by this stage.

And that made his task easier still.

All the same, he was more determined now to be patient, to take no unnecessary risks. After four o'clock, when Vicars was due to leave and the Bedford Tower closed, there would be ample time. Before then it was always possible that one of the Royal Navy destroyers which docked every day at the North Wall would bring another King's Messenger. His dispatches would be held until the *Victoria and Albert* reached Kingstown harbour after its leisurely cruise. Such things might happen before four o'clock. But when Vicars had gone home and the key to the safe had been locked away, other arrangements would be made until the morning.

So Gaudeans waited, sitting again with his back to the window wall, until the cupola clock chimed four. There was a distant sound of footsteps on the curve of the staircase, the rattle of doors being locked and tested. Stivey was going his rounds as he had the previous evening when Shackleton had left Gaudeans in Mahony's room.

Gaudeans thought of Mahony. Now that he had seen the inside of the safe, he knew that Mahony's republicans—if that was the group the young man represented—had jumped too late. If they ever had intended to jump at all. And there, somewhere in Dublin, Shackleton clutched the little packet of photographs and thought of Gaudy as his one true friend. The only kind of sportsman that a fellow could trust.

Pulling the gloves tighter on his hands, he drew the key to the

Milner safe from his pocket and stood up. There might be an art to opening the monster, but he doubted that. The key slid easily in and turned without effort. Gaudy took a deeper breath and pulled the bolt-handle. It held firm as iron.

In his dismay he took a step backwards and looked at the smooth steel door. A key that would turn in the lock without lifting enough tumblers to release the bolt? Thoughts of Mahony possessed him. A plot involving Vicars himself? For a couple of seconds he felt panic rising in his throat, the first time since he had parted from Shackleton the evening before. If the key failed him, he would never open the safe. But that was not the worst of it. He was trapped in the strong-room, either until they found him or—more likely—until he gave himself up.

Then the absurdity of it hit him, so suddenly that he wanted to laugh. Surely Vicars had turned only one key? Or had he? Or had he turned one key twice? With the blood beating at his temples again, Gaudy inserted the key and tried to turn it once more. The tumblers gave, and he heard the unmistakable sound of the bolt's being lifted.

That was it, then. A double lock, requiring two turns of the key instead of one. It was a measure of his panic that he had overlooked so simple an explanation. The time had come to pull himself together. At this rate he was unlikely to get through the evening alive.

He took the bolt-lever and pulled open the door of the safe. No one would see him from outside. The safe was too close to the wall to be seen through the window, unless the sentries pulled themselves up to look through, which was certainly not going to happen.

One by one, he began to remove the boxes which the safe contained. Five of them, small enough to be slipped into the capacious pocket of his jacket, bore names upon them. Lord Mayo, Lord Enniskillen, Lord Ormonde, Lord Howth, Lord Cork. He knew that these must be the gold and jewelled collars of the Knights of St. Patrick. Lindemann's orders were strict: the contents of the safe must be delivered unopened to the Königsplatz, their locks unbroken.

A finer case, very much larger, was no doubt the one which carried a double treasure, the Star of St. Patrick and the matching Badge of Viceroyalty. Gaudy could think only of the splendid white fire which had shot from its Brazilian diamonds in the grand ceremony of the Irish International Exhibition.

There were two dispatch-cases, their red leather somewhat worn at the corners. The monogram V.R. showed that no one had bothered to replace them when the new King came to the throne. That was odd, he thought, but perhaps not unexpected. One was marked, in tiny gold letters, SECRETARY OF STATE FOR IRELAND, and the other, ADMIRALTY. Gaudeans put them down. He guessed the Irish papers would contain a good deal of secret information which the Special Branch had acquired on Fenianism, its members and methods. In Lindemann's hands it would be invaluable if there were to be a war which promised Ireland independence with German assistance. The Irish provinces in a state of insurrection would pin down a dozen divisions of the British Army.

The other two items in the safe interested Gaudeans far more than any of the state jewels or the official papers. The first was a leather case bearing the letters P.G.M. He knew, of course, that they stood for "Peirce Gun Mahony," Within the box there lay the famous Mahony diamonds, part of the fortune which the exiled family had brought back from their service to the Czar of Russia.

Even more important to Gaudeans than the Mahony diamonds was the last box which he drew from the safe. It was made of plain black metal, about twelve inches square and ten inches deep. On its lid, in Gothic script, was the single word SCHROEDER. Gaudeans had seen the box once before, set on a table in the Königsplatz as Lindemann gave him his final instructions. But at that time it had not been decorated with the name upon the lid.

The black metal box had, of course, provided Tonia with the most innocent and plausible motive for her interest in the security of the Bedford Tower. Frank Shackleton had only to hear of the famous Schroeder necklace which his young mistress was to wear at the royal drawing-room to be held by King Edward at Dublin Castle, and to which the Dublin Herald himself had arranged her invitation.

The value of the necklace and its matching clips was such that, as Tonia confessed, even the safe of the Shelbourne Hotel was hardly worthy of it. At that moment it had seemed to Shackleton that if a private heirloom like the Mahony diamonds could claim the protection of the Bedford Tower strong-room, why could not the Schroeder necklace as well? Tonia's cautious gratitude was one more proof of her trust in her new lover. True, she had asked several pertinent questions about the strong-room and the safe, the precautions which were taken, and the routines followed by the guardians. She was, after all, a Schroeder and must have inherited some of her father's shrewdness and suspicion.

It had taken Frank Shackleton only a few minutes to laugh away her misgivings as he explained the impenetrable security of the place. And if she still felt uncertain, he would try to arrange for her to be present at the door of the strong-room when the metal box was deposited there for safe-keeping.

The memory of all this brought a brief smile to Gaudeans's face. He closed the empty safe and locked it. Now he had to work with speed and care. First of all, there was Tonia's metal box, the only one to which he had a key. As he picked it up, it certainly felt about the correct weight for a case containing a necklace. But what was inside it meant more to him than the finest stone of Golconda or Brazil. He eased back the lid and drew out a paper-wrapped bundle. Inside the paper was a tightly coiled rope, thin and very strong, perfectly calculated for his present needs.

After this, of course, the box was useless to him, merely an encumbrance. But that, too, was something he had foreseen. From his pocket he took a small screwdriver and began to undo, from the inside of the box, the little screws which held it in shape. By the time that he had finished, the bulky case was reduced to a few flat sheets of thin steel.

That left him with five little pocket-boxes, containing the knights' collars; two larger ones, with the Viceroy's jewels and Mahony's diamonds; and the two dispatch-cases. Lindemann's orders were that they should be delivered unopened. That suited Gaudeans at the moment. He had no keys to open them. To leave the broken boxes behind was to reveal something about his method, and that he preferred not to do. It would also seem odd if the debris of Tonia's box were left. Lindemann apart, it was much better to make a clean sweep of the evidence.

As a burden to be carried, the collection of boxes was inconvenient but not impossibly large. Not, at least, to a man who calculated the difficulties as precisely as he had done. Outside in the sunlit castle yard the sentries were changing places with their slow, rolling gait. Gaudeans let them settle down while he slipped off his jacket. He laid it on the floor by the window and then fumbled for a moment with his tie and collar-studs. Presently his shirt lay on top of the jacket. Underneath he wore an ugly-looking corset of thin, stout canvas with more straps than were needed merely to keep it in place round his chest and abdomen.

He undid this and, laying it on the floor as well, began to refasten it in a new shape. A few minutes later he had assembled a large and serviceable haversack. If anything, it was larger than he would have wished, but on the other hand the weight inside it would not be too great. Without bothering to dress again for the time being, he loaded the large and small boxes from the safe into it, using the flat sheets of the metal "necklace" box to give it a firmly-shaped inner floor. It was certainly no worse, he thought, than the weight which a man might have carried on a walking-tour. Except, of course, that he faced something rather more hazardous than that.

Gently and with hardly a sound, he slid the pack behind the breakfront bookcase which had been his own hiding-place. Then he put on the shirt again, fastened the studs and collar, and knotted his tie. As he slid his jacket on, he wondered how cold it would be after dark. Still, his hands would be protected in the thin grey suede of the gloves. As at the Lietzensee, it was his hands which would mean life or death to him in the hours ahead.

There was nothing more to be done until the new guard commander and duty superintendent made their inspection soon after ten o'clock. He hoped they would not be late. Every minute of delay after that must increase the odds against his escape. Through the window he watched the light thicken and the first lamps come on in the yard outside. From time to time he tried to catch some sound or other beyond the wall which divided the strong-room of the Bedford Tower from the guard-room. He had heard nothing from that direction all day, a tribute to the solidity of the structure. The builders of the place had made certain that no one would ever dig a way in or out.

Just before it was completely dark, he opened the safe again and took out the keys for the grille and the vault-door, locking the safe again afterwards. The guard commander and his companion would not be able to open the safe to check. Only Vicars had that authority. And Vicars was far away by now, at a party given by the Viceroy for his household on the eve of the royal visit. By the time that the gathering broke up and Ulster King-of-Arms had made his way back from the Viceregal Lodge in Phoenix Park, Gaudeans would long have vanished from the premises.

He waited, crouched by the window, impatience gnawing at his guts. But for the alarm system, he could have gone now. Indeed, all his instincts were to wait for the tiny click which signalled that the system was turned off, and then to make a dash before the inspecting officers could reach the Bedford Tower from the guard-room. But the tyranny of logic in the sharp little brain overruled instinct on this occasion. A dash of that kind was the very thing which might destroy him.

Two more hours passed before he heard that click. Gaudeans sidled back behind the breakfront case, where, even with the electric light burning, he would be in the depth of its shadows. As he waited there with the loaded canvas pack beside him, he wondered if there might be some sign which he had left near the safe, some indication of his presence which might betray him. It was absurd, of course. All he had to do now was to remain still and keep very, very quiet until the moment came.

He heard their voices. There was a long delay tonight, as if they had chosen to inspect the rest of the tower first. Then he knew why. The fuses, of course. Check the fuses and make sure all was well with them. No doubt the garrison engineer had carried out his repairs that morning, the duty delegated to him by the guard commander. How fortunate it was, Gaudeans thought, that an English gentleman was brought up to believe that attention to fuses and their failures were beneath his dignity.

Presently he heard a slight movement and knew that they were in Stivey's office just beyond the vault-door. But, as before, it seemed that the sound of their keys was muffled by the thickness of the armoured steel. The heavy door swung open with a whisper which suggested its glistening smoothness. Gaudeans knew at once that he had been right. These were not the voices of the night before; the duty had been changed.

Their footsteps were slow, as though they were sauntering into the strong-room. Then with a sudden glare the light went on. To either side of him, several feet away, Gaudeans saw a brightly-illuminated segment of floor, wall, and ceiling.

"Hello," said one of the men languidly. "What the deuce is this?"

There was a brief rattle on the linoleum as he picked it up.

"A screw fallen out somewhere," said the other man flatly.

"Important, d'you say?"

"Probably from one of the cases that came or left this afternoon."

It was from Tonia's metal box; Gaudeans knew it. And in that moment his professionalism was blemished.

"Rum sort of a thing to happen," said the guard commander doubtfully.

"Hardly come from the safe, would it? They don't use little chaps like that to hold it together. In fact, the way they build them, they don't *need* holding together."

"Out of a chap's pocket, perhaps?"

"Could be."

"Note it in the guard-room incident-book?" the guard commander suggested. "That all right with you?"

"If you think it necessary."

"Yes. Well, with all these Irish fellows jiggering about and threatening heaven knows what, you never quite know. Do you?"

The two men walked slowly about the room. Once a shadow fell upon a stretch of lighted wall to Gaudeans's side. He breathed through his mouth, slowly and very deeply.

"Right-ee-o!" said the guard commander with a weary drawl, and the footsteps moved slowly away.

Now! The light went out, and Gaudeans stood poised for the muffled thump which indicated that the bolt of the vault-door had locked into place. But they were still there. He knew it. Not safe to tackle the grille and door yet. Instead he slipped out from behind the breakfront case for the last time and pulled the loaded pack of canvas after him. Using the duplicate key which he had purloined a few hours before, he opened the safe in readiness, moved to the grille of the vault-door, and waited.

He heard a slam and a voice in the yard outside. They were on their way back to the guard-room, ten or twenty seconds into their journey. As he fumbled with the keys, the keen little brain ticked away seconds. Thirty remained to him—surely he had thirty before they switched the alarm on again. There was nothing to distinguish the four keys of the double locks on grille and door. He tried the first one on the grille. It entered, refused to turn, and then jammed in the lock.

Gaudeans gasped with panic and forgot to count. He wriggled it free. How many seconds missed? Never mind, he would count from where he left off. Twenty-six, twenty-five . . . The other key turned easily, and then the awkward one moved smoothly in the second lock

214

of the grille. He swung the barred iron open and snatched at the vault-door. Twenty-one, twenty . . .

This time he got the keys the right way round. Rough justice, he thought. Seventeen, sixteen . . . He wrenched the bolt-lever and the massive weight of the door swung open, but not without an effort. Fourteen, thirteen . . . For the first time he felt a crazy certainty that he could not do it in time before the alarm came on again. What then? Still time to lock the doors again and wait for his next chance. Until tomorrow? Not likely! He slung the canvas pack out into the messenger's room. Nine, eight . . . By God, he thought, it was too late. All over. There was no time . . .

But even as he thought, the wiry little figure scampered about, in a wild, running-crawling frenzy. He snatched his own key from the shelf of the Milner safe and replaced those of the safe itself, the grille, and the vault-door. Six, five . . . His slim burglar's probe tested the lock of the closed safe with its steel tip. As the bolt slammed, he was across the room and outside the closed grille. Again the steel probe triggered the automatic locking device which protected it against the cracksman's probing. The bolts went home with a double thump. Three, two . . . And how many seconds had he missed? Let them be late! Let them dawdle, gossip! Just a second or two.

One! He pulled the massive door into place. His time was up. Now the alarm was about to detonate. Why not already? The probe jabbed at the first lock and he heard the bolt slam. Now for the second. His hand had begun to tremble, his body cold with despair. It seemed to him that he must have been mad ever to believe that such a plan would work. Now, at any second, the alarm was going to go off like a mine under him.

It came like the shock of a bullet in the heart, the slam of the second bolt. Gaudeans sat down weakly on the floor of the messenger's office. After the self-confidence which had possessed him during his hours in the strong-room, his legs seemed too feeble to support him.

In contrast to the speed at which time fled during his escape, the next five seconds seemed like a new life. Before they were over he heard, more loudly than from within the room, the dry click of the alarm system's being turned on again. Not until then did it occur to him that the alarm reported only interferences with the locks while it was on, not those which might have taken place while it had been turned off. The thought that it might so easily have been otherwise was what started him giggling. He sat there, clutching the canvas pack to him, sniggering and guffawing like an ugly child.

It was twenty to eleven. There was time, of course, but he could not afford to use it extravagantly, knowing where he had to be at precisely eleven o'clock.

His hands were steadier now, and the locked door of Stivey's office, in which he sat, presented no problem to him. With a sense of professionalism he locked it again afterwards. They would dismantle the locks, of course, all of them. But he had acquired the skilled burglar's technique of wrapping the steel probe in thin flannel. When they dismantled the vault-door, he would be disappointed if they found so much as a blemish on the mirror-like surfaces of its levers or a pin out of place in the gyroscopic precision of its mechanism. And that, of course, was what would really have them on the hip.

Moving noiselessly up the curving stairs from the vestibule, he went into the little closet with its bowls and basins in flowered china. Five minutes, he thought, there must be five minutes to spare. Before leaving, he drank thirstily from the silver tap. At no time during the day had he felt hunger, nor did he feel it now. But thirst was another matter. Despite his two apples, Gaudeans's mouth felt stale and acid to him. Perhaps, indeed, the apples had been a mistake.

Still, it hardly mattered now. Glancing once at the locked door of Shackleton's room, he could hardly believe that it was only the day before that he had left it. He went up the narrow stairs to the attic floor and came to the octagonal cupola with its window, just below the clock of the Bedford Tower. Only one of the eight windows was made to open, but that was all he needed.

Outside, below him, the castle yard and the streets beyond were palely illuminated by the glimmer of gas. Gently he turned the handle of the single casement window. It had not been opened recently, he guessed, from the way in which the wood seemed swollen and jammed, the flakes of dry white paint which shivered from it as he put his weight against it. Gaudeans hoped no one would notice. He so wanted to preserve the illusion of Captain Wunder the magician.

Using the rope which had been in Tonia's metal box, he lowered the canvas pack and its contents to the flat roof of the Georgian tower, some eight feet below the cupola. And then it was his own turn.

Just below the level of the windows was a ledge, running round the octagonal lantern. He could perch there and draw the window tightly closed behind him. There was no way, of course, in which he could manipulate the handle to close it on the inside. To bang the window and jar the handle down would make too much noise. Instead, he pressed it shut with his full weight. The handle fell a little, not as much as he hoped. Still, it could have been worse. The cleaning-woman, if she went up to the cupola at all, might ease it into place without thinking about it very much. Even when the investigation began, a Special Branch officer would have to look twice at the handle to be sure that it was not, after all, in position to close the window.

In any case, it was the best that he could do. Gaudeans breathed the cool air of the summer night deeply. Far away and below him he could hear the constant rumble, the occasional shout of a drunkard, in the city streets. The castle yard and the main gate seemed still and silent. High above him the sky was veiled by torn clouds moving slowly in a windless calm. There was little moon as yet, its rising not due for an hour or more. Instead, the luminous pallor of star-light glimmered faintly through the clouds' vapour.

Gently and expertly he lowered himself to the level of the flat roof. A balustrade surrounded it; the chimney-stacks rose from it. Gaudeans stood there and began to fasten the canvas pack on his back. The rope went in a coil round his waist. In the last moments before he began the final and most dangerous part of his adventure, he decided that star-light was the best thing of all. Not as perilous as total darkness, better than the treacherous flood of full moon.

He hoped, of course, that none of the sentries below would see him. But should they do so, it would be the sight of a lifetime. A ghostly wash of starlit sky, and Captain Wunder flying above the Dublin rooftops.

Time was quite as important to him now as in his escape from the strong-room. Not the length of time but the precision with which it was used.

Gaudeans moved softly towards the eastern parapet of the roof, keeping his head and shoulders well below its level. From the edge of it he looked down upon the triumphal arch which formed the main gateway of Dublin Castle and the tall fur busby of each man who guarded it. So far as he could see, there were only two sentries of the Irish Guards on the gate at that moment. No doubt a uniformed policeman was also posted within the arch.

The brick wall of the Bedford Tower dropped away for about forty feet or so to the upper castle yard. Both the sentries on the main gate and those outside the door of the tower were very close to him. But those on the gate faced outwards with their backs to him for most of the time, while the Bedford Tower guards were just round the corner as he measured with his gaze the side of the building.

About a foot in on his side of the corner was a black-painted drain-pipe which ran from the roof to the yard below. Not that he could dare to go down to the yard without being caught. His only hope of escape was across the sky-line. But the pipe offered the easy means to a ledge of pale stone which ran round the wall at the base of the attic windows, about eight feet below him. That was the first stage, then. If the pipe gave or the ledge crumbled, he would be shattered on the stone paving below before they were even aware of his presence.

With great care, testing the balustrade for loose flakes of stone which might rattle down into the yard, Gaudeans eased himself over with the cool night air at his back. He balanced on the parapet's edge, his torso pressed upon it, his feet moving inwards to find the black iron pipe. Then he lowered his hands, gripped the roughly-painted metal, and trusted himself to its support. It held firm, and he had reached it without a sound.

The descent to the ledge below him was easy enough. His first difficulty was in turning round to stand upon it with back pressed against the sheer brickwork. No one but Captain Wunder would have dared, he thought, with brief instantaneous pride.

The ledge was no more than eight inches wide, its surface roughened by pigeon-droppings. Holding the pipe with one hand, he eased himself round. But the canvas pack on his shoulder-blades meant that he had to stand upon the precipitous shelf and lean forward slightly towards the cold, dizzy drop which fell away at his toes.

Moving only as much as he had to, looking down because his plan required him to, he uncoiled from his waist the dozen yards or so of rope which had been in Tonia's metal box. He would tie its ends so that it formed a continuous loop.

In front of him, across a vertiginous gap of about twelve feet, was the stone curve which began the top of the triumphal arch. It was slightly below his own level, sufficiently so for him to look down upon it. To jump at it was out of the question. Even if he could have thrown himself far enough from his present restricted posture, the stone of the gate sloped away and down. He would never find a hold upon it before he fell. In any case, the sound would be noticed at once.

But the stone pediment of the gate was a broken curve. It began at either end but was cut away in the middle to form a space for the statue of Justice on a small pedestal. Therefore, it provided at each end a stone capstan round which a rope could be thrown.

It was only the nearer end which interested Gaudeans. He edged to one side of the drain-pipe so that he could hold it by his left arm to steady himself. Then he gathered the loop of rope in his right hand and waited. To throw it now was out of the question. In the stillness of the castle yard, the slap of cord on the pale masonry of the arch would be heard instantly by the two sentries on the gate. Possibly by the uniformed constable as well.

Gaudeans never knew how long he waited there, perched and cramped high above the castle yard in the cool night. Logic told him it could not have been more than five minutes. But in his dry-mouthed apprehension the measurement of time by logic had ceased to have a meaning.

He listened for the first preparatory sigh of the mechanism, twenty feet above him. The clock of the Dedford Tower began the preliminary chimes of eleven. With the gesture of a man playing hoop-la, he cast the loop of the rope outward and slightly downward. It caught the curving stone projection where the triumphal arch began, failed to tighten, and fell back limply against the drop of the wall below him. But the measured chimes had concealed its sounds.

He gathered it again, waiting this time for the first stroke of the hour. It came with a deafening resonance at such short range, its echoes easily muffling the light impact of the rope. He tossed the loop again, and this time he felt it tighten and hold. By passing the ends round the drain-pipe and knotting them, he formed a continuous loop joining the drain-pipe and the masonry of the gate. It had to be done that way. There was no question of leaving the rope like a tell-tale thread across the sky when he had finished.

Before he joined it finally, Gaudeans had slipped off the canvas pack and threaded it on. As the tower-clock boomed three and four, he tightened the rope in his grip and watched the loaded canvas slide gently down until it came to rest against the stone curve of the gate's pediment. In his preoccupation he hardly stopped to think of the narrowness of the ledge on which he stood or the depth of the drop below him. He glanced once towards the place where the sentries had been, but it seemed that they were now standing within the massive arch of the gate. Of the uniformed policeman there was no sign.

As the strokes of seven and eight rang out, he entrusted himself to the rope. His weight was slight, and as he took the smooth hemp between his gloved hands and his knees, he prayed that the black drain-pipe and the stone projection of the arch would both hold. Then, with his back bent downwards toward the castle yard, he spun himself across like a spider against the starlit sky. There was nothing to be done by way of protection. If they saw him now, they saw him. A matter of bad luck. But he had done all that he could, taken every reasonable precaution. As he fed the rope deftly through his hands, he felt a sense of absolution from fear and responsibility.

The tenth stroke was still echoing as he drew himself over the curve of the gateway pediment. Holding the canvas pack securely, he freed the rope and cut it. In the last ripples of sound from the final stroke of the hour, he pulled it clear of the drain-pipe on the far wall, heard its end tap lightly on the stonework of the arch as it fell, and then gently drew it up to him.

So far as the Bedford Tower was concerned, there was now no evidence that he had ever been there. That any man could have forced the strong-room and cracked the safe was an impossibility.

There was, apparently, no means of entry to the building, nor of exit. For the first time it occurred to him that Vicars and Shackleton, the guard commander and the duty superintendent, had far more to fear than he.

Just below the broken curve which topped the gateway and below Justice on her pedestal, another narrow stone ledge ran from one side of the arch-face to the other. The Roman symmetry of the structure required that there should be such a ledge on the outer side, immediately above the heads of the sentries, and on the inner side which faced the castle yard.

But still the sentries on the Bedford Tower would be hidden from him by the projection of the building's corner for the greater part of the way. And, as he had calculated, the reception at the Viceregal Lodge in Phoenix Park meant that there were no sentries outside the official apartments here. They were unnecessary when the castle was so amply guarded in other respects. The guards outside the Bedford Tower were looking across the upper castle yard, directly towards the doors of the Viceroy's quarters, hardly twenty yards away.

That being so, Gaudeans chose the inner ledge, which faced the deserted yard. There was always a chance that there would be someone crossing the space at this time of night. But he would keep his head below the outline of the pediment. They might see him, but it was unlikely, even if it occurred to them to look up. Added to which, there was a flag-pole on top of the arch. Someone would presumably have to come up here at dawn and sunset in the course of duty. So, while it would be unusual to see a figure there, it might be explained by a flag which had been caught in the lanyard or overlooked. No one, except perhaps the guard commander, would feel obliged to inquire.

Adjusting the pack on his shoulders again and winding the cut rope round his waist, Gaudeans set his feet on the ledge. Dancing sideways with neat, silent steps, he crossed quickly to the far end.

What came next was in some ways the most difficult part of all. Between the gateway arch and the next castle building, which adjoined the Royal Exchange, there was a short connecting wall with a door in it. The top of the wall was about eight feet below his present perch. Logic and safety might have persuaded him to climb down to the ground, but at this point that would have brought him into the view of the Bedford Tower sentries. His entire plan was based upon the premise that, though they would look in all directions, they were unlikely to look upwards very often.

It had to be the top of the connecting wall. But not yet. To reach comparative safety, he had not only to cross the top of the wall but also to climb the drain-pipe of the building which it joined, and whose roof would bring him to the Royal Exchange. To attempt that at the moment was out of the question. Even if he could accomplish it without making a sound, he would be exposed to the guards on the main gate as he climbed. Clear as a fly on a whitewashed wall, he thought. It was too much to hope that neither of the men would look in that direction for the time it would take him to make the ascent.

He settled down in the shadow of Justice to wait for midnight, more than half an hour away. From the sound of voices below him he guessed that the two sentries and the policeman must be within the archway itself, rather than standing smartly at their posts. He heard a quiet laugh, and the smell of tobacco-smoke reached his nostrils. There was no doubt in his mind that he had calculated the matter down to the last detail.

Just before midnight he heard the sound of two men and the orderly sergeant being marched from the guard-room. Gaudeans drew further into the shadows of the monumental sculpture and kept his head down. A white face, after all, was the most likely feature to betray him in the darkness.

They were precise to the minute, the preliminary chimes beginning as they crossed the yard. Gaudeans knew that the men already on duty would be at their posts with rigid diligence, the two sentries at attention with their backs to the gate, the policeman standing within the arch itself. He waited until the two sentries of the new guard and their sergeant strode into the archway as well. Then, under cover of the clock's striking, he moved quickly.

The drop to the wall was easy. To run a dozen feet along it took him hardly a second. It was the climb up the wall of the building which would decide his triumph or his destruction. He snatched at the black pipe and began to pull himself upwards. Thirty feet, he guessed. Tired as he was, he could do it in time so long as they were precise in their movements and duties.

Below him, in the intervals of the clock strokes, he could hear the voice of the sergeant. The new arrivals were in the archway, where the incident-book of the previous watch was inspected. Gaudeans trembled with suppressed laughter at the thought of incidents. If only they knew! He was level with the first-floor windows now, a projecting ledge above him matching the one he had stood on outside the Bedford Tower.

This was the worst part of the climb, though he could reach the pipe above the ledge. But for five or ten seconds he had to trust to his hands, hanging by them in the cold gulf of darkness which opened below.

There was no neatness about it this time, no deftness at all. Hardly concealed by the clock's striking, he heard the tiny splinters of loose stone rattle into the yard far below him. His elbows were on the ledge and he was using them to lever himself up, racing against the gradual exhaustion of his strength. His heel caught hard on the narrow shelf of stone, sending another shower of fragments down, then his knee. He was up at last, once again braced against the wall with the dizzy drop below him.

Above him was the last projecting ledge of all, built out from the roof. But it seemed more formidable than the one he had just climbed, and he knew that he had not the strength to pull himself upwards over it. There was no pipe above it, nothing to give his hands a certain grip.

While the guard was changed and the orderly sergeant marched away with the two men who had been relieved, Gaudeans stood with the pack pressed against the wall and his eyes closed. He was high up, of course, so high up as to be almost in darkness beyond the lamps of the castle yard and gate. For all that, his worst fear now was not that they would see him but that he was trapped. Trapped forty feet above the ground on a ledge eight inches wide, running twenty feet either side of him and then ending in mid-air at the corners of the building.

From below, the roof ledge had looked comparatively easy. At close range the angle and extent of its jutting out made it impossible. To all intents and purposes the drain-pipe ended just below it, giving him no means of hauling himself up. That apart, it was simply too large to climb out and then above it.

Gaudeans was not possessed by any fear of heights, not as a rule. But as the minutes passed and he pressed back against the dark brickwork, he felt his mind succumbing to the wild thought that he would fall, that he must fall. The dark space below him would compel him to fall as his only escape from the trap.

He looked down. As though preparing to obey the compulsion, he leaned perilously an inch or two forward. Had they looked up now and been able to see him, they would have seen a man who had surrendered himself to death and was allowing the laws of nature to decide the precise moment of his last terrible plunge.

They would have been wrong. The sharp little brain in the foxy skull was racing and hurdling possibilities as it had done in the waterlogged coffin of the Specialita Theater. The wiry body was bending forward, inch by perilous inch, in the hope of seeing what was immediately below the ledge on which he stood. They were human, after all, the people who inhabited and used this building. Their needs and frailties were no different from those of the rest of humanity.

It was there. He saw it at last. Not an easy place, right at the corner, in fact. But it was there without question, a short piece of piping which vanished round the corner.

Gaudeans moved along the ledge towards the point where it ended, the corner of the building round which the pipe vanished. He was moving over the upper castle yard again, almost looking down on the sentries outside the Bedford Tower. But if he was very quiet they would never look up at so steep an angle. There was no cause for it. Best of all, he knew what was round the corner. With his back to the wall, he shuffled to the corner, the sheer drop now at his feet and his left-hand side. But as he slid that hand round the corner of the wall, he touched sleek metal and knew he was safe. It was the main soil-pipe.

Its dimensions were no greater than those of the other drain-pipes, but there was one important difference. By the laws of sanitation, a soil-pipe had to extend above the level of the roof. He was going to be all right, after all.

With great care he drew level with the end of the ledge, held the pipe by his hands, and stepped off into the empty darkness above the yard. His knees caught the painted metal curve with a gentle bump, inaudible to anyone below. Then he had only to pull himself up, slowly and easily, for another eight feet. With a stretch of pipe still rising above him, Gaudeans was able to step on to the flat surround of the roof as though strolling on to it.

Now, unless he made some lunatic miscalculation, there was nothing to stop him.

Still keeping his head down, so that the slight parapet hid him from the view of those below, Gaudeans followed the roof round to its farthest corner. It was easily done. The space between the shallow slope of tiling and the brick parapet was wide as a pathway. Once he had reached the extreme corner he was out of sight of the castle guards, at a point where the pale stone classicism of Gandon's Royal Exchange building virtually joined it. Indeed, the flat roof of the Royal Exchange with its fine central dome was close enough for him to step from one to the other. With its Corinthian balustrade facing Dame Street and the castle, the roof of the Royal Exchange gave him ample cover as he made his way round two sides of it.

He came at last to its south-eastern corner, in the depths of an unlit alley which lay off the brightly-lit thoroughfare of Dame Street itself. Cork Hill, which ran past the front of the building, made the roof on this side higher above ground-level. Well over fifty feet, by Gaudeans's judgement. It bothered him not the least. Nor did the fact that the overhang of the balustrade made a descent of the Exchange impossible.

The Exchange building formed one side of the alley. A shabby brick warehouse, its roof about ten feet lower but adjoining the Exchange at right angles, closed the end of the cul-de-sac. That was all that Gaudeans needed.

For a second time he made a loop of the rope, securing it round one of the stone pillars of the roof's balustrade. He did this at the corner which touched the warehouse wall, and then swung himself down and across, the rope under his arms as well as in his hands, until he felt the parapet of the warehouse roof beneath his feet. He had only to cut the loop of rope, as he had done on the castle gate, in order to draw it after him.

Last of all, there was another drain-pipe which ran down in the angle of the Royal Exchange and the warehouse. It was clamped to the brick of the warehouse wall, carrying off gutter-water from behind the parapet on which he stood. For a last time, Gaudeans swung himself down and clasped the painted iron tube. He came down it like a schoolboy, standing at last in the deepest shadows of the shabby little cul-de-sac.

Between him and Dame Street, the shape of a hansom cab stood against the lamplight. Gaudeans moved softly towards it and saw the driver—or perhaps the driver's boy—dozing on the box with whip askew.

"Wake up, old girl," he said with jovial impatience. "It's all over."

He opened the door of the cab and slung the haversack inside. By this time he was so weary that he longed only to throw himself down on the buttoned leather of its seat and sleep. Above him he heard a sudden scrambling and waited for the wheels to move. Instead, Tonia flung open the door and eagerly jumped in beside him.

"Is it all right?" she gasped.

For some reason the precise words struck Gaudeans as supremely comic. In the release of tension he snuffled with amusement. Then his shoulders moved until in the end he was guffawing with a helplessness which was close to hysteria. At last he wiped his eyes.

"All right?" he said incredulously. "I'll say! It's the rightest little dodge that anyone's seen in your lifetime or mine. And they're all here."

He patted the canvas shape beside him.

"The dispatch-cases?"

"Yes."

"The Viceroy's jewels and the collars of knighthood?"

"Yes!" He was beginning to giggle again.

"The Mahony diamonds?"

"Every last one."

Tonia gave a cry of exultation and threw herself in the direction of the canvas pack. But Gaudeans was her object now, as she pressed upon him, kissing him and forcing the weight of her body on his.

"I say!" said Gaudeans jovially. "I say, old girl!"

But he was not really grateful at all. It was no more than he deserved, much less than he was going to take. At last, he thought, Captain Wunder was coming to his reward. He gave her a playful slap and made her go back to the driver's box. The old horse snorted and stamped a hoof lightly. Then the wheels began to roll. Trust Tonia inside with the spondulicks while he was up there on the box? After so much trouble to get them? Not likely, missy, he thought to himself. Not something likely!

28

In the morning light, Captain Gaudeans came down the steps of Amiens Street station with a nimble clatter. It was still early, the carriages and wagons stretching in the misty Dublin sun beyond the iron railway bridge which crossed the road on its metal pillars. A long perspective of the North Star Hotel, a row of shabby little shops, and the dingy, soot-darkened brick of workmen's houses stretched away along the North Strand.

Following his plan, he hailed a cab and ordered the driver to wait while his luggage was loaded for his destination, the Holyhead steamer at the North Wall. He had, after all, merely taken the most fundamental precautions in the matter. He and Tonia had left the Shelbourne Hotel for Westland Row station, south of the river, with tickets for Belfast. Those tickets were never used. He was already equipped with others for the few minutes' journey to Amiens Street station, north of the river, on the far end of the Dublin junction railway.

Now he stood alone beneath the square belfry tower of the station, the early July sun beginning to warm the pale stone, as he watched his luggage being carried to the cab. They must travel separately to London. If the Dublin Metropolitan Police began to look for him, though there was no reason yet why they should, it would be as Tonia's companion. And if they inquired at the hotel, following the itinerary of the two fugitives, they would hear of Belfast and the Liverpool steamer. That being so, it was better to travel separately on the Dublin–Holyhead crossing.

Not that the alarm would be raised just yet. It was unlikely that the Milner safe would be opened again until the arrival of more dispatch-cases by the afternoon boat. With ordinary luck, he and Tonia would not be missed by any of their acquaintances before that happened.

Without waiting to see that Tonia's porter had found her a cab to follow him, Gaudeans let the driver pull out into the stream of horse-drawn carts and motor buses, moving south towards Custom House Quay and the river. The green dome and the cold classical elegance of the Custom House itself rose against the outline of the southern hills. The rhythm of hoof-beats, the light stirring of harness, the steady rumble of the wheels, were his reassurance that all was well. Even if Tonia should miss the early boat for Holyhead, it would hardly matter. The boxes from the castle safe were in Gaudean's own luggage. And that was what Lindemann was paying for.

The cab turned on to the long quay-side of the North Wall, below the last of the bridges across the slow, broad waters of the Liffey. Dark weed draped the lower walls of the stone embankment. Beyond the red-brick Georgian terraces fronting the river with little shops and warehouses, black smoke funnelled from the railway steamer at its moorings.

Having paid off the cab, Gaudeans followed the porter with his luggage to the first-class cabin booked for the crossing. The ship was crowded with summer visitors and red-coated soldiers going to England on leave. There was a risk, of course, that the occupant of a first-class cabin might be more easily remembered by the crew than an ordinary passenger. At the same time, he decided, there was an equal risk of being recognized by other passengers if he walked the deck or ate in the dining-saloon. Comfort was what had decided him. A private cabin certainly guaranteed that, and comfort was something he had now earned.

First of all, he went back to the deck and watched the other passengers embarking on the railed gangway. She would be there, of course, no doubt of it. All the same, she cut it very fine, coming aboard about five minutes before sailing-time. Then, as before, they withdrew and remained separate from each other.

The twin screws of the turbines churned the sluggish waters as the ship went astern from the quay. Gaudeans took a last, nostalgic look at the city, the domes and bridges, the first bunting displayed for King Edward's visit in a few days' time. Then he went down to his cabin and stood at the port-hole, staring out across the sunlit waves.

It was to be the fastest, most direct crossing of the Irish Sea. He had chosen that deliberately. The new turbine steamer would land him in Holyhead that afternoon, perhaps even before the safe was found to be empty. Gaudeans watched the cliffs and little harbours south of Dublin, the hazy outline of the Wicklow hills.

As the ship turned on to its direct course for the crossing, there was just a glimpse of the largest of these harbours. It had a double wharf, baggage-sheds, two steamers with red, black-topped funnels moored there. Kingstown, the royal landing-place. Just beyond the wharf he could see a tree-lined promenade and a pavilion which was bright with flags. Though the visit of King Edward had not yet begun, the scene was set already with rows of uniformed figures. The last rehearsal, Gaudeans thought, the dress rehearsal for the state occasion. Off the harbour mouth a slate-grey destroyer lay at anchor, the first of the escort vessels.

Far beyond the horizon, either cruising or lying at a mooring, the *Victoria and Albert* bore its royal passenger towards his twenty-one gun salutes and cheering crowds in the city streets. Gaudeans frowned and felt his one remaining anxiety. He had worked so hard to make a perfect job of it that he could scarcely bear the thought of its being blemished now. Suppose there was no occasion for them to open the safe again before the King's arrival? In his mind he had so often pictured the scene. The portly, irascible figure of King Edward being greeted by the Viceroy with news of the robbery. Was it conceivable that they would not know of it by the time that the *Victoria and Albert* docked at Kingstown? Hardly.

All the same, the misgiving was real enough. Gaudeans fretted over it in the hours which passed before he saw the Angelsey coast and the harbour at Holyhead. The humiliation of such men as the Viceroy and his master was a matter of real importance to him. It represented that long-delayed vengeance on General Thorneycroft and his kind. He stared at the valise where it stood in the corner of the cabin. It contained all, and more, than he had hoped. The dispatch-cases, every item of the Irish jewels, and the Mahony diamonds as well. Captain Wunder's triumph seemed complete. Yet Gaudeans's sharp little features were drawn with anxiety. The stained, narrow teeth worried at his lower lip. There was, after all, something not quite right in the way that he felt his triumph. Nor was it just the matter of whether King Edward would be greeted with the news of the robbery.

No, he thought, there was something else which he had not calculated. Something he knew was present in the immediate future but which he could not as yet identify.

In other words, he knew by intuition that his troubles were just beginning. And Gaudy's intuition was never wrong.

29

Major Purfoy waited from early afternoon until dusk. From his window he watched the park undergo its various transformations. First there were the nurse-maids and the prams, the girls rejecting the advances of guardsmen from Wellington Barracks with shared giggles and blushes. By four o'clock the heirs of Westminster and Belgravia had been wheeled home in their prams for tea. Then the paths between the trees came alive again with dark-suited men from their Whitehall offices striding confidently towards cab-ranks and railway stations. Last of all, as the first lamps were lit, the guardsmen reappeared, this time accompanied by young women in feathered hats. From where Purfoy stood, they might equally well have been the same nurse-maids or girls picked up in the promenade of one of the West End music-halls.

And still the message had not come. For a week he had transmitted nothing to Kurier. Nor, so far as he knew, had Kurier replied. It was possible, of course, that Sir Edward Grey or the Director of Intelligence had used some other means to communicate with the unknown man in Berlin. Possible, of course, but not likely.

Now, without further explanation, Purfoy had been detailed to stand by for the encoding of a last and supremely important instruction. This order had come to him under seal from the Foreign Office. As he went back and sat at his desk, the major half-expected the Director or Sir Edward Grey to bring the message in person.

He switched on the brass lamp and waited. Half an hour later the messenger tapped at his door and handed him the familiar envelope and its cerulean-blue slip of paper.

This time the message was the shortest and simplest of any that Purfoy had forwarded. It took him only a few minutes to translate it into a jumble of letters for wireless transmission. TOCKHIOIHQC-CHIFCUVFSJZYJNX.

He checked it through twice, letter by letter. This, of all times, it had to be perfect. Then Purfoy unhooked the receiver of his telephone and spoke to the duty signals officer at the Admiralty.

"Priority," he said calmly. "Continuous transmission to begin as soon as possible."

He listened while the young naval commander read back the code in the flat, assured tone of a man whose life would be affected neither for better nor for worse by the message he repeated. When he had finished, Purfoy acknowledged the correctness of the letters and hung up the phone. Before he burnt the bright-blue official paper. he looked at it for a last time and knew that this was the final message to Berlin.

Kurier, Kurier. You are betrayed.

30

THE THEFT OF THE IRISH CROWN JEWELS

A profound sensation has been caused in Dublin and a feeling akin to consternation in official circles at the disappearance from Dublin Castle of state jewels belonging to the Order of St. Patrick. The crime has been discovered upon the very eve of King Edward's visit to his Irish capital.

The headquarters of the Dublin Metropolitan Police, the headquarters of the Royal Irish Constabulary, and the guard-room of the Dublin garrison are all within a radius of fifty yards of the Bedford Tower, from which the theft occurred. Sentries and policemen are on duty outside the building day and night. In a word, there is no spot in Dublin or the United Kingdom which is at all hours more constantly and systematically occupied by soldiers and policemen.

It is understood that up to this evening the police, under the direction of Chief Inspector John Kane of Scotland Yard, are without any strong clue.

There is agreement that the robbery was the work of an amateur or opportunist. The Irish state jewels had been in the possession of Messrs. West of Dublin for cleaning and resetting prior to the King's visit. On their return they were temporarily housed in an old iron safe in the library of the Office of Arms. Contrary to rumour, they were not in a modern burglar-proof safe, nor were they protected behind vault-doors and alarm systems. Dublin being accustomed to honesty, this was not considered necessary. The theft was hardly more difficult to accomplish than the removal of a book from the library shelves of the same room.

That being the case, it is the three or four officials of the Bedford Tower who must first answer. It is understood that Chief Inspector Kane's inquiries are now directed to that end. The spectre of a super-cracksman to whom vault-doors and modern safes are child's play is, fortunately, not one which need concern us in this case. . . .

—Evening Post, *9 July 1907*

31

"**W**ake up, missy!" Gaudeans snapped furiously. "Wake up and read this! We've been bought and sold! The pair of us!"

Tonia stirred on the pillows of the sunlit hotel room as he rocked her to and fro by the bare shoulders. In sleep she had the weight of a corpse. Outside and far below them, the traffic of the Unter den Linden rumbled and hooted from the Schlossbrücke to the Brandenburg Gate. Her eyes opened, and she blinked stupidly at him. Gaudeans waved a bundle of the day's English newspapers in her face.

"They've done us!" he gasped hopelessly. "They've done us every colour of the rainbow!"

The girl looked at him uncomprehendingly, pulling the sheet up round her as she drew herself to a sitting position.

"Lindemann?" she said at last.

"Lindemann? Lindemann be blasted!" Gaudeans squealed. "No! The English! The King's men at Dublin! Look at this pack of lies!"

He shook the newspapers out for her to read. Under tall black headlines the story of the castle robbery was told with little variation. Tonia read it and frowned. There was no mention of the Milner safe or the strong-room. Her frown deepened, and she glanced up at him.

"Read it!" said Gaudeans insistently.

The press story described how the state jewels had been sent for cleaning and resetting to West's of Dublin. On their return they had been housed overnight in a smaller, old-fashioned safe in the library of the Office of Arms. The night coincided with Gaudeans's presence in the strong-room. On the following day, the entire collection of state jewels was found to be missing from its temporary residence in the library safe. Indeed, that safe itself was discovered to be unlocked.

"That's absurd," said Tonia thickly. "You took them from the Milner safe in the strong-room. Didn't you?"

It was the tone of her last questioning words which shocked him. If Tonia doubted his story now, what chance was there that he could ever persuade Lindemann? Who would believe that he had acted truthfully, if not quite honourably, in the matter? He, a thief and petty blackmailer, aspired to be taken for a man of truth on this occasion. Gaudeans gave a hopeless little whimper of despair, striking the page of newsprint flat.

"They've crossed us!" he said bitterly. "Haven't they just? Look at the end. Chief Inspector John Kane questioning members of the Viceroy's staff! So, it's Mahony or Shackleton they fancy for this! Perhaps even Vicars himself!"

"I don't understand it," she said, the green eyes widening under the tumble of dark-gold curls. "We know it wasn't Shackleton. He was somewhere else at the time. You said they'd watch Mahony, after your letter."

Gaudeans sat sideways on the edge of a small chair and bit his thumb-nail.

"Look," he said reasonably, "you and I took a pile of jewel-cases and two dispatch-boxes to Lindemann last night. They came from the Milner safe. I know that, though I couldn't prove it. Now, if they ain't got the jewels and papers in, what have they got? Or are they empty?"

Tonia had recovered herself now, and an uncharacteristic solemnity filled her face. She slid out of bed.

"They knew," she said suddenly. "British Intelligence knew what was going to happen, and they moved the jewels. *You* told them!"

"Rubbish," he said, dumbfounded, as if she had struck him.

"Of course you did. Your letter warning them of Mahony. You might as well have told them our entire plan!"

"Ross isn't Intelligence. He's an ordinary thief-catcher."

For the first time he stared unmoved at the pale greyhound leanness of her figure, the dark-gold curls loose on her bare shoulders. In his dismay he ignored the beauty of her movements, too, as she pranced barefoot to the basket-work stool, reaching out to retrieve the first of her clothes.

"You don't see, do you?" she said impatiently. "They've done for you both. You and Mahony. Lindemann will never believe your story of the vault and the Milner safe. And now you've told it, you can't tell another. Mahony's friends in Dublin won't believe him when he says he didn't cheat the Irish of the jewels. They'll find out it can't have been Shackleton. And that leaves Mahony, with or without some help from Vicars. He's as good as dead. And so are you, if Lindemann decides against you."

"They've done us, all right," he said thoughtfully. "Colonel Ross and his men never knew who pulled the robbery. But to them it doesn't matter. The lies they've told the newspapers! There's enough in that to make sure the Germans settle matters with the fellow who did the thieving. And the Irish with Mahony. They've saved themselves the bother and expense of two firing parties and a dozen rounds of ammunition."

"Perhaps they don't want the world to know about the vault and the Milner safe," she said quietly, drawing on long silk stockings.

"That, too," said Gaudeans miserably. He walked across to the window and stared down through the veil of the net curtains. Among the cabs parked along the side of the avenue, just beyond the main entrance to the Hotel Victoria, was a plain black vehicle. Gaudeans looked at the two men who were standing beside it. They were tall, upright, and motionless, men whose profession was visibly that of waiting and watching.

"Stop a bit, old girl," said Gaudeans quietly, raising his hand but not looking away from the window. "Lindemann's got the dogs on us. We shan't get past them like this. And we can't stay here, either. Any minute they'll have men up the stairs and lining the corridor."

For the first time since he had woken her with the news, she looked frightened.

"Undress," he said sharply. "Start again and put these on." He hurried about, snatching up clothes of his own and tossing them to her. Because he was no taller than she and his build was slight, the problem was less than it might have been. The dark trousers and coat fitted her well enough. The neat black boots she had worn when driving the cab in Dublin after the robbery were far from immaculate, but they were good enough for the present purpose.

"One thing," she said. "If they're only watching the hotel, it's probably men who have never seen us. They'll have a description, that's all."

He nodded, catching her glance in the mirror as she pushed the tumble of dark-gold curls into the cavity of the hat she was wearing. The coat buttoned lightly across at the front.

"It's not perfect," said Gaudeans desperately, "but it'll do at a distance." He surveyed Tonia's appearance as a beardless youth.

"Now, this is what we'll do. Go across to the Café Bauer and sit there. A table where you can see the front of the hotel and the two men by the black cab. If you see me taken, then you shall make the best of it. There's no more to be done. If not, I'll come over to you in a few minutes."

"Be quick," she said, as if begging a favour.

"Go!" said Gaudeans furiously. "Now!"

Tonia crossed the room towards the door. Halfway there she stopped, turned back, and came to kiss him. Then she was gone. Even in his apprehension and sickness the gesture was a new and sudden excitement. Better still, he decided, she was on his side against Lindemann. Not at first, perhaps, but now that the whole plan had gone so appallingly wrong she was left with little choice.

He gave himself two minutes to collect every coin and the smallest articles of value, shovelling these into his pocket. There was nothing more to be done then but to prepare himself as he had already prepared Tonia. But first he went back to the net curtains and looked down at the sunlit boulevard below. Both the men by the dark cab were still in position. Gaudeans saw them and waited, his heart scarcely beating, until Tonia appeared. She came out slowly and casually, so self-possessed in her manner that he could have cheered her on. At a distance of thirty feet neither of the two men did more than glance at her. Perhaps they were nothing to do with Lindemann. Possibly their presence outside had some less sinister explanation. Oh, no, thought Gaudeans, not if one knew Lindemann.

He watched the girl cross the Unter den Linden to the tree-lined promenade which ran down its centre. No one challenged her. She crossed again from the shade of the branches and walked casually through the corner entrance to the Café Bauer, the yellow sun-blinds pulled out over the tables of the wrought-iron balcony above.

That was as much time as he dared to spend on her. Standing before the mirror, he began to attend to his own appearance. First he trimmed away most of his neat ginger moustache with a pair of manicure scissors. Surveying the wreck of it sadly, he started to strop his razor.

As he worked, Gaudeans's precise little mind narrowed down the possibilities of what had happened. There were only two explanations of the lie told by Colonel Ross and the royal authorities. The first was that they had been robbed unawares and had made an attempt to discredit the robber with his masters. The successful thief would come back swaggering and boasting of his splendid work against the vault-door and the Milner safe. But the boasts were undermined at once by the story of a safe in the library, little more than an iron box. What reason had the victims to lie about it? And who would believe a word from the thief after that? Worse still, suppose the jewel-cases and the boxes did not contain what they should? Who, then, would believe in the thief's honesty after the story told at Dublin Castle?

The second possibility was a good deal nastier. It was the same as the first in all respects but one. Suppose that the royal authorities in Dublin had not been robbed unawares. Suppose, indeed, they were expecting to be robbed and had made preparations for this. In that case, they could seal the fate of a thief by ensuring that, while they protested at his having taken the treasure, they would make sure that in reality he had not got it. And who among his masters would believe him then?

Gaudeans shivered with the icy chill of someone walking upon his grave. Memento mori. The thought gave new speed to his preparations. He took a small bottle of dark liquid, added it to a basin of water, and prepared to immerse his short crop of ginger curls. As the cool dye reached his scalp he would have given a good deal to know what, if anything, was in the cases and boxes which he had taken such pains to remove from the Milner safe.

Presently he looked up at his reflection in the mirror above the basin. The ginger curls were now transformed into slick black hair plastered over the narrow skull. Despite his predicament, such skill warmed him with self-admiration. He set a match to the end of a cork, burning it until there was enough light, dusty powder to rub into his face. Working carefully, he smoothed it into his skin, as if washing himself with it. Five minutes later, with his dark hair and olive skin, he might have passed as Neapolitan or Sicilian. It would not do for close inspection, perhaps, but like Tonia's disguise it would pass at a distance.

He dressed quickly, pulling on a pair of shoes with soles and heels thick enough to add an inch or two to his height. A tall hat would aid in the illusion that this could not be the slight, gingery figure of Captain Gaudeans.

Then there was another thought which struck him chill and deep. Shackleton and Tonia. Suppose they had agreed during their nights together upon a plan for cheating both Lindemann and the infatuated

Gaudeans. It could be done, of course; Gaudy saw that clearly now. And Shackleton was just the young scoundrel to do it. Moreover, Shackleton was one of the few people who would know if the jewels were kept in the library safe overnight after their return from the jeweller's. It was possible that Shackleton and Tonia were his destroyers. All that was needed was for Shackleton to remain in the Bedford Tower, as Gaudeans had done, after it was closed. The thought of such treason caused his stomach to sink and a deep gloom to settle upon his heart.

He went quickly to the window and looked out. The traffic of the Unter den Linden made its peaceful way on either side of the broad, leafy promenade. Of Tonia there was no sign. By the dark cab the two watchers maintained their pose of studied indifference.

Gaudeans was half ashamed of himself for suspecting the girl's complicity in his betrayal. All the same, it was his own neck under the blade now. Still, if she had crossed Lindemann, she would bolt now, as Shackleton seemed to have done already. On the other hand, if she was waiting for him in the Café Bauer, her loyalty would be proved.

Whatever the answer, Gaudeans was now about to bolt as well. The royal officials at Dublin Castle might be bluffing. Lindemann might find the jewels in the cases from the Milner safe after all. Just the same, it was safer to doubt it. Best to assume, thought Gaudeans, that Lindemann had his handful of shine-rag and nothing else. Safer that way. Either Lindemann knew it already or he would discover the truth at any minute. The time had come to leave.

It was safe enough to take one small attaché-case. No more than that. However good his disguise, any guest who appeared to be making his final departure from the Hotel Victoria amid a collection of hat-boxes and cabin-trunks was bound to come under close scrutiny by the two men watching the building.

The neat leather case was such as to suggest that he was merely going about some business in Berlin. That would do. Gaudeans crammed it with everything which would be most useful to him in the immediate future. He chose hair-dye, spirit-gum, the false whiskers of the stage-magician, and all the accompaniments which were more to him now than gold itself. There was even a pair of heavily-rimmed glasses with plain lenses, but these he kept back to wear when leaving the hotel.

By wearing his light summer coat unbuttoned, he could just

manage to add an extra woollen cardigan beneath it. Now, as he made a final inspection of his appearance in the mirror, he was persuaded that they really would not recognize him as Captain Gaudeans. Not at a casual glance. He was taller and stouter. The glasses gave a new width to the thin, foxy face. Best of all, his dark hair and swarthy complexion suggested a complete change of nationality.

Approving of his work, Gaudeans had one last matter to attend to. He had prepared for escape and freedom. But there was something more important than that. Captivity. He must prepare to be a prisoner, too. When the time came, if it ever did, there would be no leisure for preparations. It was the secret of all his triumphs, this ability to meet circumstances of whatever kind. Not that there were many precautions he could take at present. Gaudeans contented himself with choosing a large handkerchief, Irish linen made in Dublin, and folding it with the most extraordinary care. The folded linen was quite enough to get him in and out of the most tightly guarded establishments.

Satisfied that he had done all he could, he glanced once round the room where the rest of his possessions must be abandoned. Then, picking up the attaché-case, he went down in the lift to the main lobby. At this time of the morning the marble-paved hall was crowded. The banquettes of cerise velvet were occupied by women in voluminous silks, the wives and daughters of Hanover or Prussia visiting the capital city. Candelabra with gilt cupids and sea-nymphs added a mild and ponderous air of impropriety to the setting.

He waited for ten minutes, long enough to ensure that his departure from the room above had not somehow been signalled to the men outside. He waited, concealed in the crowd, for them to come striding in. But nothing of the kind happened. That was good.

When the ten minutes had passed, he slipped through the crowd of men and women in the lobby and came out casually into the sunshine of the Unter den Linden. The morning was bright with banks of geraniums in the central flower-beds of the long boulevard, the light gleaming on the blue rooftops of the horse-buses. It was quite possible, of course, that they were still watching for him. Best, then, to give them no cause for suspicion. Move quietly and slowly.

Gaudeans sauntered under the red-and-white-striped awnings, past the plate-glass windows of the Café Victoria, which occupied much of the ground-floor façade of the hotel. The little tables were occupied by women, in twos and threes, eating cream-cakes and drinking coffee. At the corner, he turned into the Friedrichstrasse, with its little cigar-shops and barbers, the iron bridge carrying the overhead railway across the street to the main station. He stepped back into the doorway of a tobacconist's and waited. No one followed him round the corner. Why should they? They saw only a stout man of medium height carrying a briefcase, a figure that was possibly Austrian or Hungarian but more probably Italian or Spanish.

He had done it, then. Gaudeans crossed the Friedrichstrasse and came back to the Unter den Linden on the other side. For a moment longer he appeared absorbed by the tobacco-jars of a shop at the corner: Paul Grimm, purveyor of cigars to His Imperial Majesty Wilhelm II. Velvet and cedar-wood filled the window displays under the black glass sign with its Gothic script in gold.

No one approached him. He crossed the broad boulevard, passing under the shady branches of the linden-trees to the Café Bauer on the far side, and went through its open doorway. It was best, after all, to do the one thing they would not expect. So far as Lindemann was concerned, Gaudeans had bolted. The natural deduction would be that he had run for his life, as far and as fast as he could. The last place they would look was a café just across the street from the Hotel Victoria.

Besides which, Gaudy had always liked the Bauer. To him it was the most congenial of all the Viennese cafés to open in the city, with its sense of affluence accompanied by a congenial raffishness. He enjoyed the feeling that the tables around him on the grand parterre were crowded by the leisured society of a great capital. Fast but well-heeled. At the far end of the gilt and pillared room, beyond the red plush curtains and the unlit chandelier, a band was playing tunes from operetta. The music perfectly matched the ornate white and gold of the interior, the wall-paintings, and the central arcade of columns hung with gas-globes. The Bauer was lit by sunlight now, of course, through the skylight vaulting of its fine glass roof.

From the corner of his eye he watched Tonia at her table. She was there, after all, and that was a relief to him. It removed one possibility, the worst of all. She had not betrayed him. In that case neither, presumably, had Shackleton. It reduced the possibilities to two. Either Mahony and his chums had done the job somehow, or else the authorities in Dublin were lying deliberately. Lying to destroy the thief, knowing or guessing for whom he worked.

With a glass of rich morning chocolate before him, Gaudeans knew that such things were possible. But who had given the Viceroy his instructions to lie? If they merely wanted to avoid admitting that the vault-door and the Milner safe existed, then the jewels might after all be in the cases which he had delivered to Lindemann. All the same, it was a matter he preferred not to discuss with Lindemann. Not as things stood.

Putting the image of the young colonel from his mind, Gaudeans turned his thoughts to the other problem. How should he and Tonia live? It was to be the two of them now, he was sure of that. Not that she felt any great romantic passion for him, of course. Foolish to expect it in his case, he thought. But her reaction this morning had shown that she had as much to fear from Lindemann as he. That being the situation, there was no alternative but to stick together. The thought excited him, the knowledge that Tonia was to be his.

Perhaps it was time to resurrect Major Montmorency, an alias of Gaudeans's which had been laid to rest two years ago when the curiosity of the British and French police became rather intense.

The swindle would cost little to launch. Gaudeans had paid a jobbing-printer to imitate a page of the *Times* for him. It contained an article deploring the treatment of Major Montmorency by the English book-makers. The major had a simple and infallible gift of picking the winners of horse-races. In the face of his success the book-makers of the country had banded together in order to refuse any more of his wagers. The article also criticized the complicity of the Jockey Club, which prohibited him from placing bets in England by proxy.

Gaudeans's procedure was to send a copy of this article to rich and avaricious men and women in France and Belgium. They were countries in which he never set foot for his own purposes. He still had a list of unused victims from the time when the interest of Scotland Yard and the Sûreté had obliged him to interrupt the scheme.

His dupes were not asked to invest a penny of their own But if they would send Gaudeans's wagers by proxy from France or Belgium, which the Jockey Club could not prevent, they were to have ten per cent of all winnings. The bets were to be placed with a firm of "sworn book-makers" near Charing Cross. He liked the term "sworn book-makers," which he had invented for the occasion. It had such a ring of impenetrable honesty about it.

The men and women he had in mind would never resist the lure. He would even send them one or two cheques for wagers won, drawn on "The Royal Bank of London," which was also his own invention. It would take them weeks to discover that the bank did not exist. Long before that, they would be amazed at his infallible skill for picking winners. They would beg him to let them wager much larger sums of their own. Gaudeans would be reluctant, even adamant. Then, in their envy, they would send their cheques without even asking him.

After that, of course, they would never hear from him again. Naturally, there would be a police investigation. The premises of the "sworn book-makers" would prove to be an empty room in Northumberland Avenue or the Strand buildings, from which Gaudeans collected the cheques which his unwitting benefactors had been good enough to send there. By the time that the authorities discovered this, Major Montmorency would have been quietly laid to rest once more.

It helped to dream of such possible schemes, and the images of fantasy left a smile on his lips. He turned round to glance reassuringly and good-humouredly at Tonia. Her table was empty.

In a fit of alarm, Gaudeans swivelled on his chair, his eyes searching the wide parterre of the café for her. Alarm turned to despair as he saw the two men who had been standing by the dark cab watching the Hotel Victoria. Still, they were not looking directly at him. He kept his face lowered, trusting to his disguise, and almost leapt to his feet in panic as the waiter approached beside him.

"Colonel Lindemann's compliments, Captain. Your bill is paid. If you will now be kind enough to walk quietly to the door, the colonel suggests that this will avoid disturbance and inconvenience to the other customers."

In his mind, fear for what must happen now was matched by professional chagrin that his disguise had failed him. But it *was* good. He knew it was. How, then, had they discovered him?

Walking very slowly towards the men at the door, he tried to postpone what lay in store for him. As he came closer to the doorway and the sunlight beyond, he caught a glimpse of two people through the glass of the window. One was a young officer in field-grey. The

242

other was Tonia, still in her disguise but with the hat removed so that her dark-gold curls fell freely about her face.

They had caught her as well, then. He looked again. This time he saw Tonia smile at the young officer. With her hand on his arm they walked across to the Hotel Victoria, chattering amicably.

It was not a planned betrayal, he excused her from that. Tonia had been visibly as frightened as he during their discussion of the newspaper story. In his company, she might have been persuaded to keep faith. Left to herself, she had had time to decide that there was no refuge from Lindemann, no possibility of escape. Her only hope was in loyalty to her superiors. The sure proof of that loyalty was in betraying Gaudeans, his disguise, and his vague plans for this new emergency. There was no malice in what she had done, he supposed, just a desperate instinct for survival.

That was the end of the dapper little man in summer clothes who had haunted Merrion Square and the fashionable arcades near the Tiergarten. The spruce, comic figure was going unmourned into the darkness. Only Captain Wunder was left now, absurdly costumed in the locked coffin, fighting for his life.

He hesitated for so long that the two men in the doorway came forward and took him firmly by either arm.

32

"Whatever it is you want to know," said Gaudeans eagerly. "Anything at all. I'll tell you. I've nothing that needs keeping secret." He cocked his head to one side and looked up at Lindemann with a toothy little smile. The burnt cork on his face was smeared pale in patches, the flattened and darkened hair standing in spiky disarray.

They had sat him on a plain wooden chair before Lindemann's desk, in the strong sunlight which filled the tall rococo room through the deep window-arch. The brilliance prevented him from seeing his interrogator clearly as he looked up. Just the shape of the blond head haloed with light, the strong features thrown into shadow.

"You look ridiculous!" said Lindemann. "Contemptible! Filthy!"

Gaudeans gave a little giggle of agreement, hoping to placate the young colonel, like a child turning aside an adult's reprimand.

"Try me!" he said, softly encouraging. "Just ask me and see if I don't answer straight."

He saw Lindemann's arm move but was too late to dodge the blow which it delivered. The force of it rocked the wooden chair back against the steadying grip of one of the men who stood behind him.

"Where are the Irish jewels?" There was curiosity rather than anger in the voice. "Why are the cases empty?"

"They can't be empty now unless they were empty to begin with!" Gaudeans's voice rose to a histrionic shriek. It was not the dizziness of the blow but a hope that if only he pleaded hard enough Lindemann would believe him.

But the second time, as Lindemann struck him with the back of his open hand, the little man's head went back more sharply. He heard a dry sound of bones touching within him and felt a spasm of nausea.

"Why have you brought two dispatch-boxes full of useless papers? Where are the Irish jewels?"

"How could I know?" The protest was shrill now, the trapped and broken little animal living in pain and terrified of death. "Everything in the safe, you said. *Everything!* The papers were in there!"

He ended with a grizzle, a hopeless appeal to Lindemann's sense of justice.

"Why did you steal the Ascot Gold Cup?"

"Shackleton." Gaudeans whispered the name, as if for Lindemann alone. "Made double sure he could be sweetened if he had to be."

"Where are the Irish jewels?"

"I don't *know!*"

"Who put you up to this? This attempt to deceive the German government."

"I haven't deceived them," said Gaudeans forlornly. "What's more, I couldn't if I tried. You know that."

He was surprised at the conviction in his voice. It gave him hope.

"Why were you running away in this ridiculous disguise?"

"I was frightened!" The little mouth opened in an ugly snarl. His spirit was returning at last. "I was frightened as hell! Wouldn't you have been? Look at me now! Wasn't I right to be?"

And that was good, too, he thought in his sickness and the pain that rang in his head. Very, very good.

"Are you an agent of the British?"

Even in his misery, Gaudeans gave a pathetic, tearful laugh.

"I wouldn't have brought you the cases empty, would I? What good would that do me, or the British, or anyone else?"

"Perhaps the British have paid you, all the same," Lindemann said flatly. "If I find that is so, you will be dealt with as you deserve. In the basement below us is an indoor rifle range. You do not think a man can be shot like that, inside a building? I assure you to the contrary. There is a similar range in the Tower of London, used by the officers on duty. A young German citizen was executed there without a trial, seven years ago."

Gaudeans avoided Lindemann's eyes, watching the thin, dry lips instead. He believed every word that came from them.

"Who gave you the papers?" said Lindemann sharply.

At first Gaudeans failed to understand the implication. That earned him another blow, much harder. He fell from the chair and scrambled wildly across the floor to the window. A vague scheme of throwing open the window and flinging himself out crossed his mind. In his desperation he reached the catch and held it, struggling as they tried to pull him back. A chaotic vision swam before him. Nurse-maids and children in the groves of the Tiergarten. The long

245

tree-lined promenade of the Siegesallee with its white-marble statuary of military heroes.

They threw him back, and he crouched on the carpet at Lindemann's feet, pathetic and grotesque. Lindemann took out his handkerchief and wiped his hands clean of the burnt cork from Gaudeans's face.

"You look ridiculous!" he said, glancing down at the abject little figure. "Contemptible! A man who tries to escape disguised like a circus clown!"

Even in his sickness and terror, Gaudeans's quick little brain was fighting for a gap in Lindemann's argument.

"Listen!" he said suddenly. "If I was a British agent, they'd hardly expose me by putting out this story that the jewels were in the library safe. Would they?"

It was reasonable, he knew that. Perhaps it was even persuasive. Captain Wunder was fighting for his life now as never before.

Lindemann walked round the desk and settled himself in his own chair. He looked up at the two men who were guarding his prisoner and nodded at the plain wooden chair.

"Let him sit down again."

They faced one another across the desk. On its surface were the jewel-cases from the Milner safe which had contained the collars of knighthood and the Star of St. Patrick and Badge of Viceroyalty. The cases, forced open at the hinges, were empty.

"Where are the Irish jewels?" asked Lindemann gently.

Gaudeans edged forward on his little wooden chair, intimate and confidential, desperate to be believed. It was absurd that a man who could lie and deceive with such effect should now be trapped merely because he told the truth.

"I did what you told me to," he said softly. "I emptied the safe. Everything. If you want proof, I can tell you what the inside of the strong-room looks like. I can describe the inside of the Milner safe. I can show you how I did it. All of it."

Lindemann nodded, as though all this sounded reasonable. Then he thought better of it.

"Who would know?" he asked simply. "Who in the whole of Germany would know what those places looked like? Whether you were telling the truth or not?"

"But I *must* be!" The little man's terrified squeal brought the two guards to the alert. "This story of theirs. The jewels being taken from the library safe. It don't add up. Not two words of it add up. Can't you see? They've told the newspapers that so they don't have to describe the vault and the security system for the whole of Dublin Castle. Can't you see it? Ain't it plain as a fly on a pail of milk?"

"No," said Lindemann. "Not to me. Where are the jewels?"

It was going to begin all over again. Gaudeans felt sick in anticipation of what was coming. There was nothing he could say, no reason that he dared reveal to Lindemann, none that he could even think of. Why should the boxes be empty? Why did Colonel Ross and the Viceroy pretend that it was the other safe which had been robbed?

He shook his head, implying that Lindemann must do as he pleased. No amount of threatening and beating could alter the story. Lindemann stood up again and came round the desk.

"Mahony," said Gaudeans feebly. "Mahony and his damn Fenians. Or that swindling young gigolo Shackleton. See if it ain't one of them underneath all this. I never opened those jewel-cases. Stands to reason! I wouldn't be mad enough to bring 'em to you knowing they were empty. Would I?"

"If you recall," said Lindemann gently, "what you were doing was attempting to escape my attention disguised as a stage Indian. You and your accomplice, Tonia Schroeder. There is, of course, nothing you can do to save her. As a German subject she is more easily dealt with."

"I don't want to save her," said Gaudeans hopefully. "It's my neck that concerns me now."

Lindemann nodded.

"That's good," he said. "That is an improvement. Think like that from now on and you may find yourself a free man. Better than kneeling on the straw in the cellar below with a revolver to the back of your neck. No?"

"That's ridiculous!" Gaudeans spoke with desperate confidence.

Lindemann shook his head, still gentle rather than angry.

"Melodramatic, yes. Ridiculous, no. Where are those jewels? I shall have to begin with you again in a moment. Much worse. I prefer not to. Tell me, please. Where are they?"

A weight of despair settled again on Gaudeans's heart after the brief respite. There was nothing to say, nothing to think of. No means of convincing Lindemann that he, too, had been duped. Captain Wunder was caught now, his last power of illusion gone.

Lindemann gave him a moment. Five seconds. Perhaps ten. Then the interrogator looked up at the guards and nodded. They seized Gaudeans from behind and held him back against the chair by the throat and the upper arms. At first he tried to kick out with his feet, but when he did so they tightened the grip on his neck until he stopped. At last he sat, docile and unresisting.

Though he could not turn his head to watch, he heard Lindemann walk to the door, open it, and speak to someone outside. A second man came in, a man with the strong hands and quick eyes of an engineer or craftsman. Gaudeans's eyes flicked to and fro in horror as the implements were laid on the desk. There were tiny metal probes and wedges, little devices which could grip and twist, diminutive pincers such as a watchmaker might have used. Then the man opened a tin containing an obscene black pad.

"His fingers," said Lindemann. "His fingers first."

Gaudeans felt as cold as death, the sweat running in the folds of his clothes as his two guards held him against the chair.

"I don't know!" he shouted. "I don't know! Can't you see?"

They had stretched his right arm out now, holding it firmly for all his terrified attempts to draw it back. The man who looked like an engineer gripped him firmly by the wrist and forced the splayed fingers down on the black pad in its tin. Gaudeans screamed, convinced that they were about to burn his fingers to the bone with acid or corrosive. But there was only a cold moisture, and then nothing. Now they were forcing his hand on to something else, dry and crisp. Lindemann looked down on him, contemptuously reassuring as a man might be with a coward.

"The prints of your fingers," he said quietly. "They will set you free or deliver you to destruction."

The same process was repeated. Then one of the men held the hands and wiped the fingers over with a liquid which smelt of spirit. Gaudeans felt frightened all the same. Still, he thought, if his finger-prints could establish the truth, then he was safe. Had he not told Lindemann the truth, all of it? Abruptly a cold thought rose in his mind.

"I wore gloves," he said helpfully. "Some of the time I wore gloves."

Lindemann ignored him and spoke to the two guards.

"Take his jacket. The laces from his shoes and the belt from his trousers. Empty his pockets. Leave him shirt and trousers."

Gaudeans retrieved his handkerchief, snuffling and spitting into it. They had taken everything else from his pockets.

"Pipe?" he said hopefully. "Tobacco?" But they allowed him nothing. The handkerchief was different. Lindemann looked at the soiled, crumpled rag as Gaudeans returned it to his trouser-pocket. Not one of them could bear to touch it.

When they had drawn out his shoe-laces and taken away his belt, Lindemann paused. He surveyed Gaudeans with a calm scepticism.

"The shoes," he said suddenly. "Take them from him."

In stockinged feet, his shirt hanging loose, his collar torn, Gaudeans was pulled up from the chair by the two men who had guarded him. The last arrival, the engineer or craftsman, was beginning to work on the locks of the jewel-cases with a tiny screwdriver. A locksmith, Gaudeans thought; of course, that was the answer!

With Lindemann leading the way, they took him down to the basement vestibule, where he had been once before, on the night when he had tried his skill with the Kromer safe. That seemed as far away as a childhood dream. As on that occasion, the two military guards were at their table outside the iron wicket, beyond which ran the corridor with its little cells to the strong-room at the end.

Lindemann presented his key for the wall-safe. One of the guards unlocked it and handed him another key. After his first visit, Gaudeans had taken a professional interest in the way the keys to this corridor were cut.

That was it, then. They operated on a simple but effective system which employed a variable number of teeth on a common key-shank. Any officer who was entitled to enter the corridor could draw from the guards a key which would open the iron wicket-gate. How much it opened after that depended on his rank and authority. Probably all the keys issued would open the first little cells or storage-rooms inside the passage-way. Those were the least important. Several more keys would have teeth in addition which enabled their holders to open other rooms where some of the files were kept. So far as Gaudeans could judge, there were only two men, Moltke himself and his senior aide, Lindemann, whose keys were patterned so that they also opened the last vault-door of all. Perhaps there were other men who passed that door on occasion and even passed the grille which sealed off the Kromer safe. But it seemed to him that Moltke and Lindemann were the only two with their personal keys.

He stood between his guards, subdued as he thought out the system which they must employ. Lindemann was completing the formalities, signing a minute-book to acknowledge receipt of the key, entering the time of drawing it as he would enter the time of its return. Nothing if not methodical, it seemed to Gaudeans. That was a weakness in itself.

Lindemann turned round with the key in his hand. He walked to the iron wicket and unlocked it so that Gaudeans could be marched and pushed towards the cell just inside. When the cell door was open and Gaudeans stood within, looking back at his jailers, Lindemann spoke to him again. He was very gentle, the blue eyes concerned as those of a doctor watching the sickness of a personal friend.

"Believe me, Captain Gaudeans, I have no quarrel with you. I want only the truth. And in that matter, you will admit, you have been your own worst enemy. Tonight you shall be left alone to consider your present situation. Tomorrow, I fear, we must come to a conclusion. One way or another."

They closed the door and left him. Gaudeans heard the key turned in the lock of the iron wicket outside. He thought that he even heard the sound of their footsteps going away across the vestibule. They had left him to himself, as Lindemann had phrased it. In his self-pity, he thought how good he had been as the cracksman of Dublin Castle. How very, very good. And to what purpose? To steal a collection of empty boxes which a common sneak-thief would hardly have glanced at on a street-barrow! He realized suddenly that his stained little teeth were clenched with the outrage of it, as if pressing back some insupportable shriek of anguish.

Then he pulled himself together. He must remember where he was. The absurd aptness of the genteel phrase brought a snort of amusement, dry and sardonic. They *had* left him to himself. That was the best of it. In his own mind, as well as to the rest of them, he had played the shifty, frightened Gaudeans in the few days since his return to Berlin. And as he had deceived the world, so he had almost deceived himself. But now it was time to be Captain Wunder again. Once more. Perhaps for the last time of all.

33

S o that was that. Next day they would either shoot him or set him free. Gaudeans looked round the small electrically-lit space of the cell. Straw to lie on. A small china bowl. A bottle of water. No means of turning off the light. No window, just a small grille in the iron door. Plain stone walls, whitewashed again. If he were to shout or scream, he doubted that even the two guards in the basement vestibule would hear him. Or if they heard him, they would ignore him. Only Lindemann and his kind were entitled to use the key which opened the iron wicket.

And that, to Gaudeans, made it so much easier. Win or lose, it was all decided. The time had come to give his attention to the destruction of Colonel Lindemann.

Not yet, though; not during the day. Wait until night. He marked the passage of time by knowing he had come here at the end of the afternoon. Presumably, then, they would feed him once more and then leave him for the night. Or they might, of course, leave him without food, a persuasion to tell the "truth."

Gaudeans had no illusions as to his own courage. He was at Lindemann's mercy, and he was sick with the terror of it. If, on the next day, they took him to the indoor range and put the revolver to his neck, he would go pleading and grovelling as he had done under Thorneycroft's sentence at Ladysmith.

What he had to do now, in the harsh light of his cell, was more perilous than anything in Dublin. But that was beside the point. Whether or not they would allow him to live depended on other things which were happening far above him. The evidence of finger-prints and the opinion of a locksmith. He and Lindemann pursued parallel purposes, never wavering and never meeting.

Gaudeans was right about one thing. After several hours they brought him a bowl of grey soup and some dark bread. It was one of the junior staff officers who had a key to the iron wicket and the cell door. The grey uniformed figure stood by while one of the guards watched the prisoner eat. He tried to ask them questions, but they

-- -

ignored him. As they left, he lay down on the straw again. It was how they had found him, lying there trying to sleep.

He gave them a length of time which he judged to be about half an hour. It was possible that the guards might have looked in at him during the night, but they had no key to the wicket, he guessed. The orderly officer, if that was who he was, had no reason to do so. There was nothing Gaudeans could do but sleep. He had done his best to convey that impression.

Least of all were they likely to return in the few hours immediately after feeding him. Moreover, since Lindemann had not recalled him for questioning by now, he was unlikely to change his mind about abandoning Gaudeans to his thoughts until the next morning.

He took the crumpled, stained handkerchief. Before he had begun to use it, the white cloth had been best-quality Irish linen, ample and generously stitched. Along two sides of it ran a hem which the manufacturers for some reason always left open at either end. To Lindemann and the others, the handkerchief was a plain, empty square of linen. The sobbing, obsequious little man had displayed it at every opportunity as he blew his nose and wiped blood from his broken lip. To Gaudeans, of course, the linen square represented the best kit of tools that a man could ask for.

His pockets had been searched and their contents taken from him. Even his boot-laces and belt had gone. Anything which would enable him to escape Lindemann had been confiscated, even if the escape entailed taking his own life. But the handkerchief was a handkerchief, nothing more. They had seen more than enough of it. Not one of them was sufficiently acquainted with Irish linen to appreciate the value of the hem. It was eight inches long on each of two sides. A man could house the blade of a screwdriver in it if he chose to. Gaudeans was less ambitious.

Using his finger and thumb, he worked out from the fold of the hem a metal probe about three inches long and the size of a nail. Even a guard who picked up the handkerchief would be lucky to detect its shape. From the other side of the hem he squeezed three flatter pieces of steel, none of them larger than the area of his smallest finger-nail. They fitted together in a row on the little probe, forming the teeth of a key as the probe formed its shank. As a key, it still lacked its finger-piece. The steel probe ended with no more than a tiny metal loop. Gaudeans squeezed out the last part from his hem. Another three-inch probe which would fit tightly through the loop of the first one. This would give him the leverage to turn it, as though the key really had a finger-piece.

He owed everything to Lindemann. On their first visit to the basement of the General Staff headquarters, when he had locked the aide-de-camp behind his own strong-room grille, Gaudeans had been alone with the key for several minutes. He had seemed to be about to light his pipe, and then had thought better of it. He had later offered Lindemann a fill of tobacco, knowing that Lindemann did not smoke. Before his ill-treatment began that night at the hands of the colonel, long before he was searched, he had left the little tin of tobacco out on the table. Not that they would have noticed anything but tobacco if they had opened it.

But under the tobacco, similarly coloured and looking like a block of unrubbed shag, there was another substance. Without the concealment of the tobacco-perfume, it would have smelt of cobbler's wax. It was very nearly that. Housebreakers used it to take impressions of keys passed to them by dishonest servants. Gaudeans had never supposed that he would have one of Lindemann's keys in his possession. But ever the opportunist, he was prepared for good fortune of any kind.

When he left the Königsplatz on that rain-swept December evening, the brown wax below the tobacco covering contained an impression of Lindemann's key to the iron wicket and the vault, an impression carefully taken on both sides.

Lindemann knew that Gaudeans had had the key briefly in his possession. Would the aide-de-camp have gone to General Moltke to confess that the locks must be changed because he had been such a fool as to let Gaudeans open the Kromer safe and then close him in as a prisoner? Gaudeans thought not. However, he was about to find out.

A mere housebreaker would have rushed away and had a copy of the key cut from the impressions. And that would have hanged him. Gaudy knew more about keys than most men. In particular, he knew that the best key cut from a wax impression might be far from a perfect fit, even when the lock was of an ordinary kind. The locks of the General Staff building would be as finely balanced as that of the vault-door in Dublin Castle. No man of sense would risk a key cut to a mere pattern.

Gaudeans, in any case, favoured a skeleton key with teeth that could be moved slightly from one position to another. Given enough time, he could select and adjust teeth to fit all but the best-protected locks. Just now, he lacked the time. The lock on the cell door might not be the best-protected, but the one on the vault-door certainly would be.

Very slowly, tongue pressed between his lips in concentration, he slid the metal teeth into place along the shank of the skeleton key and tightened them into position. If there was the slightest error in the impression of Lindemann's key, he would undo them and start again. A man who had merely cut a pattern from the impression would be done for now if there was the least irregularity. Even in his present danger, Gaudeans smiled at the thought that he really was good. Very, very good indeed.

When he was ready, he listened for a moment to make sure there was no sound from outside the door. The cover was across the little spy-grille in the door, so that he could see nothing in the passage-way beyond. Taking a deep breath, he inserted the barrel of the skeleton key into the lock of the door. Like the other doors along the passage-way and like that of the Dublin Castle strong-room, this one had been made so that it could be opened from either side. There must be occasions, he supposed, when the room was used for other purposes than as a cell and when a keyhole on either side was necessary.

The key entered easily. He fitted the second probe in the metal loop of the shaft, to bring purchase to bear upon it, and slowly began to turn it. The key moved and then stuck fast. One of the teeth was slightly out of place, failing to connect with the last of the levers in the mechanism which had to be lifted to free the lock. He drew the key out, inspected it, and saw a tiny scratch on the shaft.

Patiently, he undid the teeth and altered the position of the last one by a fraction of a millimetre to cover the exact position of the scratch. Then he tried again. This time he felt the bolt move. Gently, so as not to betray himself by the sound of its falling back, he eased the key round a little at a time until it had completed its circle.

And that was all. No double lock this time, so evidently the narrow room was only a makeshift cell. Still, Lindemann had no cause for misgivings on that account. So far as he knew, Gaudeans had only his shirt, trousers, socks, underwear, and a crumpled handkerchief. Even Captain Wunder would hardly manage an escape with nothing more than that.

He slipped the skeleton key into his pocket, opened the door silently by a quarter of an inch, then closed it again in alarm. The corridor outside was in darkness. In the cell the light was full on and with no means of turning it off. So far as he could hear, the guards had not noticed the tiny crack of light beyond the iron wicket. But the moment he opened the door wide enough to let himself out, the dark passage-way would be filled with light from the bulb in his cell.

That was the end of his plan for Colonel Lindemann. Unless he could do something about the light. In his present mood, he was prepared to smash the glass bulb and have done with it. But though he could reach it, the bulb was guarded by a bowl of thick opaque glass which was strongly bolted to the wall by a steel rim. For good measure, there was even a protective steel mesh over the glass.

Gaudeans looked about him. Straw, water-bottle, china bowl. Nothing which would break the opaque glass. He knew at a glance how thick it was and what its strength would be. It crossed his mind that he might use the key as a chisel and the thick bottom of the bottle as a hammer. Apart from the noise and the explanation which he would have to devise next morning, he ruled out the idea because of the key. Any damage to it, any bending of the shaft or teeth, would make it useless for what he had in mind.

He must go barefoot. Though Gaudy had begun to perspire with the tension of what he was doing, it was cold in the little underground room, the damp chill of vaults and dungeons. All the same, he had no alternative now.

He stripped off his socks, pulling at the bands of elastic which held them up. By tearing them a little at the top he was just able to slide them, one on another, over the pear-shape of the opaque glass. The illumination in the cell was reduced to no more than a shadowy twilight. He stripped off his shirt and hung that over the bracket as well. Now, he judged, the gloom was too little to shine into the corridor itself. Too little, at least, to draw the attention of the guards in the vestibule beyond the iron wicket.

Barefoot and shivering with the cold and the apprehension, he went back to the door and opened it again, inch by inch. There was silence outside, silence and darkness. Even from the grille in the wicket he saw no light. Were the guards in darkness, or had they perhaps left him? It seemed too good to be true that they had gone for the night, or even for a few minutes. All the same, they must feel confident enough that there was nothing he could do.

He listened, his feet chilled by the stone floor of the passage-way.

If they were there, in the vestibule, he could hear nothing of them.

Softly he pushed the cell door to, without bothering to lock it. If anyone came to look for him in the next few minutes, he was done for anyhow, whether or not the door was locked. A waste of time, therefore.

He moved down the low-ceilinged passage-way, keeping his head below the level of the grille in the iron wicket. Even though he was in darkness now, there was nothing to stop one of them from flashing a lamp through and seeing him. Best, in that case, to keep well down.

Moving silently on his bare feet, he came to the imposing steel door which had no grille or Judas-hole and which he had seen Lindemann open on that first night. This was to be the supreme test of Captain Wunder's skeleton key. His teeth trembling with cold, he felt for the surface of the door in the darkness and found the keyhole. It had a steel cover which slid easily aside. On the previous occasion he had watched to see if Lindemann either turned off an alarm system or ordered the guards to do so. So far as he could make out, neither thing had happened. If there was an alarm, he was done for again. But he guessed there was not. In a place as closely guarded as this, an alarm system was hardly necessary.

The key once again entered the lock easily, once again turned, and once again jammed. That was all right. He had allowed for it. It was not to be expected that in this case, the most complex of the locks in the set, a man could be right first time. He assumed that there would be two more levers in this lock than there had been in the cell door. Two at least. All the others were similar, but here there would be two extra metal surfaces which had to be lifted to free the bolt.

Not easy in the dark, but not as difficult as it might have been. Gaudeans tasted the burnt cork on his lips. The sweat was running down his face like rain now, carrying the soft powder into the corners of his mouth.

Not too easy, then, except when a man's fingers could read a key-shaft as easily as his eyes could. Gaudeans caressed the tiny metal surface which he had polished finely in preparation. At the worst there would be two light scratches where the lever of the lock had missed the tooth of the key and grazed the shaft. Better than that. He could find only one.

To be sure, he searched the shaft again, the tiny metal probe like a broad landscape in his mind which his fingers travelled and travelled over. He had done it before with his eyes shut, practised all that might have to be performed. For the first time in all his dealings with Lindemann, it was Gaudeans who was now master of the trade.

Only one, he decided. One tooth on the key to be edged forward by a tiny distance to the place where the scratch was. In the darkness it seemed like a foot or a yard. In reality he knew that it was little more than the thickness of his finger-nail.

Again he returned the key to the lock and wound it gently through a circle. Not a double lock here, either. Surprising, he thought. Then he paused, trying to remember whether on his previous visit with Lindemann the light had already been on in the long room with its Kromer safe behind the iron grille. He thought not. Anyway, there was not much to be done now. The bolt had moved back, his fingers on the key had felt it. Open the door, then; there was nothing else for it.

All the same, he did it very slowly and gently. The door, of course, moved soundlessly on its hinges. This sort always did. Built that way. Very impressive. He opened it an inch, two inches, wide enough for the steel hide of it to clear the jamb of the doorway. Then he let out a long, quiet breath.

The strong-room was in darkness.

Easing the chill and cramp in his bare feet, he slipped through and pulled the door closed after him. No need to lock it. No point. If they found him, they found him. That was all. He was about to turn on the light. Then he paused. Could there be a device, so sophisticated that it was unknown to him, whereby an indicator at a control point would show when a light went on in a particular room? Surely not. Even if there was, it would be a control point far enough away for them to think that the visitor to the room must be either Moltke or Lindemann or some other authorized person. He pressed the switch and listened. Nothing. No sounds of commotion or alarm.

The long, vaulted room was as he had seen it with Lindemann in December. The first narrow section with its book-shelves on either side, then the iron grille and the steel bulk of the Kromer safe beyond it. Gaudeans looked briefly towards the grille and the safe, but the Kromer interested him no longer. There was no point in wasting his time trying to open that again. He already knew what was in there.

He looked at the rows of volumes on the shelves, the blue leather bindings and the gold numbers which distinguished one from another. Easy to see how it was done, of course. Saw it at once when he came with Lindemann. The seven at the end were arranged and rearranged so that their numbers matched the combination of the Kromer. First thing he had noticed as he examined them that night while Lindemann sat in cold anger behind the bars of his temporary prison. And then, when he had left, all that business with Lindemann moving the volumes on the shelf while Gaudeans waited outside. A child could spot that one. An ugly child like Gaudeans. So, he thought, he could open the safe now if he wanted to, by reading off the seven numbers. He didn't want to. That was all.

He gave them marks, though, as he looked along the row of volumes once more. A neat way of communicating the change of combination to the other man in case of an emergency. And so he had been at great pains to boast to Lindemann that he knew there was no such way. And Lindemann had believed him. Struck him first, but believed him. Lindemann, blond supercilious brute. Gaudeans stopped shivering. He must get on.

The spines of the master volumes in the Kromer safe had told him where to look on the shelves for what he wanted. He had known for months, never expecting such an opportunity as this. The number 8 was what mattered. Anything which began with it, and most important of all, the blue leather volume which carried a gold figure 8 and nothing else.

Like the Dublin Castle strong-room, Colonel Lindemann's vault was as much a study or library as a place of grilles and locks. There was a small table before the book-shelves, with paper, pen, and ink upon it. Gaudeans took volume 8 from the shelf. He sat down at the little table and opened the pages. When he saw what they contained, his shoulders moved in silent and painful laughter. It was not really funny, of course. Indeed, it was appalling to think that he had planned and connived and was now standing in the path of near-certain death for this, the smoothly bound and darkly mysterious volume 8.

Within the binding, it was an ordinary *Berliner Zeitung* railway time-table. He could have bought it from a railway station or a book-stall without ever meeting Lindemann or coming within a mile of the Königsplatz. For that matter, he could probably have got it through the post without ever leaving his fireside. This was going to be his revenge on the supercilious blond brute?

He looked again. As a matter of fact, he conceded, it would not have been that easy to get. There was no reason why its publishers should have kept a list of trains which no longer ran. The *Berliner Zeitung* time-table in front of him was already two years out of date.

He flipped through the pages, the cheap paper in its impressive binding of official Prussian blue. Someone had been doing a little travelling, it seemed. Here and there. Perhaps it had been Lindemann, or even Moltke, visiting troop depots and barracks to carry out inspections or reviews. Odd, though, that the journeys should be marked in different-coloured inks. Very rum indeed.

Then Gaudeans understood, and he smiled. Yes, indeed, this was to be the destruction of Colonel Lindemann after all. If he lived to accomplish it.

Taking one of the slips of paper from its stand, he began to write in tiny letters. "Stettin, Berlin, Hanover, Aachen." "Schneidemühl, Berlin, Cassel, Cologne." "Posen, Frankfurt am Main, Thionville." "Lissa, Dresden, Strasbourg." That was what mattered. He reached for another volume and in the same tiny script added: "Aachen, Cologne, Thionville, 36." "Strasbourg, 5." Then there were other cryptic notes which he scratched down. "Thionville, constant." "Liège, 12," "France, 22," "Abbeville, 31." The next volume offered problems in weights and measures which, to Gaudeans, were the most absorbing of all.

He took only what he needed, just enough to do his worst to Colonel Lindemann. The tiny letters, when he had scratched them all down, covered only four thin slips of paper, none of them larger than half the size of a postcard.

Returning the last volume to its place, he wiped his nose vigorously on the crumpled handkerchief, then folded the little slips of paper and slid them easily into the doubled hem. When that was done, he stood very still and listened. Still there was no sound of alarm. How long had he been away from his makeshift cell? Half an hour? Two hours? He had been so busy in his task of revenge that he really had no idea. Indeed, he was not even sure whether it was night any longer or whether it might be after dawn.

He turned out the light, opened the vault-door quietly, and edged out into the passage-way. It was still dark. Perhaps there was a cover across the little grille of the iron wicket. Patiently he coaxed the skeleton key round in the lock of the vault-door until he felt the bolt move. As he made his way back down the passage-way with head lowered prudently, his feet were so chilled that he could no longer feel the cold as anything but an invasive ache.

Then he was alone in his white cell again, the door locked behind him. He pulled the shirt and the socks from the harsh light of the electric bulb and blinked in the sudden brilliance. Before anything else, he had to get rid of the skeleton key. After all, one could never be sure. The little teeth were easily disposed of, tiny anonymous fragments of metal which could be dropped here and there in the crevices where the floor met the wall. The shaft and the lever were more difficult, too easily seen if he merely threw them in a corner.

Gaudeans looked around him. Then he thought of the electric light which had caused him so much trouble, and he smiled. It was easy enough to wedge the two little strips of metal behind the strands of the protective steel mesh, between it and the opaque glass. After all, there was no light in the underground room except from this source. And the natural human response to such light was to avoid looking directly at it. He doubted that anyone would find the two little fragments of steel for a very long time. If ever.

34

L indemann looked across the desk more amicably than on the previous morning. There was a mildness in the blue eyes now which was the closest thing in his behaviour to an apology. Gaudeans's shoes and jacket, the contents of his pockets, had been returned to him. The warm sun filling the window-arch seemed oppressive in its heat after the chill of the little room in which he had been confined.

Lindemann looked at him again.

"The truth," he said softly. "Now the truth."

His hand gestured to the desk, which had been covered by a sheet of cloth showing the outline of various objects underneath. What they were, Gaudeans could not guess. It seemed to him that his captor's present performance would have done credit to a booth in the Lietzensee fair-ground. He turned his own gaze on Lindemann, the narrowed little eyes mingling devotion and reproach. With the optimism of a dog that has been beaten and then comforted, he felt it was going to be all right now.

Lindemann slowly folded back the sheet so that it lay at one end of the desk. Beneath it were neat little metal shapes, brass- and silver-coloured; and the jewel-cases, mutilated, dismembered, and covered with a dust like face-powder. One case was open and unharmed. Upon its black velvet lining reposed a glittering river of white fire. Gaudeans stared at the brilliant facets as they caught the light of the sun from the Königsplatz window. He swallowed expectantly, and his tongue ran quickly over his fat little lips. The Mahony diamonds. And very tasty, too.

"To know whether you told the truth or not," Lindemann said. "That was what mattered. You could not convince us. Therefore we resorted to evidence which would not lie."

For the first time Gaudeans noticed a jeweller's glass lying beside the fragments of brass- and silver-coloured metal; the dismantled locks of the jewel-cases reduced to their tiniest components.

"Were you a thief?" asked Lindemann reasonably. "Somewhere between Dublin and Berlin did you open the jewel-cases and remove the contents for yourself? Skilled as you may think you are, you could not have done so without leaving a trace somewhere upon the polished surfaces of the levers within. These were therefore examined by a man whose business is the making of locks. The best of his kind. He found not a scratch or a blemish, only the marks of use left by the authorized keys. Had you opened the boxes, you would have had to press the lids down to hold them shut while you closed the lock once more. In doing so, you would have left a characteristic set of prints with your fingers. Or else the shape of gloved fingers. The prints left by the last person to close the lid are still there. Beautifully clear on polished leather. They are not yours."

"I told you—" Gaudeans began. Lindemann waved him to silence.

"Could you have substituted fake jewel-cases for those taken from Dublin Castle? No. The gold-leaf markings, the names of the Knights of the Order of St. Patrick, have been examined. The tarnish of the gold and its condition upon the leather make it impossible that these could be of recent construction or adaptation. There was no doubt, then, that these were the genuine boxes and that the authorities in Dublin were lying for some purpose of their own."

"Ain't it plain?" said Gaudeans excitedly. "They don't want the Fenian gangs or anyone else knowing about the Milner safe and the way the vault is run!"

"Perhaps," said Lindemann reluctantly. "I also had to consider whether even you would have been so foolish as to return, bringing me boxes which you knew to be empty."

"'Course you did!" The little man was almost jigging on his chair with excitement. "'Course you did! I wouldn't, would I?"

"But then"—Lindemann hesitated—"I considered that you would not have known they were empty. You had your masters, the British, who had let you believe that the jewels were still in the cases."

"Not me!" said Gaudeans confidently. "Not old Dicky Gaudeans!"

Lindemann thought for a moment, as if uncertain that he ought to make the next revelation. Then he overcame his doubts.

"One of the dispatch-cases from the Dublin safe," he said softly. "It contains papers relating to certain ships of the Royal Navy. Are they genuine?"

"Search me," said Gaudeans helplessly. "Never saw 'em."

"Or could they be papers with false information, placed there in the knowledge that they, as well as the jewels, would find their way to this building?"

"Not unless you told someone about it," Gaudeans said. "I never did."

"But then"—Lindemann was almost talking to himself now—"would the British Intelligence Department endanger their scheme by leaving the jewel-cases empty?"

"How should I know?" Gaudeans was beginning to feel uneasy at the talk of intelligence services. "I brought you what you asked for. Everything in the castle safe."

Lindemann nodded.

"And what would you say it was worth? Twenty thousand pounds? Fifty thousand pounds, perhaps, if all the items of the Irish jewels were broken up and the gems and gold separately disposed of?"

"If you say so." Gaudeans shrugged. He was weary of all this, and he felt confident enough to show Lindemann as much.

"And do you know, Herr Gaudeans, how much one battleship would cost?"

Gaudeans frowned.

"No," he said. " 'Course not."

"Somewhere between one million and one and a half million English pounds. Depending on the weight of armament and the extent of protective armour within the hull. To say nothing of the value of several hundred members of the crew, the cost of their training, the difficulty of replacing them."

"I'll take your word!" Gaudeans gave him a smile of toothy insincerity.

"A single cruiser would cost almost half a million pounds. Even a destroyer could not be built for less than sixty or seventy thousand pounds."

"You'd know, I'm sure. Better than I would. Absolutely."

Lindemann seemed poised for the coup de grâce.

"Do you suppose there is any government in the world which would not sacrifice twenty or fifty thousand pounds' worth of jewels to save even one of its battleships in time of war?"

"Sorry?" said Gaudeans ingenuously. "Don't follow you."

"The naval papers which were in the safe," said Lindemann patiently. "If they were to be planted on the German government by the British. Do you suppose that the British would hesitate to sacrifice the jewels to guarantee their authenticity? Do you think they would deliberately rouse the suspicions of their victims by sending the jewel-cases empty?"

"Dash it!" Gaudeans protested. "They were the Irish state jewels!"

Lindemann smiled.

"More precisely, they were jewels given by King George the Fourth to his mistress Lady Conyngham. The rewards of a street-woman. Not a government in Europe would sacrifice a cruiser, a destroyer, even a mine-sweeper, to save them. That is why I believe the cases in the strong-room safe at Dublin were empty for the best of reasons. The jewels had been taken out in preparation for King Edward's arrival, at which they were to be worn."

"Mahony took them from the library safe. Or Shackleton. Or both."

Lindemann shrugged, as though there were no end to what he would concede now.

"I am inclined to think that you have told me the truth. As it happens, it matters less than you suppose whether you have or not. You know too little for your falsehoods to be of much consequence."

"Just ask me anything," said Gaudeans automatically. "See if I don't answer true."

"No." Lindemann shook his head tolerantly. "Even if I were to hear the truth from you, I might be tempted to disbelieve it. Forgive me, but you are a thief and a cheat. Why not, then, a liar, too?"

Gaudeans inclined his head, as if in modest acknowledgement of his attainments.

"And so," Lindemann resumed, "the truth must be established without your assistance. You did not open the jewel-cases and steal the jewels. Did you, however, know they were empty to begin with?"

"Did I?" asked Gaudeans eagerly.

"No," said Lindemann, "I think not. Apart from being a thief and a trickster, you are also, if I may so, a coward. I do not think you would have come back to me voluntarily with cases which you knew to be empty."

"Too true!" said Gaudeans with a humorous sniffle.

"And you would certainly have pleaded your honesty in having brought the Mahony diamonds. You did not, because you thought that case empty, too, when we met yesterday."

"Yes," said Gaudeans humbly. "Yes, I did. Of course."

"Then why," asked Lindemann, "did the British authorities empty the cases before the robbery? Your companion, Antonia Schroeder—"

"Slattern!" said Gaudeans bitterly. "You start believing that little minx and you'll have cause to regret it!"

"She saves you," said Lindemann, "by her story. The letter you wrote to Colonel Ross, warning him of Mahony's plan to steal the jewels. Why did you not mention it to me?"

"You'd have been angry," said Gaudeans peevishly. "Furious."

"Yes," said Lindemann mildly, "I should have been very angry at your foolishness. But I should also have known why the authorities at Dublin Castle took the jewels from the cases. To save them from Mahony and the Irish republicans."

"I'll be paid, though?" asked the little man earnestly. "For the papers in the safe? They must be worth something?"

Lindemann smiled.

"We shall never know for certain whether the papers are genuine. The British will never know for certain whether we believe the papers. Intelligence is the great game of bluff. It belongs to the world of your shabby little card-tricks rather than to the clean-cut tactics of chess. I will ask about payment."

Gaudeans gave a sycophantic little laugh.

"Can I go? Am I free?"

Lindemann seemed surprised at the question.

"Of course. I should not set you free if it were my choice. Better, I think, that you should go elsewhere quickly and cleanly. You owe your liberty to higher authority."

"Oh," said Gaudeans meekly. "I'd like General Moltke to know—"

"Higher than the Chief of Staff," snapped Lindemann. "To put it bluntly, there are those who feel relieved at not being in possession of King Edward's Irish jewels. That being so, you are to be dismissed and given your freedom."

It was not the time to argue about money; Gaudeans knew that. He waited until Lindemann had called for a messenger to escort him off the premises In the doorway he looked back at the smart blond figure sitting upright by the desk.

"You needn't bother to hurry about sending the payment along," he said hopefully. "Any time that's convenient. I'll be at the same rooms as before. In Charlottenburg. I hope that's all right."

Lindemann, who was writing something on a pad of paper, ignored him. The door closed, and the messenger escorted him to the stairs. He was shown down the steps of the building into the sunshine of the Königsplatz. With his bandy swagger he hurried away towards the trees and the Siegessäule column at the centre of the square. But it was indignation which drove him now. His narrow face was drawn in a scowl of misery. He glowered at the long front of the Reichstag, the Brandenburg Gate through the trees, the long avenue of the Unter den Linden where his belongings still waited at the Hotel Victoria.

In its way, what possessed him now was worse than fear or sickness. It was professional humiliation of a kind which was more galling than any other. He had stolen the Ascot Gold Cup in Lindemann's interests. He had stolen the two dispatch-boxes and the jewel-cases, if not the Irish jewels themselves. He had even stolen the Mahony diamonds. And after all that, he had been paid nothing.

He looked back once at the General Staff building. The tall window of Lindemann's room on the first floor was easily identified. He could even make out a figure standing behind it in the sunlight. It was Lindemann, of course, watching him go. The distance was too great to make out the features of the face, but distance was no barrier to Gaudeans. He knew that Lindemann was smiling.

35

"**W**e're giving the Kaiser a Doctorate of Civil Law in November," said Alabaster blandly. "*Honoris causa.* I thought you might like to know. Not too much pomp and ceremony, though. He's coming up to Oxford from Windsor, during the visit. Just for the afternoon. In my opinion, a gesture of that kind will help a good deal. Now that both sides have learnt their lesson for the time being, it's quite the best thing that we should try to smooth the way."

Grey nodded and said nothing for a moment. He was sitting in the same chair in his lordship's rooms which he had occupied some months earlier when the whole business began, staring into the same fire-place. But Alabaster had got the Chancellorship now. They had installed him among scenes of unprecedented splendour in the Sheldonian Theatre. Even the Premier and half the Cabinet had watched. "The Viceroy's Oxford Durbar," C.-B. had called it sourly. Grey recalled the grotesque procession, Alabaster in his gold-embroidered gown with page-boys in attendance. The supercilious moon-face sneering out under the gold-tasselled mortar-board.

"And after all," said his lordship encouragingly, "you've caught your German spy now, haven't you? A complete confession!"

Grey nodded again, but his gloom was unrelieved.

"I thought it was Fisher," he said simply. "I really did. He *could* have sent copies of the memoranda to Berlin as a challenge, or a warning. Therefore we had our disagreeable little meeting with him. C.-B. and I, and the law-officers. He gave his word of honour that he was not guilty. One hesitates before repudiating the word of honour given by the First Sea Lord."

"And then the King owned up?" his lordship suggested.

Grey smiled, as if he found it painful to do so.

"As soon as the King read the report, he sent for Fisher. That riled C.-B., you know. To tell the First Sea Lord rather than the Premier. It seems that His Majesty was so appalled by Fisher's first proposal at Sandringham, to attack the German fleet at Kiel, that he sent a copy of the memorandum to the Kaiser, as uncle to nephew."

"Fisher knew nothing of this?" Lord Alabaster swirled the brandy round his glass and drained it off.

"Nothing," said Grey emphatically. "I understand that at a subsequent meeting on the same topic, the King demanded to know what further plans his First Sea Lord had made. Fisher has a good memory. He quoted verbatim from the other two memoranda, assuming that Edward was now rather taken with the scheme. The King remembered enough of the wording to pass that on to his nephew with some accuracy."

His lordship chuckled.

"And why was nothing said? Why the Kaiser's humbug about having got the information from his Secret Service? An imperial brag?"

"No," said Grey shortly. "A family pact, in my view. It has never been said openly, but I believe the suggestion came from Sandringham. Spike Fisher's guns by making him believe that German spies in Whitehall would know in advance of any surprise attack."

Lord Alabaster beamed.

"How very unfortunate," he said, as if enjoying Grey's discomfiture.

"How very fortunate, in its way." There was no mistaking the new tone of quiet superiority in Grey's voice. "When things went so badly wrong in Dublin, the King felt just sufficient remorse to lend his support."

"How badly wrong?" asked Alabaster keenly.

"Unforgivably." Grey stared into the empty grate. "Lord Aberdeen, as Viceroy, should have been warned. No one told him. Kurier discovered the German plan for the robbery, the bogus *Dreadnought* papers were planted in the vault, our own men removed the state jewels for safe-keeping. Then Aberdeen, knowing no better, gave the world a story in which the wrong safe had been burgled!"

Alabaster sat down in the opposite chair and began to draw invisible patterns on the grate with a poker.

"But if suspicion falls on the keepers of the treasure," he said, "you may at least have Mahony and your Fenians at one another's throats."

"You don't know, then?" Grey looked up in surprise.

"Know what?"

"After the Intelligence people briefed Aberdeen, the state jewels were kept in the castle until they could be brought back to England

268

securely. A reporter from *John Bull* saw them—every single item—being carried through the throne-room. More than a week after they were supposed to have been stolen. In consequence we have now had to put out an absurd story of replicas being made."

"May one ask what is to become of the jewels themselves?"

Grey gave a bitter smile.

"The Secret Service can hardly be allowed to keep them. At present, with the King's knowledge and consent, they are in the personal safe at Buckingham Palace. The suggestion is that, in time, they may be broken up and the individual stones reshaped for future royal use. Whether the Germans will believe a word of the *Dreadnought* papers they now have is anyone's guess."

Alabaster stroked his chin.

"It depends, I suppose, on what they have been told."

"Fisher's department," said Grey wearily. "Reports of her trials and battle-practice mingled with papers of little importance. The papers in the Irish Secretary's box are entirely genuine, of course. Lists of the Fenian activists known to the Special Branch. Suspected assassins and dynamiters. One or two of our own agents as well."

"Excellent!" His lordship was beaming again. "If the Germans have those, you know precisely whom to watch in the next war. What about the *Dreadnought* papers? Anything genuine in them?"

"Quite a lot," said Grey cautiously. "Anything that German Intelligence was likely to know already was put down accurately. That was Fisher's scheme. Turbine performance, use of solid bulkheads rather than water-tight doors—all that is genuine enough."

"And where, precisely, is the deception?"

Grey smiled more easily.

"On Fisher's advice we aimed for one deceit only, in the description of *Dreadnought*'s armour. The Germans are led to believe that the Armstrong guns are designed for battle at three thousand yards with armour-piercing shells. The torpedo-tubes indicate the same distance. In short, the document is an invitation to the High Seas Fleet to close with her at that range, about a mile and a half."

Alabaster nodded. He guessed what was coming now.

"They would never live to get that close," Grey continued. "Her new shells are not armour-piercing, but their effective range is six thousand yards. The torpedoes are the new Whitworths, accurate at the same range according to the Sheerness trials. The aim is to tempt a future enemy into *Dreadnought*'s range without that enemy's realizing it."

"Anything else?" asked his lordship sceptically.

Grey tightened his mouth defiantly.

"Speed of fire. The papers do not include such items as the new articulated hoist, feeding the gun-turrets from the magazine. Electrically-driven. It works like the belt of a Maxim gun and doubles the rate of fire. In the first minute of battle, at six thousand yards, *Dreadnought* would drop twenty-four twelve-inch shells on an enemy. Half of them would be direct hits, according to her gunnery practice."

"But not armour-piercing?"

"No," said Grey, "not armour-piercing. But as Fisher pointed out, if the deck of a battleship is in flames, her control platform blown to smithereens, her steering gone, what does it matter whether she has neat holes drilled in the armour-plate of her hull above the water-line?"

Lord Alabaster stood up.

"Fisher is a good mechanic," he said suavely. "I told you as much."

They walked together towards the door and the entrance to the quadrangle beyond. His lordship turned to his guest.

"Purfoy did well," he said suddenly. "Didn't he do well? And his man Kurier, too?"

Grey looked as if he might bite his lip with resentment.

"Kurier has disappointed us."

"Really?" said Alabaster mildly. "You do surprise me. I had thought you were rather taken with him. He did all that you asked."

"Kurier has disappeared," said Grey indignantly. "He may be dead or merely elusive. When the last wireless code was sent he was certainly still alive. I assume, and Major-General Ewart agrees with me, that he is at large somewhere. That being the case, Major Purfoy has been sent to find him and bring him home."

His lordship gazed up at the summer sky through the interstices of the horse-chestnut leaves.

"What a rackety sort of people," he said philosophically. "Sir Arthur Vicars disgraced and dismissed, the Dublin Herald bolted to South America or Africa, Mahony hunted by the Fenians. And now Kurier, too. If I were you, my dear Grey, I should let them all go. Kurier included. Find something more elevated for Purfoy to do."

Sir Edward Grey turned to his host with an expression which bordered on anger.

"Out of the question!" he said sharply. "Kurier is at large, of that I am convinced. What he has in his possession now, heaven knows. Damn the crown jewels! He may be walking about with the plans of an entire fleet of *Dreadnoughts,* or the mobilization orders for half the armies in Europe."

"Or perhaps nothing," said Alabaster helpfully.

Grey nodded.

"Perhaps. No one can rest easily until we know, for better or worse. Make no mistake about it, Kurier must be found. Kurier *will* be found—by one side or the other."

But despite Alabaster's helpful promptings, Grey refused to say another word on the subject.

36

The beat of the steamer's paddles carried clearly across the smooth waters of the lake in the mellow Italian afternoon. With her tall white hull, the candy-striped awning over the upper deck, a thin black funnel trailing its banner of smoke, she was a familiar sight to the summer visitors. Just short of the landing-stage on the western shore, the purser's voice began to call monotonously, "Gardone! Gardone!" And then followed his recitation of the other little towns yet to be reached: "Malcesine! Limone! Torbola! Riva!"

They were serving tea on the shaded upper deck, where a three-piece band played its gentle accompaniment to the fragmentary murmurs of conversation. Men in linen suits and straw hats strolled between the tables, exchanging questioning glances with women whose summer dresses had the frail beauty of moth-wings or the coquetry of ribboned kites.

Approaching Gardone, the steamer was now level with the pink-gravel terrace of the Grand Hotel, the oleanders in terra-cotta urns. In the little square beyond, there were dim café interiors, banks, and ticket-offices. On the cream walls of the Hotel Savoy, bougainvillaea swarmed to the upper windows in a splash of ecclesiastical purple.

Captain Gaudeans had taken one of the cabins below, near the paddle-box. For the moment, however, he leant on the steamer's polished rail and watched the paddle-wash subside to a hissing froth as they came alongside the little jetty.

He was not frightened any more, hardly even nervous. Someone had been very decent to him. There was no money, of course, except for the modest sum remaining in the account at Coutts Bank in London. Gaudy had drawn that at once. His true reward had come in a small wooden box. Inside it were the Mahony diamonds. That was decency, after all. They might have palmed him off with real dead lead. Like the Ascot Gold Cup.

And there was more to come. He looked up at the tall hill-side above the town, its silvery olives and lemon-groves, the dark spears of cypress against an intense blue of Italian sky. Much, much more.

Still, there were problems in disposing of the diamonds, even for so shrewd and knowledgeable a little creature as himself. He had contacts, of course. Men who would buy. Men who *must* buy, for their own sakes. Throughout his furtive little journeyings from Berlin to Vienna, to Innsbruck, and down to Verona, this thought had been his chief consolation. It was time, then, to settle up his affairs and move on.

The passengers from Gardone were coming aboard now, filing up the gangway. In the interstices of this human screen, Gaudy watched the tall man in the Raglan coat who stood near the stern of the vessel. The man was scrutinizing the new arrivals as they embarked. There was a wry, woe-begone expression on the pale face, two flaps of dark hair coming down on either side of the bald dome of intellect.

Of course, the man was looking for Gaudy. But like the cautious little animal that he was, Gaudy had been most careful to board the steamer at the beginning of the excursion, observing the woe-begone figure while ensuring that he was not seen himself. He chuckled at the deception. After all, he meant the man no harm. His intention was simply to come upon him unawares and unexplained, true to the tradition of Captain Wunder.

It was all very nicely calculated. Across the northern end of Lake Garda lay an invisible frontier, dividing Italy from Austria-Hungary. Torbola and Riva, the steamer's destination, lay within Austria-Hungary. The customs officers and officials owed their allegiance to Vienna and, ultimately, to Berlin. Gaudy had no illusions as to that. But he intended that all his transactions should be completed before then. Perhaps in a few minutes' time. He would reach Riva with clean hands.

A rope splashed into the water, and the paddles began to churn. The criss-cross journey up the lake continued as the steamer's bows swung out towards Malcesine, ten miles away on the eastern shore. He watched the pink and white oleander flowers of Gardone, the magnolias and the creeper-covered walls of lake-side villas, drop away across the oily, smooth water. Above him, with a vibrato like Venetian mandolins, the little band was playing "O Sole Mio." Gaudy smiled. The plaintive notes, the clink of knives, and the rattle of bone china drifted away towards the sharp, cold ridges of the mountains above the lakes.

Gaudeans, smiling innocently to himself with the thought of the

273

surprise he would give to the man waiting at the stern, froze suddenly with uncomprehending fear. Someone spoke, in German, on the deck above him. He knew without turning that the speaker was so close as to be looking down directly upon him.

"I think, Eisner, you should go ashore at Limone. After that, we are in Austrian waters. I can manage him quite easily. I should prefer to deal with him alone."

The voice was Lindemann's. But why? Looking round, from the corner of his eye, Gaudy saw only a pair of tall, polished riding boots, knickerbockers, the glint of a monocle. But Lindemann had done with him. Surely? Surely?

In an agony of despair he saw that his movements had drawn the attention of the tall, woe-begone figure as well. The second hunter was closing upon him. He could have whimpered with the unfairness of it all and the sick realization that Lindemann would connect him with the other man at once.

Had they still been close enough to Gardone, he would have flung himself overboard, risking the spinning blades of the paddle-wheel, and struck out for the creeper-hung walls of the lake-side gardens. But the distance was too great for him now.

Were they rival hunters? Or had the two men made a compact for his destruction? Thrusting aside straw-hatted children and an elegant widow in black bombazine, the little man raced for the companion-way and scampered down the steps to the subaqueous light of the saloon below. It was almost deserted. He found the door of the hired cabin and the steward who stood in attendance outside.

He closed the door behind him and looked round at the rosewood panelling, polished to a liquid gloss, and the two banquettes in deep pink velvet. It would take them a while to find him here. Five minutes? Perhaps ten?

The door had a keyhole but no key. No security there. As for the port-hole, it was too narrow even to permit Gaudy's escape. He tightened his fists and emitted a whine of frustration and helplessness. As if trying to burrow deeper, he went into the cabin's little water-closet and bolted the door. That would hold them for a minute or two longer. And then what?

In his attaché-case, which accompanied him all the time, was the box with the Mahony diamonds. A small portmanteau contained his remaining possessions, several of which were distributed on the marble top of the little stand in the closet. He looked at the badger-bristle shaving-brush, the hairbrushes with their tortoise-shell backs. All were the accoutrements of the dapper Captain Gaudeans known to Dublin society.

Picking up a small, round travelling-mirror, backed like the hairbrushes, he watched the face which looked up at him. All the shallow, sporting optimism of the trickster had gone. The eyes were vacant and hopeless, the cheeks sagged, and the pudgy lips quivered. Even the ginger moustache appeared thin and ragged. But as he looked at the glass, he knew what must be done.

To be a little animal now was to submit to his own destruction, hiding his eyes in the burrow as the ferrets tore at his limbs. But surely he was something else, too. Captain Wunder. He was not trapped at all, so long as he remembered that. Laying down the mirror, he walked back into the cabin with his hands unclenched. There was always a way. Compared with the underwater coffin and the steel walls, this was nothing. He knew now how the trick could be done.

Opening the cabin door, he spoke to the steward in his execrable Italian.

"Tea for two. *Tè per due personne.*"

The steward ducked his head.

"*Pronto, signore.*"

Gaudeans went back to the closet and made his preparations. It mattered nothing to him which of them found him first. Either or both would serve his purpose. Presently he heard the steward tap at the door and set down the tray with the tea things upon it. Gaudeans peered out of the closet.

"*Grazie.*"

"*Prego, signore.*"

The steward would have been bought, of course. Probably by Lindemann. Gaudeans expected that. He came out into the cabin and surveyed the tea with a gentle smile. It was not elaborate, just tea, milk, sugar, and a plate of fancy cakes, sugared and iced in white, yellow, and pink. With a paper in his hand, Gaudy made passes over the sugar bowl and two of the four sticky cakes, as if he might have been blessing the feast.

Then he had only to wait, but not for long. They were at Malcesine. Through the port-hole he saw several horse-drawn carriages waiting beyond the jetty, their luggage-racks empty. Porters in white caps with dark peaks attended by the gangway.

He was still standing there, watching the steamer draw away, when the door opened without a preliminary knock. It was Lindemann.

"Hello," said Gaudeans amicably. "I thought you'd be down. They've just brought the tea in."

In the light suit and riding-boots, he thought, Lindemann looked his magnificent and beastly best.

"Sit down!" said Lindemann sharply.

"Certainly." Gaudeans took his place at the table. "Tell me, though, what brings you here? A message for me, perhaps?"

For the first time in their acquaintance, he saw that behind Lindemann's impatience and arrogance there was a deep uncertainty. For all that, the blond young colonel retained his manner of urbane scepticism.

"You have betrayed us," he said lightly, "and you must know the penalty for that."

Mastering his terror, Gaudeans gave a shrill little laugh.

"Betrayed you? Ain't I done everything in the world you asked?"

He poured a dash of milk into each cup and added tea. Lindemann sat down, his voice softening almost into pity.

"Did you truly suppose you had escaped? That your story of Dublin was believed? That you would not be watched by us, when so much was at stake?"

"Sorry," said Gaudeans, preoccupied. "I never asked if you took milk. Old man, I don't give a damn who watches me. I've nothing to hide, provided the Mahony sparklers are mine."

Lindemann sighed.

"Except for boarding this steamer to keep a rendezvous with an agent of the British intelligence services."

Gaudeans whinnied at the outlandishness of it.

"I haven't spoken to a soul since I got on this boat! If you've been watching, you know that. If there's a British agent on board, which I very much doubt, he's here for the same reason as you. To watch me. Only now he's likely to be watching you as well. Confidentially, old man, I'd say you've muffed it."

"A desperate lie," said Lindemann wearily.

"Tell you what." Gaudeans licked his lips eagerly. "If this chap really is on board, why not get rid of him for both our sakes? You think I'm his friend? I'm not! Sooner he's over the side in a weighted sack, the better, if what you say is true. By the way, old man, is it one spoon of sugar or two?"

Lindemann helped himself, unimpressed by Gaudeans's offer.

"I'm sorry," he said sincerely, "truly sorry for what must happen to you. You will be held in this cabin until we reach Riva. There you will be taken to the Franz Josef Infantry Barracks. The rest, I imagine, you can guess. I would not wish such a thing upon you, but you know that these things must be. You are—have been—a soldier."

Gaudeans swallowed down the prayer which would have had him on his knees by Lindemann's chair. Captain Wunder was in control now; the deceit alone occupied all his energy.

"I'm not frightened," he said, "not this time. I've done nothing against you. Nothing. I know that. And I can show it. You've been watching me, so you must know it as well. Old man, do have a sticky bun, they're very good."

Gaudeans mashed his with the fork and lifted a mouthful to his fat little lips. The uncertainty in Lindemann's eyes was deeper still. Even in his peril, Gaudy felt a surge of pride, knowing that he had never woven falsehood with such poise and dexterity as this before.

"I shall take you ashore at Riva. There is no alternative to that."

Gaudeans, listening, heard a sudden catch in the other man's voice.

"Of course, old fellow. Absolutely."

He watched Lindemann lift the fork to his mouth again and gave him a gentle, encouraging smile. Then he saw that where Lindemann's tongue touched the pale skin of pastry, it left a tiny pink blot.

Somewhere above them, the purser was calling, "Limone! Limone! Limone!"

"More tea, old man?"

The gangplank was down, the passengers going ashore. Lindemann drew breath with a sharp intake.

"What I think, old man, is that you should round up this agent of British Intelligence, if that's what he is. Take him ashore. Put him through the mangle and see what his story is. I'd say you'd find it was me telling the truth all the time."

"You will not dictate such matters to me." The words were both a statement and a command.

"Try it, though," Gaudeans urged. "See if I'm not right."

Lindemann gave a quick, light cough, covering it with the edge of his hand. On the side of the finger which had been nearest to his mouth there was a faint reddish print of his lips.

"See if I'm not right." Gaudeans repeated the suggestion distantly. His mind was lost in a conflict of dismay and self-admiration. He had half-expected that nothing at all would happen. Certainly he had never imagined that the drama would move to its gruesome climax with such speed as this. He sat motionless, watching Lindemann. Between the two men a patch of reflected sunlight lay upon the bone china and silverware, the bright little cakes and the amber slops of tea.

Lindemann opened his mouth, as if to reply. Instead, he uttered a faint, wordless sound, like the catch of laughter. He stopped and then made the sound again. And again. The hand went back to his mouth. Above it his eyes seemed immobilized by a depth of suffering, so that he looked past Gaudeans rather than at him.

Spasmodically, the hideous little sound in the throat broke out again. Lindemann, apparently beyond speech, nevertheless managed to get to his feet and turn to the door. Gaudeans made no effort to prevent him. It was better this way. No doubt the colonel was struggling to reach Eisner. But the little jetty of Limone with its flower-baskets and pony-carriages was now receding in their wake. Eisner was ashore. If Lindemann had not realized that, he was even further gone than Gaudeans supposed.

Gaudeans watched the tall figure crash against the door with an impact which caused the steward outside to open it. After that, it was hard to follow in detail what happened as the door closed again. Gaudeans had only a momentary impression of Lindemann's collapsing into the steward's arms.

Quick and thoughtful, the little man scooped the top of the sugar on to a napkin. He threw both the napkin and the last of the fancy cakes out of the open port-hole. He rinsed the other cup, discharged it through the same opening, and then tipped slops into it. Finally he went into the little closet. It took him only a moment with the shaving-brush and a sheet of paper to sweep up the bright little slivers and the snowy powder of glass from the broken hand-mirror. He brushed the heel of his shoe as well to remove any traces. Then he lobbed the brush, paper, and mirror-frame as far into the water as he could manage.

Captain Wunder washed his hands, stroked his moustache into place, and ran the two tortoiseshell-and-silver brushes over his hair. Then he returned to the cabin and poured himself another cup of tea.

37

Gaudeans waited for ten or fifteen minutes, long enough to be sure that no one but the steward would try to prevent him from going out. It was time to resume his negotiations where they had been interrupted by the arrival of Lindemann. He went to the door and opened it. Outside in the pale green light of the saloon stood the tall woe-begone man with the absurd flaps of dark hair. His general attitude suggested that he had been standing like that for several minutes, facing the door and watching.

Beside the tall man was another, burly and coarser. Gaudeans tried to side-step, but he was too late. The pair of them advanced upon him, driving him back through the doorway of the cabin. In that moment the woe-begone look lifted from Major Purfoy's face, to be replaced by a brightness which was not far removed from a smile.

"Well, well," he said pleasantly, glancing about the cabin as the other man closed the door behind them. "Well, well, Kurier. What a chase you have led us, to be sure!"

Gaudeans clutched his brown attaché-case to him. The sharp little face, cocked slightly to one side, smiled up at Purfoy.

"Chase?" he said humorously. "Didn't I promise to meet you here? And ain't I done it?"

Purfoy shrugged off his Raglan coat and threw it on a banquette. He laid his stick carefully on top of it, as if he might be needing it soon. Gaudeans watched the movements of Purfoy's hands with a nervous glance. The major nodded to his silent companion, who leant his broad back against the door to prevent interruption.

"Now then, Captain Gaudeans," Purfoy began, crowding the little man back until he was obliged to sit down heavily on the pink banquette, firmly embracing the attaché-case. "It is still Captain Gaudeans, is it?"

"It's my name, old man." There was no doubting the intense sincerity of his grin.

"Quite so," said Purfoy vaguely. "Sometimes one never knows."

"You know with me." The little man's eyes crinkled persuasively. "You always know with me."

Purfoy sighed.

"Whatever possessed you to think that you could abscond when all this was over?"

"Abscond?" squealed Gaudeans. "Ain't I here, waiting for you?"

"In the company of a German officer," said Purfoy. "One who has long been identified as a controller of spies."

"Him!" Gaudeans's mouth quivered with triumph. "You don't need to worry about him. Any case, old man, it was you that brought him here. Don't suppose you knew that. And thanks to you, they nearly killed me in Berlin."

"Nonsense," said Purfoy coolly. "Thanks to me, or rather us, you remain alive. All the time you were in Dublin we had the messages tapped out to Berlin, just as if you were there answering them. Even I had no idea at the time. The Germans were actually permitted to discover the code word."

Gaudeans looked up sulkily.

"I'm not talking about messages. It's the Irish jewels I mean. You could have said the boxes were empty! And that story in the newspapers about them being in a different safe. That could have killed me. They wouldn't believe at first that I'd ever been inside the strong-room."

Purfoy sat down beside him on the banquette.

"You really don't understand, do you?"

"No," said Gaudeans huffily. "I'll be damned if I do."

The major spoke gently, as if to an awkward child.

"There was a problem about letting you steal the Irish jewels in earnest. A royal problem. It was felt, if I may say so, that you were a thoroughgoing little thief. 'Slippery little rat' was another term employed. Instead of returning to your duty in Berlin, you might have left Dublin with the jewels and never been seen again. In that judgement we were mistaken. I apologize. The Mahony diamonds were another matter. No one cared about them. Least of all Mahony."

Gaudeans made a muted sound of derision, and Purfoy continued.

"But however honest you were, we had to throw some suspicion upon you. Temporarily. Your report on your visit to the cellars of the General Staff building with Lindemann, last December, was quite fascinating. How could we get you down there again? Preferably alone. You had a key. It merely required a pretext under which you should be confined in one of the little rooms you referred to as cells.

We know, from experience, that people are held in that manner when necessary. Myself, I hardly dared hope that they would actually put you down there. I assure you, all the same, you never were in any real danger."

Gaudeans emitted a whinny of outrage.

"Twice I was beaten almost senseless! They even threatened to shoot me!"

Purfoy sighed and stood up. This was getting him nowhere.

"And the Mahony sparklers!" Gaudeans persisted. "Someone was to be sent to buy them off me. You, I suppose. How much are you paying? Go on!"

Purfoy glanced at the burly man whose back secured the door. But the man was looking at the ceiling, as if he heard none of this.

"The Mahony heirloom has become a liability," said the major soothingly. "It would, after all, be impossible for you to keep it."

"Why?"

"The Fenians had a plan to rob Dublin Castle, as you suspected. They wanted King Edward's jewels for the sensation that would create, and the Special Branch files for their own purposes. They believe that Mahony deceived them and forestalled them. It is essential that this belief be maintained. If the Mahony diamonds were to reappear on the market, that would put paid to the story."

"Fenians?" Gaudeans looked up at the major, his mean little face creased by incredulity. "They'll slaughter young Mahony."

"Yes," said Purfoy equably, "they probably will."

"But even his chums must know that Mahony couldn't do it. Not even from the library safe. He wasn't up to it."

Purfoy nodded.

"They believe he was assisted, probably by Vicars himself. That is quite a common opinion. To that end, Vicars is being dismissed as Ulster King-of-Arms. His enemies will need no more proof."

"Two men condemned to death," said Gaudeans caustically. "And what about me? If I can't sell the Mahony sparklers on the market, you'll have to find the price. Eh? I'm entitled to that. Ain't that what you're here for?"

Purfoy turned to the burly man behind him and raised his eyebrows. The two of them stood over Gaudeans and wrenched the attaché-case from the grasp of the struggling little figure on the banquette. Purfoy opened it.

"They're mine!" There was such energy in the desperate cry that

Gaudeans seemed about to launch himself against the major in a wild assault. The other man held him back. Purfoy forced the locks of the case and took out the box inside it. He opened this, too, and gazed for a moment at the white fire of the stones as they nestled on the black velvet lining. He closed the lid.

Gaudeans began to gabble urgently with the apprehension of what lay in store for him.

"Don't!" he cried. "Don't! You've no idea what it cost me to lay hands on those! They're mine! By every law of natural justice they're mine! Get this ruffian of yours away from me! Give them here! They're not yours! You know they're not *yours*. . . ." And then the voice died in a piteous whine.

Purfoy turned away from him, pulling the catch of the port-hole and opening the circle of glass. A cooling stream of air from the foot-hills of the Alps blew down across the village of Torbola at the north-east corner of the lake. The hand with the jewel-box went out, extended above the paddle-wash.

"No!" Gaudeans screamed as he had never done under Lindemann's ill-treatment. "Don't! Wait! Wait until you know what you're doing!" He fought ineffectually against the powerful arms of Purfoy's bully.

But the hand returned empty and the port-hole was closed again. The box had fallen in the centre of the lake even before the last words of Gaudy's intercession had been uttered.

"Come now," said Purfoy, as if to a fractious infant. "Come on! There may well be a customs search at Riva. The Austrian police have been informed that the Mahony diamonds are missing, as have all the police forces in Europe. Be sensible!"

Gaudeans's arms were wound round his head and he was sawing to and fro on the banquette in a pantomime of anguish.

"You were to buy them! You know you were!"

Purfoy looked at him with cool distaste.

"Military Intelligence does not buy stolen property from thieves."

The absurdity of this remark calmed Gaudeans's outburst of self-pity. He stopped acting and looked up, the little head cocked to one side again.

"Don't talk rot," he said quietly. "Buying stolen property of one sort and another is almost all their business. On both sides."

But Purfoy had turned away and was talking quietly to his subordinate. Gaudeans caught the name "Lindemann." The burly man, before leaving, looked at Gaudeans and then glanced back at the major.

"That's all right," said Purfoy smoothly. "We shall have no trouble now. The captain and I understand one another."

As his companion went out and the door of the cabin closed, Purfoy sat down on the banquette next to Gaudeans.

"Now, then," he said, "the information. After that we shall see what can be done. I take it you *have* the information?"

"Oh, yes." The honesty and enthusiasm in the upturned face approached the level of devotion previously displayed towards Lindemann.

"Then perhaps we might discuss it," said the major, prompting him.

Gaudeans drew a deep breath and closed his eyes. He began to recite, as if reading from a page which he could recall only behind his closed lids.

"Fourteen-day mobilization period." Then he stopped.

"We know that," said Purfoy, gently as a doctor encouraging a patient to reveal his symptoms. "Go on!"

"Railways. All done by railways."

"We know that, too."

"Trunk routes identified by colours in *Berliner Zeitung* time-table. Green: Stettin, Berlin, Hanover, and Aachen. Blue: Schneidemühl, Berlin, Cassel, Cologne. Brown: Posen, Frankfurt am Main, Thionville. Red: Lissa, Dresden, Strasbourg."

"Just a minute."

Gaudeans peeped and saw that Purfoy was searching for a pencil. He gave the major no respite.

"All written down," he said reassuringly. "Just listen."

"Wait!"

But Gaudeans babbled faster and faster.

"Accessible bridges: Schönhausen, Magdeburg East, Zierenburg, Schweinfurt."

"Stop!"

"All written down. This is just samples I carry about in my head. Listen!"

His voice rose close to falsetto in the excitement of it.

"Twelve kilometres per hour. One hundred and eighty trains per army corps. Seven armies in five-and-two grouping. Thirty-six corps and seven corps. Liège, day twelve. Thionville to Maubeuge, day twenty-two. Thionville to Abbeville, thirty-one. General Staff holds doubts as to rail detour via Aachen. Further doubts as to superior French mobility in the final stages when supported by the rail network of the Paris region. There's more."

"Start again!" said Purfoy grimly. "Slowly this time."

Gaudeans shook his head.

"No. Sorry. All written down on paper. Need a bit of an understanding over that first. Eh?"

Though he tried to stop himself, he gave a sickly little giggle.

"Then give me the paper!" snapped Purfoy. "Now!"

Gaudeans looked surprised.

"But you've got it. Gave it you in front of a witness."

"The paper!"

"Eight thin sheets. Tucked under the black velvet of the Mahony jewel-box. Box not for sale, you see. Sentimental reasons."

"I don't believe you." But from the sudden apprehension in Purfoy's voice it seemed that he did.

"I did try to stop you," said Gaudeans, mild but chiding. "I can't imagine what they'll say to you back in Queen Anne's Gate."

"Once again, then," said Purfoy, a pencil now in his hand. "Slowly. That recital of railways and towns and dates."

"Oh, no," said Gaudeans with mock gravity, "I couldn't do that. Not possibly. Not without an understanding. That was just a trade sample. Doing business is something else again. More like compensation for the sparklers. Eh?"

Purfoy clenched his teeth. Presently he relaxed.

"If we have to take you back to London, you may be sure you will divulge the information there. Our methods may not be Colonel Lindemann's, but I promise you that in the end you would beg us to listen to you."

Gaudeans looked surprised.

"London?" He laughed at the absurdity of it. "I ain't going back to London, old fellow. And you shan't take me, either. There's not a trick stacked against old Gaudy now. No diamonds, no jewels, no nothing. First thing I do, when I get off this boat, is give you in charge for threatening behaviour and breach of the peace. Whatever they call that in Austria or Italy. You'll be lucky to get back to London yourself, never mind me."

"Nonsense!" said Purfoy, but there was no strength in the contradiction.

285

Gaudeans nestled closer to him on the banquette.

"How I see it is this. The price of the Mahony sparklers and the bits of what you call the Schlieffen time-table go together. One price for the two. See?"

Purfoy drew away with an instinctive grimace of repulsion.

"As things are," he said, "I doubt if anyone in London would offer you twopence for your beastly little plan."

"You try 'em," said Gaudeans encouragingly. "Try 'em and see. But when you do, be sure to tell 'em that all the prime bits are safe and sound. Locked away tight, up here."

He tapped his temple knowingly and favoured Purfoy with another ghastly little smile.

Before either of them could argue the point further, Purfoy's assistant returned. Turning their backs to Gaudeans, the two men spoke quietly and intently together. Then the major swung round, his face drawn in a mask of incomprehension.

"You maniac!" he said softly. "What the devil have you done to him?"

"Done to whom?" Gaudeans asked mildly.

"Lindemann, of course!" Outrage and horror caused Purfoy's pupils to dilate magnificently.

"Oh, him." Gaudeans shrugged. "I shouldn't worry if I were you. I don't think you'll have any more bother there."

"It's the bleeding, sir," said the other man softly. "Italian doctor with him says it doesn't usually happen so quick. Only a fluke. Cut two big veins. Throat and abdomen. He won't last till Riva. White as veal."

"Plain murder!" Purfoy swung round on Gaudeans, awe-struck and shrill. "You murdered him!"

Anxiety clouded Gaudeans's face briefly.

"I don't think so, old man. A chap can defend himself, surely? That's just nature, ain't it?"

Purfoy shuddered.

"Glass!" Another spasm seized him at the sound of the word.

"I'd do it again," said Gaudeans encouragingly, as if to placate the major by the reasonableness of his act. "See, chaps like me don't get asked to name seconds. Dawn in the park. Pistols for two, coffee for one. We just get beaten and killed."

"Be quiet!"

"Not supposed to fight back, am I? You know where that brute was taking me! You ever had two people holding you while you were knocked about? Kicked till you were sick with it? Head held under water to half-drown you? Scalded like a lobster? I've had that since I was twelve! Not any more, thank you!"

Purfoy marvelled at him.

"So a brave soldier had to die by a vile and cowardly trick?"

"You bet he did!" said Gaudeans emphatically. "What would you have done? Sorry, I forgot. It'd be pistols in the park for you. An affair of honour they call it. Eh? I wasn't offered that."

"You foul little reptile!" Purfoy turned his back. Gaudeans sighed. Useless to argue the matter with such people.

Despite the loathing which he felt, Purfoy was obliged to act as Gaudeans's protector. In the late afternoon the stately paddle-steamer came to rest against the quay of a little harbour which formed one side of the main square at Riva. Gaudeans peered nervously from the port-hole at the little town with the precipitous limestone hills rising behind it. He saw the olive-trees planted along the quay-side itself, the palms straining in the southern breeze. On one side his view was bounded by a tall signorial tower with a belfry, on the other by the institutional drabness of the new Franz Josef Barracks. Away towards Gardone the sheer cliffs came down in a series of headlands to the glitter of the lake, shading into the mist.

Purfoy's companion had gone to make certain arrangements. By the time that the gangway was down and the Austrian customs officials had come aboard, the burly assistant had gathered up Gaudeans's possessions and gone. Then Purfoy escorted the little man across the saloon to another cabin.

Presently there was a rap on the door and a peremptory official voice:

"Zollrevision! Zollrevision!"

Gaudeans's stomach grew cold and tight. He need not have worried. Purfoy went to the door and opened it. At first it seemed that he might be about to bribe the Austrian officials, but the protection was much more thorough than that. There was a shuffling of thick and splendidly embossed papers. Even in his rising apprehension, Gaudeans was impressed by the foresight with which they had made their preparations in London. The Austrian in the dark uniform looked carefully at each of the three papers containing a diplomatic laissez-passer. Then he saluted and withdrew. Gaudeans had no idea what name, his own or another, appeared on the parchment which had shielded him from his enemies. As Purfoy folded it again, he caught only a glimpse of the familiar crown supported by lion and unicorn, *Honi soit qui mal y pense.* . . .

Despite Purfoy's contempt, they wanted him badly enough. That was good. The information stored in the sharp little skull was a saleable commodity. Better still, it was clear that Purfoy almost believed that the fuller details of the Schlieffen plan were at the bottom of the lake. Gaudy had them safe enough. And what he could not lay hands on conveniently, he could always invent. Purfoy and his masters would find it a most expensive business.

The steamer cast off and turned south again into Italian waters on its evening return to Desenzano. They took him off at Sirmione, a little town on a peninsula with an ancient castle and tree-lined squares of yellow and pink hotels open to the calm lake on their western sides. It was in one of the more expensive of these that Purfoy and his companion were installed.

Major Purfoy had missed a good deal of Gaudeans's babbled account of the German strategy. However, he had enough of the general outline to send a cryptically-worded telegram to London the next morning. His companion was dispatched with fuller details.

For three days, under Purfoy's supervision, Gaudeans was confined to the hotel suite. Not that he minded. Only a fool would run away from the prospect of a fortune. Besides, as he told himself, he was getting rather a taste for hotel life of this kind.

In the meantime, of course, there was leisure to study Major Purfoy. Whether the major really believed that he had thrown away an abstract of the Schlieffen plan with the Mahony jewels hardly mattered. The main thing was that he seemed increasingly convinced of Gaudeans's possession of it, either in his head or written down elsewhere. That was good. Gaudeans gazed out across the square at the calm waters of the lake. He watched the coming and going of the elegant steamers, the couples strolling among the trees. There was a girl with a blond coiffure, her dress of plum-coloured satin taut over her hips. A splendid waist. He caught the name. Francesca. He would know where to find her.

On the third afternoon the reply came.

"It seems," said Purfoy with pleasure in his voice, "that you can be of no further service to us."

Gaudeans blinked at him, certain that he must have missed

something in the major's words. He repeated them incredulously, seeking an explanation.

"No further service?"

"That was precisely the phrase used."

"But look here"—Gaudeans assumed a desperate, tormented little grin at the foolishness of it—"I've got everything you want! Everything they've always wanted in London! The whole Schlieffen business! Mostly in the old brain-box, but, tell the truth, a bit written down, too."

"Then I wish you joy of it." Purfoy folded the paper and put it away.

"But why? After all this?"

"Because," said Purfoy simply, "no one believes you. Imagine that you had not been incarcerated in the cells of the General Staff building. Suppose you had merely visited them with Colonel Lindemann and then made up a plausible-sounding plan to be sold for your own profit. You see? No one could believe that a creature like you had laid hands on the key to the Schlieffen plan. A lesser falsehood might have convinced us. You have simply been too greedy."

"But it's the truth!"

Purfoy heard the whimper of defeat in the words and sniffed with contempt.

Presently Gaudeans tried again.

"Look, suppose they were to take the details on spec. Not pay anything until they've seen 'em. Seen if they stand up to the test. Eh?"

Purfoy lowered the newspaper he was now reading.

"They could never be sure. In any case, interest in Count von Schlieffen and his proposals is not what it used to be."

"How d'you mean?"

Purfoy had begun to raise the newspaper again. He put it down once more.

"It is no secret," he said patiently. "The papers have been full of it for weeks. If another war should come, the choice of battle-ground will be in the hands of the Royal Navy."

"How?"

"The enemy will have no leisure to invade France. All his forces must be committed to defending Schleswig-Holstein and the north German plain against a sea-borne invasion, supported by superior naval power."

"That's absurd," said Gaudeans thoughtfully.

"The future very often appears to be so," said Purfoy, returning to his newspaper, "but Schlieffen belongs entirely to the past. Now please be quiet."

Fretting at his lower lip with sharp, spasmodic movements, Gaudeans kept his silence for a quarter of an hour.

"What about me?" he said suddenly.

Purfoy sighed and took the telegram from his pocket again.

"You are to remain here until the orders are confirmed by messenger. Probably for two or three days. Then, of course, you are free to go."

"Where?"

Purfoy shrugged.

"A matter for your choice."

"But I'm penniless! Destitute!"

"People of your sort very often are." Purfoy rattled the newspaper irritably. "Now do shut up, there's a good fellow."

It was not Gaudeans's nature to remain despondent for long. This resilience was one of the qualities in himself which he most admired. Now that he knew the worst, he had to plan and calculate, as Captain Wunder might have done. For an hour or two he ignored Purfoy and sat at the window, gazing out across the pollarded trees and the placid lake beyond.

Already he could see what the Schlieffen secrets offered him. London might not be interested, but Paris was another matter. Much better. France, after all, was the intended victim. They would have a few details of their own, no doubt. By checking these, they would see at once that what he had to sell was the genuine article. And when his stock of information ran out, he had only to invent whatever they seemed most anxious to hear.

Most promising of all was Purfoy's revelation about Schleswig-Holstein. That was very good. Gaudy had every intention of resuming his trade in secrets with the Germans, as soon as possible. To that end, he had begun to imagine how Lindemann's fate might be turned to his own supreme advantage.

A simpler mind than Gaudy's would have invented a tale of the brave colonel trapped and murdered on a lake steamer by British agents. No one would be taken in by that alone.

The story they would swallow like butter was so obvious that he stared at it for hours without seeing. Then inspiration took flight. Lindemann was Kurier! It dropped into place with such neatness that Gaudeans himself could have been persuaded. It was Lindemann, not he, who had been in Berlin when the coded messages were tapped out from Whitehall. It was presumably Lindemann who "discovered" the code word. Lindemann had twice taken a British officer down to the vaults of German Military Intelligence. And Lindemann was responsible for accepting the naval secrets of Dublin Castle as genuine.

Gaudy's story would fit their minds like a hand in a glove. Eisner was sent ashore at Limone, leaving Lindemann free to rendezvous with two British agents. Then, his usefulness over, the colonel was foully done to death by Purfoy and an accomplice on the orders of their perfidious masters. With that quality of material, Gaudeans's persuasive powers would have sold water to a drowning man.

Then would come the most astonishing coup of all. The sale of England's plans for the invasion of Schleswig-Holstein. Here again, the German General Staff would know of the thing in principle. That was half the battle.

Gaudy imagined himself writing an admiring letter, either to a British military commander or perhaps to a military attaché. He might offer a handsome donation to the man's pet charity. Anything to obtain an answer in the dupe's own handwriting. With this to copy from, it would be easy enough to draw up letters and memoranda in which the proposed invasion of Schleswig-Holstein was discussed with a few appetizing hints and details.

Basking in the thought of it, he sat back and relaxed. At every stage of the game there would be payment. A reward for every item of information disclosed. He would require that recurring type of fee known to British lawyers as a "refresher." With his doggy optimism he knew that in a few months' time he might be the most refreshed little trickster in the whole of Europe.

Gaudeans smiled down upon the strollers in the square and thought again how very good he was. He saw the girl who was called Francesca walking with two other young women, sensuous and undulating. Captain Wunder, he told himself, must belong to no woman and to all women, to no country and to all countries. That was the secret of his achievement. Sooner or later, when war came, he would have no great preference as to which countries fought which others, nor even as to the eventual outcome. It was his pride that, whatever the triumphs and the catastrophes, Captain Wunder would survive them all.

The future excited him by its opportunities. Every hour of every day threw them in one's path, if only one knew how to exploit them. He alone, perhaps, in the dark storm which was gathering over France and Germany, Austria-Hungary and the Balkans, would prove indestructible. The meek would inherit the earth.

For the moment his requirements were very modest. The money that Purfoy had in his pocket would do. During the next half-hour Gaudeans contented himself by playing patience at the little table in the window. He did not cheat, of course. There was no point in playing this particular game if one cheated. Behind him he listened for sounds of Purfoy's boredom and restlessness. Ironically, the jailer must now depend upon his prisoner for company.

When he had heard what he wanted, Gaudeans stood up with the pack of cards in his hand. He ran his fingers affectionately round the edges. Then he went across the room and sat down, facing Purfoy. He drew his chair intimately close. As Purfoy looked up, Gaudeans moved to the very edge of his seat and fanned out the pack, face-down. He gave the major a look of earnest, toothy sincerity.

"Take a card, old man," he said encouragingly. "Any card."

>>> If you've enjoyed this book and would like to discover more great vintage crime and thriller titles, as well as the most exciting crime and thriller authors writing today, visit: >>>

The Murder Room
Where Criminal Minds Meet

themurderroom.com

9 781471 904424